Dear Reader,

My love affair with all things Australian began almost a dozen years ago when my family and I had the opportunity to spend four months in Adelaide. Two years ago when we had the opportunity to return, I knew that the time was ripe to research and write a story that had haunted me since my first visit.

At the beginning of this century there really was an unlucky pearl found off the coast of Broome. Some years later that pearl was lost in a storm at sea and lives on only in legend and in the seed of this story. But in the same way that a pearl is formed, that tiny seed grew and transformed itself over the years into this tale of two families tempted and torn apart by their own flaws and by their lust for a pearl that has none.

I'm grateful to so many people for extending the hand of welcome along the way, but none more so than the congregation of the Unitarian Church of South Australia. I found, on both my visits, that Australians are among the world's most generous people, always willing to help and unwilling to take credit for their kindness.

But may I say thank you, anyway?

Emilie Richards

EMILIE RICHARDS

Beautiful Lies

ISBN 1-55166-492-5

BEAUTIFUL LIES

Copyright © 1999 by Emilie Richards McGee.

Printed in U.S.A.

Beautiful Lies

"Australian history is almost always picturesque;
indeed, it is so curious and strange that it
is itself the chiefest novelty the country has
to offer.... It does not read like history,
but like the most beautiful lies."

—Mark Twain, *Following the Equator*, 1897

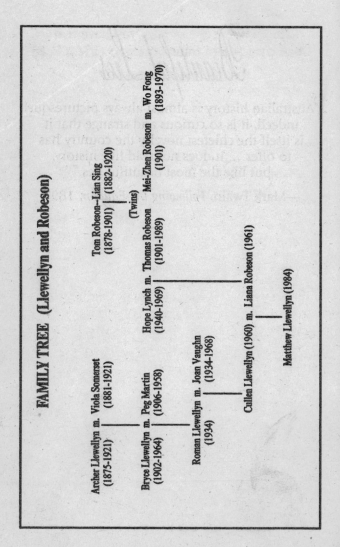

FAMILY TREE (Llewellyn and Robeson)

Archer Llewellyn m. Viola Somerset
(1875-1921)   (1881-1921)

Tom Robeson—Lian Sing
(1878-1901) (1882-1920)

(Twins)

Mei-Zhen Robeson m. Wo Fong
(1901)   (1893-1970)

Bryce Llewellyn m. Peg Martin
(1902-1964)   (1906-1958)

Hope Lynch m. Thomas Robeson
(1940-1969)   (1901-1989)

Roman Llewellyn m. Joan Vaughn
(1934)   (1934-1968)

Cullen Llewellyn (1960) m. Liana Robeson (1961)

Matthew Llewellyn (1984)

The liquid drops of tears you have shed
Shall come again transformed to Orient Pearl

—Homer, *The Odyssey*

For Leslie Wainger,
who loves Australia as much as I do.

1

San Francisco—Present Day

"Hey, lady! Better watch out for sharks."

In a different context, the warning might not have seemed so ominous to Liana Robeson. Spoken by a mother lecturing her adolescent surfer, or a retiring CEO handing over the reins to his young and eager replacement, it might have seemed like good advice. But in the middle of a San Francisco sidewalk, when she was fast approaching the epicenter of the worst panic attack she'd experienced in months, the words sent a screech of alarm up and down Liana's rigid spine.

She was surrounded by sharks, and she could feel them circling.

"You won't forget now, will you?"

Liana batted at the hand puppet the homeless man continued to wiggle in front of her face. "No...no, I won't forget."

The puppet, a grinning dolphin, fell away. The man, dark-skinned and lean, moved a little closer. He spoke over the clanging of a cable car across the busy street. "You all right, honey? You looking pale."

"I'm...." The words wouldn't form. She wasn't all right. She was a thirty-eight-year-old businesswoman who could not walk down a sidewalk by herself. She was afraid of open spaces, afraid of the unfamiliar, terrified of all the forces in her life that she couldn't see or control. She was a mother who just hours before had committed her son to a 737 and the great unknown. At 8:16 that morning she had watched her only child board the plane that would deliver him into his father's arms. Now she was paying the price.

Concern filled the man's eyes, but he waited for the cable car to depart. "Didn't mean to scare you. Flipper here, he won't hurt you."

Liana squeezed her eyelids shut, so tight that the tentative sun rays piercing the afternoon gloom disappeared. For a moment she was in her own little world, fog sliding along overheated skin that would quickly turn icy cold if she didn't pull herself out of this.

Skin icy cold, heartbeat faster than a firing squad drumroll, a million fiery needles stabbing at her extremities—oh, she'd been here before. She knew what she could expect.

"Honey, you had anything to eat today?"

Liana opened her eyes. The man was still there. She was dressed in Thai silk and Irish linen; his T-shirt had been old five years ago. Under his arm he held a stack of newspapers published by a coalition of the homeless. She always had her driver buy a copy, but she'd never actually read one.

"I'm fine, thanks." In an effort to take charge, she pointed to the papers. "I'll take one."

"Well, that's just fine. Flipper says thank you." He and Flipper began to shuffle through the papers, looking for the best of the stack.

Belatedly, Liana wondered if she had any money. She was a vice president of one of the Bay Area's largest development companies. In the hours since she had accompanied Matthew to the airport, she had represented Pacific International Growth and Development at two meetings and picked over a seafood salad at Tarantino's with real estate magnates from four continents. As always, she had been driven from one location to another with no thought of carfare or parking fees.

Then she had made the mistake of abandoning the limo to

walk the final three blocks to the Robeson Building. She had forced herself to take this journey down California Street on foot, forced herself because her world was growing narrower, and she had to fight.

Or one day she would wake up and find herself unable to leave her bedroom.

She wrenched open her purse, but a search turned up nothing except a crumpled dollar bill. Officially it was more than enough, but she didn't often encounter kindness.

"Look, take this." She shoved the dollar bill at him as a bicycle whizzed by. She was not surprised to find her hand was trembling. "And this." She put her hand on the lapel of her black blazer, which was embellished with a brooch from the days when she was young and foolish enough to believe she should follow her heart. The pearls were small but pristine, six of them tucked in a spray of lily-of-the-valley forged from fourteen-carat gold. The only man she'd ever loved had created the pearls. She had created the brooch.

The clasp gave way, and she took a second to lock it before she held it out.

His eyes widened. "I can't take—"

"Sure you can." She reached for his hand and curled his dusty fingers over the brooch. "Take it to a good jeweler."

He was staring at the brooch in fascination when she turned away. The look on his face carried her to the door of her building and across the black-and-white marble floor to the brass filigree elevator screen. Inside the empty car she pulled the emergency lever and closed her eyes.

Why should she be surprised that today of all days panic had burrowed straight through to her soul? This was June, and in June her beloved son belonged body and soul to his father, Cullen Llewellyn. Right now, if all had gone well with his flight, Matthew was already at LaGuardia, wrapped in Cullen's hearty embrace.

For weeks Matthew had thought of nothing but being with his father. They were going on a camping trip to the White Mountains, then to the coast of Maine, where Cullen had rented

a boat and a primitive fisherman's cottage. Cullen, raised in
the Australian outback on kangaroo milk and water-buffalo
meat, Cullen, who was part Mad Max, part Crocodile Dundee,
was going to teach their son to be a man.

At fourteen, Matthew was already tall enough for the role,
but he still had a child's sensitivity. He was broad-shouldered
and big-hearted, this man-child who was the very center of her
existence. He had never by word or deed communicated that
he preferred his father to her, but each June, despite an ironclad
custody agreement, as she watched Matthew board his flight
into Cullen's arms, she was never convinced he would return.

And why should she be convinced of anything where Cullen
Llewellyn was concerned? A century ago an ancestor of Cul-
len's had nearly destroyed the Robeson family. Ten years ago
Cullen had nearly destroyed her.

Liana sagged against the wood paneling and covered her
eyes with her palms. She told herself she was sheltered securely
in the building that was her second home. Matthew was gone,
but of course he would come back.

She was safe.

Eventually the comfort of the familiar began to work its
magic. Her mind continued to race, but mixed with adrenaline-
laced forecasts of doom was the beginning of logic. By the
time she restarted the elevator and waited for it to reach the
offices on the top floor, she was in control again. When the
doors opened and she stepped out of the car, her eyes were
wide-open and her spine was as straight as the path she cut
through the crowded hallway.

"Good afternoon, Miss Robeson."

She nodded to personnel as she skirted walls of opalescent
white hung with calming pastel seascapes. The decor was
soothing, but the atmosphere was not. The most expensive interior design firm in the city hadn't found a way to veil the
tension that permanently infused the air. The world of real-
estate development was always cutthroat, and nowhere more
so than in this building.

"Liana?"

Frank Fong, director of marketing, stepped into her path, forcing Liana to swerve and slow her pace. Oblivious to Liana's stony gaze, he fell into step beside her. "Your ex called. Twice."

Liana didn't slow. She nodded to her stepbrother, Graham Wesley, Pacific International's CEO, who was having a conversation with another employee in the hallway outside his office. He returned her nod, but unlike Frank, he heeded Liana's somber expression and didn't approach her. At the desk nearest her office, her secretary, Carol, a quiet young woman who was easily wounded, didn't even meet her eyes.

Liana waited until she was inside her office with the door shut before she faced Frank. "He sounded upset," Frank said. "Carol put him through to me. She was shaking in her Guccis."

"Frank, this is a game divorced people play. Cullen calls to tell me Matthew's arrived, then he launches into a list of complaints. He doesn't like the clothes I sent along, or my arrangements for Matthew's flight home...."

"This sounded like more than picking a fight about blue jeans or Dockers."

Liana clipped each word. "Cullen is incapable of repressing his feelings. When we were married, that made him great in bed and a complete washout the rest of the day."

Frank affected a lisp. "Well, dahling, I wouldn't have been so quick to divorce him. On the timeclock of life, that puts him at least an hour ahead of the men I'm acquainted with."

Liana leaned against the edge of her desk. Frank smiled, and, reluctantly, she did, too. She and Frank were distantly related, but any resemblance was subtle. Frank, one hundred and fifty pounds of honed muscle, had a ready smile that was as appealing as the streets of Chinatown, where he had grown up. Serious, tightly-wired Liana had a thin, angular body that barely topped five feet. But the shape and set of her dark eyes and the parchment tint of her skin hinted that she, like Frank, had family roots deep in the fertile soil of the Far East.

Liana glanced at her watch, a Cartier that was much less her style than the brooch she had given away. "Did Cullen say if Matthew got in on time? I heard there were storms expected over the Rockies. And he was changing planes in Denver."

"No, he insisted he'd only speak to you."

Liana didn't show her annoyance. "Well, he's not going to have the chance. Graham and I are leaving in ten minutes for an interview."

Frank turned away. "I told him you had an appointment and might not be available."

Liana looked up again. "And he said?"

"Fuck the bloody appointment." Frank managed a credible Australian accent. At the door, he faced her again. "Do you think a war with your ex is a good idea? What if he really does have something he needs to discuss?"

Liana thought of all the discussions she and Cullen had engaged in during the years of their marriage and the ten years since. There had been a century to discuss, a century in which the Robeson and Llewellyn families had murdered and betrayed each other. She and Cullen were star-crossed lovers, but there had been a time when they believed they could forge a future, despite the intrigues of the past.

They had been wrong.

Frank grew impatient. "Liana?"

"If I'm still here the next time Cullen calls, tell Carol to put him through. Otherwise, he can call me at home tonight. In the meantime, see if Carol can talk to Matthew. Maybe she can find out how the flight went."

As the door clicked shut, Liana's shoulders sagged, but before she could take a deep breath someone rapped on the door again. It swung open, and Graham walked in.

"I saw Frank leaving. I'm not interrupting, am I?"

She told him part of the truth. "I'm just preparing myself to make PIG look like the best thing to happen to San Francisco since sourdough bread."

She watched him wince at her nickname for the company he ran so effectively. "We could do without the acronym."

"Sure. Let's be even more direct and call ourselves Pacific International Land Swindlers."

"Maybe you ought to stay here and let me handle the interview."

Liana motioned him inside. She and her stepbrother were not friends—her father, Thomas, had seen to that. But she and Graham understood each other. Together they had lived through Thomas's abuse, his tantrums, his plots and intrigues. In the end they had survived being pitted against each other to develop a grudging mutual respect. Blond-haired Graham, who at forty was still battling baby fat, did not resemble Liana, but underneath a thousand differences, one similarity bound them together: a helpless connection to the despicable man who had raised them both.

Graham closed the door and stood with his back against it. "Jonas called a little while ago."

Jonas Grant was a reporter for the business section of the *San Francisco Chronicle*. Liana shrugged. "I sent him complete portfolios of everything we're involved in right now—at least, everything we want him to know about. Does he need something more?"

"He wants you to bring the pearl."

For a moment Liana just stared. There was only one pearl Graham could be referring to. The Pearl of Great Price. The pearl that had been shifted back and forth between her ancestors and Cullen's since it had been plucked from the Indian Ocean floor. The pearl that was featured prominently on PIG's glorious logo.

"You're kidding," she said at last.

"No. He claims the pearl will make a nice lead for his article and a good visual reference. They want a photo."

Liana fell silent, mulling over Jonas Grant's request. The panic, which had subsided to a distant nagging buzz, threatened to rise inside her again. She circled her desk to gaze at the city stretching toward the bay.

"I don't like handling it, Graham." She didn't add the postscript. The Pearl of Great Price had a tumultuous history. For all its rare, flawless beauty, it had never brought good luck to anyone. She didn't like the idea of handling the pearl today, not after Matthew had just left for the East Coast. She turned. "It's not like I can throw it in my purse with my tissues and lipstick."

Graham nodded in sympathy. "Then don't bring it."

Despite his casual tone, Liana knew Graham was hoping she would take his suggestion. Then he would have one more story about her reluctance to give her all for the corporation.

She faced him. "We'll need security, of course. Will you ask Frank to see to it?"

"If you really don't want to handle it, I can do it for you. It's only a pearl."

She didn't pretend to consider his offer. "I just want to be sure we make the appropriate arrangements to protect it."

The door closed behind Graham, and after several seconds she crossed the room and locked it. Then she leaned back against it and stared at the Georgia O'Keeffe print hanging on the wall to the right of her desk.

For the first time since her return, the room was silent except for the dull grumble of traffic beneath her window. But even with the door bolted, Liana knew she was never quite alone here. This office had belonged to her father, and the ministrations of an interior designer hadn't erased Thomas Robeson's ghost. Worse yet, inside the wall lay tangible proof that some things endure forever.

She echoed Graham's words, but her tone was bitter. "It's only a pearl."

Before she had time to consider what she was about to do, she strode to the O'Keeffe print and carefully removed it, placing it face-up on the credenza before she turned back to the paneled wall.

Four tiny screws held this narrow section of paneling in place, and she removed them with the help of a screwdriver from her desk. When the paneling was lying neatly on the floor, she stared at the brass-adorned wall safe with the imposing lock.

Graham and Frank knew the pearl was here, of course, and so did the rest of the management staff. The paneling fooled no one, although it might deter a random burglar. But the safe itself was as secure as any device of its kind. Her father had demanded the best and gotten it.

"You were a son of a bitch, Thomas Robeson."

Her hands were clammy as she reached for the dial. Some days she could almost forget that the pearl was embedded deep in the heart of the room, its moonbeam glow extinguished in velvet darkness. When she remembered its presence, she told herself that hidden behind cast iron and steel, shielded by sheets of redwood and the endearing O'Keeffe poppies, the pearl had no power to harm her.

But there were days when she felt the pearl watching her, speculating, laughing....

"Tell it to a psychiatrist, Liana." She grimaced and thrust out her hand. The dial was cool to the touch, and her hand, sweating now, slid right over it. She wiped her palm on her skirt, then reached for the dial again. She imagined it grew warmer as she began the long series of numbers that would open the safe. Only three people in the world had ever known the combination. Her father, herself, and the man who had calibrated the dial.

She stepped back before she set the final number, preparing herself to remove the pearl.

Her intercom buzzed, and Carol's high voice came over the speaker. "Miss Robeson, Mr. Llewellyn's on line one."

She flinched, and her heart sped faster. She was suspended between the pit and the pendulum, the pearl and the man who had even more power to hurt her.

"Miss Robeson? Are you there?"

She heard Carol coughing softly. She turned the dial to the final number, then she threw open the door and abandoned the safe, marching to her desk. She punched the intercom and cleared her throat. "Has he told you how Matthew is?"

"No. I'm sorry, but he sounds furious."

Liana sagged against the desk. Clearly she had no choice but to take the call. "Thanks."

She lifted the receiver, and her finger hovered over the blinking button before she punched it savagely. "Cullen, don't start with me. Just tell me how Matthew's flight went."

A silence ensued. Somewhere at LaGuardia there was an announcement over a loudspeaker. The line crackled. She had no patience to lose. "Damn it, Cullen. Don't play games."

A familiar voice with a broad Australian accent rumbled across the lines. "What do you mean, how his flight went? What flight? Do you take me for a bloody idiot?"

There was a soft rapping at her door, and Graham's voice sounded from the other side. "Liana, it's time to leave."

Liana put her free hand over her ear. "You're not making sense," she said into the receiver. "It was a simple question. Did he get there on time? Did he have rough weather? Look, if Matthew's there, just put him on the line. I'm in a hurry. You and I can talk another day."

"Get here? He bloody well didn't get here, Liana. You know he didn't, because you didn't put him on the fucking plane!"

For a moment her heart seemed to stop beating. "What are you talking about?"

"Matthew wasn't on the plane! He was never on the plane! Where's my son? Either you tell me what's going on, or I'm taking the next flight to San Francisco to shake it out of you!"

Graham grew louder. "Liana, we're going to be late."

Liana pressed her palm against her ear. "You met the wrong flight, Cullen. Damn it, he's there at the airport somewhere, waiting for you. I sent all the information. You told Matthew you had it."

"I met the flight. He wasn't on it. In the past hour I've met every flight coming in from Denver and two directly from San Francisco. He wasn't on any of them!"

"I took him to the airport myself. I saw him board. I saw the plane take off!"

There was silence again. The line didn't even crackle. Finally Cullen spoke. "Then somewhere between San Francisco and New York, our son went missing, Liana."

The receiver slid through her hands, and she felt the blood draining from her face. She could hear Cullen's voice from the desk, small, so much smaller than the man. Graham rapped on the door again and called to her.

She turned slowly and stared at the open safe, as if the Pearl of Great Price—the flawless, hideous pearl that for a century had determined the destiny of her family and Cullen's—had rolled from its velvet pedestal and kidnapped her son.

As she stared, she realized how foolish that was. Because the safe was empty.

Like the child who meant more to her than anything in the world, the Pearl of Great Price had vanished.

Full fathom five thy father lies;
Of his bones are coral made;
Those are pearls that were his eyes....

—William Shakespeare
The Tempest, Act I

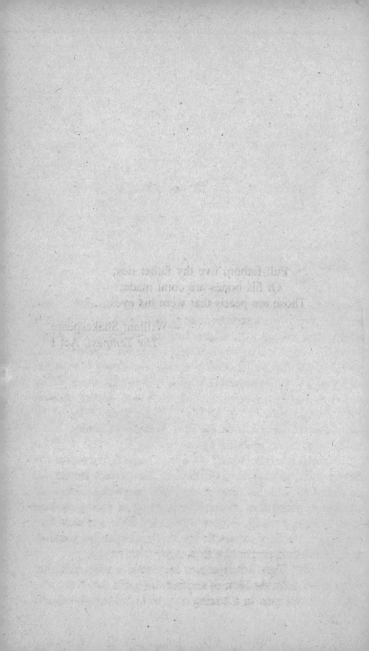

Full fathom five thy father lies,
Of his bones are coral made;
Those are pearls that were his eyes ...

—*William Shakespeare,*
The Tempest, Act I

2

Broome, Australia—1900

Australia fed on the souls of men, grinding them into a fine red dust that swept across treeless gibber plains and sifted into stagnant billabongs. She was a land of promises that would never be fulfilled, a sky choked with unfamiliar constellations, a year of seasons so tormenting a man was forced to long for whatever hell he'd recently left behind. And still, none of that mattered. For better or worse, Australia was Archer Llewellyn's new home. In 1898, in Cuba, in the thick of battle, he had murdered an officer of the First Volunteer Cavalry.

He could never go home again.

"I'll take this one, Tom." As a man came flying across the rickety table, Archer ducked; then, at the perfect instant, he battered him with his fists to send him sprawling. When his attacker, a gargantuan specimen who stank of rotting oysters, tried to right himself, Archer tipped the table and sent him crashing to the floor, where he lay still, eyes open but puzzled, as if no one had taught him to contend with failure.

"Thanks!" Tom Robeson sent his friend a swift grin that fragmented under the blow of another stranger's fist. Tom, who could hold his own in a boxing ring with padded gloves and

Marquess of Queensbury rules, never watched for the unexpected.

"For Chrissake, Tom, keep your head down!" Archer wrapped Tom's attacker in a crushing bear hug, battering the stranger's skull with the side of his own. For a moment the stars he saw were blessedly familiar—unlike the ones he'd seen every night for the past two years. Then the stars disappeared, his head cleared, and the man in his arms stopped struggling and collapsed to the floor.

"Anyone else want to give it a try?" Archer stepped a good distance from the two downed brawlers. "Anyone else in this godforsaken town got a score they want to settle?"

The half-dozen men who had been lounging on the sidelines turned away as if nothing had happened.

"You okay?" Archer turned Tom's cheek to the light.

Tom cheerfully slapped away his hand. "What about our mates?"

Archer's gaze flicked to the defeated men. The smaller was helping the giant to his feet. As they stumbled toward the door, neither spared a glance for the two Americans. Archer grimaced. "Looks like they'll live to fight another day."

Tom rubbed his jaw. "You saved my neck. Again."

Archer touched his chin to his chest, his ears to his shoulders, checking for damage. "You'll never learn, will you? You think other people pay attention to the rules. Well, no one fights fair in a place like Broome. It'll get you killed."

"Apparently not as long as you're around." Tom held out his hand. It was an aristocratic hand, with long, calloused fingers, a strong hand, despite its appearance. It was a hand that didn't mind dirt or sweat or reaching out to help a friend.

Archer grimaced again, but he clasped it in his broader one for an instant before he pushed Tom away. "Let's get on with it."

Tom had an easy smile, even when his lip was swelling. "Get on with what? Brawling, drinking, or plotting how we're going to make our fortune?"

Archer had already tired of the first, and what remained of

a tumbler of square-face gin was now a puddle on the warped plank floor. That left plotting their future, which looked grimmer by the minute.

"I'll shout you another one. For saving my neck." Tom waved his friend toward an up-ended chair and started for the front of the room.

Archer hauled the chair to their table and settled into it as he watched Tom maneuver his way toward the bar. The boardinghouse, their temporary home, hardly deserved the title. It consisted of a few rooms behind this bar, with filthy bedding and a view of the bathhouse. The bar itself—known locally as a grog shop—was built from sheets of corrugated iron propped into alignment by the misshapen trunks of native trees. No glass or gauze graced what passed for windows, and the door was nothing more than a gap between two sheets of iron, hung with cork-laced fishing line to discourage flies.

There were decent hotels in Broome, where pearling masters in crisp white suits and solar topees told stories of pearls they had won, and European pearl buyers came to quench their thirst and scout for the gem of a lifetime. But the boardinghouse was the best Tom and Archer could afford, and before long even *it* would be beyond their reach.

As he wound his way toward the front, Tom, with his elegant stride, his proud bearing, looked like a king sympathetically assessing the plight of his lowliest subjects. He wasn't unusually tall, but he held himself as if he were seeking the rarefied air reserved for the gods. He was dark-haired, fine-boned, pale-complected, a man with a quiet smile for everyone and a warmer one for the people he cared about. Archer, in contrast, had a wiry, compact body, the sandy hair and freckled complexion of his Irish mother and the impaling blue eyes of his Welsh father. And although usually he was as cheerful as his friend, today his face was etched with an uncharacteristic scowl.

A chair scraped the floor beside Archer, and a deep voice boomed, "Just where is it you hail from, stranger?"

Archer turned to see a man who had just come through the

door pulling up a chair beside him. Archer evaluated him quickly. "Who wants to know?"

"John Garth. Skipper John Garth." The man, both older and cleaner than the other patrons, held out his hand. He was tall, with a ruddy complexion and a slickly waxed mustache. He wore the formal white uniform of the pearling masters, but his tunic was casually unbuttoned over a spotless singlet. "Call me John."

Archer, having taken his measure, relaxed a little. "Archer Llewellyn. And I hail from America."

John made himself comfortable. "We don't get many Americans in Broome. If you're here on a holiday, you've jolly well come to the wrong hotel. You'll get nothing but a scuffle from the patrons and crook from the tucker. By the time the cook's finished his morning pipe, he can't tell if the meat's fresh or flyblown."

"Then what are you doing here?"

"That was my shell-opener and bosun you laid out just now. I saw them dragging themselves out the door. I came to investigate."

"How do you know I'm the one who did it?"

John smiled. "From the looks of this mob, you're the only one who could have."

"Your sheller insulted my friend."

"Do you always stick up for a mate?"

Archer shrugged carelessly. "When he needs sticking up for."

"Loyalty's a fine thing. If it weren't for loyalty, we wouldn't have any order in town, or out on the water, either. It's loyalty we look for when we're hiring our crews."

"And I suppose you're loyal to your men, and you've come to finish what they started?"

John raised one brow. "Shall I show you loyalty?" He reached inside the pocket of his shirt and pulled out a drawstring bag. "Have a look."

Frowning, Archer spread the opening with his thumb and forefinger and peered inside. Three pearls, small but seemingly perfect, gleamed back at him. He looked up to find the skipper watching him closely. "A man could get himself killed over pearls like these," Archer drawled.

John held out his hand, and Archer returned the bag, which the skipper tucked back in his pocket. "I'd say you're from Georgia, or maybe the Carolinas?"

"Texas."

"And your friend?"

"California."

"So why are you here?"

Archer was still thinking about the pearls. He wished he could have rolled them lovingly in his hand. Off Broome's coast lay the finest mother-of-pearl in the world, which was in constant demand worldwide for buttons. Men were making fortunes from pearl shell alone.

But the by-product of the oyster that produced the mother-of-pearl was pearls like these, pearls considered some of the finest ever brought up from the sea. Unfortunately, in the three days since Archer and Tom had arrived in town, Archer hadn't held a one.

Tom returned with two grime-streaked schooners and set them on the table, offering his hand to the skipper before he sat down. "Will we have to fight you, too? Can we at least finish our drinks?"

John signaled, and the Amboinese landlord, who hadn't moved from behind the counter since Tom and Archer came in, drew another schooner from a large wooden keg and brought it to the table. John held it in the air. "To mates."

The men drank in silence for a moment. The beer was sour and nearly flat.

"I was just asking Mr. Llewellyn why you're here." The skipper set his glass on the table.

Tom answered easily. It was a story he and Archer had agreed on a long time ago. "We fought with Roosevelt in Cuba. Afterwards we decided to see some of the world. We went looking for luck and tried your gold fields, among other things. So far, we haven't been well favored."

"There's luck here in Broome. For some." John shrugged.

Archer pushed his glass away. "I've seen some of your poor twisted bastards who haven't been so lucky. Sitting outside in Chinatown like the living dead, waiting for the sun and the sandflies to finish them off."

"The divers?" John looked properly regretful. "Pearling has hazards as well as treasures. Some of our men die, some are crippled for life. Others find enough shell and pearl to go back home and live like sultans. The Muhammadans are sure their fate's determined in advance. The Japanese put paper charms under their suits to protect themselves. Me, I think a man just needs to educate himself and be cautious. The rewards are fine enough to take a risk or two."

Archer considered all the risks that he and Tom had taken since the day they had been mustered out of the United States Army. And the risk he had taken the day he killed a man to save the life of his friend. In the years since his escape from certain court-martial and death, he and Tom had crewed on a rumrunner's ship in the Caribbean, harvested the giant kauri trees of New Zealand, ridden boundary fences in New South Wales and scoured the Kimberleys for gold.

And through it all, the rewards had been meager, the work filthy and degrading. Archer Llewellyn had been born for better, but better had eluded him all his life.

"Broome's no place for a white man." Archer scraped a fingernail through the grime on his glass. "Tom and I are experienced sailors, but unless a man has enough money to buy his own lugger, he won't have a chance of work. The town is teeming with slant-eyed bastards and native niggers who'll do what any white man would only do for three times the pay."

"Do I take that to mean you can't tolerate the company of our Asians and Aborigines?" the skipper asked.

"Me?" Archer grinned. "I could tolerate the company of Old Nick himself if I thought there was a dollar in it. I'm just saying there's a difference in how far that dollar goes for me and those bastards living ten to a room or sleeping on the beach. I require more."

"Yet you say luck has abandoned you...."

"That's the thing about luck, isn't it?" Tom interrupted. "When you least expect it, there it is."

Archer lowered his voice. "About those pearls..."

"Right-o, the pearls." John toyed with his mustache. "There's a certain class of men who'll do anything, cheat anyone, to make a shilling. The stones I showed you came off my own lugger, the *Odyssey*, but I never saw them until today. Cambridge Pete, the bastard you laid low, found them in shell he opened. He hid them, and sold them when he got into port yesterday. The man to whom he sold them is known to buy snide—"

"Snide?" Tom asked.

The skipper waved his hand. "Stolen pearls. Smuggled off luggers by crew members. Divers, sometimes. Anyone with the opportunity to do it. This time Cambridge Pete hollowed a rope and hid the stones until he could take them safely ashore. The man who bought them sold both the stones and the tale back to me this morning. He and I, we have an understanding...."

"And you're sure he was telling the truth?"

"Pete wasn't expecting me to be in port, so he was careless. I found the rope in question where Pete always sleeps. Hollowed like a reed, it was. Pete wasn't smart enough to throw it overboard."

"Then you're out a crew member or two."

The skipper nodded. "And Pete and his mate won't live long enough to see the sun set if they don't board the afternoon steamer to Perth. Of course, they'll be boarding with nothing in their pockets after we've had a private chat."

Archer wasn't surprised. Broome was a frontier town, with a jail that was often filled to capacity. But in towns like this one, teeming with the flotsam and jetsam of a dozen island nations, justice was often administered by those who hadn't been sworn to uphold it.

John leaned forward. "I need a new shell-opener. Unfortunately, I can only hire a white for the job. The colored crews can't be entrusted with that sort of authority."

Tom grimaced. "Hiring a white man doesn't seem to be a guarantee, does it? If I don't miss my guess, Cambridge Pete is white enough under the dirt and stench."

"My friend grew up with Chinese servants," Archer explained to the skipper. "He has a fond place in his heart for any yellow-skinned man with a queue."

"Don't get me wrong," John said. "I respect any man who does his job, but this is one job a white man must do. My shellers report directly to me, and they share in my profit. We have to understand each other perfectly." He paused. "Do *we* understand each other? Perfectly?"

Archer leaned back in his chair. "There were two men. A bosun, too..."

"Precisely. There are two openings on my lugger. There are two of you. You say you're sailors. I know you can take care of yourselves. You've shown me you know how to be loyal...."

"And we're white," Tom said.

"I've always been a gambling man, and my instincts are good. The season's almost over. You can learn what you need from the rest of my crew. You can share the jobs if you like. The *Odyssey* only came in to port because the bosun claimed she needed repairs and supplies. But she'll be ready to sail again tomorrow. Tell me, gentlemen. Will you be sailing with her?"

John Garth had two luggers that worked independently, with the largest under his direct command. He had begun pearling two years ago, increasing his fleet by one lugger this season, and if he continued to find good shell, soon he could afford a schooner, which would act as his mother ship. Then he could store and dispense supplies out on the water, so that the valuable days when the ships could be at sea would not be wasted. The pearling masters with the largest fleets had the tightest control over their crews and an enviable income.

But even the smallest lugger, with a skeleton crew, could bring in a fortune if a diver brought up exactly the right shell.

"*Pinctada maxima.*" Tom let the words roll off his tongue. *Pinctada maxima* was the name of the oyster that lived in the coastal waters of Western Australia, the oyster that produced the finest pearls in the world—the oyster that was about to provide the two Americans with a place to sleep and food in their bellies. "Did you ever think you'd be prying open shells to make your living?"

Archer favored him with a grin. With a little money in his pocket, Tom had discovered, Archer was always more agreeable. "No, and I never thought I'd see a place as unholy as this one, either. Will you have a look at that?"

Dampier Terrace in Broome's Chinatown, like a small sliver of Singapore transported to the Australian continent, was overflowing with people. The street itself was so narrow only a few men could walk abreast. It was lined with whitewashed shops and dwellings of galvanized iron and timber, leaning one against the other. Rickety balconies strung with laundry perched above their heads, and the smoke of cooking fires and perfumed joss sticks darkened the humid air.

Tom obediently gazed down a dusty alley. "What exactly am I supposed to see?"

"What do you suppose those bastards are doing? Christ, I'll never get used to men wearing dresses."

Half a dozen dark-skinned men in brightly-colored sarongs huddled in a circle in one of the numerous narrow alleys snaking to either side. Judging by their rapt concentration, they could have been gambling or performing a religious ritual.

Tom was swept by nostalgia. He knew these smells from the Chinatown of his boyhood in San Francisco. He had gone there occasionally with the family cook, when his mother was otherwise occupied and didn't suspect. Ah Wu had guided his fascinated charge through lanes of shops adorned with paper lanterns and brightly colored silks, around carts piled with tantalizing vegetables and fruits that would never appear on the Robesons' table. Now, surrounded by familiar sights and smells, Tom could almost feel the firm hand of Ah Wu on his shoulder.

"Can you imagine what this place will look like in the lay-up season?" Tom tried to picture it. Since a majority of the men in Broome made their living in the pearling fleets, they were gone during the months from April through October, when the fleets were at sea. When they returned to Chinatown and the camps beside the water, Broome would take on a different flavor entirely.

Archer made a sound of disgust. "Typhoons will come when the crews do, and the heat, as well. This place stinks now. Christ almighty, imagine the stench in a month or two."

Tom admired the colorful vitality of Chinatown, but he was accustomed to his friend's narrower vision of the world. He knew Archer to be basically fair-minded and steadfast, even though he was occasionally intolerant. Archer was a contradiction in many ways. He was an impulsive man, but he could still calculate the odds in a situation and come out a winner. He was a man whose self-interest was paramount, but he would also cheerfully lay his life on the line for a friend.

Tom knew the last from experience.

Now he rested his hand on Archer's shoulder, and gently steered him, as Ah Wu had guided him, past the alley. "Be sure you don't miss the good Broome has to offer."

"A job finding pearls I can't own myself?" Archer spat in the street.

"We have to learn the business one way or the other. We'll find out how it's done, and maybe by next season we'll have a lugger of our own. I still have funds in California."

"Not enough for a lugger, you don't."

"But enough to help us get a start. In the meantime, we have to keep an eye open for the main chance. That's what Garth said he did. Don't forget, this is just the beginning."

Archer's dreams were big ones and not easily deferred, but, as Tom knew, he wasn't one to brood. He shook off Tom's hand. "Right now I'll settle for something to eat."

John Garth had given each man an advance on the pay he would receive at the season's end. They had already moved their meager belongings to the Roebuck Bay Hotel, more suitable quarters than the hovel where the skipper had found them. All that remained was to find a laundry that would return their clothes by the morning. Then they could go back to the hotel to fill up on cheap, nourishing food. John had warned them to expect nothing better than rice and fish once they were on board the *Odyssey*.

"There's the laundry John recommended." Tom pointed out the sign at the end of the block. "Sing Chung's."

Chinatown, called Japtown by some, was the home of a dozen Asian nationalities, with various social clubs and businesses, but here, as in other parts of the world, the Chinese had honed and bartered marketable skills they had brought with them from the old country. The Chinese washed and pressed the uniforms and incidental clothing of those pearling masters who couldn't afford to send their laundry to Singapore.

"Do you suppose the poor bastards work all night long? Don't they need sleep the same as you and me?" Archer said.

"They're exactly like any man. They do whatever they can, whenever they can, to survive."

"I wouldn't stand over a kettle of boiling water in this heat."

"You would if that was all you could do to support your wife and children."

Archer flashed a winning grin. "I'm planning to marry a woman who can support me."

"And I'm sure you'll find a dozen like that in Broome. If you can find a dozen women."

"I won't be staying in this hellhole long enough to find anything except a pearl. I'll make my fortune quick, then I'm going to Victoria. I'll buy a place, settle down and raise cattle. That's what I know. And when I'm done, I'll have a kingdom to leave my sons."

Tom understood where his friend's ambitions had originated. Archer was the only child of immigrants who had traveled to Texas with dreams of their own. His father had died in a West Texas jail with nothing to show for years of struggle except a prison sentence he hadn't deserved. His mother, destitute and sickly, had been forced to place her young son in an orphanage.

Archer had spent the remainder of his childhood on the ranch of the local mayor as an unpaid laborer.

Tom clapped him on the back. "Let's dispose of the laundry, then you can fortify yourself so you'll have the strength to build that kingdom."

Archer was laughing as they walked through the door.

The room was dark and cramped, and the heat was almost unbearable. Tom supposed the wash was boiled in the curtained partition behind this one, adding ten degrees to the temperature. The only light came from the doorway behind them. As his vision adjusted, he saw a slender figure behind a low table. As it sharpened, the figure became a woman, a young woman with a delicate heart-shaped face and eyes that were modestly fixed on the table before her.

Archer, who was in a hurry to get back to their hotel, stepped forward, slinging his bundle to the table. "We have to have this back by tomorrow morning. Early. Can you have it finished by then?"

Tom joined him. The girl hadn't answered. "She may not speak English," he said softly.

"I speak very good English." The girl still didn't look up. She had a musical voice, and although her words were accented, they were clear.

Archer tapped his foot. "I don't want a runaround. If you take them, they'd better be done on time."

Tom spoke. "Look, go back to the hotel. I'll take care of this. Order something for both of us. I'll join you in a few minutes."

"There are plenty of laundries in Chinatown," Archer warned as he headed for the door.

Tom waited until his friend was gone before he spoke. "He's in a hurry to eat. He doesn't mean to be rude."

"And you are not in a hurry?"

Tom was in no hurry at all. He had seen few beautiful women since arriving in Australia. He was certain there were many, but they didn't live on the vast tracts of land that the

Australians called stations, nor did they inhabit the gold fields. And Broome was heavily populated by men.

This young woman, with her long black hair, her smooth ivory skin and feathery eyelashes, rivaled any beauty he'd ever seen. Even with perspiration dotting her forehead and staining her clothes.

Tom placed his bundle on the table beside Archer's. "We wouldn't ask you to have these finished so quickly, but we were just hired to work on a lugger, and we're leaving in the morning. This is our last chance for clean clothes. Not that they'll stay that way very long."

He smiled and hoped she would lift her eyes. She did, and her gaze was surprisingly candid. "I will do them tonight."

"You're very kind." Despite the heat, he wanted to stay and gaze at her. He was reminded of the rare lovely Chinese women he had seen as a young boy. The merchants' wives with their embroidered clothing and festive holiday headdresses, the servant girls in their drab tunics and trousers. This woman wore similar garb, a black cotton tunic with only a thin line of embroidery ringing the high collar. But the stark contrast to her skin and the accent of a silken braid falling over her shoulder made her even lovelier.

She didn't seem to be in a hurry, either. Perhaps she enjoyed the escape from the laundry tubs in the rear. "You are not from here?"

He was pleased at the question. "No, I'm from California. And you? Have you always lived here?"

"No. I come here from China, just ten year ago."

"I miss California. Do you miss China?"

"I return soon to marry a man from my village."

He felt an absurd stab of disappointment. "He'll be a lucky man." Color rose in her cheeks, and he knew he had overstepped the considerable boundaries between them. "I'm sorry."

"Perhaps that is how things are said in California." She began to untie Archer's bundle.

Since Tom had already stepped into forbidden territory, he

ventured a little farther. "No, in California I would say something like, are you sure you want to go all that way home to China when you could stay here and marry me?"

The color deepened in her cheeks, but she smiled shyly. "My father does not let me talk to men. Now I understand."

"Where is your father today?"

"He is ill and sleeping."

"I'm sorry. I hope he feels better soon."

She looked down at the clothes spread out in front of her now and named a price.

"I'm sure that will be fine," Tom said.

"The same for yours."

"But you haven't even counted mine. There might be more."

"The same or less."

Clearly she didn't want to spread his clothes in front of him. He smiled his acceptance. "Shall I pay you now?"

She looked up again. She had winged brows and lovely dark eyes, but it was the intelligence in them that captivated him. "You may give me money when you return tomorrow."

"Will you be here? Or will your father?"

She shook her head, as if to say she didn't know.

He told himself it was despicable to hope her father would remain ill. "Will you still be here for the lay-up? Or will you be in China by then?"

"If my father is ill, I will stay and care for him."

"I'm sure you'll be sorry to delay your wedding."

As he expected, she didn't answer.

"I keep saying things I shouldn't," he said. "I'm sorry again."

"The man I am to marry is old, already with two wives."

The idea of this young woman—hardly more than a girl— marrying an old man upset him. Even more, he did not want her to marry a man with wives who would treat her as their slave. He didn't understand Chinese customs, but he knew this lovely young woman deserved better.

"Please, you leave now. Come back tomorrow." Before he

could respond, she gathered up the clothing and disappeared through the faded curtains into the rear of the shop.

He stared after her until the curtains stopped swaying and the heat finally drove him outside.

3

Archer ordered dinner for himself and Tom, then found a table in the corner where he could sit with his back to the wall. The Roebuck was primitive by city standards, but a great improvement on the boardinghouse where he and Tom had met John Garth.

Here, for the most part, he was surrounded by his own kind, although there weren't many of them. Men in informal khaki and dusty moleskins and men in formal white dotted the room, talking and drinking with their mates. No one had paid attention when he entered, but he was sure that he was already known here. In a town like this one, no stranger went unnoticed.

From his vantage point he could see into the billiard room, which was already crowded, and around the rest of the dining area, where most of the tables were empty. But as he waited idly for service, a middle-aged man in pristine white strolled in, accompanied by a hatchet-faced woman in a dark dress so stiff it didn't even rustle as she moved. They were seated quickly, and although Archer wouldn't have guessed deference was part of the town character, the couple immediately had two fawning hotel employees at their sides.

"A bit of royalty there, hey?"

Archer looked up at the publican who dropped cutlery in

front of him along with a healthy shot of whiskey. "Who is he?"

"Him? That could be you one of these days, if you just found a pearl or two fit for Her Majesty's crown. Or a maharajah's."

"One of your pearling masters?" Archer had figured as much on his own.

"Top o' the heap. Sebastian Somerset and his missus. Has his shirts tailored in Singapore, his cigarettes rolled in Egypt and his champagne bottled in France." The publican, bell-shaped and sweating profusely, gave the table a quick flick with a rag and lowered his voice. "Me, I wouldn't trade all the pearls in the world for living with the likes of her."

Archer imagined the starch in the woman's dress was limper than that in her soul. Somerset, a dark-haired man who held himself as straight as a mast, looked every bit as unyielding. His features were even and fine, but his scowl was permanently etched. "So Somerset's been successful?"

"Captain Somerset's got a fleet of sixteen luggers and at least two mother ships, with a big camp up by Pikuwa Creek. Regularly pulls out pearls as big as emu eggs."

Archer laughed. "And enough mother-of-pearl to pave the streets of heaven?"

The publican gave the table another swipe. "He's a rich man, that's no joke. The richest in town. There's not a bachelor between here and Perth who doesn't dream of marrying his daughter."

"Does this daughter look anything like her mother?"

"Viola? She's pretty enough, I suppose, but she's got a tongue like a death adder. Poisoned every man in town."

"Sounds like she needs taming."

"T'will take a rich man to do it." The publican wandered back to the bar at the same moment Tom wandered through the door.

"The laundry will be ready by morning," Tom said as he pulled up a chair.

"Good, because I'm planning to take an early stroll before we set sail."

"Stroll?" Tom looked perplexed.

"Yeah. It seems there's a part of Broome we haven't yet seen."

"Where, exactly?"

Archer crossed his arms over his chest and grinned. "The part where my future wife is living."

Viola Somerset despised Broome. For that matter, she despised Australia. When she was a young girl her mother had promised to send her to England to finish her education, but her father had never allowed it. Viola was too willful, he claimed, too intent on having her own way. He was certain that if he allowed her to leave the Southern Hemisphere, he would never see her again. And any chance he had for influencing future generations would be gone forever.

Pleading with Sebastian hadn't helped Viola. When she was fourteen she'd starved herself for a week, and in response he had taken to eating all his meals in front of her without offering up a morsel. At fifteen she had given up hope that England might be in her future and begged him to send her to a finishing school in Perth. Viola had claimed that she needed refinement, that she required all the skills of a proper lady so that someday she could take her place as the wife of the man who would succeed Sebastian.

Her father had claimed that no finishing school could make a lady out of a girl who was so obviously deceitful.

Sebastian Somerset was as stubborn as his daughter, and although Viola despised him right along with town and country, she also admired his tenacity. He had gone against conventional wisdom to establish himself in Western Australia, building his empire one lugger and load of pearl shell at a time, until now he was a wealthy man. He had brought his wife and newborn daughter to live in Broome when the town was thought to be no place for white women. And by establishing his family before it was the fashionable thing to do, he had been in the best position to reap the rewards when others followed suit.

When her father had finally relented long enough to allow Viola to spend her sixteenth year visiting a cousin who lived on a large sheep property in South Australia, Viola had thanked him like a dutiful daughter, while silently promising herself that she would disembark in Adelaide, sell the pearl necklace she was taking as a gift to her aunt and find another ship sailing anywhere that wasn't Australia.

She hadn't, of course. Her cousin Martha had been waiting when she arrived in Adelaide, and Viola had seen immediately that Martha was a kindred spirit. The two girls had spent the next months caught up in the social whirl of the South Australian pastoralists. Viola had attended city balls and country race meetings, whipped high-spirited thoroughbreds over rock-strewn pastures, and danced and flirted at week-long house parties. Martha had taught her to wear her golden curls high on her head and her evening dresses low on her shoulders, but the art of making a man fall in love with her had come as naturally to Viola as wildflowers in the Wet.

Finally forced to return to Broome, Viola had carried with her the knowledge that she could control her future by the toss of her curls and the sweep of her long, pale lashes. Sebastian might have plans for her life, but she would find a man who gloried in the pastoralist's life and leave pearling and Broome behind forever.

Now, months later, she was beginning to despair that she would find that man. As she watched her parents step out of their buggy and start toward the door of the family bungalow, she told herself not to pout. Her father was always displeased with her. No good would come of making him more so.

"Did you enjoy your tea?" she asked her mother with a strained smile.

Jane Somerset sniffed. "There was no one of consequence at the hotel."

"That's a pity." Viola offered an arm to help her mother up

the stairs. As always, stout Jane wore an old-fashioned corset that was laced so tightly it restricted her movements.

Even with Viola's help, Jane breathed heavily as she climbed to the lattice-shaded veranda. "The roast was tough. I don't know what their cook could have been thinking of."

Sebastian ignored his wife and removed his hat. "Viola, I don't approve of the way that dress bares your chest."

"Don't you?" she asked sweetly, abandoning her resolution not to upset him. "Would you prefer it bared more?"

"I would prefer that you speak to me the way a daughter should speak to a father!"

"And I would prefer that you not criticize me for every little thing." Viola tossed back her curls. "There is no one here to see what I'm wearing. There is never anyone here who matters."

"Then what do you call young Freddy Colson? He's here often enough to suit even you, I wager."

Freddy Colson did not suit Viola in any way. He was her father's choice as a potential husband, a slight young man who devoted himself to overseeing and investing her father's profits. Freddy knew the price of every nail that studded the Somerset luggers, every barrel of rice carried on board and every basket of shell removed. She was certain he dreamed of pounds and shillings.

She was also certain that Freddy did not dream of her or any other woman.

"Freddy would be happiest if he could marry you," Viola said. "If this were a race, I would finish a distant second."

Her father began tugging angrily at a mustache that was more luxuriant than his hair. "You're determined to infuriate me, aren't you, girl?"

"I am determined to point out I won't marry Freddy Colson, no matter how much he knows about Somerset and Company." She settled her wheezing mother on a chair. "If I marry any man from this town, it will be one who wants to leave it!"

"And if that happens, I will disown you!"

"And if *that* happens, I will consider myself blessed!" She turned away, angry at her mother for remaining silent, angrier at herself for becoming provoked, angriest at her father, who was determined to ruin her life. She left her parents on the veranda and retired to her bedroom.

Archer's bed was hard and narrow, but better than anything he'd slept on for weeks. The bedding was clean, and the window was covered with a light gauze that kept out the bulk of the mosquitoes but not the night breeze. He had slept soundly at first, his stomach filled with mutton stew and his head foggy from too much whiskey. But just before dawn something had awakened him. Now, just seconds after he had been pulled from slumber, he lay tense and alert.

At first he heard nothing out of the ordinary. Dogs barked in the distance, but the town was filled with mongrels who fought over every scrap tossed their way. He heard the dull thud of a gong from some pagan temple in nearby Chinatown, and from the hotel itself he heard the clanging of glasses and cutlery as someone in the dining room readied it for business. But none of these sounds could have disturbed his sleep.

"No, don't, Linc. I don't want to fight...not you. Don't be a fool—" Tom mumbled the words, then turned restlessly on the bed next to Archer's. "Linc... No..."

Archer realized what had awakened him. In the first year after the war with Spain, Tom's nightmares had been frequent and occasionally so violent that restraining him was necessary for his safety. Even if Archer woke him, it sometimes took Tom minutes to realize the nightmare had been only that.

Now, from the words he'd uttered, Archer knew what his friend was dreaming about, and he debated what to do. Sometimes, after minutes of tossing, Tom fell into a deeper sleep. But sometimes the nightmares consumed him, and for Archer's own peace, he was forced to shake his friend to bring him awake.

Archer lay still and waited to decide which would be best.

"We're not here...to fight each other." Tom mumbled something else; then, for a moment, at least, he fell silent.

Even in his sleep, fair-minded Tom got the story right. The men of the Volunteer First Cavalry, known to the world as the Rough Riders, hadn't been sent to Cuba to fight each other. They'd been an odd mixture of trail-roughened cowboys and idealistic aristocrats guaranteed to have both the brains and brawn an Army unit needed. Despite the difference in their education and background, they had come together to fight a common enemy, the Spanish, who were said to have sabotaged the *Maine* and enslaved the Cuban people.

Archer hadn't enlisted because he gave one damn what happened to the dark-skinned denizens of an island too distant to be a threat. When the call went out from Teddy Roosevelt, Archer had signed on because the army was a way out of trouble. A certain rancher wasn't pleased that he had lost most of his hard-earned savings to Archer in an Amarillo poker game, and he had threatened to prove that Archer had cheated. Since Archer *had,* he had seen the free trip to Cuba as a way to hold his head high and still keep his neck out of a noose.

Of course Tom hadn't joined the Rough Riders because he was in trouble, or even because he wanted to explore the world. He was a man who felt the suffering of others as if it were *his* stomach that rumbled with hunger, *his* throat that was parched with thirst. Tom, a skilled athlete, horseman and sharpshooter, was also the sole heir to a fortune. His father was a railroad tycoon in boomtown San Francisco, and someday Tom would inherit a significant part of the city. Without thought of the riches that would someday be his, he had pledged his destiny to Roosevelt even after his father had threatened to pledge Tom's inheritance to distant relatives.

Although both men were assigned to K Troop, at first neither had taken notice of the other, content to seek out their own kind. Then one night, in a beer garden near Riverside Park in San Antonio, K Troop's drill sergeant, a miner named Linc Webster, began to turn his considerable talent for torment against Tom.

Despite the hardships of training, Linc had always managed to find enough liquor to stay one drink beyond belligerent. That night he had objected to an innocent remark of Tom's, and without thinking, Archer, who always relished a fight, inserted himself between the bully and the aristocrat. Linc threw a punch, Archer pushed Tom out of the way, and Linc was thrown by the force of his own swing to the ground, accompanied by the laughter of everyone who witnessed it.

Tom and Archer, bound together by Archer's action, became firm friends. But from that moment on Linc made revenge against Tom his life's mission. In San Antonio, and later in Tampa, Tom was given the dirtiest jobs. When mounts were assigned, Tom's, not surprisingly, was a knock-kneed, wall-eyed gelding he was glad to leave behind when the Rough Riders discovered they were going to ride shank's mare during their conquest of Cuba.

Linc's campaign against Tom grew dirtier as the days passed. As often as he could, Tom ignored the escalating hostilities—which infuriated Linc still more. When Tom discovered that the buttons had been slashed from his blue cavalry shirt, he sewed them on again without a murmur. When someone stuffed his slouch hat with horse patties, he emptied and cleaned it without protest. Tom was not immune to anger, but he reasoned that too much was at stake to lose his temper. He believed that reason and patience would win the day.

Archer, who had never set much store in either, was certain Tom was wrong.

The tension between the drill sergeant and the private seemed to dissolve after the Rough Riders stepped off the transport ship at Daiquiri on Cuba's southern coast. At first it seemed as if Linc had a new focus for his rage, or even that the jungle heat and punishing afternoon rains had sapped his interest. During their first battle at Las Guasimas, Linc, Tom and Archer fought the hidden Spanish soldiers without incident, each surviving without a wound, although eight of their comrades were killed. But a week later, after a hellish advance to the outskirts of Santiago, everyone's temper was short, Linc's most of all.

On the night before the charge up San Juan Hill, Tom'received a warning that Linc had not forgotten him. All day the men had marched in the worst of conditions over paths a foot deep in mud, slashing their way through jungle inhabited by tarantulas and giant-clawed land crabs. Some of them had succumbed to fever; others were beginning to suspect they had been infected, too. No time or opportunity presented itself for comforting army routine. They threw down their blanket rolls and collapsed to the ground. Talking and smoking were prohibited, and most of them simply closed their eyes and hoped for sleep.

Tom was sinking into oblivion when he heard Linc's whisper close to his ear. "You won't survive tomorrow, Robeson. I'm the one who'll see to it." Tom opened his eyes and saw Linc's sneering face just inches from his, but in the next moment Linc dissolved into the darkness. In his exhaustion Tom wondered if Linc's words were only his own worst fears spoken out loud. He was already uncertain whether he would survive another day of this hell, much less another battle, and he fell asleep convinced he had dreamed the threat.

They were on the move again by four the next morning. Tom and Archer marched together, and Tom told him about the dream. Archer suspected Linc's visit had been real. Even in the face of threat, Tom was altering facts to make them palatable. But Archer had his own safety to worry about. He could only warn Tom to avoid Linc.

The attack on Santiago was to be two-pronged, with the Rough Riders swinging west across San Juan Creek to the heavily defended San Juan Heights. San Juan Hill stood to the left and a smaller hill to the right. As they waited for orders, the Rough Riders crouched beside the riverbank or wriggled into position in the tall, waving grasses.

Archer and Tom settled themselves along the bank in a position where they were least vulnerable to the savage Spanish gunfire that was steadily picking off their confederates. Out of sight, the wounded moaned pathetically, and curses filled the air.

"I'm going to see if I can get a better look." Archer took

off for a pocket in the bank. He was tired of waiting for the charge and eager for action. He made the pocket without incident and squirmed into position so he was hidden from view. Then he looked back to see if he could spot Tom.

From his new vantage point Archer could see that Tom was exactly where he had left him, but that behind him, creeping stealthily forward from mound of dirt to rock outcropping, was Lincoln Webster. Archer didn't have time to think. He raised his rifle, and at the exact moment that Linc aimed his own rifle at Tom, Archer fired.

No one except a dismayed Tom should ever have known what happened. No one else would have suspected that Linc was not just another casualty of a Spanish Mauser, but as Archer lowered his gun, he caught and held the gaze of a reporter from a New York newspaper who had been hidden behind another outcropping on the riverbank. From the man's horrified expression, it was clear he had witnessed the entire incident, minus the crucial detail of what Linc had been planning to do.

The man rose, his face draining of color, as if he was certain that Archer would not let him live to tell this tale. He scurried from behind the rock and dove for better cover. And as he did, a Spanish bullet knocked him to the ground.

The story would have ended there. Even Tom, with all his integrity, would not have sullied the outcome of the subsequent charge up Kettle and San Juan Hills by relating what had happened just before. Linc was dead; the reporter was dead, too. Both Archer and Tom had survived the charge. No good would come from reporting what had happened that morning at the riverbank.

But well after the bugles had announced Spanish defeat, and days after the bands had finished their victory marches, Archer discovered that the reporter had not died that morning after all. At the brink of death from a head wound complicated by malaria, the man had been taken by ship back to the United States. No one knew for sure what had happened to him after that.

Every day until the *Miami* carried the victorious Rough Riders north to Long Island, Archer expected to find himself bound and chained. And on the day in September when the First Volunteer Cavalry Regiment was disbanded, he realized that he couldn't stay in the United States any longer. That morning he discovered that the reporter was recovering slowly in a sanitarium in Albany. And someday the man might remember exactly what he had seen.

That night Archer told Tom he was leaving the country for good, but Tom protested. Tom was convinced that even if the truth was revealed, Archer would be exonerated. But Archer knew he was doomed if the military ever made an inquiry. The reporter had a major newspaper standing behind him, a newspaper that thrived on sensation. And what was more sensational than one of the Rough Riders murdering another? Archer was nothing but a cowboy turned soldier. If he lied, no one would believe him. And if he told the truth, he would probably face a firing squad.

"Then I'm going with you," Tom told him. "My family won't help us, but I have money saved. If we throw our lot together we'll be able to establish a life somewhere. And even if I don't stay, I can help you make a start."

Archer, who knew that success in his new life depended heavily on cash, welcomed Tom to join him.

Now, as Tom flailed from side to side on his narrow bed in Broome's Roebuck Hotel, Archer listened to his mutterings. By saving Tom's life, Archer, who had never been anyone's hero, had become Tom's, a position that suited him, since it brought with it Tom's resources and loyalty.

But even after years of seeking their fortune together, Tom was still a mystery to him. Linc's senseless persecution hadn't taught Tom anything. He still believed that, deep inside, everyone was good. He excused the faults of those he encountered and looked for redeeming virtues in the unlikeliest places, but most of all, he loved Archer without reserve. Archer, who had not been loved since the early days of his childhood, found this the strangest mystery of all.

Archer was a daredevil who acted without thinking, and this was the real reason he had saved Tom's life. But even though murdering Linc had not been without personal consequence, he wasn't sorry he'd done it. Since fleeing the country, he had grown accustomed to, perhaps even dependent on, Tom's friendship.

As Archer stared at his friend, Tom sat up suddenly and looked around, although his vision was still focused inward. Then, as if the dream had been shaken into a new chapter, he sighed, slid down against the rough cotton sheet and turned to his side. He was silent at last.

Archer stared at the ceiling, but sleep had fled. He no longer thought about the circumstances that had brought him here, but about the ones he found himself in now.

He savored adventure, but he was tired of knocking around the world, living by his wits and Tom's dwindling bank account. He had little to show for his life, and the lure of the unknown was quickly becoming a curse. Like his father, he wanted to build a dynasty. He wanted land and sons and a herd of cattle stretching farther than a man could see. Even if it had been safe to go home to Texas, his chance of obtaining enough good land to build an empire was slim.

Here in Australia there was land at the right price. Granted, some of it was bleak, barren land that could sustain few cattle, but there was also more of it. All he needed was a stake to buy or lease property. He could do the rest with sweat and savvy.

He needed a bride from a rich family; he needed a pearl to make a woman like Viola Somerset look at him.

Archer sat up and felt for his clothes. He dressed quickly and let himself out without waking Tom. The early morning air was heavy and still. The faintest light tantalized the horizon. Last night he had asked the publican where the town's wealthiest citizens lived, and the man had pointed toward a road leading away from the center of town.

Archer had been too busy trying to find work to pay much attention to the way Broome was laid out. Now, as he strolled along the pindan dirt road and slapped lazily at mosquitoes, he saw that there was more to this slice of frontier than Chinatown, the jetty where the luggers docked and the ramshackle foreshore camps.

Society was beginning to make inroads in Broome. There were a customs house, a police station and a jail. He passed bungalows surrounded by deep verandas, some of which were shuttered or screened for sleeping. As the road began to climb and the sun spread its golden glow, the houses grew larger and finer. Archer knew he had discovered the lair of the pearling masters.

Archer had spent enough time on ships to know that by nature he wasn't a sailor. But for a moment he could appreciate the quaint charm of this coastal town with its exotic profusion of bougainvillea and feathery poinciana trees, its skies filled with circling terns, noddies and gulls. Broome nestled between mangroves and mud flats and the red pindan sandhills, but the faintest scent of salt was always in the air.

He stopped and surveyed the landscape, wondering which distant house belonged to Sebastian Somerset. If Somerset was the most successful pearling master in Broome, than it stood to reason that his would be the finest residence. But nothing Archer had seen was worthy of a man with so much influence. He trudged farther up the road until just ahead of him he saw a dark-skinned youth dressed in neatly pressed Western clothes, obviously somebody's houseboy on his way to work. Broome was a town where even the poorest sea captain could afford a houseful of servants.

Archer easily caught up with the boy. "Hey, can you tell me which house belongs to Sebastian Somerset?"

The boy looked puzzled and turned up his hands, but he didn't move away.

Dozens of languages were spoken here, but the universal one seemed to be an oddly adulterated English. Archer tried a version of it. "House belonga Mr. Somerset? Big pearling boss?"

The boy didn't move or speak.

Archer reached in his pocket for his smallest coin, but instead of giving it to the boy, he flipped it into the air and caught it, repeating this several times before he asked his question again in the same pidgin dialect.

The boy pointed down the road. "Three house. Bigfella fence."

Archer considered pocketing the coin, but instead he grinned and let it drop into the dust. The boy scrambled for it as Archer continued up the road.

Had he just kept walking he would still have recognized the third house as Somerset's. Although it didn't begin to compare with the houses of rich men in Texas, in contrast with its neighbors, Somerset's home was a castle. The house was imposing, but it still fitted into the local landscape and architectural traditions. The verandas surrounding it were cavernous, trimmed lavishly with lacy gingerbread and trellises smothered with vines. The floor was raised off the ground on blocks, and the green metal roof was peaked, with a door facing the front and a narrow walkway leading off it. Archer imagined that the pearling master could catch sight of his luggers going off to sea from his private vantage point.

The grounds were lovely, with a variety of palm trees and young specimens of the other-worldly boab trees with their massive bulbous trunks. The trees and a collection of shrubs rose in landscaped clusters to soften the edifice. A golden shower tree drooped beside a sober iron fence that looked as if it might have been imported from across the seas. He stood sheltered by the tree's weeping branches and stared.

Archer wondered what life must be like for the daughter of this house. Had she lived here always, or had her father sent her away to become a proper lady? Did she love this town, with its pungent smells, exotic vistas, its barbaric population? Would she refuse to leave, no matter what the enticement?

As if he had conjured the image, a woman in a nightdress glided across a veranda on the western side of the house. Through the sheer gauze at the windows he could see her moving silently, gracefully, toward the veranda railing. She lifted the gauze-draped frame and stood looking out over the garden.

Archer held his breath, not certain if she could see him. For a moment he had been afraid that Sebastian Somerset's wife would be staring back at him, but this woman was young and slender, with a single braid of golden hair draped over one shoulder and the hint of a softly rounded figure under the fabric of her white gown and robe. He couldn't see her face clearly, but he saw enough to realize her features were pert and symmetrical. She leaned against a veranda pillar and folded her arms.

The sun rose higher, and the sky brightened with the passing moments. The birds, like everything else in the heathen town, were too brash for Archer's tastes. Now one landed in the tree above him, flashing the colors of the rainbow and chattering as if it expected him to answer.

At the noise the woman turned and saw more than the bird. She leaned forward, her hair spilling over the railing like Rapunzel enticing her lover. Archer stepped out from the shadow of the tree and held up a hand in greeting. She moved to the steps and stood just above them.

"Do I know you?"

She didn't speak loudly, but even though the distance between them was considerable, Archer heard her.

"Not yet." He flashed his best devil-may-care grin.

"Really? And why would that change?"

"Because I'm the man you're going to marry."

She didn't seem disturbed by his impudence. "Do you think so?"

"I've made up my mind."

"And why is that?"

In the most dangerous moments of his life Archer's intuition had always been keenest. That sixth sense had saved Tom in Cuba. Now he sensed that Viola Somerset was a formidable woman, one who would want to know the truth because it would help her plan her next move. This was no shy virgin who expected a devotion no man was capable of. This was a woman who would scheme to get her heart's desire. He just wished that he knew exactly what that desire might be.

"You're going to marry me because we're two of a kind,"

he said at last. "I want you because you'll give me pleasure in bed, strong sons and a wealthy father-in-law. You want me because, in trade, I'll give you whatever you want most."

"And that is?"

"Sorry, princess. But I don't have that part figured out."

"Then how do you know you can give it to me?"

"Because if I can't, I'll die trying."

She had a tinkling laugh. "I want to leave Broome and never, ever return. Will you give me that?"

"The very moment I can. Because I want the same thing."

"I want a husband with property. I want to be the mistress of a station, not a man. Do you have property?"

"I don't have much of anything, but that's going to change, and soon."

"Really?" Her tone dropped several degrees. "Come back if it ever does." She lifted her chin, and sweeping the hem of her nightdress away from her feet, she started toward the door.

"Princess?"

She turned her head and stared icily at him.

"My name's Archer Llewellyn. You can embroider bridal handkerchiefs while I'm out at sea."

"And my name's Viola Somerset. You can dream about me until the day they bury you forty fathoms deep."

He was laughing when she closed the door behind her.

4

"Whale him badfellow. You-me no come-up long pearling grounds."

Bernard, the *Odyssey*'s tender, a massively built Koepanger from Dutch Timor, shook his head philosophically and went to take the tiller to continue steering the little lugger away from the waterspout spraying the waves ahead of them. Tom remained where he was to stare at the unmistakable evidence that the crew was not alone at sea.

"If it's not one thing, it's everything put together." Archer joined Tom, folding his arms over his chest like a sultan issuing orders to the royal executioner. The boat groaned as Bernard and two crew members adjusted their course.

Silently Tom turned to watch the waterspout growing more distant as the sails of the *Odyssey* snatched the wind. They were well away from the uninterested whale before the lugger changed course and continued toward the pearling grounds. The crew, a mixture of nationalities that stretched from Japan to Malaysia, knew exactly what was expected of them, and each man worked quickly and quietly at his job, only trading words when absolutely needed.

"Have you ever seen so many thugs and murderers gathered in one place before?"

Tom inclined his head toward Archer. He saw the diversity of the crew as an adventure. "These thugs and murderers can make or destroy us," he said, quietly enough that no one else could hear. "Best if we try to get along with them, don't you think?"

Archer went on as if he hadn't heard him. "And what exactly do you make of Bernard? Yesterday he and Ahmed argued, and he lifted him three feet off the deck with one hand. Mark my words. He'll gut us while we sleep if he can get the rest of the crew to go along with him. Not that any of them speak English well enough for a mutiny."

Tom thought the crew communicated well enough, using their own sort of pidgin, to plot any number of heinous acts. But unlike Archer, he doubted they were interested. "Did you get any sleep last night?"

"Not a wink."

Tom wasn't surprised. By day the lugger was comfortable enough, but by night it became the playground of a thousand winged cockroaches that dined on the remnants of oyster gristle in the hold and—if they felt the need for variety—on the toenails and calluses of the crew. Every night since he had come on board, he had felt feet skittering and wings whispering over his bare skin. And if that wasn't bad enough, the air below was thick with the smothering odor of rotten fish, Oriental curry and mildew. He and Tom had been sleeping in the mainhold on planks laid over hogsheads of water. The rest of the crew slept on deck beneath an awning.

He turned to Archer, whose scowling face was sprouting the beginning of a full beard. "It's only going to get worse. Juan told us we wouldn't want to sleep below. Tonight I'm going to spread my bedroll up here with the rest of the crew. There'll be a place for you, too, if you want some sleep."

"Sleep up here with cutthroats and murderers? When Juan is sleeping in the cabin?"

Juan Fernandez was the *Odyssey*'s diver, indisputably the most important man on board. He had come to Australia from Manila, and although he wasn't the best diver in Broome, his record, measured in tons of pearl shell, was good.

"Go ahead and take the other bed in the cabin, then," Tom offered. "I'll be just as happy out here in the fresh air."

Archer's sour expression dissolved into something more pleasing. "If one of us doesn't take the space, someone less deserving will. After all, we're the ones who open shell."

Two mornings ago, just before their departure, John Garth had given them a quick lesson on shipboard life. Like the other pearling masters, John had made it a point to hire men of many differing backgrounds. A crew with inbred animosities and no common language was less apt to band together against a captain's interests. So the lugger had a Manilaman diver, a Koepanger tender, a Chinese cook, two strong young Malayan boys to pump air when Juan was down below, and an old sailor from Japan whose years as a diver had left him nearly deaf and blind in one eye.

And despite the fact that all the crew had extensive experience on pearling vessels, when decisions had to be made, Tom and Archer, who were brand-new, were in charge.

"What do you suppose it's like underwater?" Tom said. "Juan's a lucky bastard, don't you think?"

"Lucky? You had a good look at Toshiharu? That's what diving will do to a man. I don't know why Garth put him on this crew. He can't hear. He can barely see. He stumbles and trips every time something gets in his way."

"He's here because he was John's diver on his first voyage, and John feels responsible."

"The skipper's not much of a businessman, is he?"

"You would do the same." Tom had lost sight of the spout, and he wondered idly where the whale was headed. "I know there are dangers down below, but I'd gladly take my chances."

"Ask Juan, why don't you? Maybe he'll let you take his place." Archer wandered off in search of a more active way to spend his time.

Juan came up from the hold, swaggering with a rolling, bow-legged gait, as if practicing for the long hours he spent on the ocean floor. An hour out of Broome he had abandoned his trousers and shirt in favor of the more practical sarong. His only other adornment was a gold cross around his neck.

"What is it you looking at out there?"

Tom already liked Juan, a deeply religious man who had erected an altar to the Virgin Mary in his cabin. "Eternity."

"Too many men seen eternity here."

"Tell me what it's like down below."

Juan was of average height and dark-skinned, with cropped hair as shiny and sleek as the pelt of a mink, and long-lashed, languid eyes that took in everything around him. Now his eyes grew dreamy. "Below's not so lonely as this. Lot of fish. Lot of company. Up here a man keep looking for something but find nothing. Me, I think of home up here, but down below I think of nothing but shell." Juan wandered away, too.

Tom had thought of home hardly at all since he and Archer had left the United States. He wrote his parents regularly, but he had only received one letter in his years away. His father had demanded that he return immediately or lose his inheritance.

Tom had never shared his father's infatuation with wealth. He was happier now than he had ever been as the heir to a great California fortune. He needed very little to stay alive, and he couldn't think of any reason why that would change. The Van Ness Avenue mansion his parents called home was as close to a prison cell as he ever hoped to come, and the chic young heiresses who'd bid for his attention had, for the most part, been dull or shallow.

He thought about the woman who was neither of those things, the woman who, even as he stared at the horizon, was probably preparing for her bridal journey to a small village in China.

He tried her name out loud. "Lian."

Tom was still surprised at his own strong response to the young Chinese woman. He had seen her only twice. And the second time, on the morning he had gone to pick up the laundry, she had been carefully watched by her father, Sing Chung, a hollow-eyed old man with a scraggly queue who had shivered convulsively on a stool in the far corner.

She had been even more beautiful at their second meeting, her tunic freshly ironed, her face unflushed by heat. She had pinned her hair high on her head with an ivory comb, but he had missed the seductive length of it lying against her breast.

"Did you stay up late to do our clothes?" he had asked in greeting.

She didn't meet his eyes. "It was no trouble."

He lowered his voice so her father wouldn't hear. "I'm sure it was. Thank you."

She nodded, her eyes downcast.

"Your father seems very ill."

"He will not rest today."

A torrent of rasping Cantonese issued from the man in the corner, and the young woman blushed. "I must take your money." She named the price they had agreed on.

Tom took his time finding the right coins. "I'm leaving this morning, and you'll probably be gone by the time I return. Will you at least tell me your name so I'll know what to call you in my mind?"

She lowered her voice to a near whisper. "Why would you think of me?"

He didn't respond directly, because the answer eluded him. "My name is Tom. Tom Robeson."

She hesitated.

He turned his pocket inside out as if he were still searching, although by now the money was cupped in the palm of his hand.

She met his eyes quickly, then looked away. "Lian."

"Lian."

"In English, I am a tree. A willow."

"Willow." He grinned. "How well it suits you."

"Perhaps. My mother told me I must always bend."

Tom thought about the life that awaited her and hoped that she would be able to bend without snapping in two.

The old man barked hoarse orders at his daughter again. She

released a breath that was almost a sigh. "I will take your money. You must go."

He held out the coins. He didn't know what else he could say. There was probably no life for a girl like Lian in Broome except servitude or prostitution. Perhaps it would be better for her to return to her homeland, where at least her place in the community would be respected.

"May your voyage be successful," she said as she took the money.

"May your future be happy," he responded.

She looked up at him, her eyes clear but sad. They stared at each other for a long moment until the old man began to shout sentences punctuated with shallow gulps.

Tom lifted his laundry from the table, turned and left without looking back.

Now he *was* looking back. He wondered at his own strong reaction to Lian when he was so unmoved by women of his own background. He certainly pitied the girl, and he admired her beauty. But his feelings were stronger than either. He had been tempted in that moment when they stared into each other's eyes to reach across the table and touch her cheek. Hell, he had been tempted to grab her and pull her outside into the sunshine and a future with him.

Instead he had walked away. Now he wondered if he would walk away again if he found she was still in Broome when he returned. He was not impulsive like Archer, nor did his passions run as erratically, or as deep. But in that moment, staring out at an unknown sea, he wished he could sail back to Broome.

"Willow," he said, trying the name softly. The woman who must always bend would remain Willow in his mind for the rest of the voyage.

Archer had never done a job he despised more. Just days after leaving Broome with their own private flock of seagulls in tow, the *Odyssey* had arrived at coordinates off the Eighty Mile Beach where the crew had been successful earlier in the season. Juan was anxious to try the area again, and Bernard, whose job was to keep the lines free as Juan drifted below scouting for shell, believed the area was both safe and potentially fruitful.

The take had been small at first, which was just as well. After removal from the ocean, the shells were left out on the deck at night, where they gasped for air as the temperatures cooled. The next morning Archer and Tom practiced using tomahawks to scrape away the sea growth that clung to them; then, with thin-bladed knives, they learned to cut out the oysters without damaging an undiscovered pearl. The first day Archer had felt the thrill of adventure every time he gouged the oyster from its shell. The next step, palpating the slimy mass with his fingertips, had been like searching for buried treasure. A pearl could be lodged there, anything from a tiny misshapen baroque pearl, worth little more than the time it took to discover it, or the huge, perfect pearl of a century.

Now, three weeks later, there had been no pearls at all, nothing more than a few blisters attached directly to the shell, which would probably prove to be hollow and worthless when removed by a more expert hand than his.

The thrill had vanished quickly, and all that remained was a stinking, filthy job that left his hands slimy and tainted no matter how thoroughly he scrubbed them.

The lugger had been transformed, as well. Strips of drying, malodorous oyster muscle adorned the rigging to be bagged and sold later in Singapore. In the hold, the cockroaches seemed to double in number and size each night, and the stench of the pearl shell reached above deck and infected every breath of air.

The constant rolling and creaking of the ship. The enforced inactivity. The boredom. Everything added to Archer's feeling that life was passing him by. While he ate, slept and worked with heathens who spoke in tongues he didn't understand, his dreams, like the Australian coastline, seemed to move farther from reach.

Strangely, Tom, who had been Archer's friend and champion

since the war, seemed not to understand his feelings. Tom was thriving on the pearler's life. He had made a place for himself on board, and the crew both respected and liked him. Even now, as Archer stood to one side, the crew was gathered around him. Tom, thanks to Juan's generosity, was going below for his first dive.

Tom looked up at that moment and grinned. "Hey, Archer. Come over and give me a hand."

Tom didn't need his help, of course, and Archer knew it. But he ambled over because there was nowhere else to go. "You're sure you want to do this?"

"By and by him go," Bernard answered for Tom with a shrug of his massive shoulders. "So him go-long now."

Every one of the crew members was a fatalist, unlike Archer, who believed a man made his own fortune. But he could see that the men believed Tom was destined to try his luck under the water. Tom, who had talked of it often, had convinced them.

"It's a good time to give it a try," Tom said, as he allowed Juan to begin wrapping his chest and abdomen in flannel. Although it was scorching on deck, the ocean would be cold. "There's no shell to speak of here, so I'm not wasting time Juan could use productively. And it'll be tomorrow before we can sail to different grounds. So I might as well use this time."

Archer would prefer walking naked through a bonfire to donning the canvas diver's suit and copper helmet, but he didn't point that out, sure that if he acknowledged any weakness in front of the crew, it would come back to haunt him. "Don't fool around for too long," he said gruffly. "We have more important things to do than give you a little underwater holiday."

"It best he not stay down long first time," Juan said. "We bring him up, he wants to come or not."

Tom was wearing two layers of flannel pajamas in addition to the flannel wrapping, as well as two pairs of thick wool socks. Now, with the gnarled and lame Toshiharu's help, he donned woolen drawers and a sweater, and over them a long pair of wool stockings that reached to the tops of his thighs.

"You step in suit now," Juan instructed. "Then we fix."

Tom did, and the men pulled the suit around his feet, encasing them snugly before pulling it up and over his shoulders. Tom thrust his hands through the greased rubber cuffs and stood silently as they adjusted the rubber collar around his neck. Juan led him to the hatch, and he sat as Juan and Toshiharu shoved on the diver's boots with their fourteen-pound lead soles. As they did, Bernard sank the plumper, the line that would help guide him to the bottom.

Bernard lifted the copper corselet off the deck and held it in front of Tom's face. Tom grinned, and Bernard set it over his head and carefully screwed it down over the rubber collar of his suit, checking once, then again, to be certain every nut, every screw and valve, was in place and in working order.

"Him ready-fellow."

Archer had an odd sensation in the center of his belly. "You're sure you want to do this?"

"You bet."

Juan moved forward again, repeating last-minute instructions, as Tom listened carefully. Then, at Juan's nod, he turned and plodded slowly to the side. He lowered himself to the rope ladder and carefully descended until his corselet was even with the rail. Bending over, Bernard set a mantle of weights over his chest and back to keep Tom from capsizing if he lost his balance underwater. Then, after making sure the air pipe was unobstructed and the lifeline rose properly from its position on the back of the suit, Bernard lifted the bell-shaped helmet and screwed it down over the corselet.

Now all that was visible was Tom's features through the square glass opening. On deck the two Malayan boys bent to the pump wheel, and air began to hiss into the helmet. Toshiharu held the air pipe, and Bernard, after making some adjustments in the helmet valves, grasped the lifeline and nodded.

Tom hesitated for a moment; then he pitched himself off the ladder backwards into the water.

"Now we see if he remember good," Juan told Archer.

Tom flailed for a moment, and Archer almost expected him to overcompensate and flip face down into the water. But after a moment he seemed to relax. He adjusted the valve at the side of his helmet; then, as if he'd done it all his life, he held tight to the plumper and began to descend to the ocean floor.

"Your friend be a real sailor," Juan said. "He belong here with us."

Archer felt the quiet sting in the Manilaman's words. "I gather you don't think the same of me?"

Juan lifted an eyebrow. "You looking for pearl. He is looking for better something." He moved off to consult with Bernard, and Archer was left by himself to watch the bubbles from Tom's suit dance along the ocean surface.

Evening was Tom's favorite time aboard the *Odyssey*. When the final flagrant rays of sunset faded away and the anchor had been set for the evening, the lugger rocked lazily, and the men, tired from their chores, settled along their favorite places on deck to consume Wong Fai's curried fish and rice, and drink countless cups of strong tea fresh from the cooking fire.

Tom liked to listen to their conversations. He was becoming adept at the clever pidgin that united them despite the variety of their native tongues. He particularly enjoyed conversations with Juan, whose English was far superior to Tom's Spanish. Juan was an educated man with a taste for poetry and a talent for guitar, which made the long evenings easier to bear.

Juan joined Tom after dinner on the evening of his first dive, offering his slice of tinned beef, which was an infrequent item on their shipboard menu.

Tom smiled but shook his head. "I can't take that. You need every bit of meat. You work hard. I found that out today."

"Today you work hard, too. Take it."

Tom complied with murmured thanks. "I've never seen anything like it, Juan. A whole world out of reach to everybody but those lucky enough to go below."

"How is your ears?"

Tom swallowed to test them. The pressure had been fierce, and he had been stunned to discover blood seeping from his ear canals when he surfaced. His nose had bled, too. But both had stopped quickly. He had not gone too deep, and he had not stayed under long. Bernard believed that bringing divers up slowly was safest, and it seemed to Tom that he had spent much more time going down and coming up than exploring.

But he had found shell.

"Ears good?" Juan asked.

"They seem fine."

"Crew say it's good luck, you find shell below. Say you be luck for this lugger."

Tom laughed, and the sound rattled oddly in his head. "I'm afraid if we had to count on my finding shell, we'd go home with our hold half empty. There's a real art to seeing it. I don't know what led me to the few I picked up."

"God of the shell?"

Tom inclined his head. "Do you believe in such a thing?"

"No. Nobody believes."

Tom laughed again, and Juan smiled. They finished in silence, each enjoying the other's company. The other men were scattered over the deck. Archer was throwing dice with Toshiharu and Ahmed, the older of the two Malayan boys. Archer never seemed to lose, and the crew members had quickly learned not to play him for anything more than a pinch of tobacco.

Tom set his plate to one side and leaned back to stare at the stars. When he had decided to accompany Archer on his travels, he had not considered what he might do with all the years ahead of him. Despite his father's threats, he knew that his old life waited for him back in San Francisco if he wanted to reclaim it. At first he had half planned to go back after Archer was settled. He felt a duty to his parents, even though he had little affection for them.

But now, with the moon glistening like a celestial pearl on the calm water, the boat rocking gently beneath him, the men's voices murmuring in the cool evening air, he wondered if what he really wanted was to stay in Broome, acquire a lugger and make his own fortune. He was happier than he could remember. The pearling life suited him. Broome, with its colorful cultures, suited him. Australia, with its frontier values, its infinite and ancient stretches of land, its wondrous animal and plant life, suited him.

"I met a woman in Broome." He didn't look at Juan. "She was Chinese. Lian, the daughter of Sing Chung, at the laundry on Dampier Terrace. Could a man marry a woman like that in Broome?"

"Color bar in town. Not so good to mix. White people not approve. They not understand and turn back on you."

"Is that so?" Tom wasn't surprised.

"Girl want to marry you?"

"No, it was only a question. She's going to China to marry a stranger. She'll probably be gone by the time I return."

"Not so. Sing Chung die soon. She be there to care for him meantime. Still be there when we return."

"How do you know that, Juan?"

"Crew makes bet. Every man want her."

Tom grinned. He wondered if Lian knew she had a boatload of admirers. "The nice thing about Broome is that if a man was shunned by his own people, there would be plenty of others who would be his friends."

Juan got up and went to get his guitar. He came back to sit beside Tom and strum. "'Nother lugger in distance. Riding light there." Juan pointed out to sea.

Tom followed the direction of Juan's finger and squinted into the darkness. Finally, after a moment of total concentration, he saw a tiny dot of light from a lantern at the top of a distant masthead.

Since leaving Broome the crew had seen other luggers. Although there were many miles of ocean, the pearling boats worked the same grounds. Several times they had even gotten close enough to spend an evening in each other's company.

"Too bad they're so far away," Tom said. "It would liven up our night if they were closer."

Juan put down his guitar and sidled to the railing. He stared for a long moment. Archer and the others, sensing that something was up, abandoned their game and joined him.

"Dinghy coming," Juan said at last.

"Really?" Tom joined them. "So we'll have company after all." Juan's eyes were sharper than his, and moments passed before he saw the rowboat approaching.

Juan stepped back. "Nakanishi, the diver. From the *Sophia.* One of Somerset's fleet. Two others in boat."

"Somerset's fleet?" Archer asked, interest in his voice.

"Big camp down on coast at Pikuwa Creek." Juan pointed to the east. "Mother ship comes to pearling grounds when month begins and brings supplies."

Archer grinned at Tom and rubbed his hands together. "A night of gambling for me. With Somerset's men, yet. Maybe I'll own the company before I'm finished."

"Better watch it, Archer. I don't know those men. I can't stop them from throwing you overboard if you win everything they bring with them."

Archer laughed and gazed back out at the water where the dinghy was now just a hundred yards away. "I don't know, they look—" Archer stopped, leaning forward. "Good God!" Then, before anyone could ask him what was wrong, he stepped up on the railing and made a clean dive into the water.

He surfaced several yards from the lugger. "Launch the dinghy!" he yelled. Then he put his head down and started to swim.

"Jesus, what's he doing?" Tom yelled. "Archer, turn around!"

"Man fall in." Juan pointed at the dinghy, which had stopped now. Only two men were left inside. Tom could just see a head bobbing in the water many yards from it. "He stands up and falls in," Juan said. "Nakanishi."

"Well, why aren't they trying to get him?"

"Waves picking up and pushing boat toward us, away from him."

"Juan, that water's freezing. Archer's not that good a swimmer. He's not going to make it."

Juan didn't seem perturbed. Tom glanced at the diver's face and saw the truth. If Archer rescued Nakanishi, that would be fine. If he went down, that would be fine, too.

Tom readied himself to dive, but strong arms wrapped around his waist and pulled him back to the deck. "Boat belong boat, he go long. You-me, stay."

Tom tried to push Bernard away, but the man's massive arms tightened. "You-me stay."

Behind him, Tom heard the others launching the dinghy to help rescue the two men.

"He makes it," Juan said, as if he were talking about something of no consequence. "Archer, he swims better than you think. Nakanishi, he find drink tonight and have too much. Or he got touch of diver's sickness."

Tom saw that Juan was right. Archer was only yards from Nakanishi, who was inexpertly treading the water. Out of his diving suit he had little rapport with the waves.

Bernard released Tom, and Tom saw there was no point in throwing himself in to help. The *Sophia*'s dinghy was closing in on the two men; the *Odyssey*'s dinghy with Toshiharu and the two Malayan boys was on its way. And Archer, with the reflexes and impulses of daredevils the world around, had reached Nakanishi and was now helping him stay afloat.

"Nakanishi, he makes Somerset a rich man. Somerset, he not want to lose him. He hears of this, he be glad. He make Archer glad, too."

Tom wondered if, in the split second before he dove into the water, Archer had thought of that. There were sharks in this water and other menaces besides. But once again, Archer hadn't hesitated to risk his life.

He pushed down the thought that Archer had only jumped in to rescue Nakanishi so he could bathe in Somerset's good graces. It had to be a coincidence that Nakanishi was Somerset's diver, and that Somerset was the father of the woman Archer jokingly claimed he would marry.

"Do you believe in coincidence?" he asked Juan.

"All things have purpose." Juan shook his head. "But sometimes, man makes own purpose."

Tom watched silently as Archer struggled to keep the Japanese diver's head above water as the dinghies grew closer, and he wondered where Archer would be right now if the man in the water had been anyone else.

5

Viola Somerset was even more beautiful up close than from a distance. Her long golden lashes shadowed eyes the same vivid shade as her blue-green gown, and her features were delicately executed. When Sebastian introduced Viola to Archer, one finely molded eyebrow lifted just a fraction of an inch before she held out a gloved hand.

"You're the man who saved Nakanishi's life."

Archer took her hand and made a quick bow, but he grinned as he did, to belie the formal gesture. "I'm not certain I saved him, but we did have a nice chat while we were floating in the water waiting for the dinghy."

Sebastian, dressed in the blinding white of the pearling master, interrupted. "Don't let Mr. Llewellyn tease you, Viola. If it weren't for him, my best diver would be at the bottom of the ocean—and *not* gathering shell."

"How courageous you were," Viola murmured to Archer. "What makes a man risk his life for a stranger? And with no thought of reward." The same eyebrow rose higher.

"He was in trouble, and I was there. There was nothing complicated about it, Miss Somerset. I would have done the same for you."

She smiled sweetly. "I'll sleep better at night knowing as much."

Sebastian gestured toward the parlor door. "I see someone

I must greet. I'll leave you two to become acquainted. Viola, please don't forget that you're to sit on Freddy's right at dinner."

Archer heard the steel in Somerset's voice and saw the flicker of rebellion in his daughter's eyes.

"How could I forget, father dear? For the past three days you've reminded me every time the clock strikes."

"That seldom motivates you, does it?" He excused himself and left them alone.

"My father and I are not the best of friends," Viola told Archer. "Freddy Colson is his assistant. Perhaps I should introduce you to Freddy now, and we can make bets on which of you will climb higher in my father's estimation tonight."

"It almost seems you believe I rescued your father's diver just to impress him."

"You certainly have endeared yourself."

"Have I endeared myself to his daughter?"

"Have you suddenly acquired money?"

"Sadly, no."

"Then I am not endeared or impressed."

Archer was almost certain Viola had recognized him from their dawn encounter some months before, but he left nothing to chance. "I gather this means your handkerchiefs don't carry my initials?"

Her gaze didn't flicker. "I'm quite sorry you're a poor man, Mr. Llewellyn. You have a certain brash charm that, together, we might put to good use. But I have no interest in a man who can't get me out of this town." She turned away, as if she was bored. But Archer stopped her with a hand on her arm.

"Miss Somerset…"

She turned back, her gaze drifting languidly to his hand.

"I promise I'll sweep you off your feet and out of Western Australia. But I'll need just a little time to do it. Is there anything that will prevent you from waiting?"

She seemed to consider. "Only Freddy Colson. My father is determined to make me marry him. And I don't know how much longer I can refuse."

"Then Freddy must go."

"Go?" She favored him with a tinkling laugh. "Freddy clings to my father like an oyster to its shell."

"I opened shell until the lay-up season. It only takes one swipe of the knife to separate an oyster from its home."

"Maybe you're the man for the job, but may I propose you separate Freddy from my father with a touch more finesse?" She bowed her head; then, lifting her skirts, she stepped around him and crossed the room to speak to someone else.

Tom joined him. Sebastian Somerset had come to the Roebuck Hotel yesterday, just an hour after Archer and Tom had left the *Odyssey* at the jetty following their long months at sea. Somerset had wasted no time thanking Archer for saving Nakanishi's life and inviting him to this dinner. Archer, surprised that Somerset had moved so quickly, had requested that Tom be allowed to accompany him. Now he was glad. Tom, with his polished manners and elegant bearing, lent Archer credibility.

What society Broome could claim was gathered at the Somersets' tonight. There were bankers, pearlers and staff from Cable House, which administered and oversaw the submarine communications cable stretching from Broome to Java. As a boy, Archer had played servant to people like these and witnessed the gracious behavior expected of guests, but he was already impatient to be done with this. He wanted Viola and her inheritance, and to have both he needed her father's regard. But he was not a man who enjoyed the subtleties of getting ahead.

"What do you think of this house?" he asked Tom. A formally dressed string quartet played quietly in the background, but not one of the musicians was as talented as Juan Fernandez.

"Nice. The architecture has an Asian feel to it, and Mrs. Somerset has obviously been to Singapore for her shopping. It suits the climate. I could be happy here."

The house was the finest Archer had ever visited, and Tom's words brought home the differences between them. Archer snorted. "Well, you won't have a house like this one—or any house, for that matter—if we don't acquire a lugger and start getting shell of our own.''

"That's still your intention?''

"What else is there for us? It's the best gamble I know.''

"Even with the money I can lay my hands on, we're a long way from buying our own lugger. Maybe in a year or two.''

"We'll own a lugger by the time the weather clears and we can go out again.''

"What do you know that I don't?''

"I know I don't have time to waste.''

Tom frowned. ''Don't be in such a hurry that you take too many chances, Archer. Or that you hurt anyone. We're young. We can wait.''

But Archer hadn't been young since the day his mother had abandoned him at the orphanage door. He sent Tom a reassuring grin. ''Don't you worry. We'll have that lugger. And I'll have Miss Somerset. You'll see. Now put a smile on that handsome mug and let's go charm the natives.''

Tom excused himself after dinner. The rest of the guests, including Archer, were to be treated to another concert by the string quartet, with the addition of a local soprano who specialized in Stephen Foster. Tom explained to Jane Somerset that since he'd just arrived back at port, he had business to attend to, and after a sufficient number of compliments on her house and hospitality, she let him leave without protest.

He was relieved to go, already nostalgic for quiet nights at sea and the rough-hewn company of the *Odyssey*'s crew. He had endured too many events like the dinner at the Somersets'. The shell of Tom Robeson had behaved impeccably, but his heart had been somewhere else.

Since arriving back in Broome, he had been too involved in overseeing the unloading of the *Odyssey* to try to locate Willow. This morning, in between watching crew members disembark with baskets of shell, he had found a few moments to visit the laundry. But the stifling room where they had met was now an eating house where food was served to Chinese men who sat at plank tables chatting in a language he didn't understand. He had tried, without success, to discover what had happened, but no one had been willing to help him.

Now he decided to try Wong Fai, the *Odyssey*'s cook. He knew where Wong was living, and since the two men had developed a comfortable rapport during their days at sea, he hoped Wong would help. Tom had little hope Willow was still in Broome, but he couldn't persuade himself not to look for her.

He found Wong's room in the back of a tailor shop in an alley off Sheba Lane in Chinatown. With lay-up season, the population of Chinatown had tripled. Wong probably shared the room with other men, so when the door opened, Tom was glad to see he was alone.

Wong was a thin man who had managed, despite the diversity of tastes on the crew, to prepare meals that were as pleasing as a steady diet of fish and rice could be. He kept to himself on board, content each night to find a space on deck to toss coins in the air to divine the future or to silently smoke his pipe. Although he was small, he was tough and wiry, and the few skirmishes he had been involved in had ended in his favor.

"Something wrong, boss?" Wong asked, moving out of the doorway with a courteous bow.

Tom stepped inside, although he was embarrassed. The room would have been tight quarters for one man, and now he was taking up far too much of it. "Nothing's wrong, but I have a favor to ask you. I'm looking for Lian, the daughter of Sing Chung. The laundry is gone, and I can't find her."

Wong was silent, but he managed to communicate disapproval by his stance and tightly drawn lips.

"Look, I know this is crazy," Tom said. "But you know I'm not going to hurt her. I just want to be sure she's all right."

"How you know this woman?"

Tom related the story of their two meetings.

"She give you laundry? No more?"

"Yes, that's all. But I liked her. And I want to be sure she's all right. Do you know if she's still in Broome? Did her father die?"

"Father dead."

"Oh. Then she's probably gone back to China."

Wong didn't respond.

"*Has* she gone back to China?"

"Why you care? She laundry girl. No more."

"I don't know why, but I do."

Wong hesitated; then he folded his arms and shook his head. "She in China now. Married woman. Here no more."

"I see." But he didn't, because despite the cook's carefully blank expression, Tom suspected he was lying. Wong was giving him too many clues to think otherwise. The way he shifted from foot to foot, the way he refused to meet Tom's eyes. Tom tried a new tactic. "If Lian *hadn't* gone back to China, where do you suppose she might be now?"

Wong looked relieved, as if he had done his duty and now he could speak the truth. "Girl like that, she have many men want her. Maybe one take her, hide her."

Tom felt alarm spreading through his belly. "Where would a man hide her, do you suppose? If she were still here in Broome?"

"Many place hide girl. On boat. In room." He hesitated, then shrugged. "Or if man own gambling house, he hide her upstair with others he keep."

The alarm was growing, but Tom nodded patiently. "A man who might want a girl like that would probably be Chinese, wouldn't he? If the girl wasn't already married and back in China."

"Yes. Big man. Big money."

"And if something like this had happened, how would people feel, do you suppose, if someone went to find and help her?"

"Some be happy. Others try to kill man who help."

"How could the man who tried to help protect himself?"

"Maybe man bring friends. If man come from boat, he bring

crew to gambling house. Crew make trouble, he go upstair, get girl.''

"Thank you, Wong." Tom turned to go.

"Remember. Sing daughter in China. Married now."

The door closed behind Tom before Wong's final words were spoken.

Bernard and Juan were easy to find. Ahmed and his friend Reece were more difficult, but once Tom located them, they were equally as enthusiastic about the fight. Even Toshiharu, whose limp was worse on land, was anxious to come along. Together the *Odyssey*'s crew carried a variety of hastily gathered weapons, including some that Tom had never seen before and prayed he would never experience. The only crew member besides Wong who was missing was Archer. Apparently he was still at the Somerset's listening to renditions of "Jeannie with the Light Brown Hair," and although Tom regretted not having his friend along, he didn't want to wait. Under the circumstances, time was more important than numbers.

He had reported every word of his conversation with Wong to Juan, who had lived in Broome the longest. Juan had two guesses about who the mysterious owner of the gambling house might be. Gambling was as much a part of the local character as mosquitoes or mangroves, and all the nationalities had their own games and their own places to pursue them, including the British and Australians, who were partial to billiards and horse racing. It wasn't uncommon for a man to lose an entire season's wages in his first days on shore. Even the local police cooperated by turning their eyes the other way in exchange for tickets in the various weekly lotteries.

"First man, he has a big house, but don't think he's the one. He plays nothing but mah-jongg there, and his wife, she lives above." Juan drew a finger across his throat. "That one, she be unhappy if he bring Sing Lian to stay."

"What about the second?" Tom was trying not to imagine what might have happened to Willow already.

"That's my guess. Wild place, that one. Lotta money come

and go there, and landlord, Bobby Chinn, he gets rich enough to buy village at home.''

"Do you know anything about him?''

"He's bad. He be sent back to China fast, but he gives too much money to town. How he makes his money, that's bad, too. He brings in opium. Not just a little for good time, but too much. He makes his own people sick.''

Juan had already told Tom that the Chinese had several gambling games they preferred. Fan-tan and a numbers game called *pai-gow* vied with mah-jongg.

"That's where we'll go, then,'' Tom said. "Let's just pray it's the right place.''

The house in question was in Dampier Terrace, behind a general store run by Chinn. Entry was through aisles lined with bolts of fabric, sacks of flour and an assortment of straw sandals and hats. Tom and the others ignored the protests of the clerk, who followed behind them shouting. At the back of the store Juan nodded to a door, and Tom flung it open and braced himself for a fight.

The room was thick with smoke and noise. Laughing, gossiping men lolled on benches or stood in clusters around tables piled with fan-tan beads. Charts filled with Chinese characters lined the flimsy iron walls, and one man stood in front of them, altering them as another man shouted in his ear.

Tom and the *Odyssey* crew didn't have to wait long. The sound dimmed gradually as the occupants saw the new arrivals. One of them, a man in a dark shirt and khaki trousers, separated himself from the others and came toward them.

"Not welcome here,'' he said, making slashing motions with his hands to drive them away.

"Bobby Chinn,'' Juan said.

Tom didn't move. He addressed Chinn. "We're just here to spend our money.''

"Not welcome.''

Tom was inches taller than Chinn, just as Bernard, who was behind him, was inches taller than he was. They were international stair steps, each measuring the other and refusing to move aside. Tom let the silence extend a moment as he surveyed his opponent. Then he moved forward until they were nose to nose. "Do you want to make trouble, Chinn? I'll have one of my men call a police officer." It was an empty threat. Broome's law officers would just tell him he was a fool to force entrance where he wasn't wanted.

Chinn's expression darkened, and Tom pressed his advantage. "If I were you, I wouldn't want the sergeant and his men in my place. No telling what they might find, huh?"

"You stay short time. Just short time. No trouble."

"Trouble?" Tom smiled. "Why would I make trouble?"

Chinn didn't move. Then, just as Tom was about to push his way past him, he stepped aside.

During the struggle to get in, Tom hadn't had time to make more than a quick survey of the room. Now, as he strode into the center with his crew behind him, he did a thorough evaluation. At first glance he hadn't seen any way out of the room other than the way he had entered. But now he noted a door that fitted so snugly into the corrugated iron walls it was hardly visible. He and Juan had carefully inspected the building before going inside. It was two stories front and back, and obviously this was the entrance to the second floor.

Tom pulled out a one-pound note and placed it on the nearest fan-tan table. "How do I play?"

The man behind the table consulted in Cantonese with Chinn. Chinn cut him off with another slash of his hand and turned to Tom. "Why you waste time?"

Juan came up beside Tom. "They divide beads into four piles. You bet how many beads left over."

"Quick and to the point." Tom pushed his money forward. "Three."

Other men came up to place bets, and Tom sidled to the edge of the group as the man behind the table began to divide the beads so quickly Tom's eyes could hardly follow his hands. It didn't matter, though, because at that moment, Bernard let out a loud whoop and turned over a table on the other side of the room.

"It begins," Tom said under his breath. Juan was already on his way to join his tender, flanked by Toshiharu, who had wrenched a leg from the table and was brandishing it with surprising skill. Ahmed and Reece jumped on the backs of two men trying to grab Bernard, and the population of the room rushed forward to pull them off.

Tom sidestepped the table and headed for the door.

"So this your game." Bobby Chinn stepped in his way, but Tom, who had expected as much, knocked him to the floor with one perfectly placed punch. He leapt over Chinn's body, flung open the door and took the steps two at a time.

The upstairs was a warren of rooms off a narrow hallway. He threw open doors as he passed, finding the first two empty. At the third door he found a bleary-eyed young woman in a dirty silk wrapper sitting listlessly on the bed. "Where is Sing Lian?" he shouted at her.

She didn't move, and she didn't look afraid. She stared past him with vacant eyes, as if he wasn't even there.

He moved on, sure that he would have better luck searching than trying to get a response. "Lian! Where are you? It's Tom."

He heard someone behind him and ducked reflexively. Bobby Chinn crashed into him, hands punching and feet kicking. Tom ducked and feinted, for once putting into practice all the advice he'd gotten from Archer. Chinn was adept, but Tom had more to lose. As Chinn hurled himself forward one more time, Tom leapt to the side, whirled and kicked Chinn against the wall. Then, fingers locked together, he slammed Chinn on the back of the neck with the heel of his hands.

Chinn crumpled to the floor, but Tom knew he only had moments to find Willow before others followed.

"Lian!" He moved down the hallway, flinging open doors. He heard a noise behind the last one just as he tried to open it. The door rattled when he turned the knob, but it was locked.

"Lian? Willow?" He rattled the door harder. "It's Tom. Can you open the door?"

He heard a sob, but no other response.

"Lian, is that you?" Frustrated, he backed up as far as he could, then hurled himself at the door again and again until it flew open.

The room was dusty and dank, with no window and no lantern. In the feeble light from the hallway, he saw that Lian was sitting on a dirty blanket in the corner, sobbing.

"Willow." He knelt and put his hands on her cheeks to turn her face to his. Her hair was unbound, and it hung in tangled strands to the waist of her dark tunic. "It's all right."

"I am dead," she said. "Leave me."

"No, you're alive. And I'm here to help."

"Bobby Chinn has killed me."

"Damn it, I'll kill Bobby Chinn. Has he hurt you?"

She sobbed harder.

"Whatever it is, I'll help. I'm with you now. But we have to get you out of here. He may kill us both if we don't."

"I am not worthy. I am a fool."

He stood; then he took her hands and pulled her to her feet, even though she resisted. "You have to help me. It'll be easier if I don't have to carry you out of here."

"Leave me."

"I'm not going to leave you. Willow, you have to help me."

She gulped air, and for a moment he thought she was going to refuse again; then she gave the barest nod.

"Good girl." He started toward the door, but he held her hands, pulling her as he went until they were in the doorway together. He could hear shouting from downstairs, but now that he had his prize, he wondered how he was going to get her outside. Surely if he tried to take her through the gambling house they would never make it.

"Is there another way out?"

She seemed confused, and he realized she wasn't going to be any help. "Come on." He pulled her into the room opposite her own, searching for a window, an attic door, some way of escape. The room was connected to another, and he dragged her after him. The second room had a window leading to a rickety balcony. He took one look and realized this was the best they could do. The window was painted shut, but he made quick work of it with the heel of his boot, stepping out to the balcony and pulling her carefully through the broken glass behind him.

"Look, here's what we have to do. It's not a long drop to the alley. I'll go first, then I'll be down there to catch you. Watch how I do it and do the same thing. Can you manage that?"

She was still sobbing. He wasn't even sure she had heard him.

He shook her gently. "Willow, a lot depends on this. Can you do this?"

She managed a nod.

"Watch me. And do exactly what I do. I'll be there to catch you." He heard noise from the hallway and knew their time was short. He considered picking her up and dropping her over the side, but he was sure she would be injured if he did. Instead he held on to the railing and flung himself over the side; then, sliding his hands down the posts, he lowered himself as far as he could before he let go and dropped to the ground. Despite the impact, he remained on his feet, staggering backwards before he regained his balance. Once he was stable, he moved back under the balcony and held out his arms.

"Jump. Do it now, before they find you."

He had expected her to hesitate. He had even wondered if she would do as she'd promised, but as he watched, she lifted herself over the railing and slid down as he had, falling into his waiting arms.

Willow brushed her hair with trembling hands. She was alone in a room, just as she had been at Bobby Chinn's. But this time she was dressed in a clean robe and the door was unlocked. The room was simple, but tidy, and there was a bed with a new blanket stretched over the mattress and a dresser beside a window.

A knock sounded at the door, and after a moment, the door swung open and Tom appeared. "I brought you some supper."

He moved inside and closed the door. Then he placed a tray on the dresser. "I don't know what you like. I brought what they had at the bar. It looks like shepherd's pie. And I have a pot of tea and some bread." He fussed with the meal, and when there was nothing else to do, he turned. "Are you feeling better? Even a little?"

She liked to look at him. She had since the day he had come into her father's laundry. She had thought of him often in the days since, thought of the easy way he moved, the way he held his head, the way his dark hair curled over his forehead. But she had never expected to see him again. And she had never expected Tom to see her like this.

She looked away, hoping he might look away, too. She was not worthy to be looked at. "Why do you help me?"

"Willow, you don't deserve what happened to you. Did you think I could leave you in a place like that once I found out?"

"You should not have come."

"How can you say that?"

"I am dead."

"You are breathing. Your heart is beating."

"Bobby Chinn killed me."

"Will you tell me how you ended up in that place?"

She glanced at him again and shook her head.

He didn't look angry at her refusal, only sad. "No matter how it happened, it doesn't matter. You're safe now. We'll find a place for you to live." He hesitated. "Or will you go back to China now?"

"I cannot go back. I am dead."

"Because Chinn kidnapped you?"

There were no words to answer him.

His next words were soft. "Because Chinn raped you?"

She wasn't shocked by the word, and she wasn't shocked Tom had asked. Nothing would shock her again. "It does not matter what he did. I was an obedient daughter. I was to be married to an honorable man. But when my father died, I did not go to China as I knew I must."

Tom moved closer, but he stopped several feet from the bed,

then he squatted so that she no longer had to look up to see him. "What happened?"

"I am from a village in China, but I am not. Do you understand?"

"You were born there, but you have not lived there since you were a child?"

"I did not want to go. I am stranger with no family. Here I learn to speak English, to read and write. My father, he did not understand. He punished me when I tried to explain."

"Go on."

"Broome is my home."

"Yes."

"When my father die, I took the money left for my passage, and I rent a room. I did not want to go to China. I knew there would be work here. I disobey my father. And I am cursed."

"Chinn found out you were a woman alone, and he kidnapped you?"

"I was promise a job at his store. I knew he was not a good man, but I thought I could stay away from him."

"But you couldn't."

His voice was so gentle, so accepting, that the hated tears rose in her eyes again. "You should not be so kind. I was a disobedient daughter, and I have been punished."

"No, you're only a woman who believed in others who didn't deserve it."

"Bad things happen because I did not listen."

He reached for her hands, and she didn't shy away. She let him hold them. She was dead, and it didn't matter.

"Willow..." He squeezed her hands. "If you had been brought up in China, you would have felt differently about your father's plans. But you were brought up here, where women have more to say about their fate. You were educated, you had a different view of things. What you did was understandable. But because..."

She looked up when his words trailed off. "Because I disobeyed my father?"

He shook his head, and his eyes were sad. "No, because

you're Chinese, you had no one here to stand up for you after your father's death. Chinn's a powerful man, and your own people were afraid to cross him. And the others in Broome, they wouldn't interfere.''

"You were not afraid.''

His tone hardened. "If I had been here, none of this would have happened. I'm sorry.''

She didn't understand. She had done something terrible, something unforgivable, yet Tom sounded as if he thought he was to blame. "I am the one who is disgraced.''

"Disgraced, not dead?'' He reached out and touched a tear sliding down her cheek. "We're making progress.''

"Now I cannot marry. My sons will be outcasts. No woman will let me be a servant in her house. I can only live as Bobby Chinn planned for me.''

"As a prostitute?''

"I am dead.''

He sat back on his heels. "When did you last eat?''

She shook her head.

"Are you starving yourself, then?''

She looked straight through him. "A dead woman does not eat.''

"A dead woman doesn't speak, either, or walk or cry.''

She lifted her chin. "Soon I will not do those things.''

"Willow, you're not to blame for the things Bobby Chinn did to you. And if there's no place for you with your own people, then you have to find a different place away from them. You're educated and intelligent. I'm sure the wife of a pearling master will take you in as a nursemaid or housekeeper. I met some important people tonight. I can find a job for you. Trust me.''

She was dead. She felt dead inside. And yet Tom insisted on breathing life into her, life she wasn't worthy to feel. Something like anger stabbed at her, and that made her feel alive, too. "And what must I do for your help? The things I was to do for Bobby Chinn? The things he would have sold me for?''

He cocked his head. "How long were you at Chinn's, Willow?"

"Long enough to die."

"Why were you alone in that room?"

"A man was to give him much money for me. Chinn kept me away from other men."

"Then Chinn didn't…" He shook his head. "Do you really believe I came to get you because I want something from you?"

"This is something all men want."

"All men may want, but all men don't take. I would never touch you, unless that was what you wanted, too."

"I want nothing! I am—"

"Dead. Yes, I know you think so."

The anger jabbed at her again. "You think you know? You are a man. I am nothing. I am alone!"

"No, you're not. You have me, and I'm not going to let you starve yourself, or sell your body, or allow this to defeat you."

"I want to die." The anger was gone, and she felt such a profound sadness that she could hardly bear it. She rested her head in her hands and began to sob again. Not hopeless tears, as she had shed at Bobby Chinn's, but tears wrenched from a soul still encased in her unworthy body.

Tom joined her on the bed and pulled her into his arms. "Go ahead, sweetheart. The last days were terrible. But I promise, things are better now." He brushed his hands over her hair, soothing her. "I won't let anyone hurt you again. Not ever again. I'll take care of you. I promise. I promise."

"Why?"

He didn't answer.

"Why you did come to look for me? Why you did fight for me?"

He still didn't answer.

"Why?" she repeated.

"Shh… Isn't it enough I did? That I found you and I'm going to help you?"

She pushed against his chest until he let her go and she could see his face. "What did you hope for?"

"This won't make things better."

"Tell me!"

He sighed, and his face was sad. "I thought of you often while I was at sea. I knew I shouldn't, that you were to be married. But I couldn't forget you. So when I came back, I just had to be sure you were gone. Then, I thought, I could let you go."

"You have *not* let me go. I am dead, but you have not let me go. Not even now."

"No."

She was disgraced and undeserving. But this man, this handsome American man with the kind eyes and the peaceful soul, did not care. He had come to find her. He had risked his own safety, and he was asking for nothing in return.

Yet he wanted her. She could see he did. And this was something good, something to wash away the sickness of Bobby Chinn and the other man, who had stripped her naked and gazed at her breasts with cold, hard eyes before he offered Chinn money. She was dead to her own people, but she was not as dead inside as she had believed.

"I will do for you the things I did not do for Bobby Chinn and the man who was to pay for me," she said softly. "I will do them for you because you would not let me go, even when you should."

He shook his head, but his hands tightened on her shoulders. "No. You don't even know me. And you're a good woman, despite what you believe about yourself. You deserve marriage, and I don't know if I'll even be allowed to marry you here, or what kind of life I could give you. There will be another man who'll overlook what happened to you, a man who will take you as a wife, despite Chinn."

"No, there will be no man like that. Because what I did not do for Chinn, I will do with you." She leaned toward him before he could protest and pressed her lips against his. He was warm, and his chin was smooth and smelled of soap. He groaned against her lips and tried to push her away. She lifted her head and saw in his eyes what he denied. "You say I am not dead, Tom Robeson. If this is so, then you must show me."

"Willow…"

She kissed him again, and he said her name once more. But this time differently. She felt his hands under her hair, warm and strong through the thin cloth of the robe. She pressed against him, pressed the breasts the men had stared at against Tom's chest, until she was cleansed by the hot sweetness of his body.

"I will give you what they would have taken," she whispered.

He groaned and pulled her closer.

And she found she was alive after all.

6

Archer kept an eye on Viola for the rest of the evening, but Freddy Colson interested him more. Colson was a colorless man with thinning hair he slicked back so rigorously that strands clung like leeches to his scalp. He had an odd habit of repeating the final words of a sentence, as if he thought no one he spoke to was really listening, and an even odder habit of staring reverently at Sebastian Somerset. Colson could quote facts and figures like a textbook on the pearling industry, but he had no conversational skills beyond discussions of the weather—with emphasis on how it related to business.

"You seem to enjoy yourself here," Archer told Colson when the string quartet and warbling soprano had finished for the evening. "Tell me, is there anything in Broome that could make life more pleasant these next months?"

Colson looked shocked, as if a pleasant life was the first step on the road to degradation. "I work long hours for Mr. Somerset, and I find that rewarding enough. Rewarding enough."

Bringing Colson to his knees had been a business proposition at first, but now Archer decided he was going to enjoy it. "Really? You don't drink? Gamble?" He lowered his voice. "You don't chase the ladies? A man with such prospects for the future? I was sure you would be in high demand."

Colson flushed. "I work too hard to worry about such things."

"You know what they say about all work and no play. Why don't you spend the rest of the evening with me? I'm new in Broome, and I don't know where a gentleman spends his time." Archer lowered his voice. "There aren't many true gentlemen in town, are there?"

Colson succumbed to temptation. "There aren't too many places where you'll feel comfortable."

"That's why I need your help."

"I suppose it wouldn't hurt. Wouldn't hurt," he said.

"Good man." Archer clapped him on the back. "Then shall we say our good-nights? I believe Miss Somerset is coming our way."

Viola moved gracefully toward them, as if she had come to help. "Did you gentlemen enjoy the music?"

"I'm a great admirer of Stephen Foster's songs, particularly when they're sung on key," Archer said with a grin.

Viola made a face. "My mother's choice. She has a tin ear."

Colson looked shocked. "That hardly seems like something you should say about your dear mother."

"Freddy, my dear mother is always more concerned about her performers' pedigrees than their talent."

"Mr. Colson has agreed to show me a little of Broome," Archer said.

"I'm sure you'll be in excellent hands. Freddy won't lead you astray, will you, Freddy?"

Freddy looked mildly shocked that Viola would even know such a thing was possible. "Mr. Llewellyn is interested in a proper look at our little burg."

"Mr. Llewellyn strikes me as a man whose interest in what's proper is…" She hesitated with a smile hovering at her lips. "Words fail me."

"Acute?" Archer offered. "Heartfelt?"

The smile blossomed. "Are words just one of your many talents?"

"We'll see."

Archer and Freddy said their goodbyes, and Archer made a

particular point of thanking Viola's parents for the invitation. Then he and Freddy set off for town on foot.

"Miss Somerset seems quite taken with you," Archer said, once they were on the road.

Freddy sounded unsure. "Did you think so?"

"From long experience I'd say all the signs are there."

"I rather thought she was trying to humiliate me."

Archer gave a conspiratorial chuckle. "As lovers so often do."

"Her father would like us to marry."

"Then what could stand in your way?"

"I owe Mr. Somerset a great deal. I'll marry Viola, if it pleases him."

Archer considered wringing the man's neck right then and there, but he knew he would be the first suspect, since they had left the Somersets' together. "It doesn't sound as if marrying Miss Somerset is your own preference."

"I suppose it makes sense to solidify my place at Somerset and Company."

"Of course a man like you would be in high demand, Freddy. I'm sure every business in town wishes it had someone of your talents."

"I've considered…considered—"

Archer could hear him struggling. "Moving? Taking another offer?"

"Others have wanted me, of course. But I owe Mr. Somerset my allegiance."

"You're a loyal friend and employee." Archer clapped him on the back. "Worth your weight in gold."

"Yes, I suppose. I suppose." Freddy sounded pleased with himself.

Archer was pleased, too. Now he knew exactly how he was going to bring Freddy Colson to his knees.

"We'll start over at the Conti," Freddy said. "It's the place for men like us."

"Lead on," Archer said. "I'm certain I can count on you to show me everything I need to know."

* * *

Willow was sleeping when Tom heard Archer return to the room beside his. She didn't awake when he rose. She was so exhausted, nothing would wake her for hours. He pulled on his pants and a shirt and went to Archer's room, rapping softly before he opened the door.

"Did you just get in?"

"I made a long night of it." Archer beckoned him inside. "I went on a tour of the local bars with Freddy Colson, Somerset's assistant."

"There must be more to the man than meets the eye."

"Precisely," Archer said with a grin. "What did you do this evening?"

Tom wasn't sure where to start. "Look, Archer, something happened while you were gone. Something you need to know about."

Archer stripped down to his underwear and poured water from the pitcher into a pottery bowl. "Is Garth back?"

They had beat Garth to port, and Tom knew Archer was anxious for the rest of his money. "No. It's something else." He took a deep breath and launched into the story of the night's events.

Archer mopped his face with a hand towel. "Let me get this straight. You and the crew went to Chinn's and stole the girl? Are the others all right?"

"They're all fine. They were waiting outside by the time we escaped. Just a few bruises."

"What happened then?"

"I brought Willow here."

"You brought her here and took her to bed?"

"That wasn't my intention. It just happened."

"She's Chinese! There's no telling what you can pick up from a woman like that."

Tom felt anger knotting dangerously inside him. "There's no chance I picked up anything. She was innocent."

Archer just stared at him.

"This complicates things," Tom said. "I'm sorry."

"Things? It complicates everything. She's a Chink! You can't trust those people, Tom. I know you have some romantic notion that she's good and pure. In some twisted way she probably reminds you of home. But she'll exploit that. And for God's sake, what will your parents say if they find out you have a Chinese lover? Do you think they'll let you come home?"

Tom told himself that this was Archer, and that Archer cared about him. Archer had saved his life. "Chinese *wife*."

"Oh, tell me you're not going to marry her! Have you lost your mind? Where would you go? Where could you live?"

"Here, I think. Maybe some people will cut us, at least for a while. But that hardly matters, does it? We'll make friends. And we'll raise our children to be good citizens."

"And who will they marry? Chinese? White? Maybe they'll try something new and different! Can you do that to them? Don't you want better?"

"I want *her*."

Archer fell silent.

"I want you to get to know her."

Archer shook his head. "No. I know everything I need to. You've been without a woman for a long time. You've found a virgin who let you take her to bed, and you think you're in love. She's going to destroy your life."

"She's going to make me happy."

"Have you given any thought to what this will do to me?"

Tom frowned. "What do you mean?"

"Everyone knows you're my partner. Any chance I have for respectability will be destroyed."

"You don't want to settle here. You just want to make enough money to buy a place in Victoria."

"And I can't do that unless people in Broome trust me!"

Tom didn't want to see Archer's side, but he was nothing if not fair. "Do you want to stop being partners?"

"I want you to think about what you're doing. Other white men probably keep an Asian girl on the side. People will look the other way if you keep a mistress, but you'll destroy us both if you marry her. If you're going to do something that stupid, wait until I'm out of the picture. We're partners. Mates, the way they say it here. Doesn't that count for something?''

"You know it does."

"Will you think about this?"

Tom didn't like it, but Archer's concerns were not unreasonable. Tom's actions *would* reflect on his friend. And he owed Archer his life. That, coupled with his own insecurity about whether he and Willow would be allowed to make a real life together, forced him to nod. "I'll think about it."

"Good."

"She's everything a man could ask for in a wife, Archer."

"No. She's not white. Somehow you completely skipped the most important criteria, Tom."

Tom settled Willow in a bungalow in a section of town where a mixture of people lived. The house had three rooms, but there was a tiny garden and a lattice-lined veranda that looked over it. She was as pleased as if he had built a castle for her.

The day he moved her in, he went to see Bobby Chinn at his store. He chose broad daylight as a precaution.

Chinn stepped around the counter when he saw Tom. "You have girl belong to me. I take back what's mine."

"Do you? That would be unfortunate. I have all manner of information about you that I could share with the local police. Interesting facts, like how much opium you've brought into the country, and how many immigrants you've smuggled in. I even heard a story about some men being put ashore north of here and dying in the wilderness."

"Nothing you tie to me."

"Don't you think so?" Tom took a thick envelope out of his jacket pocket and rattled it in front of Chinn's nose. "I have statements here from people who were involved in all those operations, people you cheated. They were more than willing to help me. Now, I'll keep all this to myself unless my hand is forced. But since I despise you, Chinn, I'd be happiest if I could give this right to the police."

Chinn didn't look upset. He regarded the envelope the way he might have regarded any business transaction. "What I have to do?"

"Just leave Lian alone. You aren't to speak to her. You aren't to go near her. Someone will be watching over her, even when I'm out to sea. And if you or your people bother her, the police will have this in a matter of minutes." He rattled the envelope again.

Chinn considered. "I could find you better girl," he said at last. "Younger. Prettier. You like Chinese girl."

Tom grabbed him by his shirtfront and hauled him closer. "You are despicable. And I will kill you myself if you ever, ever speak to me or mine again."

Chinn shoved Tom away and straightened his shirt.

"Do we understand each other?" Tom asked.

Chinn didn't nod, but clearly an understanding had been reached. Tom, who had nothing in the envelope but a written account of rumors everyone had already heard, had won.

Archer was winning, too. Every time Tom saw his friend, he heard stories of successful bets and money pocketed. His favorite game was ninepins, played more often than not with champagne bottles from cases that had to be emptied by the willing participants before the game could start.

Archer was spending more hours with Freddy Colson than with him, but Tom suspected this was because of Willow. Most of the time Archer refused to visit the house he and Willow shared, and except for the mornings he spent overseeing repairs to the *Odyssey*, Tom spent most of his time with her. He was happiest in her arms, happiest watching the nightmare of the past weeks recede from her eyes. He didn't want to shut out his old friend, but the current arrangement suited him. If Archer refused to visit, Tom had that much more time alone with her.

On the day John Garth finally returned to Broome, Tom headed off to the Continental Hotel to meet Archer and celebrate the relative success of the season. Although Garth had been laid low by a fierce gale and forced to pull into an inlet for extensive repairs on his ship, he had collected good shell. Better yet, he was well pleased with what the *Odyssey* had collected.

By the time Tom arrived at the hotel, Garth was giddy from too much liquor and too many overblown plans for the future.

"I'll be adding a lugger to the fleet next season. No, two." He poured Tom a drink from a half-empty bottle of square-face gin and topped off Archer's. "Maybe three. I'll sell the *Odyssey*. She's seaworthy, nothing better. Small, she is. Too small." He shook his head. "Not good enough for my fleet."

"I like her," Tom said. "She's small, but she's sleek. She sails over the roughest waves like they aren't even there."

"She's yours, if you can afford her."

Tom looked at Archer, whose face was completely expressionless. Tom knew his friend well. The only time that Archer's considerable range of feelings was secret was when he was gambling. "Name your price," Tom said.

Garth did, and Tom's heart sank. He had paid six months' rent in advance on the cottage for Willow, and he had hired a girl to help with the cleaning and gardening. There wasn't much left from what he had earned in half a season on the pearling grounds. He had sent for the last of the funds he could access in San Francisco, a small trust left by a grandmother and the remains of his bank accounts there. But even combined with the money Archer had made during his recent lucky streak, they wouldn't have nearly enough.

"I don't suppose you'd let us pay you a bit at a time," Archer said.

"Can't. I need the money to increase my fleet."

Archer nodded. "I understand you're a gambling man, Skipper. Is the reputation larger than the reality?"

Garth laughed. "I was, once upon a time. All pearlers are gamblers. Haven't you seen that?"

"Once upon a time? Then your luck ran out?"

"The best gambler is one who has nothing important to lose.

When I reached the point where I could lose my chance at a future, I put down the cards forever.''

"That sounds smart," Tom said.

"I have nothing to lose except the wages you still owe me," Archer said. "You have nothing to lose except a lugger you don't want anymore."

"Your wages for the *Odyssey*? Are you joking?"

Archer shrugged. "We could just play for my wages, then. If I win, you double them. If you win, you don't owe me a thing. You save what you would have paid me, and coupled with what you can get for the *Odyssey*, you can buy those two new luggers."

Garth stroked his waxed mustache. Tom had expected him to refuse immediately, but Archer obviously knew their employer's reputation better than he did. "And what would you live on during lay-up if you lost?"

For obvious reasons, Archer didn't mention his gambling wins. "I still have more than half the advance you gave me when I signed on. That will take care of things."

"If I win, you stay on with me next season and open shell."

"I have nothing better to do."

Garth turned to Tom. "What about you?"

"What *about* me?"

"Will you stay, too? I'd rather not lose either of you."

Tom saw Archer give the barest nod to encourage him. If he'd had other plans he might have refused, but he was intending to work the next season anyway. "All right," he conceded. "I'll stay, too. But watch him, Garth. He's slick, and he's good."

"You Americans think you're better at everything, don't you?" Garth called for a deck of cards and another bottle of gin.

"I'll have that lugger by the evening's end," Archer said in a conversational tone. "Don't say we didn't warn you, Skipper."

Willow wasn't sleeping when Tom came home that evening. She didn't want to sleep while he was awake. She had been raised to be respectful and dutiful. She had not been raised to expect pleasure in her life. What shreds of pleasure were destined for her would have come from fulfilling her role in a society of ancient customs and laws, of meeting the stern, demanding standards of her ancestors. Instead she had abandoned all roles and standards to live as the concubine of a man who adored her.

And how she adored him in return. Tom was handsome and kind, but still strong enough to frighten away Bobby Chinn. He had brought her to this house with its garden of flowering shrubs, its veranda where she could sit unseen and breathe in the fresh sweet air. The crowded alleys of Chinatown, the heat of her father's laundry, the filthy room where the old man had bartered to buy her body, were fading farther away each day.

Now Willow thought constantly of Tom and what she could do to please him. He often bought her presents when he was in town. One day a small hand mirror, another a painted tin box, and another a jade necklace to place inside it. In return she tried to give him what she could. A single hibiscus beside his plate. A steaming cup of rare jasmine tea bought with money she carefully saved from the household accounts. An etching of mountains and ocean on a thin slab of melaleuca bark.

She knew, though, that nothing she gave him was as valued as her love. At first he had treated her like a rare and precious ornament. He had been so gentle, so concerned about her, so afraid she would suffer. But as time had passed, she had uncovered the passion she had seen under the surface. She had shown him that she could be passionate, too, that she was more than a delicate blossom to admire and care for.

She had never thought she might someday know a man with whom she could share her heart. But Tom wanted to know the smallest things about her. He encouraged her to talk, and he remembered the details so that he could adjust his life to hers. If she told him she liked candles on the table, he made certain to light them each night without being asked. If she told him she liked to watch the full moon rising, he made certain to walk with her in the evenings when the moon's reflection was like stair steps over the town mudflats.

Because their moments together were precious, she didn't want to waste them. So even when he went out in the evenings, she was always waiting for him when he returned.

Tonight he returned much later than she had expected. The glaze of pleasure that adorned the simplest of their days had begun to wear thin by the time he arrived. She worried that Bobby Chinn had sought revenge after all, or that a fight had erupted at the hotel and Tom had been injured. When he walked through the door, straight and strong and held out his arms, she ran into them like a frightened child.

"I was afraid." She rested her cheek against his chest as he folded his arms around her.

"Why? Did something happen?"

"No. I was afraid you would not come back."

"Willow tree, I would never do that to you."

"But another might do it to us, Tom. Another could hurt us."

"I won't let that happen, either." He lifted her face and kissed her lips. She could taste strong drink and knew now why he hadn't returned earlier.

"I have prepared food," she said, when he let her go.

"I'm not hungry. Will it keep?"

"Yes. Perhaps tea?"

He hauled her against his chest and held her there, hugging her fiercely. "You won't believe what happened tonight, Willow. I still can't believe it myself."

He was holding her too tightly, but she didn't care. "What? What is it?"

"Archer and I have our own lugger. The *Odyssey*, the boat we worked on this season. Archer won it tonight in a card game."

She broke free so she could see his face. "You won this boat?"

"No, Archer did. But we're going to be partners. His boat and my money to fund next season."

"A man lost this boat in a game? How must he feel?"

"Well, not good, of course. But he's a man, and an honorable one. He gambled and lost. He could have stopped any time, but he refused. And at the evening's end, when Archer offered to bet everything he'd won against the lugger, Garth chose to take the bet."

Willow frowned. "Gambling is not honorable."

"I don't have the heart or the instincts for it myself. But I can't very well condemn Archer for winning tonight, can I? Not when it's going to mean so much to you and me."

"Mean so much?"

"We'll build a fortune together, Archer and I. He's going to become an Australian citizen right away, so there won't be any trouble about a license. Archer isn't a pearler by nature, so once he has enough money, he'll buy land. He'll raise cattle and sons and find some happiness at last. I'll stay here with you, Willow. You and I, we'll have a whole fleet of luggers one day, and we'll raise our sons in Broome and find our happiness right here." He enfolded her in his arms again, kissing her hair, then her forehead, and finally, once again, her lips.

She wondered why, when his heart was so light, hers felt so heavy. Tom had just outlined a perfect life, a life beyond any she had ever hoped for. But when she closed her eyes, she didn't see the golden glow of a happy future. She saw nothing but darkness.

Archer had considered many ways to bring Freddy Colson to his knees. At night, when he stumbled into his room at the Roebuck, he lay in bed and pondered the possibilities until he fell asleep with a smile on his lips.

He had discovered the secret to Freddy's downfall on their first evening together, but the ways in which he might bring it to pass had been a source of considerable delight since then. The months of the lay-up were interminable, and the weather was so foul a man had to entertain himself any way he could.

When the streets of Broome were awash in rain and mold bloomed on every surface, when the rats, the spiders and snakes slithered inside for shelter, and the heat grew so intense the rain turned to steam, Archer thought about Freddy and what he would bring to pass.

One night between storms, when a king tide had risen so high it washed barramundi through the streets of Chinatown and the deadly local crocodiles into the gardens of the prettiest bungalows, Archer waited in the front bar of the Roebuck for the Somersets' houseboy. He had cultivated the young man on his infrequent visits, making certain to give the boy small gifts and show him small kindnesses. Two nights ago he had called in the favor, begging the boy to carry a private note to Viola. As he had expected, the boy had complied.

Now Archer waited for Ashwar, as he had last night, hoping the boy would return with news. In his note he had asked Viola to meet him, or at the very least to let him know when he could visit her in secret. He had implied he had news she would be glad to receive.

The clock ticked on, and the mood in the bar grew glummer. Lay-up was a time of intrigues, of melancholy and suspicions. When the rain and heat were at their worst, men plotted against each other and swore lifelong enmity against their best mates. A fight had broken out just minutes ago, squashed quickly by the publican and his assistant, but another would crop up by the evening's end. By eleven, when a policeman arrived to be certain the front door was closed for the night—then settled down for another hour or more of drinks with the patrons who came in through the back—hostilities would be reaching their peak.

Archer could feel his own tension building to a climax. He understood why men lost their minds in this weather. Forced into inactivity, he had no outlet for his energy except his thoughts. The glow of winning the *Odyssey* from Garth had long since dulled. Even if he and Tom had an exceptional season, they would be a long way from a fortune. Viola, and the real fortune she represented, would still be out of reach. And by the time he could afford to claim her, she would be married to someone else.

But not to Freddy Colson.

"Sir?" Archer felt a tug at his jacket hem, and he turned to see the houseboy, Ashwar. He was a lad not yet fifteen, slight, but tall for his age, and he always had a shy grin for Archer.

"Ashwar." Archer held out his hand. "Did you finally bring me some news?"

"Very wet outside. Take time."

"You look like you swam here."

"Walk almost as bad." Ashwar dug in his trouser pocket and pulled out a canvas-wrapped package. "This for you."

Archer unwrapped the canvas and pulled out a single sheet of paper that had been folded and sealed. "Wait, would you?"

Ashwar put his hands behind his back and looked deferentially at the floor.

Archer broke the seal and saw one short paragraph. Viola's parents were away. He was to come at nine, but not by buggy, in case her parents arrived home early. Ashwar would lead him.

Archer slipped the paper into his pocket. "It looks like I'll be going back with you. Wait on the veranda while I get my duster." Archer returned to his room for rubber boots and a cape-shouldered duster that would keep off some of the rain. He wrapped a sheaf of documents in the same canvas Viola had used; then he went to find Ashwar.

The trip to the Somersets' took twice as long as it should have. Even with Ashwar looking for potential dangers, they still had to pick their way through trash heaped high by the tides and wade through treacherous stretches of water.

By the time they reached the Somersets', Archer was thoroughly wet and filthy, and the thrill of sharing his news had diminished considerably. Under cover of darkness and a new storm whipping up from the east, he followed Ashwar to the back of the house and waited on the veranda while Viola was called.

She appeared at last, and he was certain she had made him wait on purpose. She wore a violet skirt and a shirtwaist trimmed in embroidered flowers. One long curl trailed over her breast, clinging tenaciously when she moved.

"Such an odd night for a visit," she murmured in greeting. "If Ashwar becomes ill, it will be difficult to explain."

"Perhaps, if I'm so unwelcome, I should leave before I give you the gift I brought."

She cocked her head. "A gift? I'm intrigued. What could a man like you give a woman, Mr. Llewellyn?"

"What would you want most, Viola?"

She didn't blink at the use of her name. "A ticket out of town. But I doubt you've brought me that."

"No, but I've brought you something nearly as good. Something you requested."

"Freddy's head on a platter?"

"Nearly."

For once the cultivated ennui of her expression livened into something more appealing. "Tell me."

"I think not."

"Then why have you come?"

"I'm asking myself as much. I come at some personal expense, and I'm greeted as if I'm a nuisance. A man prefers a warmer reception."

"Is that so? But you're nearly a stranger, Mr. Llewellyn."

"Archer."

She lifted an eyebrow.

He didn't smile. "My name is Archer. Say it."

"Has the weather affected you badly?"

"This business is affecting me badly. You are affecting me badly. Good night, Viola." He turned, fully prepared to leave.

"Archer...please. What did you bring?"

He faced her again. "Are you glad to see me, Viola?"

"I can't say until I know why you've come."

"That's not what I want to hear."

Her expression was pensive. He recognized a woman sorting through her options. He tipped his hat and turned away again.

"Oh, all right. I am glad to see me. I'm bored. I'm miserable, and the rain is driving me insane. I hate this country. I hate this weather. And I am positively dying to find out why you're here.''

"And me, Viola? Do you hate me, as well? Or do you have no feelings whatsoever?''

"I find you...exciting.''

It was already more than he had hoped for. But being a gambling man, he pushed on. "How exciting?''

Her eyes widened, and she smiled. "Excitement has no measurement.''

"No? Don't you think so?'' He reached for her, hauling her firmly against him and pressing her lovely white shirtwaist against the dripping canvas of his duster. "Shall we see about that?'' She squirmed against him, but before she could issue more than a word of protest, he sealed her lips with his, taking his time and using his considerable strength to show her who was in charge.

He let her go at last, sputtering and pounding against his chest. "You bastard!''

"My birth was completely legitimate.''

"How dare you?''

"Did you like it at all? Even the tiniest bit?''

She raised her hand to slap him, but he grabbed her wrist. "I'm not Freddy Colson. He might let you slap him, but I never will. I'll answer my own question, Viola. You liked it. More than a bit. And you'll like everything that comes with it once we're married.''

"I would sooner marry Freddy!''

"Is that so?'' He stepped away and reached inside his duster, taking time to unfasten it slowly and pull out the canvas package. "Then I've wasted my time, haven't I? I can tear up these papers. You can do what your father demands, and I'll find a woman who wants the things a woman wants.''

He unwrapped the canvas and held up the papers, then twisted them in his hands as if he were going to tear them to shreds.

"No!'' She laid her hand on his arm.

"No?''

"What is that?"

"Freddy's demise. I'll tear this up as a wedding present to the two of you. For Mr. and Mrs. Freddy Colson. I would save it as a gift for your children, but I doubt there will be any. As it turns out, Freddy prefers men. I don't know that he'll ever be able to do his duty to the future."

"Is that what's in there? Is that what you've found?"

"No. I've found Freddy considered an offer from a company based in London to open up an office here in Broome in their name, taking every trick he learned from your father and using it for his own profit. I have letters he wrote, an application to a bank in Perth, documents that spell out the whys and wherefores. He would have used everything he learned at your father's knee to undercut him. Information about Freddy's perversions would be less important, wouldn't it? I'm afraid your father values Freddy's loyalty more than happiness in your marriage bed."

"You say he planned to open a competitive business?"

"Of course he told me himself that he decided against it. He holds your father in highest esteem."

"Then how can this destroy him?"

"I have proof Freddy made the contacts. There's no proof he decided against moving ahead. Only his word. The loan is still pending."

"Freddy…"

"Freddy is no longer a threat to you. Or to me. If I give you these papers."

"If?"

"Tell me, Viola. Did my kiss mean anything to you at all?"

She was silent, her eyes on the papers in his hands.

"You aren't giving me your hand in marriage. I'm not asking you to accompany me to my hotel room. Simply tell me if the kiss meant anything. Either way, I'll give you the papers."

She stomped her foot and rainwater splattered them both. Then she met his eyes. "You think too well of yourself!"

"A man can't think too well of himself, particularly if there's no one else who does."

"It would be a sin to encourage such a fatal flaw."

"Quite probably." He waited.

"Yes, it meant something," she said at last. "But don't ever take a kiss without my permission again. Do you understand?"

"I understand that you and I will battle this way for the rest of our lives. Is that something to look forward to?"

"You definitely do think too well of yourself!"

"Do you want the papers, Viola?" He held them out.

She grabbed them away from him.

He waited.

"I'll let you know what happens when Father sees these," she said.

"Of course, you won't tell him where they came from."

"I'm not a fool."

"Are you a woman who's willing to wait for a man who's proved he has her best interests at heart?"

"I *could* wait—now that Freddy is out of the picture."

"But *will* you?"

She smiled. "I make no promises except that I will marry a rich man. If that man is you?" She turned and walked to the door, turning back with her hand on the latch. "I suppose I would not be heartbroken." She stared at him for a moment, then she laughed. He grinned as she flipped her hair over her shoulder and closed the door behind her.

7

The crew of the *Odyssey* was loyal to Tom, and when forced to choose between him and John Garth, they stayed with the new owners. Only Toshiharu was missing when the pearling boats, scrubbed and freshly painted, were launched for another season. In February Toshiharu had died in his sleep, and now he lay beside other divers in the Japanese cemetery, a delayed victim of the dangers of deep water.

For Tom and Archer, the season began well enough, with friends of the crew taking the town's only rail car out to the jetty to watch the *Odyssey* sail away. Tom had only reluctantly agreed to let Willow come to say goodbye. A neighbor, the West Indian wife of a local shopkeeper, had agreed to accompany her. But Tom didn't want to watch Willow growing smaller on shore as the *Odyssey* departed. Although she had never said as much, he knew she didn't want him to go. He had given her a comfortable home, and both the neighbors and household help would watch over her during his absence. But Willow seemed disturbed. No matter how encouraging he was about their future, in the final week before his departure, her eyes remained sad.

Archer attracted a well-wisher, too. Just as he was about to board, he looked back to see a well-appointed buggy pulled by a sleek thoroughbred. Holding the reins were the slender white hands of Viola Somerset. Her appearance at the jetty was enough for him. Freddy Colson was out of the picture now, dismissed by Viola's father and cut from all society functions. Viola's silent farewell was a good omen, and when the lugger finally set sail with gulls and gannets wheeling in the sapphire sky, Archer was filled with hope.

Hope reigned for the first weeks. They found shell almost immediately, and although Archer would never have believed it, he found the smell of rotting oysters could be a pleasure when the oysters were his. He discovered a pearl in the second week at sea, a baroque pearl of irregular shape, but it, too, seemed a good omen. In the third week a storm blew the lugger off course, but when Juan tried a dive just to see what was below, he found the richest patch of shell they had encountered.

Archer and Tom sat up on deck that night, contemplating their future. "It's not such a bad life in Australia, is it?" Tom had been down on a dive himself that afternoon, after Juan had come up early with a headache, and he had been in a particularly good mood ever since. "No one's shooting at us. No one's telling us what to do. We won't be rich men, at least not for a while, but if we keep this up, we'll bring home enough shell to make ourselves comfortable."

"Comfortable?" Archer gave a snort. "Is that what this is about?"

"Not for you, perhaps. But for me."

For months Archer had wondered why he had ever paired up with Tom. The bulk of Tom's attention was elsewhere much of the time now. He had made good friends with every man on the crew, and he was nearly revered by Bernard and Juan. Even worse, his infatuation with the Chinese girl hadn't wavered. Archer had expected Tom to realize how foolish such a liaison was, and to abandon her. Instead, Tom and the girl were keeping house like newlyweds, and Tom had even had the bad judgment to be seen with her at the jetty.

Archer shook his head in disgust. "Once upon a time you wanted more out of life than a miserable shack in a foreign country and a little Oriental pussy to warm your bed."

Tom was silent for a long time. Finally he turned to Archer, and his eyes were blazing. "By tomorrow I won't remember you said that. So don't say anything else that might make it harder to forget."

Archer's temper flared, too. "You could have everything a man wants, but you've given it up without a thought. I don't understand you."

"No? Well, if I hadn't given up my life in California, I wouldn't be here on this boat with you."

"If you hadn't given up the rich man's life, you wouldn't have joined Roosevelt in the first place, and I wouldn't have had to risk a firing squad. I'd be back in Texas right now!"

"Maybe you should have looked the other way when Linc decided to kill me."

This time Archer fell silent. He was a man who nursed few regrets. He did not regret saving Tom's life, but he did regret the way things had changed since they arrived in Broome. "Maybe you should just remember who your real friends are," he said at last. "Maybe you should remember who proved he'd stand beside you when things get rough."

"That's never been in doubt, Archer."

But Archer wondered.

The argument changed their luck, or at least that was how it seemed. The patch of shell they'd discovered by accident died out quickly, and the next few areas they scouted yielded little, too. They spent one day trying to scare away a lovesick whale determined to mate with the lugger and another repairing the mainsail when a sailfish, in a stunning leap, ripped a hole a yard wide before flopping in panic to the deck.

During lay-up, the *Odyssey* had been sunk in a creek off the coast of Broome to rid it of cockroaches. Archer had witnessed thousands of the creatures abandoning cracks and crevices throughout the ship to scurry up the mast in one last vain attempt at survival. The crew's first weeks at sea had been blessedly pest-free, but now a new swarm was hatching from eggs harbored over lay-up or brought on board in their supplies. Sleep became a struggle, and a spate of severe storms warred with the cockroaches to rule the nights.

After a particularly treacherous storm, the crew gathered on deck to discuss the coming weeks.

"I don't think we want to stay here," Tom said.

They had encountered half a dozen luggers in the past days, and none of them reported having luck. Even Archer, who had little faith in his fellow man, was inclined to believe they had been telling the truth. "I talked to a skipper at the Continental during lay-up who claimed the best place for shell is Cygnet Bay in King Sound."

"Good shell, bad luck," Juan said.

"What's the problem with it?" Tom asked.

"Bottom drops off like this." Juan floated his hand through the air, then suddenly his hand fell below his waist. "And like this." This time his hand extended down as far as it would reach.

"You can't tell when it's going to drop?"

"Holes hide in sea grass. A man don't know until he's falling. Line snaps…" Juan shrugged. "Man gone."

"Then it sounds like this place is out of the question," Tom said.

Archer waved his hand impatiently. "The skipper claimed that, with the right precautions, it was worth the risk."

"To whom, Archer? Juan's the one who'll be risking his life."

As he had too many times in the past months, Tom seemed to be taking someone else's side of an argument. Annoyed, Archer was suddenly willing to fight for something that had been a casual suggestion. "Do you think I want to risk Juan's life? Even if I were heartless, I could still see how much time and money we'd lose going back to town and trying to hire another diver midseason. But I still think this is worth discussing."

Support came from an unlikely quarter. "Discussion is good," Juan said. "Cygnet Bay, she's called the Graveyard. Graveyard bad luck for some divers, but not for all. Careful man, good tender…" He shrugged. "They make lotta money, little time. Men like that retire, go back home and live rest of lives with no worries.''

Tom's brow furrowed in concern. "I'd rather go home with my diver than with a hold full of shell.''

"Pearls down there. Lotta pearls come from Graveyard. I go there as young diver. I make more money that season than ever again."

"Why didn't you mention this place before?" Archer asked.

"Friend die there. Another Manilaman, from home village."

Tom grimaced. "I don't know why we're discussing this."

If Tom truly sympathized with his need to be rich, Archer knew he wouldn't be so quick to dismiss the possibility. "I say we leave the decision up to Juan," Archer said. "He's the one taking the biggest risk. If Juan's willing, let's go for it. We can always go elsewhere if it proves too dangerous.''

Tom could hardly argue, not without insulting Juan. He shrugged and waited.

"I work ten seasons, more than most," Juan said, as if he were thinking out loud. "Now not many left. Pearls make a difference to me."

"Then you're for setting sail for the Graveyard?" Archer said.

Juan nodded.

They were only about three days away from the Graveyard if the winds were good, and they set about preparing for the voyage. Archer waited until he was alone with Tom before he spoke of the meeting. "There are some things more important than caution, Tom. Even the crew realizes it."

"You're a gambler right down to the bone, aren't you?"

"I didn't hear you complaining when I won the *Odyssey* from Garth. If I weren't a gambler, that shell in the hold wouldn't belong to us."

"I just hope you know what you're doing."

Archer was sure he did, but it was a symptom of the tension between them that Tom seemed unconvinced.

Tom relaxed after two weeks in the Graveyard without incident. He had questioned Archer's proposal to look for shell here, even questioned his motives, but as each day passed, he worried less. The crew worked well together, putting aside their small differences to focus on the task at hand. Although the first week had yielded only an average haul, the second had been well above average.

And they had found pearls. Tom found his first good pearl on a morning when the crew was helping Juan don his diver's dress. At first he thought the peculiar lump at his fingertip was gristle; then, as he dug deeper, he realized the truth. He lifted the pearl between thumb and forefinger and rolled it around and around, savoring the slippery feel.

He knew better than to alert the crew. There was an unwritten law on pearling vessels. The shell opener kept his find to himself, stowing it in a special box kept in the captain's cabin and designed to be impervious to theft. Later, in private, he shared the good news with the diver, who would receive a percentage. But everyone on board was safer if no one else knew. Envy and greed had to be avoided at sea.

He pocketed the pearl and waited until later to show it to Archer, who had spent some portion of lay-up learning what he could from pearl buyers. "What do you think?" he asked, as Archer held the pearl to the light.

"The best we've found so far." Archer gave it back. "Worth a hundred quid maybe, if it cleans up well. It has a tiny flaw, but that might peel right off."

Tom laughed, foolishly delighted with himself. "I'd like to keep it and give it to Willow. My first pearl."

"Why? Then if she takes off with some man who makes her a better offer, you'll lose the pearl *and* the girl."

Tom swallowed what was now familiar anger. "I'll take this as part of my share of the profits at the season's end."

"I should know by now you won't listen to reason."

Archer found a small pearl the next day, too, but better yet, Juan continued to find good patches of shell, working eight long drifts a day and sending up a full mesh bag more frequently than ever before.

At the beginning of the third week, Juan stepped into his diver's dress one morning, then, before he could lower himself to the ladder, he bent over the lugger's side and began to vomit.

"What's that all about?" Archer asked, when Juan seemed finished.

"Something sick inside." Juan folded his arms over his stomach. "No dive today."

"Rot!" Archer pounded the heel of his hand against the tiller. "What, do you think it's something you ate?"

"Could be curry last night."

Archer turned to Tom. "Did you eat the curry?"

Tom, whose tolerance for spicy food was low, shook his head. "No, did you?"

"Not me. What about the others?"

Bernard looked fit, but both Ahmed and Reece were now hanging their heads over the side. And while Tom and Archer exchanged knowing glances, Wong Fai came up from the hold looking pale and shaky.

"That curry last night," Tom asked him. "Juan said it was hotter than usual. Did you spice it up because the fish smelled bad?"

"Fish smell strong. All fish strong."

"Wong, it's better not to take chances. Fish smells strong from now on, get rid of it."

"No new fish two day. No bully beef. No meat."

They had gotten supplies from a camp on the Eighty Mile beach before setting out for the Graveyard, but Tom knew their stores were getting low again. Soon they would have to sail into Broome to unload shell from the hold and get more supplies. He was glad for the opportunity, since it meant he would see Willow, but it wasn't economical to make the trip until the hold was full.

"We'll go without, then," he said. "Just don't serve anything spoiled again. Understand?"

"All fish strong." Wong Fai punctuated this brave statement with a trip to the side to join the others.

"All men not so strong," Archer said. "Jesus. A day off. Just what we need."

"Could be longer," Tom warned. "Juan can't go down until he's completely over this."

"Don't you think I know that?" Archer ran his fingers through hair that was in need of cutting. "And just when we were really on shell. By the time the crew's better, we'll have to go for supplies. And we won't want to brave the riptides and other hazards of the sound to come back."

The trip through King Sound, with its islands and sucking tides, *had* been harrowing. Tom sought a solution. "Look, while we're here, why don't I dive?"

Archer examined him as if he'd lost his mind. "This isn't play, Tom. You want a holiday, find a better moment for it."

"I'm not talking about a holiday. Juan can't dive, but I can. I'll go down and see what I bring up. We're stuck here for a while. We might as well give it a try."

"Who's going to man the air pump?"

"You can."

"It takes two men."

"Then the others can take turns. They should be able to manage short shifts. They won't have anything left in their stomachs before long."

"This is no place for amateurs."

Tom fell silent. He realized the irony in his suggestion. Just weeks before he had argued against coming to the Graveyard. Now he was arguing for making a dive himself.

"We're a long way from help if you're injured," Archer warned.

"I've done enough dives to know what chances I can take. Juan hasn't had any problems. I know you're anxious to get shell. We need to fill the hold before we go back. Let me give it a try."

"You'd do this for me?"

"You risked your life for me, didn't you?"

Archer hesitated, but at last he gave a short nod. "Don't fool around down there. If you spot trouble, signal and we'll bring you right up."

Tom clapped him on the back. "I will. I promise."

"Anything you want me to tell your next of kin?"

Tom sobered quickly. "I'm coming up in one piece. But if anything ever does happen, Archer, take care of Willow for me. Please."

"Take care of her?"

"Give her my share of whatever we own together. Help her invest it."

Archer gave a reluctant nod.

Tom thought about their exchange as Bernard and Archer helped him into the suit. It was a piece of luck that he and Juan were so close in height and only a few adjustments had to be made. Tom would never equal Juan in skill, however, or the Japanese divers who seemed to be taking over the profession. He was too lanky and too easily absorbed by the wonders of the deep, but he was able to spot shell.

Tom was glad to be going down today. The lugger wouldn't be a pleasant environment until the sick men began to recover. And Archer's frustration was like a fierce wind pounding at a boat without sails. If Tom could find some shell, everyone would feel better, and he would have the pleasure of the dive to divert him.

He thought of Willow as Bernard fastened the helmet in place. He had thought of little else since taking to sea. She was always with him, and he missed her even more than he had expected. He wished he could show her the ocean floor, with its brightly colored fish, its coral formations and rippling vegetation. Each time he dove, he felt more confident, and each time he explored more aggressively. He had seen sharks as large as dinghies, deadly sea snakes and underwater battles for survival that were a solemn reminder of how fleeting life could be. But so much of the ocean was miraculous. Few men had seen what he had, and he knew he would always look forward to the next dive, the next exploration.

"Test with foot," a pale Juan said, as a last warning. "Take small steps. Don't step in grass. Watch always."

"I'll be careful." Tom signaled for Bernard to fasten the faceplate of the helmet. Then he stepped off the ladder, adjusted the valve of his helmet and began his slow descent.

He was accompanied on his journey by the steady clicking of the air pump above him and the gurgling rush of his own air bubbles to the surface. The sounds were comforting, and although they grew fainter as he descended, they would stay with him. If the time came when he ceased to hear them, the minutes of his life would be numbered.

When he was nearly to the bottom, he tugged once on his lifeline to let Bernard know he was all right. Before Juan had let Tom dive, he had carefully instructed him on the codes a diver must know. The lifeline and air pipe were the only forms of communication a diver had, and the signals had to be instinctive.

The water was cloudy, but clearer than the last time he'd gone down. A school of tiny silver fish darted past—herring, he guessed—pursued by a smaller school of something larger but clumsier. He stood perfectly still, hoping not to be involved in the deadly game. Both schools passed him by like a useless stand of coral, and when he was sure the herring wouldn't return to attach themselves to his suit in terror, he began a slow, thumping walk across the bottom, searching for shell.

He remembered Juan's instructions. A man falling into a deep crevice was in mortal danger from the pressure in his own suit. The long fall would be so swift, there would not be time to adjust valves before a diver was jammed into the top of his own helmet, eyes bulging, body exploding in horrifying ways. He tested the floor as he moved, concentrating on avoiding areas hidden by the lush, mysterious meadow of underwater growth.

He hummed as he searched, his tenor buzzing against the faceplate. Archer had marked this place with a red buoy when yesterday's dive had ended, but Juan had warned him he would find little shell here. Juan had already gathered what was present, and had expected to drift to find more. When Tom was satisfied there was no point in combing the area again, he signaled Bernard to lift him from the bottom and set sail.

His job now was to drift under the boat, hanging from the lifeline and trying to picture the boat above, the currents, the wind, the waves, while he scouted for shell. If he saw promising terrain, he had to judge whether the boat could carry him there and how best to signal his wishes to Bernard. He had only drifted once. His other dives had simply been to explore the bottom, and what shell he'd found was luck. But today the drift was serious, and if he found even a little shell, it might ease the tensions above him.

Juan had given him hints on how to judge the best underwater landscape, but guessing accurately was a skill that took years to learn. He swung from the line, floating over the bottom like an angel hovering over earth. He tried to distinguish one area from another and judge the potential value of each section of reef. But when they had covered some distance and it was increasingly clear his skills needed honing, he tugged to signal that he wanted to stop and explore.

He was disheartened already, and the day had just begun. The possibilities were limitless, and if he explored them all, he could spend his life underwater and never find an oyster. He lowered himself to the bottom and began the weighted, cumbersome walk again, bending once to dislodge a suspicious mound, then dropping it back in place when it turned out to be a lump of coral dressed in tuberous black vegetation. Gold and white fish, iridescent in what sunlight made its way to the bottom, frisked back and forth in front of his helmet, and several larger fish, blue-black and eyes bulging, appraised them from the sidelines, like overweight matrons at a lawn tennis match.

The hunt was unsuccessful. He signaled and began another drift, only choosing to stop again because his frustration had built to a climax. His experience here was much the same. He could imagine the men above him growing sullen and impatient. Keeping a diver underwater was never an easy task, and with so many of the crew sick, it would be harder than usual.

After a time he gave up on this spot, too. He was already growing tired, and he knew that soon it would be time to surface and rest. He doubted the men would send him down again.

He signaled for another drift and was almost surprised when Bernard complied. He concentrated on the undulating sweep of the floor, searching as he passed for telltale clumps, for the foliage he had mechanically chopped off Juan's shell on the lugger. He tried to remember how the shell he had found had looked when it was on the bottom, what kind of sea life it had been near, what kind of setting he had found it in.

Fatigue began to eat away at him, or perhaps disgust. He had believed he had some talent for this, but today was proof he didn't. He would stop once again, but the effort would yield nothing. Bernard would haul him up, and he would have to tell the men he had failed. Archer, always impatient, would be curt and sarcastic. The others would be disappointed.

He jerked sharply for Bernard to stop. The signal was automatic, and only afterwards did he realize he'd signaled before the thought had fully formed. He gazed at the floor to his right. The reef was subtly different here, the plant life more verdant. He and Archer had not prospected for gold long enough to know the thrill of a strike, but he suspected it was something like this. This section of the bottom looked different, and it felt different. He signaled where he wanted Bernard to go, and he waited until he was close enough to begin his exploration.

The floor felt right under his feet, and he moved easily and well, as careful as he needed to be but not overly cautious. For once the fish seemed to melt into the background. He was dimly aware of brilliant blue binghi fish, but he passed them by without a real look. A small shark swam by, but it was easily intimidated by his air bubbles and disappeared quickly.

He found his first shell just fifteen feet from where he had touched the bottom. He was not a diver, but he did know shell. This one was old, and perhaps the largest he had ever seen. He grinned with delight as he stuffed it into his bag and began the search for more.

8

There was a celebration of sorts that evening. Most of the men were still feeling too ill to eat, but not to toast Tom's success with strong tea. He hadn't set any records. In fact, his find had been less than Juan's on an average day. But the fact that he'd brought up any shell at all had seemed like good luck.

"You open shell tonight. See what you got," Juan told him. "Good luck follow you today."

Tom had expected to pile his shell with the shell that hadn't been opened yesterday, but he could see Juan thought this was important. Tom had the diver's right to anything found inside.

"Want some help?" Archer asked later, when the men, worn by their illness, were asleep before the skies had completely darkened. Even Bernard, who had assumed extra duties all day, was snoring somewhere at the stern.

"With the two of us, we can finish before the light's too poor." Tom settled down to the task. He was used to opening shell, but he never enjoyed it. He was sorry to separate the oysters from their opalescent homes.

"What's it like down there?" Archer said, chopping growth from an oyster before he tossed it to Tom.

"Like another world."

"I don't know why you go down. It's not a white man's place."

"It's a magnificent sight."

Archer was silent, working at another shell. He tossed it on the pile at Tom's feet before he spoke. "I couldn't do it."

Tom had never heard Archer admit there was anything he couldn't do. He felt a swell of affection for his friend. "Sure you could. You just don't want to."

"Every time someone puts that helmet over your head...?" Archer shook his own. "You could die like that."

"Or I could die in my sleep, or from falling off a horse, or from Wong Fai's cooking."

Archer laughed. "I never said Wong's curry was good for you, either."

"I like being down there. When I was a boy, I'd stare at the sky and wonder who was living on the stars. I'll never find out, but the ocean floor might as well be a star or a planet."

"I was too busy to stare at anything. Too busy riding after somebody else's steers and hoeing their weeds. Too busy getting whupped if I didn't work fast enough."

Tom knew how completely Archer's childhood ruled him. "The way you're working, you'll have your own steers someday, Archer. See if you don't."

"My pa worked all the time. He got up way before dawn, and he kept right on working till he dropped in his tracks at night. And all that work never got him a damned thing."

"That doesn't mean the same thing's going to happen to you."

Archer tossed another shell at Tom. "You're right, because I'm not the same as him. He thought if he lived right, good things were bound to happen. Me, I know better. A real man grabs whatever comes his way—and some things that don't."

Tom gave a wry smile. "Yeah, that's what my father did. He grabbed everything within grabbing range and made himself a rich man. But he never grabbed enough to make him happy."

"And you think you'll be happy if you live the way you're planning?"

"I'm already happy."

Archer abandoned the shell for a moment. "Happy? Now?"

"Damned right. I've got you. I've got Willow. I've got the *Odyssey*. I like being out on the water. I like Australia. What else do I need, Archer?"

"Good sense."

Tom waited for his friend to launch into another tirade against Willow, but Archer passed up the opportunity. He picked up the next shell, and Tom glanced at it as Archer turned it over and over in his hands. "This one's a monster."

Tom recognized the shell by its size. "That's the first one I found today. I'd about given up hope, then there it was."

Archer scraped off what little growth clung to it and silently passed it to Tom.

"I almost hate to open it," Tom admitted. "As oysters go, this one's somebody's grandpa."

"Throw it back, then. I don't care."

Tom weighed the shell in his hands, but he doubted it would live after so much time out of the water. "Too much sentiment and we'll never get you the first cow." He jimmied his knife into the crack and pried open the shell. But he was almost reluctant to probe. Oysters had no personality, he told himself, and he'd opened thousands of shells; but this one was different, because of its size and the good luck he associated with it.

He felt along the rim with his finger, poking and pressing. Then he stopped.

Archer looked up from cleaning another oyster, and he stopped, too. He didn't ask the obvious question. The crew was asleep, or so it seemed, but someone could still be awake, listening and hoping....

He lifted a brow in question. Tom looked down at the shell, sliding his forefinger a little farther. Then he dug with his thumb, stretching it wider and farther than he'd ever guessed he would need to. He was breathing faster, and his heart sped up to fill his chest with the crescendoing resonance of a drum tattoo.

Archer leaned forward. Tom slowly squeezed his fingers together and brought out a pearl.

"My God." Archer whispered the words so softly they disappeared against the creaking of the chain and the waves lapping against the lugger's sides.

Tom stared at the pearl in his palm, the largest, most magnificent pearl he had ever seen, a pearl larger than a sparrow's egg. A pearl was the only gem that emerged from its natural home in nearly finished form. No gem cutter chipped it from its surroundings or ground and polished it. Washed and shined by a soft cloth, it immediately glowed like the precious freak of nature it was. Tiny flaws might be peeled away, one skin at a time by an expert, but many pearls were perfect from the moment they left the oyster.

Perfect was too poor a word to describe this one.

Archer held out his hand. For a moment Tom was reluctant to hand over the pearl. He rolled it in his palm once more, treasuring the feel of it, then he dropped it into Archer's hand.

"I don't believe it." Again Archer spoke so softly that even Tom had trouble making out his words.

"Is it as valuable as I think?" Tom mouthed.

"More so." Archer held it between his thumb and forefinger, turning the pearl around and around. "Superb. Priceless."

"Shall we wake up Juan and examine it in the cabin?"

Archer nodded. There was no way to hide this find from the diver. The cabin was the only place they could really take a good look at the pearl, and Juan's bed was there, alongside Archer's.

Tom looked down at the oyster that had given him this treasure. There was no way it could survive this assault, but somehow, he could not cut the animal from its home and throw the shell in the hold to be made into buttons. He bundled it back together as best he could and went to the side. He dropped it over as gently as he could to let the oyster die in familiar surroundings.

"You're a fool," Archer said at his side, but he said it with affection. "A damned stupid, sentimental fool, but one hell of a diver."

Tom had been wealthy, but never because of his own efforts. "We're rich men," he said.

In the moonlight, Archer's eyes glowed. "Let's see how rich."

They woke Juan, who was tossing back and forth fretfully in discomfort. Tom waited until the lantern had been lit and Juan was fully awake before he told him what had transpired.

Then Archer took the pearl from his shirt pocket and laid it on a white handkerchief on the bunk beside Juan.

In the stronger light, the pearl was transformed. Its luster was celestial, its shape a perfect sphere, its size immense enough to be the dominant jewel in any monarch's crown.

Juan's eyes widened, and he drew a deep, shaky breath. "Such a stone I never seen."

"It's as silver as it is white," Archer said. "A rare enough color. And I can't see a flaw on it anywhere." He rolled it over with his fingertip. "It's as big as a marble. Bigger."

"Price will be great for this pearl," Juan said.

"The pearl of great price." Tom shook his head.

"Am I supposed to understand that?" Archer asked.

"It's from the Bible. I learned the verses as a child. 'The kingdom of heaven is like unto a merchant seeking goodly pearls, who, when he had found one pearl of great price, went and sold all that he had, and bought it.'"

"This is a pearl men will sell anything they own to possess." Archer stared at the pearl. "And it's ours. We could buy the kingdom of heaven with what we'll get for this pearl, or any other kingdom we desire."

Tom stared at the pearl, too, but he didn't see kingdoms. He saw a contented future with Willow in a spacious pearler's bungalow, sons and daughters who would enrich his days, the satisfaction of knowing Archer could now embark on the life he had always dreamed of.

"This pearl make one man very rich," Juan said. "Make two men sorry they be partners."

"Surely it will sell for enough to give us both a good start?" Tom picked up the pearl and rested it in his palm. He savored the weight.

"Start, maybe, not kingdoms. Whatever you sell it for is not enough."

Tom knew that what pearlers got for their stones in Broome was only a fraction of what the same pearls brought in cities like London and Paris. But neither he nor Archer had the contacts or the income necessary to sell them elsewhere. "So it may take another season or two before we both have everything we want. At least we're on our way."

"We'll be on our way to the jetty tomorrow," Archer said. "We're going back to town to get supplies and take care of this. I don't want to risk anything happening to this pearl."

Tom squeezed his fingers closed, wrapping the pearl in his own flesh. "Don't you think we should stay here as long as we can? The moment Juan feels better he can dive, but I can muddle through until then. The shell is good."

"Do you really want to keep this pearl on board?"

Tom knew what Archer was asking. A pearl the value of this one could cause untold problems if the men discovered it. He trusted his crew. He genuinely liked and admired them all. But smaller pearls than this had caused mutinies.

"We'll have to keep it a secret," he conceded. "Juan, you have to promise not to tell anyone."

Juan gave a gruff nod.

Tom believed him. "I think we can take the risk. A few more days in the Graveyard and we can fill our hold. Then we can go back to town, unload everything and get fresh supplies." Tom expected Archer to argue, but he didn't. He had been staring at Tom's hand. Now he looked up.

"For now you'll put it in the box?" Archer said.

Tom nodded. The pearler's box had been designed for moments like this. Copper tubing ran from a slot in the locked lid, making it impossible to get the pearl out once it had been placed inside. The only key was back in Broome at their bank.

"One more look."

Tom straightened his fingers and arched his palm. The pearl gleamed in the lantern light. "Gentlemen, I give you the Pearl of Great Price."

They were silent, each gazing intently at it, as if to memorize the sight and keep it with him. Then Tom pinched the pearl between his fingers and ceremoniously slid it into the box.

Archer hardly slept. Every time he closed his eyes, he saw the pearl gleaming in Tom's hand. Tom, who had been born for pearls like this one. Tom, who had never been poor, who had never been alone, who had never wanted something so badly he couldn't sleep nights for thinking about it.

On the bunk beside his, Archer could hear Juan's restless tossing.

It wouldn't surprise him if they all sickened and died out on the ocean. Between the roaches, the rats, the sour drinking water, the poor quality of their food, they were doomed, at best, for disease. He hated the pearler's life, the ship, the heathen crew. But most of all, tonight he hated the joy he had felt when seeing the Pearl of Great Price for the first time, lying in Tom's hand.

What a fool he'd been. For more than a few moments he had believed the pearl would make a difference in his life. He had envisioned going back to Broome to tell Viola about it and to show the pearl to her father. After the first show of gratitude over Nakanishi's rescue, Sebastian Somerset had grown cooler toward Archer, as if he sensed Archer wanted more from him than an introduction into Broome society. But the pearl would have changed that.

Would have, if the pearl belonged to Archer exclusively.

The pearl was out of sight now, waiting in the pearler's box until the day when it would astound those lucky enough to glimpse it. But he could almost feel its presence and all the promises it made, simply by its existence.

Archer had not, in all the months of the lay-up, seen any pearl that was comparable. One owner would be rich enough to buy land *and* cattle, particularly if he had a lugger to sell and a hold nearly filled with shell.

But joint profits would have to be plowed back into the partnership. The money could be used to increase their fleet. They could be two-lugger admirals, or even three- or four-lugger, competing with men like Somerset with his vast number of ships, his quality equipment and talented divers. They could be small players in the pearl industry, reinvesting in themselves when the season was good, holding tight when it wasn't. In the end they could be, as Tom had said, comfortable.

Archer wondered if Viola would accept that life. If he gave up his dream of land and stayed in Broome, could he convince her to marry him anyway? When her father passed away, everything Sebastian owned would be hers, and she and Archer could sell it all and buy a spread as far away from Broome as Viola wanted to go. But even as he considered it, Archer knew she wouldn't wait. She would marry someone else, someone who could take her away while she still had youth and beauty to barter.

If the pearl were his alone, he could have the life he wanted. With Tom as his partner, that life would be denied him.

He wondered if Tom would consent to selling the pearl and buying land together. There would be room for two men, two families. But even as the possibility entered his mind, he discarded it. Tom liked the pearling life, and he was set on marrying the Chinese woman. Even if he could be persuaded to leave Broome, he would certainly bring her with him. And Archer was sure Viola would not accept Willow.

If the pearl were his alone, he thought again, he could have the life he wanted. With Tom as his partner, that life would be denied him.

Juan moaned and tossed noisily on the bunk beside his, but Archer hardly heard. His own thoughts kept him awake.

The next morning, just before dawn, Bernard hung his head over the side and emptied the contents of his stomach.

"Humbug belonga belly," he muttered as he stretched out close to the outrigger platform where he crouched when he was tending the diver. He closed his eyes and rested his hands on his chest like a man about to be buried.

Tom, who had heard the tender move to the side, brought a blanket and covered him.

"How do *you* feel?" Archer came out of the cabin wearing nothing but trousers. He stretched, like a man who'd just had a welcome night's sleep.

"Better than I knew I could." Tom grinned to let Archer know he was talking about the pearl. He had thought of little else since finding it last night.

Archer looked away. "I'm still all right. Bernard's so big, maybe it just took a while for the bad fish to strike him down."

"This may not be the fish at all. It could be something else, and we may not be able to hold it off, whatever it is."

"Well, with the rest of the crew down sick, we'll have trouble sailing back to town. I don't think they'll be much help. We should wait a day or two and see if they start to recover. If they don't, and you and I are still feeling all right, we can make a run for it then."

Reece and Ahmed came over to check on Bernard and reported that both of them were feeling a little better.

"Too bad we don't have a tender," Tom said. "With Reece and Ahmed sharing turns with you at the air pump, I could dive."

Archer stroked his unshaven chin. "I could be the tender today. Bernard's here if I get into any trouble, but I've helped him before, and I've watched him every time. I know what to do."

The tender's job was probably the most important one on a pearling lugger. Although the diver determined the success or failure of a season, the tender determined the diver's survival.

"I don't know what to say." Tom gazed at the outrigger, as if he might find his answers there. "I'm a novice, and you're a novice. Shouldn't one of us know exactly what he's doing?"

"Tom, when you go down below, you're alone. If you make a mistake, there's no one there to advise you. Up here, I have the whole crew. Bernard's sick, but he's not too sick to tell me what to do if I think you're in trouble."

Archer's argument made sense, and Tom guessed his answer

mattered to his friend. Last night had seemed like old times. The tensions that had permeated this voyage had disappeared. The pearl had changed everything. Archer seemed different already, more resolute, more determined to make this trip an even greater success. He was offering to give Tom what he desired, a chance to dive today to see if there was more shell waiting. They were solidly partners again, two men seeking their destinies together.

"Let's do it," Tom said. "I don't want Ahmed and Reece to get completely worn-out, so I'll only do a few dives. But let's give it a try. Maybe we can fill the hold after all before we set sail for Broome."

"Good," Archer said, turning to stare at the outrigger. "That's what we'll do, then. You can make your first dive after breakfast. I'll see what hints Bernard has to offer before you go down. We'll take every precaution."

Tom clapped him on the back. "It'll be like old times. You'll have my life in your hands again. That seems to be our fate."

"It does, doesn't it?"

They stood side by side in silence and watched the sun rise.

A few minutes later, Juan joined Tom on the deck as he finished breakfast. Juan was pale and shaky, but he claimed the night had done him some good. "But no dive today," he added, as if it might have been in question.

Tom poured him tea from a pot Wong Fai had made and wished that their supply of coffee wasn't gone. "I'm going to dive again, and Archer's going to act as tender," he told Juan.

Juan looked troubled, but he didn't respond.

"Do you have any advice?" Tom said. "Anything I should look for that might help us? The sooner we fill this hold, the sooner we can start back to Broome."

Juan folded his hands around the cup. "We go back now. Better that way."

"It's a long trip, and everyone's still sick. We think it would be easier if we wait."

"Tender needs steady hand. Needs to follow signals. Be patient and pay attention. Needs to feel things that happen."

"I know, Juan."

"Bernard knows this. He knows when things happen underwater. He feels them."

"I know he does. But Bernard is sick, and Archer's willing to give it a try. He won't let anything happen to me."

"Bernard and me, we're not friends. Tender and diver should not think of anything but what goes on in the water. Should not think about rest of life."

Tom slapped Juan's arm affectionately. "I'll tell him not to think about a damned thing except bringing me back up, I promise. You and Bernard can keep an eye on him."

Juan frowned, but he didn't repeat his warning.

Archer returned from taking tea to Bernard. "Bernard won't move. I think we're going to have to step over him all day."

Tom stood. "I'll go get the flannels. Finish your breakfast. Then we can get started."

"The sooner the better."

Tom donned what portion of the diver's dress he could by himself. Despite the undiminished thrill of finding the pearl, he wasn't really looking forward to today's dive. He was anxious to get back to Broome to tell Willow about their good fortune. He had something concrete to offer her now. He knew that he didn't have to be wealthy, that she would stay with him no matter what, but he was pleased to be able to offer her more. And he yearned to see her face when he told her the news.

Now he wished that he had not requested they stay at sea and fill their hold. If he had anticipated Bernard's illness, he would have voted to sail back home, but now that he had made a case for not returning immediately, he was loath to admit he had changed his mind. Archer had volunteered to be tender, and Tom didn't want to seem ungrateful or worried that Archer wouldn't do a good job. Archer was a man of swift reflexes, a restless man who enjoyed challenges. He would master this one quickly, and when he had shown that he could, he would gladly hand the job back to Bernard.

In the meantime, Tom had little choice but to dive or risk a return of the tensions between them.

"Are you ready for the rest of it?"

Tom hadn't heard Archer come up behind him. Now he managed a smile. "How about you?"

"I'm set. Bernard gave me some reminders. But I know exactly what I'm doing."

Tom let Archer help him into the diver's dress. Juan assisted where he could, but he never smiled. He grew more sober as Tom disappeared into the canvas folds. Tom wondered how much Juan regretted not being the one to find the pearl. The chances that he would have stopped the boat at the same place or found his way to that spot and that shell were small, but it must have occurred to him that his illness had destroyed the possibility. Now he would not get the biggest commission of his career.

"You'll be well soon," Tom told him. "And there's plenty of shell waiting for you to discover it. Don't look so gloomy."

"I think I will not dive again." Juan shook his head. Then he turned and walked away.

Tom nearly called for him to come back and explain. "What do you suppose that's about?" he asked Archer.

"Who knows? All colored people are superstitious. Anything sets them off."

The sun was warm, but Tom felt a sudden chill. For a moment he considered calling off the dive. Archer might be upset, but Tom could make it up to him. Then he glanced at his friend's face and saw that Archer expected him to change his mind. His posture was rigid, as if he was waiting for Tom to disappoint him, and Tom knew he owed Archer too much to question his competence.

He turned and started toward the hatch, waddling gracelessly. Seated, he thrust out his feet for the weighted boots, then the corselet. When Archer helped him up again, he made his way to the side and stepped over and on to the ladder. Archer signaled Ahmed, who brought the weights to slide over his shoulders.

Archer made all the necessary checks, taking his time and making adjustments, as if he had been readying divers for years. "You're good at this," Tom told him. "Bernard had better get well soon, or you might just take over his job."

"I wouldn't have volunteered if I didn't know what to do."

"Good luck," Tom said.

"You, too." Archer lifted the helmet. For a moment, despite its weight, he held it over Tom's head, as if he wanted to change his mind, then, with his gaze locked with Tom's, he lowered the helmet and began to fasten it in place.

"Archer..."

"What?"

"Remember what I said yesterday about Willow?"

"What's wrong? Did you change your mind about her already?"

"No. It's just easier to go down there if I'm really sure she'll be taken care of if something happens to me."

"I'll take care of Willow. Don't worry about anything. Just find us some shell."

"That's what I'll do." Tom waited until Archer was in place on the outrigger, holding the lifeline and air hose. Then, with Ahmed and Reece steadily pumping air into his helmet, he pushed off and began his descent.

Just as he had yesterday, he thought about Willow as he floated to the bottom. He wondered about the children they would have together. Perhaps she was even pregnant now. Suddenly he was sorry that he hadn't married her right away. He had been sure there was plenty of time to find ways to make their relationship more acceptable. Oddly, now he felt certain that he had been wrong to wait, and he wondered if it could be arranged quickly when he got back to town.

Yesterday he had wished he could bring her here, to this exotic world of undersea creatures and alien vistas. He had wanted to share it with her and broaden her horizons. Today he wanted nothing more than to be in their tiny bungalow, in the familiar surroundings he had learned to love, with the clock ticking on the mantel and rice steaming fragrantly in the kitchen. He wanted Willow in his arms, her heart beating strong and steady against his chest.

He felt a stab of sadness that he hadn't always appreciated the smallest things about his life. The way the San Francisco fog crept along the ground in whirling wisps. A scarlet splash of bougainvillea against a rusting iron fence. The fragrance of jasmine tea.

His eyes felt heavy, and he realized he was feeling exactly the way he did just before he drifted off to sleep. He wasn't sure why he felt so tired. He adjusted his air valve. He could hear the steady clanking of the air pump through the hose, but today it seemed as soothing as a mother's lullaby. His eyelids closed, then, startled, he forced them open. He drew a deep breath, or tried to, but despite the reassuring rhythm of the pump, despite his frantic attempts to regulate his air, he couldn't draw enough into his lungs.

He told himself not to panic. He adjusted the valve on his helmet again, but now the air seemed in even shorter supply. His head began to ache and his fingers to tingle.

He tugged frantically on the lifeline. Something was wrong, and he didn't know what. The helmet needed adjustments. The line was compressed somewhere along its length. Whatever the problem, he couldn't fix it alone. He had to surface—and soon, before the air flow stopped altogether.

He readied himself to rise, tugging at the lifeline again to signal Archer to bring him up. But there was no answering tug.

Something must be wrong above him, too. Something was wrong with the equipment, and Archer must be trying frantically to repair it. In a moment Archer would respond. Tom's helmet would fill with air, and he would be safe. Archer would bring him up, and they would discover the problem together.

He tugged once more, but now his fingers were so numb he could hardly bend them to signal. His head felt as if it were being flattened by stones. He landed on the ocean floor and staggered backwards until he fell.

He cried out Archer's name, but there was no one to hear him. Above him, the air pump continued its life-giving rhythm, and in the cabin, a pearl waited to be sold to the highest bidder.

He died quickly, but not quickly enough. He knew, as he struggled unsuccessfully for a final breath, that his best friend had sacrificed him for the Pearl of Great Price. He himself had paid the greatest price of all.

9

Archer buried Tom above the high-water mark, on the beach nearest the place he had died. He marked the spot with a primitive wooden cross while the crew looked on. They had refused to help him dig Tom's grave, and he had been forced to keep a pistol ready. They stood near the water and watched, and when the deed was done, they came and laid small tokens at the site. But only after Archer had climbed back into the dinghy.

He knew every man on board was certain he had murdered his friend. But Juan was the only one who said so.

"You think you have done a good thing for yourself," Juan had said, when the grisly task of removing Tom's distorted body from the diver's dress and wrapping him in a blanket and length of canvas was finished. "But now we see to it that no man works for you. And the other masters will know what you did. We see to that, too."

"I tell you, Juan, Tom didn't signal. I had no idea he was in trouble, not until I felt his body dragging!"

"You think I don't know? You think I don't see what you do to the valve in the helmet?"

"That's ridiculous. It was damaged when we had to cut him out. You've got to believe me. Tom was my closest friend."

Juan closed his hand over the gold cross he always wore. "You will never have another."

Archer hadn't slept for the two days it took to return to Broome. He was careful never to turn his back on the others and to keep his gun in reach.

In Broome, the men left the lugger without a backward glance, even after Archer swore he wouldn't pay them if they didn't help with the unloading. He gave up when it was clear they weren't going to respond to his threats. He secured the lugger and locked the hold. Then, with the pearler's box under his arm, he made his way to the bank that held the key.

He had occupied himself during the voyage back to Broome by making plans. He had considered selling the pearl immediately, but the pearl was so dramatic, so magnificent, he hated to part with it without taking advantage of all its potential. He wanted Sebastian Somerset to see the stone, to know exactly what kind of man would be asking for his daughter's hand. He wanted Viola to see it, too, so she could view the proof that he'd made good on his promise. He had returned a rich man.

After retrieving the key, he went to the Roebuck to rent a room. The clerk assigned him one, but he didn't seem inclined to chat. Archer told him about the tragedy on the *Odyssey,* and the man peered unsympathetically over wire-rimmed spectacles until the story was finished.

"I liked Tom," he said without expression. "He was a gentleman."

"You don't seem surprised by his death."

"I knew."

Even considering Juan's threats, Archer was surprised the word had gotten out so quickly. "The crew blames me." He gazed off into the distance, like a man tormented by things out of his control. "But I did everything I could to save him. We were mates. I would take his place in the grave, if I could."

"It's too bad such a thing's not possible." The clerk turned his back before Archer could respond.

In his room, Archer unpacked, then he opened the pearler's box and gazed at his bounty. On land, in natural daylight, the Pearl of Great Price was no less beautiful than it had been at sea under a flickering lantern. He held it carefully in his palm

as he considered what to do with it. He could hide it somewhere in the room, but any man who wanted it badly enough
to search would be diligent and thorough. No hiding place, no
matter how clever, would be secure.

He could take it to his bank to be locked in their safe, but
how could he be certain that the mere sight of it wouldn't turn
an otherwise honest bank officer into a scoundrel? The pearl
represented the answer to man's most unattainable dreams.
Who wouldn't steal it, if given the opportunity?

At last he decided to keep the pearl with him. If he were to
lose it, he would prefer to die, anyway. He untied the kerchief
he wore knotted around his neck and rewrapped it so the pearl
fit snugly against the hollow of his throat.

With that taken care of, he penned a note to Sebastian and
a separate one to Viola, to be delivered to Ashwar, the houseboy who had helped him before. He told Sebastian the sad
circumstances of Tom's death, how something had gone wrong
and a panicked Tom hadn't signaled his distress. How Archer
had tried to no avail to rescue his friend. He ended by saying
that he had something to show Sebastian, something he needed
advice on.

In his note to Viola, he condensed the story of Tom's death
and asked her to meet him in secret. Then he went to find a
messenger.

Archer had one more thing to do before he put Tom Robeson
out of his life forever. He had promised Tom he would take
care of Willow. To keep himself awake and on guard during
the voyage back to town, he had considered what to do about
her.

He knew that when the story of Tom's death was told, people in Broome would be suspicious. He even half expected to
be questioned by the local police sergeant. If he did nothing to
help Willow, his reputation would suffer more. If he made a
show of helping her, even when it wasn't required, it might
cast doubt on the rumors that he had caused Tom's death.

Now, before getting sleep or even a decent meal, he changed
his clothes and made the trip by foot to Tom's bungalow. He

was not looking forward to facing Willow or seeing one final time the house where Tom had lived. He knew Tom had left touches of himself there. A garden he had planted for Willow. Wicker chairs on the veranda. Shells and driftwood he and Willow had collected and arranged in curiously artistic displays.

His decision to let Tom die had been a sudden one, hatched during a sleepless night amidst dreams of the future. He had saved Tom's life in Cuba, giving him more than two extra years to live, and it had almost seemed fair that Archer take his life, too. Those extra years had been a loan, and he and Tom had grown apart. Tom no longer looked up to him as he once had. Soon their paths would have separated, anyway. Archer was deeply sorry he had been compelled to kill his friend, but he had learned a long time ago that no matter what other people claimed to feel, in the end, every man looked out for himself. And Archer had to look out for Archer.

Now he was anxious to finish this business with Willow and begin his new life. There had been moments since cutting Tom from the diving dress when Archer had almost been sorry that Tom had found the pearl. But he had never been a man who looked back. Tom was dead now, and it was up to Archer to use the pearl to his best advantage.

At the sound of wailing, he slowed just before the bungalow. He knew who was making the sound, and why. He steeled himself and turned into the walkway.

A woman barred the front door, and he recognized her as the West Indian woman who had accompanied Willow to the jetty to say goodbye to Tom. She was dark-skinned and wide-hipped, and her eyes condemned him before he spoke.

"I'm here to see Willow," he said.

"What for? You come to kill *her*, too?"

"Let me through, stupid woman. I haven't killed anyone. I'm here to give her something."

She had thick black brows that she drew together in an ominous line. "Juan Fernandez say you kill Tom."

"Juan just wants to blame somebody."

Her expression made it clear she didn't believe him. But it didn't matter, because she turned at the sound of steps behind her, and her face softened. "I tell him go away," she said to the woman behind her.

"Please."

The woman twisted her face into a frown, but she stepped aside so that Willow could move into the doorway.

"Why you have come?" Willow said.

Her face was swollen and her eyes red-rimmed. Her hair streamed wildly around her shoulders. But even in this disheveled state, Archer still had to acknowledge her beauty. He could understand why Tom had acted like such a fool over this woman, although he still couldn't forgive him for it.

"I promised Tom I would give you this if something happened to him. Neither of us ever thought I'd have to do it. But I'm honoring my promise." Archer pulled a handkerchief from his pocket and unwrapped it. The first pearl that Tom had found, the small one he had said he would give Willow, lay inside. "He wanted you to have this."

She looked as if she wasn't going to take it. He continued to hold out his hand.

She took it at last and turned it over in her hand for a moment before she looked up at him again. "Juan Fernandez says there is another."

Archer didn't answer.

Willow lifted her chin. "Pearl of Great Price. Half of that pearl belongs to Tom."

Archer folded the handkerchief and put it back in his pocket. "Even if that were so, Tom is dead. I'm giving you this pearl because he wanted you to have it. Not because I owe it to you."

"Owe? You owe me nothing. But you owe child of Tom what belongs to Tom."

"Tom *has* no children."

Willow touched her belly. "You are wrong."

Archer felt something stirring inside him, something he couldn't name. He had never considered that Tom might have fathered an heir. For a moment he felt vulnerable, even afraid. He had rid himself of his partner in order to have full title to everything they owned together. Had it been for nothing?

Then the absurdity struck him, and as relief filled him, so did anger. "You little bitch. He rescued you from a whore-house. Do you suppose anyone would believe that child is his?"

"It is child of Tom."

"So you say." Archer knew that she spoke the truth. On the night Tom had told him about Willow's rescue, he had also told him she was a virgin. But Archer was sure Tom would never have told anyone else.

He started down the steps. At the bottom, he turned and faced her again. "I've given you Tom's pearl. Sell it, keep it. I don't give a damn. Maybe when I sell the shell in our hold I'll send you a little money. But not if I hear you've been spreading false rumors about me. And not because I owe you anything."

She drew herself up straight, and her red-rimmed eyes focused like shafts of light traveling through him. "I tell the truth. You cannot buy the truth from me. And you cannot buy peace in your mind. I have child of Tom, but you have nothing. No peace. No sleep. No friend. Only a pearl, and this pearl will haunt you for rest of your days. I will haunt you, too!"

She had not cursed him, but Archer felt cursed. Exhaustion dragged at him, along with something that he didn't recognize. He wanted to throw her words back at her, but he found that his tongue was tied. He turned and started back to the hotel.

For two days Archer waited for Viola or Sebastian to contact him. On the second day he wrote identical notes to the ones he had already sent and had them delivered by a different messenger. Another day passed, and although casual inquiries turned up the fact that the Somersets were in town, he heard nothing from either of them.

He rarely left his room except for meals, and what little sleep he managed was fitful. He slept sitting up, with his pistol cocked and ready, and the kerchief knotted at his throat. He longed for the moment when he could sleep soundly again, when the pearl was sold and his money deposited safely. He longed to share his good fortune with Viola and receive her promise of marriage.

Most of the time he kept himself awake with visions of his future, the land he would buy and the cattle he would breed. But sometimes, despite his best efforts, his eyes closed and pictures of Tom filled his head, Tom with eyes bulging and skin a hideous blue.

Tom, who had been his friend.

On the fourth morning he knew he couldn't go on this way. He had wanted to see the envy on Sebastian's face when the pearl was revealed, and the pleasure on Viola's, but Archer couldn't wait any longer. He dressed carefully to visit the most successful pearl buyer in Broome. Fabian Wells was an Englishman who was said to handle all the Somerset pearls. Archer arrived at his house precisely at nine and was ushered into his hallway by an Aboriginal housekeeper.

Fabian Wells dressed like the wealthy man he was. He wore a beautifully tailored suit and a silk waistcoat with a gold watch gleaming at his waist. A pearl stickpin adorned his lapel, but in no other way did he advertise his profession. He looked like a banker, middle-aged and portly, and he spoke in a nasal voice.

"You've brought me something?" Fabian said, after he shook Archer's hand.

Archer had imagined this moment, but now he was too exhausted to do much more than nod.

"I have an appointment," Fabian said. "But I'll be back by one. You're welcome to wait or return any time this afternoon."

"There's nothing you'll see at your appointment that will be as fine as what I've brought you."

Fabian inclined his head. "Nevertheless, I can't afford to upset my regular clientele. I hope you'll return."

Archer struggled to hold on to his temper. "Maybe I will, and maybe I won't."

Archer used the rest of the morning to hire help to unload the shell in the *Odyssey*'s hold. He found two men at the Japanese Social Club who were willing to do the job, and he took them down to the jetty to see the lugger. At the jetty, no one spoke to him, not even the Asians who had joked with him in halting pidgin before Tom's death. There were white men lounging and talking along the water's edge, men with whom he had drunk and gambled, but now they looked straight through him.

The same had been true at the Roebuck. Since his return, no one had spoken to him unless it was absolutely necessary. And when he entered a room, all conversation stopped.

By one he was ready to return to Wells's house to sell the pearl. When he arrived this time, he was kept waiting on the veranda. Just as he was about to give up and find another buyer, the housekeeper ushered him inside. "Mr. Wells tell me take you to office."

"It's about time." An angry Archer straightened his shoulders and flicked the kerchief to one side.

He followed the woman through the hallway to the back of the bungalow. He glimpsed a European woman holding a child dressed in spotless white, but he was not introduced, and neither child nor mother glanced at him. The housekeeper abandoned him at a door, and Archer knocked.

Fabian called for him to enter, but he was not alone. With him were Sebastian Somerset and Broome's police sergeant.

Archer's pulse soared, beating perceptibly in the hollow of his throat, right behind the pearl he had come to sell. "It seems you're having a meeting." He didn't enter. "Should I ask if I'm the subject?"

"Come in, Mr. Llewellyn," Fabian said. "And please close the door behind you."

Archer moved into the center of the room so as not to appear hesitant or nervous. "I came to conduct business with you, Mr. Wells. Private business."

"Mr. Somerset and the sergeant have asked to join us. They've heard you have an extraordinary pearl to sell, but there seems to be some question about how you got it."

Archer let his gaze settle on Sebastian, whose face was expressionless. "Mr. Somerset heard about the pearl directly from me. I didn't expect to discuss it with him quite this way."

"We'll come straight to the point," the sergeant said. "Your crew insists that you killed your business partner at sea so the pearl would belong entirely to you."

"They all liked Tom—everybody did—and they want somebody to blame. Maybe it was my fault. He wanted to dive. Our tender was sick. I thought I knew what I was doing. But he never signaled me. I waited. Everything seemed fine. Then I felt the line dragging—" He closed his eyes, swallowing, like a man trying not to lose his composure.

"Juan Fernandez claims you damaged the helmet, that the air couldn't fill it properly."

Archer opened his eyes and shook his head. "How could he possibly know something like that? How could anyone? We had to cut Tom out of the helmet when we brought him up. We destroyed it getting him free."

"Suppose you tell us your theory on what happened, then?" Sebastian said.

"I checked the equipment before he went down. Everything was fine. But he had only dived a few times. Those dives had gone like clockwork. So when this one didn't, he panicked. He shouldn't have been diving in the Graveyard. He was too inexperienced. Maybe he stepped in a hole and couldn't adjust his air. He didn't signal, and I didn't know anything was wrong. We were pumping air to him, but he wasn't getting enough." Archer shook his head. "That's all I know. That's all anyone ever will."

"Convenient that you had to cut up the helmet," Sebastian said.

Archer narrowed his eyes. "Do you think I should have buried him inside it? Don't you think I owed him better than that?"

The sergeant looked at the other men. "There's nothing to be done about this. We have Mr. Llewellyn's word against the crew's. Any proof of tampering has been destroyed. Mr. Llewellyn certainly had a motive for killing Tom Robeson, but without any evidence of foul play, a motive is meaningless."

"I would have spoken to you about this anywhere, any place," Archer said. "You didn't have to arrange a surprise meeting. If I had anything to hide, I would have left town immediately."

"You haven't left town because you're planning to take my daughter with you when you do," Sebastian said, before the sergeant could answer. "My daughter *and* the promise of everything she'll inherit."

"That's absurd." Archer knew better than to deny he wanted Viola. "I love your daughter, it's true. But not for anything but herself."

Sebastian smiled coldly. "I know you were the one who assembled the evidence against Freddy Colson, Llewellyn. And I believe deep in my heart—where evidence *isn't* required—that you murdered your partner. A man like you would taint the Somerset bloodlines. If Viola marries you, she will be dead to me."

Archer drew himself up straighter. "As to Freddy, I really believed you should know the caliber of the man working most closely with you. I thought I was doing you a favor. As to Tom, I can only say again that I am falsely accused."

"And as to my daughter?"

Archer was frantically trying to think of a way to convince Sebastian that he was not the scoundrel he appeared. Without the promise of her inheritance, what point was there to marrying Viola? "I can't speak for her, can I? She's a good daughter, and your regard means too much for her to take this—"

Sebastian threw back his head and hooted. "My regard? You don't know my daughter, do you? She would kill me as I slept if she thought no one would find her out. Now that you have money she'll go anywhere with you, if you ask her. Just know that when she goes, *nothing* of mine goes with her."

"It seems your best bet is to sell the pearl immediately and leave town," Fabian said, speaking for the first time since the interrogation had begun. "I'm prepared to give you the best price in Broome to facilitate your departure. And I'll find you a buyer for the *Odyssey,* as well, although I warn you, the price will be low, since no crew will want to sail on her again."

Archer knew that refusing to sell the pearl to Fabian was tantamount to slitting his own throat. He would get the best price right here, and he needed every cent he could muster. What was the point of continuing this conversation? He had no desire to remain in Western Australia, and what these men thought of him was immaterial now that marrying Viola was out of the question.

He unknotted the handkerchief and removed it carefully. Then he walked to the table in front of Fabian and laid the handkerchief on it. "Tom called this stone the Pearl of Great Price."

"Apt description, considering he paid for it with his life," Sebastian said.

"Not at my hand!" Archer unrolled the handkerchief slowly until the pearl was revealed.

The other men stared at it for a long time before anyone spoke.

Finally Fabian reached out to touch it with one trembling finger. "It is a pearl worth killing for."

Archer had known that the pearl would bring him a fortune. With a relatively untrained eye he had seen its worth. But even *he,* with all his hopes and dreams, had been stunned at Fabian's offer. He had taken it without bargaining or considering his options. He was now a wealthy man.

And the pearl, with its dangerous beauty and the memories it stirred, was gone from his life.

He went immediately to the bank and deposited most of the money so he could sleep that night without fear. He would rest and recover from the past weeks, then he would prepare for a lengthy journey to find land. Without the promise of Viola's inheritance, he would have to choose carefully. Land he couldn't develop immediately would be useless. But with luck and proper husbandry, he could still establish the dynasty he had dreamed of for so long.

It was just too bad that Viola couldn't be the mother of his sons.

At the hotel, he slipped off his boots and fell on the bed, fully expecting deep sleep to claim him at last. But to his own surprise, sleep eluded him. He had what he'd worked and killed for. He was safe from the law, and once he was rested, he could begin the life he'd dreamed of since childhood.

Yet despite that, sleep wouldn't come.

An hour later he was still staring at the ceiling when a knock sounded at his door. He crossed the room and opened it with one hand resting on his pistol. Viola stood on the threshold, looking even more beautiful than he'd remembered.

He released the butt of his pistol and pulled her inside, closing the door behind her. "What are you doing here?"

"My father locked me in my bedroom when he heard you were in town. He's been paying Ashwar on the sly to bring him notes from my admirers before I receive them. When he got yours, he locked me away."

"Your father thinks I killed my partner."

"So he's told me repeatedly."

Archer waited for her to ask whether it was true, but it seemed that did not interest her. "Why are you here?"

"I told you I would marry you if you became a rich man."

"Your father will disinherit you if you do. He's warned me."

She didn't ask if he would marry her anyway. She seemed to have no illusions. "But he didn't tell you everything, Archer. He didn't tell you that I *have* an inheritance. With or without his consent. That's why he locked me away."

Archer touched a curl lying provocatively over her shoulder, and she didn't object. Hope stirred inside him, and something more. "What inheritance would that be, Viola?"

"My mother's brother died a year ago. He owned land all

over Australia. Land foolish, my mother always said. She had no use for him.''

Archer fondled the curl, and still she said nothing. ''He left it all to you?''

''No, he left each parcel to a different niece or nephew. Mine is the largest, a station in the Northern Territory. He called it Jimiramira, an Aboriginal word, but I don't know what it means.''

''Why didn't you mention this before, when we were discussing the future?''

''It's only just been settled, and I only found out after you'd sailed away. My father wants me to have nothing to do with it, of course. He says it's worthless, that nothing will come of land there. But I've seen my uncle's letters about it. My land's near a river. So there's water there, and rich grazing plains. He said the area is largely unsettled now, but others will flock there when the word gets out. The man who gets there first and establishes a homestead...why, he'll be like a king, won't he? And the woman who stands with him will be a queen.''

''And what will you do with it, Viola?''

''I don't know. What should I do with it, do you suppose?''

He tugged at the curl, and she came willingly toward him. He gazed into her eyes and saw she was simply proposing a bargain. They could help each other and, perhaps, find some pleasure doing so. Each of them was the other's best choice for a future.

''I will be the mistress of a great station that will thrive with the money you put into it,'' she said, as if reading his thoughts. ''And in return I will give you my land and sons.''

He kissed her, and she didn't resist. She didn't resist everything that came afterwards, either. In fact, she seemed to genuinely enjoy it.

But when they were lying on Archer's bed together after the lovemaking had ended, both of them stared at the ceiling.

Neither of them slept.

They were married as quickly as the law allowed. Viola was permitted to take her clothes from the house, but nothing more.

Her mother smuggled several good pieces of family jewelry to her but refused to meet with her one final time to say goodbye.

They found an Aboriginal man who knew the route to Jimiramira and would guide them there. Archer bought the best horses and wagon he could find and all the supplies they would need for the trip, which would be grueling at best. Viola wasn't looking forward to making what promised to be a treacherous journey, but she agreed that the reward would be worth it.

On the morning they left Broome, they were halted just outside of town by a man blocking the road in a familiar black buggy. Sebastian Somerset climbed down, leaving his groom in charge of the horses, and walked over to look up at his daughter sitting proudly on the thoroughbred Archer had bought for her.

"I couldn't let you leave without a wedding gift," Sebastian said.

Archer looked on silently. There was nothing Sebastian could do now that interested him.

"What is it?" Viola asked. Her hands were folded on the reins, and they didn't even flutter in anticipation.

"You'll have to open it to see."

She hesitated and looked at Archer. He nodded, and she extended one gloved hand toward her father. He gave her a small package and stepped back.

"Thank you," she said stiffly.

"I want you to open it now," Sebastian said. "It would mean the world to me."

For a moment Archer thought she would refuse, just to spite Sebastian, but she shrugged and tore it open. Her eyes widened, and she looked at him as if she couldn't believe what she saw.

Archer pulled his horse closer and gazed down at the object in her hand. The Pearl of Great Price gleamed up at him.

"It's yours, Viola," Sebastian said. "Yours, but not your husband's. It's yours to do with whatever you will. You could sell it, of course, but it's a rare pearl, and you'll be an even rarer sort of woman if you keep it. It's truly one of a kind."

Sebastian looked up at Archer. "And though you don't own it, Llewellyn, it will always be a reminder of your days in Broome, won't it? And everything that took place here. Sometimes a man needs a reminder." He smiled, as if he were genuinely pleased with his own generosity.

"But why?" Viola said. "You hate me. You have since I was a child. Why have you given me this?"

"Consider it the final word in a lifelong conversation we've had. And, Viola, since the pearl is almost beyond price, I don't have to warn you to hide it from everyone. Men have killed for pearls, haven't they, Llewellyn?"

Viola still looked bewildered, but Archer understood. "She is my wife! We share everything. I would never harm her."

"I'm immeasurably comforted, my boy. Immeasurably. Take good care of my daughter and her pearl. And may the good Lord give you both the life you deserve." Sebastian turned without another glance at either of them and strolled back to the buggy.

He climbed in, took the reins and pulled off the road so they could pass.

Archer could hear him laughing until they were far away.

Errors, like straws, upon the surface flow:
He who would search for pearls must dive below.

John Dryden
—*All for Love,* Prologue

10

San Francisco—Present Day

"Of course you had to let him go, Liana. He's the heir to a fortune, but he needed to see his father."

Liana didn't face her stepbrother. Instead she stared out Graham's study window at San Francisco sloping gently to the bay. A century ago her grandfather, Tom Robeson, might have stared at the same body of water from nearly the same place. When she was eight, her father, also named Thomas, had taken her to the former site of the Robeson mansion on Van Ness Avenue for a brief history lesson.

He had stood with his arms crossed, his face devoid of emotion. "This is where my father was born. But not in this building. Oh no, once there was a house on that site, larger and finer than anything you'll see today."

Liana had waited until she was certain he was finished. She had spent her early childhood away from Thomas. Since her mother's death several months before, she had learned never to interrupt this man, this giant stranger who claimed to be her father.

"Why isn't it there anymore?" She narrowed her eyes to peer at the apartment building, which was pale and plain.

"There was an earthquake in 1906. I was only a boy, on a

ship that sailed into the bay that morning. I was coming to live with my grandparents. The waves were so high I fell and hit my head on the deck, and when I came to, the woman who had been caring for me was gone. Later they dynamited this street to stop fires raging through the city. We heard the explosion at the harbor. Blew up all the houses. Boom!''

She jumped when Thomas shouted the final word. She wanted to cry at the death of all those beautiful houses, but she had learned not to do that, too. "Was your father killed?"

"No, he was already dead, murdered in a place called Australia by his best friend. That's what happens when you trust people, Liana. Never, never trust anyone. That's the lesson I learned that day."

She had nodded, as if she understood. But now she didn't nod. She was grown and much wiser, and her father was dead.

"Cullen insists on his month with Matthew. Legally, I couldn't refuse him if I wanted to." She continued to stare out the window of the house she had lived in with Thomas, the house Graham continued to live in with only a small staff for company. At his request, she had made this detour after filing a missing persons report at the police station.

"No one expected this. I didn't dream…" She couldn't continue. She could hardly think, much less argue. Her son was missing. Matthew was *missing*. The truth of it seemed to elude her. Why hadn't her heart stopped beating at the moment of his disappearance?

"You couldn't have known."

"I'm second-guessing *everything*." She pushed a lock of hair over her ears, wondering when it had come loose from the clip.

"Tell me everything. Exactly what did the police say?"

"They're checking into it. They're contacting the airlines, the authorities in Denver. They say they'll phone as soon as they know something. But they warned me he might have run away."

"Run away?"

"That's right. I told them Matthew has no reason to run, but they blew me off. Usually they don't respond to this sort of thing too quickly. Most teenagers come home on their own in a day or two."

Liana had conducted an agonizing debate with herself over whether to tell her stepbrother or anyone else about Matthew's disappearance. What she knew of kidnappings she had learned from bad television movies, but in the hours since Matthew had boarded the airplane, there had been no warning phone calls, no whispered messages or instructions. Still, she had told Graham, who, with Pacific International's resources behind him, could be an enormous asset to the search.

But so far Liana herself was the only person who knew about the missing pearl.

She turned away from the window. "I know we're going to find him. He's almost fifteen, and big for his age. And he's smart. He's so smart. We know he got on the plane. I saw him. He wouldn't have gone off with strangers after he landed."

Graham motioned her to a pew salvaged from a church on Geary, just before demolition. Liana's father had been a confirmed atheist, but it had pleased him to have bits and pieces of the city's historic churches adorning his home. The devil, masquerading in ecclesiastical garb. "How are you?"

Liana wasn't sure. She was a kite without a tail, soaring on winds that threatened to destroy her. She had no equilibrium and no control.

When she didn't answer, Graham continued. "I told Stanford not to spare any expense." Stanford Brown was the head of Pacific's security division. He had come to the company directly from the FBI, and his contacts were legion. Graham had arranged to have Stanford drop everything else and work on finding Matthew. "He'll do his job."

"Where could he be, Graham? Do you know how hard every mother works to be sure her children won't go off with strangers? Well, I worked harder!" She took a breath and let it out slowly. She could not fall apart, not until Matthew was on his way home.

"I know you don't want to hear this, but maybe he really did take off on his own. Maybe..." He shrugged.

"Don't stop there."

"Maybe he feels a little smothered." He patted her shoulder, as if to take the sting from his words, but he dropped his hand when she glared at him.

"Who smothers him? He goes to private school, but he gets there on public transportation. He visits friends all over the Bay Area, even in places *I* don't feel safe. I don't wrap him in cotton."

"No, you don't."

"Then what are you talking about?"

"He's a kid, Liana. Kids need to try their wings. Matthew knows if he's one minute late, you'll have Stanford and his team out looking for him. He's the Robeson heir. No matter what he does, somebody's always watching him."

"He has never complained. Never. He's happy. He's not on drugs. He has more friends than I can count."

"Is someone checking with Matthew's friends?"

"Of course. That's the first thing Stanford asked for. I keep a list and update it, just in..." Her voice trailed off.

Graham grimaced. "That's the kind of thing I mean."

"Where would I be right now if I hadn't?"

She rose, and they left the study to start down the hallway. Graham was silent until they had descended the stairs into the wide foyer with its Waterford chandelier. "Are you going to tell anyone else?"

So far, only a handful of people knew, and they had been sworn to secrecy, but she realized that was going to change before long. "Not right away, but other people will have to know eventually. Stanford will want to question them."

"What are you going to do now?"

"I'm going home to wait. Stanford may be there already. He thinks I should stay by the phone, in case Matthew or—" She cleared her throat. "Or someone else calls."

"I'll come with you, if you'd like."

"Thanks, but I don't think so. I won't be much company."

"I wasn't expecting a party."

She tried to smile and couldn't. "I know. But until I sort this out a little, I'd rather be alone. I'm sorry."

"I'll stay home tonight, in case you need me. I'll be a phone call away." He put his hand on the doorknob. "Liana, what about Cullen?"

"What about him?"

"Could he have anything to do with this?"

"No. He loves Matthew."

"What if Cullen's using his so-called disappearance as a cover so he can take him out of the country?"

"That just doesn't make sense. Cullen has Matthew for the next month, anyway. If he was going to take him to Australia, he'd have plenty of time to do it without making up this story and involving the authorities. Besides, Matthew knows full well he can't go to Australia with Cullen. He's promised he never will."

"You know what your father said before he died. There are two things your ex wants that he'll never be able to have. One is his son. The other is the Pearl of Great Price."

At the mention of the pearl, Liana's heart squeezed painfully. "Yes, and Thomas was certain Cullen spent his days scheming to get them both."

"And you aren't certain?"

Liana didn't know what to think. Who but Cullen would risk everything to have them?

Her voice caught, and she cleared her throat. "If Matthew's with Cullen, then he's perfectly safe. The terrible thing about this is that of all the alternatives, Cullen kidnapping his own son is one of the best."

The Robeson family home, where Graham lived, was by all standards a mansion. Constructed with red Arizona sandstone and quiet Georgian lines, the house, built immediately after the earthquake, had none of the flirtatious frills of the city's painted ladies. It was a massive house, extensively remodeled through-out its history to integrate developing technology while retain-

ing its considerable dignity. Thomas, not a man with soft spots
or sentiment, had chosen to remain there after the death of his
grandparents because a business rival had expressed an interest
in acquiring it.

The house was somber both inside and out. The interior of
dark wood, heavy drapes and massive leather furniture suggested a men's club. The exterior, with towering trees and geo-
metrical shrubs extending halfway up narrow windows, was
largely hidden from view by a brick fence that diminished the
remaining light. As children, Liana and Graham had only been
allowed to play in a side yard where a fountain divided the
narrow space. At play, as in every other facet of their lives,
Thomas had encouraged them to choose different sides.

In contrast to the Robeson house, Liana's apartment near
Lafayette Park was designed to let in sunshine. She had the
penthouse of an eight-story building constructed in art deco
style, with intriguing, quirky spaces and dozens of windows.
Additionally, glass doors opened out to a roof garden with
views of Nob Hill and the financial district. She had combined
contemporary decor with warm woods and subtle, elegant fabrics. The apartment was her haven, and Matthew's, too. Nothing in it was off-limits to him; nothing was too precious for
him to handle or play with.

Matthew was her only truly precious possession.

That morning, when she had left the apartment to take Matthew to the airport, she had realized how silent it would seem
when she returned that evening, even though she wouldn't be
alone. She and Matthew had a live-in housekeeper, Sue Lo,
who drifted quietly through their lives. Sue was not a friend
but never a servant. She was more than both, a piece of their
lives, a wise middle-aged woman with little education, who
gave her opinion and kept her counsel, each when it was required. But with Matthew gone, Sue would disappear into her
private life more fully, leaving Liana to live her own.

Liana had dreaded opening the door to see a month of evenings, looming before her, without her son. Now she opened
it and saw a lifetime of them.

"Miss Liana?" Sue, her broad, square face no study of her feelings, came into the hallway. She took the briefcase that Liana wasn't even aware she was carrying and set it on a table, then helped with her coat. "Mr. Brown's in Matthew's room."

"Thank you. Have there been any calls?"

There was a break in Sue's serene mask, a quick glimpse of her misery. "No. I wish."

"Has Stanford asked you any questions?"

"Just a few. He wanted to know if I had any ideas where Matty might have gone."

Sue was the only person who was still allowed to call Matthew "Matty." The name brought tears to Liana's eyes, but she stubbornly blinked them away.

"I told Mr. Brown the names of some of Matty's friends. But he says you gave him those."

"Keep thinking. Maybe you'll remember something."

"I won't be thinking of anything else."

Liana squeezed Sue's hand and got a gentle squeeze in return. "I'm going to talk to Stanford."

She wound through the hallway, past walls filled with photographs of Matthew as a baby, then Matthew as a toddler. Her son grew older as she walked, until just before his bedroom the photographs showed a handsome, grinning teenager in a soccer uniform, a boy, all legs and arms, poised on the brink of adulthood. The photos stopped there. The hallway beyond was adorned with Japanese scrolls until Matthew grew older.

If Matthew grew older.

"Stanford?"

Stanford Brown, whose legal first name was easily forgotten, was a dark-skinned, wide-shouldered African-American who had been Stanford University's prize linebacker before heading off for the FBI Academy. He faced her, his hands filled with papers from Matthew's desk. "I wanted to get started as quickly as possible. I knew you wouldn't mind."

"Did you find anything?"

"Just school papers. I was looking for topics that might give us a clue. When they're upset, some kids use class assignments as a signal.''

''Did he?''

''Not unless he left home because he was worried about the ozone layer or the effects of the 1906 earthquake on the city's Chinese community.''

''I don't think he *left* home, Stanford. I would have known if he was unhappy. We're close, too close for him to hide something like that.''

''He's almost fifteen. I was that age once. And I can guarantee a boy doesn't share everything he's thinking with his mother.''

She pressed her lips together to keep from protesting.

Stanford looked down at the papers in his hands. ''First thing in the morning, I'll track down the teachers he had this year. He might have kept a journal at school. Do you know?''

''Not that he told me about. And no one mentioned a journal during conferences.''

''This is a pretty sophisticated computer.'' Stanford gestured to the one at Matthew's desk. ''Does everything but cook supper.''

Liana touched the monitor, as if somehow it could bring her in contact with her son. ''Computers are one of his passions.''

''I turned it on and checked out a couple of things. He spends a fair amount of time on the Internet. Did you know?''

''It seemed harmless enough.''

''I checked the mail he sent and received recently. No obvious leads, but I want you to E-mail everybody he's corresponded with in the past two weeks and find out if anyone has an idea about where he's gone. Are you computer savvy?''

''I use the database at Pacific. Matthew showed me how to go on-line, but I rarely do. Just occasionally, to please him.''

Stanford explained exactly how to do what he'd requested using Matthew's computer. ''Do it tonight, after I leave. Then check for answers before you go to bed.''

She might go to bed, but Liana knew she wouldn't sleep. She would be checking for answers all night long, even though she suspected Stanford was just trying to give her something to do.

Stanford continued. "An expert could extract anything he posted earlier than about two weeks ago. Most of it's been deleted. We'll do that if we have to. I checked websites he visited in the past few days, but again, no leads. It looks like he was checking prices on some new computer equipment. And he logged on to a couple of camping sites."

"He and Cullen were going camping in New England."

"Well, we know camping was on his mind as recently as yesterday. He was looking into the best ways to pack a backpack."

"He was trying to impress Cullen."

"About your ex-husband…"

Liana folded her arms. Here in Matthew's private sanctuary she felt even more vulnerable. The room was spacious, and every inch was filled with clutter. Her son couldn't bear to throw away anything, as if every object he had once treasured might feel personally rejected. Shelves lined the navy blue walls, filled with the plastic space ships and baseball cards of a younger boy and the stereo equipment of a teenager. One wall held a well-loved baby quilt of multicolored stars that Liana had stitched herself.

"Go on," she said. "Stanford, ask me anything. I don't care. I just want my son back."

"How did Mr. Llewellyn sound when he reported that Matthew hadn't shown up at LaGuardia?"

"Furious. He thought I hadn't sent him."

"How about later, when you told him you'd put Matthew on the plane this morning?"

She closed her eyes and remembered. After the shock, after realizing that both Matthew and the pearl were missing, she had managed to pick up the receiver to finish her conversation with Cullen. "What are we going to do?" she had whispered.

She could hear Cullen breathing harshly. "You really didn't know, did you?" he'd said at last.

"No."

"I'll find him. We'll find him."

She opened her eyes and stared at Stanford. "Cullen was broken up," she said. "He's as worried as I am."

"He has a reputation for being a good liar."

She exhaled sharply.

"I'm sorry," Stanford said. "But that's what I've heard."

"Cullen's a gambler. When we were married and he lost big, he lied about it. Yes."

"Could he be holding Matthew to extort money from you?"

When she shook her head violently, he grimaced. "I know you don't want to believe it, Liana, but think. Could he be desperate? Could he have lost so much money that this is the only way he can get it back?"

Cullen owned and managed Southern Cross Pearls on Pikuwa Creek in Western Australia. It continued to amaze Liana that the pearl farm was still in business, considering Cullen's gambling addiction, but, somehow, through the years, Cullen had held on.

But gambling was one thing, kidnapping his own son another. "Cullen loves Matthew." She had said the same thing to Graham.

"You're saying your husband would never use his son, even if he'd lost so much money his life was in danger?"

She didn't answer, because she couldn't say that. In the final year of their marriage, Cullen *had* been that desperate.

"I see," Stanford said. "I'll be investigating him right along with everyone and everything else. Be prepared."

She gave a short nod.

"I've got enough for now. Do you want me to stay the night, to help you man the phone?"

"No. I'll be all right." She led the way out of Matthew's room and walked Stanford to the door.

"This is my beeper number." He handed her a card. "I can be here in ten minutes. Try to get some sleep if you can. I've put a trace on your line, but it's fairly primitive. If someone does contact you, the FBI will step in, and their equipment is state-of-the-art."

"Tell me the truth. Do you think Matthew's been kidnapped?"

Stanford seemed uneasy. "The truth?"

She nodded.

"I think he's going to turn up on his own. But we have to consider every possibility."

On the trip home she had agonized over whether to tell him about the Pearl of Great Price. Perhaps Stanford could be trusted not to spread the news of its disappearance, but if she told him, would he turn his considerable powers of investigation to that and slight, even for a minute, the search for her son? She had discovered the pearl's disappearance at nearly the same moment she had discovered Matthew's. But was there a connection? It had been weeks since she had last opened the safe, perhaps months. The pearl could have been missing since then.

"Is there anything else?" Stanford said.

She decided to consider all the possibilities before she committed herself. "No."

"Don't hesitate to call if you think of anything new, or if you hear anything at all."

"Thank you."

He nodded before he let himself out.

She stared at the door her son had walked through that morning. Then she rested her head in her hands and let the tears flow.

11

Cullen Llewellyn was dog-tired. He had covered every inch of LaGuardia, spoken to authorities of every stripe and color and watched them file useless reports, as if paper in proper little compartments would help anyone find his son. Then he had flown to Denver to begin the same process all over again.

No one in either place remembered Matthew. They were all terribly sorry, but since the boy was fourteen and flying alone, there was little they could do. No one had alerted them to watch out for a teenager named Matthew Llewellyn.

And why *should* they have been alerted? Cullen wanted to blame somebody. In the worst way he wanted to blame the airlines or Liana, who had put his son on the airplane and blithely walked away. But what should she have done differently? Cullen had criticized his ex-wife for holding too tightly to Matthew, for keeping him a child when he needed to become a man. Liana refused to fly, but for years she had paid an escort to travel with their son, and only after Cullen had sent Matthew home by himself last summer—just to prove the boy could do it—had she agreed to let him travel alone in the future.

If he was going to blame anyone, Cullen had to blame himself.

"Here you are." The taxi driver slowed, then stopped in front of an apartment building at the top of a hill. Matthew had described his mother's apartment, but Cullen still wasn't prepared for the lights of the city rippling in waves down to the bay. The closest town to his home had less than a thousand people. And even if Broome was growing by leaps and bounds, it would be a millennium before it rivaled this.

"Looks a bit like Sydney," he said, reaching for his wallet. "Grander, though."

"First time here?"

"More or less." Over the years he had reluctantly made the occasional business trip to California, and several times he had met Matthew at the San Francisco airport. But he had never wanted to tour the city where Liana and his son lived. He didn't want to picture them here, making the pain of their absence from his life more immediate and defined.

He paid the fare and reminded himself to add a tip. He grabbed his bag and closed the door; then, as the taxi drove away, he wondered if he should have paid the driver to wait. There was no guarantee Liana would let him in the door to ring another.

Since there was nothing to be done, he hoisted the bag over his shoulder and crossed the street to her building. When no doorman appeared, he buzzed her apartment, stepped back and waited. Time passed, more than he had expected, before a woman answered. It was not his ex-wife.

He announced himself and added, "I have to see Liana."

He expected a wait this time, but there was none. The woman, who was probably Sue, the housekeeper Matthew had told him about, buzzed him inside. In the small but elegant lobby he found the elevator, flanked by ficus trees in red lacquered pots, and took it to the top floor. There was only one apartment and one door. Liana stood in the doorway, gazing silently at him.

Sometimes still, on the blackest nights out on the Indian Ocean, Cullen tried to picture Liana's face. Over the years he had aged the image, adding tiny lines and slacker skin. He had imagined a woman whose fear and turmoil were mirrored in her eyes and in dark hollows beneath them.

The woman staring up at him from the doorway was older,

but no less stunning than she had been the day she walked out of his life forever.

Of course, *this* moment proved how relative forever could be.

Liana didn't move aside. She was wearing a white silk robe, Chinese in style, piped in gold and embroidered with bloodred roses. Her black hair hung loose at her shoulders, and her pale face was scrubbed clean. But she hadn't been sleeping. Her hair was neatly brushed, and her slate gray eyes were shadowed with grief, not slumber.

She spoke at last. "What are you doing here, Cullen?"

He lowered his bag to the carpet. "Has there been any word?"

She shook her head. "Nothing."

He hadn't expected different, but he had hoped. He felt his shoulders sagging. "I had the airline route my flight through Denver so I could question the authorities myself. There's no word of Matthew there, either."

"The police are looking into it. The Pacific security team is working on it."

"But nothing so far?"

"Nothing. If he calls, or someone else calls about him, we can trace the call. But the phone hasn't rung."

"Has he been upset about anything? Bad marks at school? A girl?"

Her veneer of composure slipped. "We could have covered this on the telephone."

He was too exhausted to be tactful. "I had to see your face. To be sure."

"Sure he wasn't here? That I wasn't trying to keep him from being with you?"

"I don't know what to think, Lee. My son's gone missing. I have one month out of twelve to be with him. And instead of holding him in my arms, I'm filing police reports."

A flicker of compassion softened her expression, but her words belied it. "Too bad he had to disappear on your time."

"Don't twist my words."

He wanted to start again, to go back to the beginning when he had stepped off the elevator to find her in the doorway. But he knew that the most carefully worded sentences wouldn't change a thing. The animosity between them went back years. Some might say as far as the turn of the century.

"I didn't come here to fight with you." He took off his hat, a battered Akubra that was as familiar as a body part, and raked his brown hair back from his forehead. "I want to find my son. Maybe if we share everything we know, we can sort this out."

"Sort it out?"

"Would you rather sit back and wait?"

He expected more sarcasm, but she shook her head, sending hair swirling against her cheekbones. "Come inside."

"Thanks, I have to ring a taxi."

"Where are you staying?"

He smiled tiredly. "After I ring a taxi, I have to ring a hotel."

"This isn't the outback, Cullen."

"No, you've got a sight more hotels here."

She turned and led the way through a tiled hallway into a sitting room with pillowy couches in neutral tones and bright contemporary art on the walls. The only representational painting was a beautifully wrought portrait of their son standing beside the water, a portrait Cullen had never seen. Matthew Robeson Llewellyn at eleven or twelve. Sun-streaked brown hair and cowlick like Cullen's, dark angled eyes like his mother. Cullen's grin, Liana's straight nose. Cullen's large frame, Liana's long fingers.

Their son.

Cullen couldn't bear to look at the portrait any longer. He dropped his bag beside one of the couches facing away from it. "Can we talk a bit before I go?"

"It's the middle of the night."

"Is *that* why it's so bloody dark out there?"

"I could have been sleeping."

"Bugger it, Lee, you know you weren't."

"How do you know?"

"Because I know what you look like when you wake up. Until Matthew's found, you'll hardly close your eyes."

She didn't deny it. She chose a couch across from his and carefully pulled the robe around her as she sank into the corner. "Tell me what you discovered at the airports."

"Not a flaming thing. They spent their time making sure I understood they had no liability. They took Matthew's photo to make copies. I made sure they'll be watching for him, and questioning people who might have seen him, including the crew of the plane you put him on today."

"Yesterday."

Cullen didn't want to believe a day had gone by, but Liana was right. The count had begun. "What did you do after I rang you?"

"Notified the police. Got our security division working on it." She hesitated. "Then I went over everything with my step-brother."

"Does he have any theories?"

"He wondered if this is one of your schemes, Cullen. I was in the familiar position of having to defend you."

"And what do *you* think?"

She looked away, as if the granite sculpture behind him had captured her fancy. "I think you wouldn't go this far."

"Good on ya. Loyalty above and beyond."

"What have you done to earn my loyalty?"

He was silent, but his gaze never left her face.

She looked at him at last. "You didn't have anything to do with it, did you?"

"Is there any point in answering?"

"Try me."

"I didn't have a thing to do with it. You didn't. Someone else did."

"You don't think he's run away, do you?"

"I know it's hard on our egos, us being such a happy family and all, but I think we'd better hope he has. The alternatives are worse."

She looked as if he had struck her. "He *is* happy! We have

a good life here. I spend every minute I possibly can with him. He goes to a wonderful school. His grades are excellent.''

He leaned forward, twisting the Akubra. ''His father lives on the other side of the world, and Matthew isn't allowed to visit him.''

''You have him for a month every summer, Cullen. One entire month.''

''On your terms. In your country. And it bothers our son. He's told me as much.'' He hesitated, then exhaled slowly. ''But I don't think that's why he's run off. *If* he's run off.''

''Maybe he's run off because he didn't want to spend a month with you. Have you thought of that?''

The words hurt, but he had to consider them. ''Did he give you cause to think he didn't want to be with me?''

She struggled over her answer. Her arms were folded over her chest, and she tightened them, as if locking her feelings inside. ''No. He tries not to mention you, but this time he couldn't help himself. He talked about the New England trip. He even pulled out that hat you gave him.''

Cullen smiled, thinking of his son in the Akubra like his own. Then the smile died. ''Our son isn't welcome to mention me in your home?''

''Of course he is. I never criticize you in front of Matthew. And I've never asked him not to talk about you. But we're divorced, Cullen. Quite obviously we aren't the best of friends.''

They had never been the best of friends. Lovers, yes. Wildly obsessed with each other. Passionately absorbed in the minutiae of each other's lives. Unwilling to live apart but unable to live together. Idealistic, impetuous and foolish. But never really friends.

''It's a dead cert we aren't getting anywhere, isn't it?'' Cullen closed his eyes for a moment, and for the first time he realized how heartsick he was. ''I meant it before, Lee. I don't want to fight with you. I just want to find our son.'' He opened his eyes. ''We can work together more effectively than we can apart. Are you willing?''

He expected an argument, but she nodded. "I'd do anything to get Matthew back."

He heard the postscript. *Anything, Cullen, even suffer your presence.* He pushed himself wearily to his feet. "I'm all in. I'll ring the taxi. Can you suggest a hotel?"

"There are probably at least three major conventions in town." She stood, too, silent and watchful, as if she had never seen him before. Then she released a breath. "You can stay in the guest room for what's left of the night."

He was seldom speechless, but now he couldn't think of anything to say.

Liana's eyes were huge, dark frightened eyes that told him even *his* presence was welcome, even *his* help was better than facing this crisis alone. "If we're really going to work together, you should be here tonight, in case Matthew calls. Or if someone else does."

"Thank you."

"By tomorrow we'll know something, and you can make whatever arrangements suit you best."

"We may not know anything tomorrow, but we'll find our son. I promise I'll do everything in my power. Do you remember the morning Matthew was born?"

She looked away, but he could see her eyes filling with tears. Despite everything between them, he wanted to gather her in his arms and hold her. He wanted to feel his own heart beating against the red embroidered roses.

Instead he thrust his hands in his pockets. "I came into your room in hospital, and you were holding him. You looked up and said, 'Our families tried to destroy each other, Cullen, but look what a miracle we've created together.'"

The tears didn't fall, but they were in Liana's voice. "Why are you bringing this up now?"

"Because Matthew is a miracle. If we can work together to bring him home, maybe we can finally put everything else to rest."

"I remember that morning," she said. "No one knew where you were. No one could find you until the delivery was over and I didn't need you anymore. You were off in a back room, gambling away the money I'd saved to pay for our stay in town.''

''I remember that, too.''

''So you'll have to forgive me if I'm out of practice trusting you to keep your promises.''

Cullen wished there was some way of erasing a century and a past that had doomed them both. But he could only tell her the truth. ''I just hope someday you'll be able to forgive me.''

Liana couldn't believe that Cullen was only two rooms away. She had excised him from her life so completely that even her memories of their years together had grown dimmer and more tolerable. But Cullen had lurked in the shadows of her mind, and now that he was here in her apartment, the memories refocused in painful clarity.

Their relationship had been cursed from the start. They had been too young when they met, too isolated from the world when they married, too caught up in daily problems after Matthew's birth to realize the larger difficulties they would face. Cullen was the great-grandson of Archer Llewellyn. Liana, whose father had been sixty-one at her birth, was the granddaughter of Tom Robeson. They had known from the beginning of the tragic connection between their families and the story of the Pearl of Great Price. But in their youthful idealism, they had thought they would never be touched by it.

She had met Cullen in New York, followed him to the ends of the earth, and married him when it was clear that her morning nausea was not caused by the heat and humidity of Western Australia. She had fallen insanely, desperately in love, a free-spirited jewelry designer besotted with a man who created pearls.

And then, four years later, after a slow slide into distrust and disillusionment, the bottom had fallen out of their lives.

She gave up trying to sleep when she realized that every time she closed her eyes, she saw Cullen's face or, worse, Matthew's. The faces were not one and the same, although

Matthew strongly resembled his father. Cullen's features were rugged and sensual, while Matthew's were more refined. Cullen's eyes were a smoky blue, lit by temper, warmed by laugh lines—because the world had always been a laughing matter to Cullen. Matthew's eyes were boyishly innocent, trusting cinder gray eyes that mirrored whatever they saw.

And what did they see right now? Where was her son? Under the control of a stranger, terrified he would never come home again? Or running from some personal demon he hadn't been able to share with her?

She sat up, in the grip of a panic attack that made the one outside the Robeson building seem like a twinge. Even with her eyes wide-open, she could still see Matthew's face. She could almost reach out and stroke his cheek, but when she tried, her hand trembling so hard it fanned the air, Matthew's face disappeared.

She swung her feet over the bedside and stood, stumbling in her panic until she gripped one slender cherry post. She was dizzy with anxiety, but she couldn't bear to lie still and think about her son and all the things that could be happening to him.

She forced herself to breathe slowly, and bit by bit she calmed until she could stand alone. She found her robe and put it on once more, tying it tightly at her waist. Then, barefoot, she made her way to her son's room and stood in the doorway.

Matthew's computer was on, and the screen lit the dark room with an eerie green glow. She had spent the hours between Stanford's departure and Cullen's arrival carefully wording messages to everyone in Matthew's Internet address book, as well as everyone from whom he had gotten E-mail in the past weeks. All the mail she had sent had been similar. She was Matthew's mother, and somehow, through a communication error, she had temporarily lost touch with her son. Did the recipient know where Matthew could be? Was it possible to get a message to him?

She supposed anyone capable of stringing two thoughts together would see right through her request. But she wasn't ready to advertise Matthew's disappearance on the information superhighway. Not until she had more information.

Before Cullen's arrival she had checked for responses, but the only new mail had been from a school friend who didn't seem to know he was gone.

Now she didn't turn on the light, afraid she would alert Cullen, who was in the room next door. She found her way to Matthew's desk chair and sat, fingers poised on the keys. Then she logged on to the Internet, using Matthew's password, which was stored in the program. She listened as the modem dialed and watched the steps flash by as the computer connected, and finally as it retrieved his mail and logged off again.

She clicked the appropriate box for incoming mail and saw that three messages were waiting.

The subject of the first message was "More Diabolical Danger." Her heart slammed in her chest as she opened it, until she realized it was an advertisement for an updated adventure game Matthew had downloaded on-line at Christmas time. The second message, "School Sucks," was from a cyber-friend in Massachusetts who was just finishing final exams. Since this was someone she hadn't written to earlier, she responded with the same message she had sent everyone else, to be posted later.

The third message, "Guess I'm Late," wasn't signed, but the sender was SEZ, another unfamiliar screen name. "Problems with the server. Hope you get this before you go. Lots of luck. Wish I was going, too."

She was staring at the screen, trying to decide if anything could be read into the message, when she heard a noise behind her. She swivelled in the chair and saw Cullen leaning in the doorway.

"What's going on?"

She was still shaky, as dizzy as if an abyss had opened at her feet. Cullen, jeans low on his hips, shirt unbuttoned and untucked as if he had just pulled it on, was not what she needed.

"I'm checking Matthew's E-mail. Nothing's going on."

"You won't be any good to anyone if you don't sleep a bit."

She faced the screen. "Suppose you tell me how to manage that, Cullen."

"Climb in bed and close your eyes. You see how successfully it worked for me." He came to stand behind her. "Hasn't somebody checked this before?"

In as few words as possible, she explained what she was doing.

"Did you find any of my posts?"

"Yours?"

"Right. Sometimes we post back and forth a couple of times a day. Not the last few weeks, of course, since I've been on the road."

She knew Cullen had been in New York for the past week on business, which was why he had made arrangements to meet their son at LaGuardia. "I didn't know Matthew was mailing you."

"Maybe he thought you wouldn't like it."

She could feel him behind her, almost as if some indefinable charisma filled the space between them. "I should have guessed. He hasn't asked to call you as often."

"We send photographs back and forth, as easy as attaching a file to an E-mail. That way he gets a taste of what I do, and I can see how much he's changed."

This secret correspondence unsettled her, as if Cullen and Matthew had been plotting to find ways around the custody agreement. "Are you trying to make me feel guilty?"

"No, I'm trying to tell you what your son's been doing. I thought you'd want to know."

"You get a month with him, Cullen. Isn't that long enough to catch up?"

"Would it be long enough for you?"

"That's different. I wanted to be his mother. Everything Matthew does matters to me."

"And to me. That's why I use every way I can to show him I'm interested in his life."

"You didn't want him."

"I didn't want to be a father. There's a difference, Lee."

"It's too subtle for me."

"It's simple. I didn't want to be a father because I knew I wasn't ready to be a good one. But I loved Matthew from the moment he was born."

"You had a strange way of showing it."

He didn't reply, and she felt a stab of guilt that when they were both legitimately terrified they might never see their son again, she had waved Cullen's faults in front of him.

"I sound so bitter," she said. "And spiteful, too. I'm not really that way. I rarely even think about the past. It's just that Matthew's disappearance—"

"And my appearance..."

"That, too, after all these years," she admitted. "I don't seem to have much self-control." It was as close to an apology as she could come.

"I hurt you. I can't change that. But I can help you find our son. And I will."

She listened to his footsteps and finally, the closing of the guest room door. She stared at the computer screen, willing it to make sense of Matthew's disappearance and of her life. But in the end, the computer was only a machine, with no miracles to offer.

Stanford arrived not long after dawn. Liana, dressed and showered but not rested, met him at the door, waving Sue back into the kitchen, where she was already hard at work scouring an impeccably clean tile floor to keep herself busy.

"Have you heard anything?" Liana asked before she even allowed him to step across the threshold.

"Nothing much. May I come in?"

She moved aside. "Nothing much sounds like something."

"I had a telephone interview this morning with the woman who was sitting beside Matthew on the flight to Denver. She remembered him because he was so polite, and she found that unusual in a teenager. Matthew told her he was transferring to another flight in Denver, but unfortunately she didn't ask his destination. She hates to fly, so she was preoccupied. She said he told her his mother won't get on an airplane. And that's all she remembers.''

Liana shook her head sadly. "He told me once that if I'd just get on a plane with him, he'd make sure everything was all right. He wasn't even eight at the time.'' Her fear of flying had preceded the panic attacks by almost a decade. It had narrowed Matthew's world, too, making it impossible to take vacations away from home.

"There's one more thing. The passenger said Matthew was in a good mood. He seemed to be looking forward to the rest of his trip. She said if he was worried or upset, he hid it well.''

"That doesn't tell us anything, does it?''

A voice answered behind her. "It tells us if he's running away, he's bloody well glad to be doing it.''

Liana turned and examined Cullen, who was wearing fresh clothing, dark trousers and a knit shirt. He had shaved and showered, but he still looked as if he had spent the remainder of last night staring into the gaping chasm of Matthew's absence.

Stanford drew himself up to his full height, which made him just slightly taller than Cullen. Liana made the introduction. "Cullen got here late last night,'' she finished.

Stanford extended his hand, and Cullen moved forward to grasp it. "I guessed who you were from the accent,'' Stanford said. "I'm sorry we're meeting this way. I know you must be worried.''

"Too right. I gather you spoke to someone on Matthew's flight?''

Stanford filled him in. "I wish there was more, but that's it.''

"I spoke to the authorities in Denver on my way through. Nothing there, either.''

"We've been in touch with them. They seem particularly aware of everything. You light a fire under them?''

"They won't forget about my son.''

Stanford gave a weary smile. He had probably slept more than either Liana or Cullen, but he didn't look rested, either. "Did you have any luck with the E-mail?" he asked Liana.

"Nothing. The computer's on. You can see what I got."

"No calls?"

She shook her head.

"You have a cell phone?" At her nod, he continued, "Use it to call the office this morning, and tell them to put all your calls through to that number. We want to keep the regular line free. What do you have planned for the day?"

She hadn't wanted to think that far ahead, but when she had gone to her closet, she had stared at one jacket near the front for minutes. Then she had known what she had to do.

"If you think it's all right to leave for a little while, I'm going to see my aunt."

"Your aunt Mei?" Cullen asked. "How is she taking this? She's what, in her nineties now?"

"Ninety-seven. And she doesn't know. I didn't see any point in telling her yesterday."

"Do you see a point today?"

She had thought of nothing else since she'd stared at the antique jacket that was Mei's most recent gift to her. It was red silk brocade, with a Chinese collar and beautifully knotted black silk buttons, a lovely gift that had been intended as a reminder of Liana's heritage.

Liana faced Cullen. "If I don't tell her and she finds out from someone else, she won't forgive me."

"Wouldn't she forgive you anything?"

"Not where Matthew's concerned. I think she's lived as long as she has because she doesn't want to die and leave him."

Stanford addressed Liana. "They're close?"

"As close as a ninety-seven-year-old woman and a fourteen-year-old boy can be. My aunt believed Matthew was special from the moment she saw him. She treats him like a grandson."

"Is it possible he might have shared secrets with her?"

"You're asking if he might have told her where he was going?"

"Is it possible?"

Cullen answered for her. "I know my son. He wouldn't ask an old woman to keep a secret like this."

Reluctantly Liana nodded. "Cullen's right."

Stanford pressed her. "But if she knows him as well as you believe, maybe she has a theory on where he's gone."

"She might. If I can just find the words to tell her."

"I'd like to come with you." Cullen continued before she could protest. "When we were married, her letters to me were always more than cordial. She'll want to meet me now that I'm here. I can help you give her the news."

Oddly enough, Liana knew Cullen was right. Since Liana and Cullen had lived in Australia during their marriage, her aunt had never met him face-to-face, but she had always wanted to. Mei had not counseled Liana to stay with Cullen when their marriage neared its end, but neither had she tolerated criticism of him. After the divorce, Mei had become the one person with whom Matthew could happily discuss his father, and Liana had been grateful for that.

"Liana?"

"You're right. If she discovers you're in town, Aunt Mei will be upset if I come alone."

"This is what we'll do, then," Stanford said. "I'll stay here to answer the telephone. We'll put the company limo at your disposal, and if I need to reach you, I'll call the driver." He looked at his watch, then back at Liana. "Have you had breakfast?"

Her mind went blank. Nothing that mundane had made an impression on her.

"No, she hasn't," Cullen answered for her. "Lee, hot tea and toast? You've got to eat something."

She nodded numbly. The fact that Cullen was taking charge alarmed her, but she didn't have the defenses to fight him.

"I'll speak to Sue." He disappeared into the kitchen, and

Liana could hear the low rumble of his voice, the sexy, accented voice that had first attracted her to the man.

Stanford spoke quietly. "Did you know he was coming?"

"I knew." Liana realized it was true. Of course she had known, way down deep inside. Except that some time in the past years, she had disconnected her instincts from her mind. Inside, where feelings dwelled, she had known that Cullen would come to San Francisco to help find their son, she just hadn't acknowledged it.

"It's better he's here," Stanford said, as if he understood. "And now, at least, it's clear Matthew's not with him."

"But where is he, Stanford? Where is our son?"

It was only after the words had escaped that she realized what she had said. Not her son, and not, for this one isolated month of the year, Cullen's. *Their* son.

Our son.

Liana closed her eyes. Cullen Llewellyn had been gone from her life for ten years. She had exorcized him from her heart, from her thoughts, from the passing moments of every day. She had made a new and better place for herself in the world.

And now, despite everything, she, Matthew and Cullen were a family again.

12

Mei Fong was an imperious matriarch in a withering body. She did exactly as she pleased, and at ninety-seven, it pleased her to do everything she could. She thought nothing of inspecting the homes and lives of her family without invitation, and reordering their schedules to suit herself. She controlled her sons and grandsons and exasperated her daughters-in-law, but she was still loved by all for her warm generosity and loyalty.

Mei lived on Waverly Place in Chinatown, two short blocks that were replete with temples and family associations. For decades she had resisted all attempts to move her away from the tourist crowds and commercial clutter of a culture under siege. She gladly suffered the smell of American-style chop suey and fried prawns from a basement restaurant on the corner. She tolerated the sidewalk stands on nearby Grant Avenue, with their plastic cable cars and T-shirts that shrank in heavy fog.

Once, as a young woman, Mei had stood on a corner of her block and beaten off a gang of local toughs who attacked her oldest son, Sam. She had given birth to three more sons in the apartment in which she still lived, played mah-jongg with neighbors in the tiny living room, and made offerings of oranges and vegetable oil in the temple to the goddess Tien Hon, protector—among others—of sailors, fishermen and prostitutes.

Waverly Place was home, and most recently, when Sam, in ill health himself, had insisted that she move into a nursing home, she had promised she would cease breathing immediately if anyone tried to evict her. Since the family knew Mei never made idle threats, she remained in her apartment with a live-in helper. And she had only submitted to that indignity a year ago when her vision failed so dramatically that she couldn't cook and clean properly, or read the labels on her prescriptions.

As the limo pulled up Clay and stopped on the corner, Liana leaned forward and peered around Cullen at her aunt's apartment. "This could kill her."

"I don't think so, Lee. She'll want to be certain Matthew's all right before she dies."

"Even Aunt Mei has limits."

Cullen touched her hand, one brief brush of his fingertips for reassurance.

Liana leaned forward to speak to the driver. "You'll probably have to circle. We'll come back here and wait for you." She opened her door before anyone could do it for her. She told herself that she wasn't far from the door into her aunt's building. She had less than half a block to walk. She would be all right.

Her own platitudes failed, and the familiar trembling began deep inside. And today there was someone other than a stranger to witness the panic. Cullen was right beside her.

"You'll have to lead the way," Cullen said.

She didn't speak. She took a deep breath and exhaled slowly. Then she began to walk toward the building, silently counting steps and breathing carefully each time she reached five. She felt a hand at her elbow, though Cullen didn't comment. He didn't ask how she was feeling, or mention the sweat misting her brow, the colorless hue of her cheeks.

"So this is where Mei lives." He spoke as if nothing was wrong. "Now I can see why she likes it so. She told me about this place in her letters. I'm glad she's still here, that her family didn't cart her off somewhere that would never be home."

He continued to talk, his voice low and soothing. She sensed that somehow he understood exactly what she was feeling. She wanted to shake off his hand, to scream at him to leave her alone. But all she could manage was one breath, then another.

Inside the building, at the bottom of the stairwell leading to Mei's apartment, Liana leaned against the wall and closed her eyes. "How did you know? Did Matthew tell you?"

Cullen didn't pretend confusion. "He mentioned it."

She was so drained, it was all she could do to stand erect. She tried not to imagine her son telling her ex-husband about his mother's weird bouts of fear, about the difficulty she had going outside, how the panic got worse with each passing month. She had tried to keep the truth from Matthew, to medicate herself or play it down when her fear was too obvious to ignore, but clearly she hadn't succeeded.

"I try not to let it affect our lives. I...I go with him anywhere he has to go, even if..." She shook her head.

"That's above and beyond the call of duty, Lee. You don't have to be Superwoman, do you?"

"Yes, I do." She opened her eyes. "I have to be his mother and father."

"He has a father."

"Don't try to use this against me, Cullen. I can still be a good mother. I'm fighting this thing, and I'll beat it."

"I've known about the panic attacks for some time. If I planned to use them against you—meaning, I suppose, another custody battle—then I would have done it already."

"Would you?" Anger blazed inside her, a flame that had smoldered for years. "Oh, I doubt it. Because if you try to get custody, I'll expose *you*. I'll tell Matthew what you did and why I finally divorced you, and that's the *only* reason you haven't tried to take him away from me!"

His eyes didn't waver. "I will never take him from you." When she attempted to start up the stairs, he put a hand on her shoulder to hold her against the wall. "But just for the record, I reckon you would never hurt our son that way, so you don't have to make empty threats. I made a bargain with you when we parted, and I intend to honor it."

He straightened and dropped his hand. "And now that we've finished that, let's get on with telling Mei, shall we?"

Liana knew Cullen was perfectly capable of using all her weaknesses against her. But he *was* absolutely right that she would never tell Matthew why she had divorced him. She was just surprised that Cullen, who had so few scruples of his own, would be so certain of hers.

She drew herself up to her full height, as if those fractions of an inch would make her more of a threat. "We'll get on with finding Matthew. But once we find him, don't underestimate what I'll do to keep him."

"Let go a bit, Lee, why don't you? If you try so hard to control everything and everybody, the world's just going to get more and more terrifying, isn't it? There's only so much impact any one of us can have. Then we have to trust the universe."

"Our son is missing, and you're telling me to trust the universe?"

"You have to trust me and everyone else who's trying to find Matthew. You can't do this alone."

She was furious that Cullen, of all people, would lecture her. "When did you get all the answers, Cullen? Between a full house and a straight flush? Or maybe somewhere in between win, place and show?"

"I can see what's right in front of me. You're so tightly strung you're going to shatter into a million pieces. And I don't want that to happen."

His expression was understanding, almost compassionate. Despite everything she had said to him, he didn't seem angry. This was not the man she had known.

"If I weren't so tightly strung, I *would* shatter." She looked away. "But there's no chance of that. I'm going to do everything to find Matthew. And right now I'm going to talk to my aunt." She started up the stairs, and this time he didn't try to stop her.

Cullen watched Liana prowl Mei's tiny sitting room like a convict in a jail cell. The room was unseasonably warm, as if the windows hadn't been opened in months and the radiators had sucked away every molecule of fresh air, leaving a residue of sandalwood and jasmine. The walls were freshly painted, the furniture recently reupholstered, but the rest of the room was in a slow state of decay. Gilt on picture frames was flaking into dust; nap on the patterned carpet was wearing thin. Even the lilies in an onyx vase on a sideboard were thinning at the edges of their fragile petals. In another day they would be compost in an urban rubbish tip.

And what of Mei? he wondered. Mei Robeson Fong. The twin sister of Thomas Robeson, the stabilizing force in Liana's adolescence, the joy in Matthew's. Cullen had known Liana's aunt only through her letters, but she had surprised him with her quiet warmth, her acceptance of this Llewellyn in her life— despite the history that had nearly destroyed their families. She had talked of the good luck they would have, of the future— never of the past—of children he and Liana would raise, of joys anticipated and horizons conquered.

Now he was here to tell her that the only child born of their union had disappeared.

"She naps frequently," Liana said from the window, where she was staring down at the street below. "And it takes time to get her up and dressed."

"No worries. Where else would I go?"

She moved restlessly to the second window, as if the few meters between them might change her view. "I don't know what to say to her."

"I think it's best we not point out all the possibilities."

She seemed about to snap at him again, but she contained herself, giving a short nod instead.

Gazing at Liana wasn't easy. She was thirty-eight now, moving into midlife. In his experience, women who cared most about what was in their hearts were the ones who grew more interesting with age. Even tangled in her own emotions, Liana was still more interesting than younger women Cullen knew. The woman he saw in the curve of her cheek and chin, the soft lines at her lips, was the woman he had married. Free-spirited, generous, loving, a woman who would fight to the death for those in her care, a woman who contemplated her own fragility and tried in every way to overcome it.

Not the angry, rigid, frightened shell she had presented to Cullen since their reunion.

"Lee?"

She faced him, her arms locked over her chest.

He searched her face. "I'm asking this because it might matter. Is there a man in your life? Somebody Matthew's close to? Or even someone he doesn't get on with?"

For a woman so filled with emotion, she was a dab hand at hiding it. Her expression didn't flicker. "This has nothing to do with any man in my life."

"I'm trying to sort through the possibilities."

"Well, that's one less to sort through."

"Matthew mentioned someone named Jay...."

"Yes, and last time he came home from his month with you, Matthew mentioned someone named Sarah."

"I doubt Sarah nabbed him. She's too busy managing my office to nick off to California and steal our son."

"Jay moved to Honolulu about six months ago to marry his childhood sweetheart." She paused, and her expression softened. "A guy named Max."

Despite himself, he grinned. "That must have given you a bad moment."

"I knew about Max. Jay and I were just friends. I miss him."

"Friends are rare enough, aren't they?"

She seemed surprised. "How would you know? You always had dozens."

"Too right. A bloke who loses more than he wins is always in demand."

"Is there someone you owe money to right now, Cullen? Someone you can't pay? Someone who might have taken our son in retaliation? Or for blackmail?"

"No one."

"Stanford's looking into your activities."

"If he doesn't, he's not worth a whoop, is he?"

"It would help everyone if you'll be absolutely honest. Matthew's life could depend on it."

"I don't owe money. I don't have a mortgage on my house, a loan on my car. I don't even keep credit cards. I don't need that temptation." She looked as if she didn't believe him, and how could he blame her? "That doesn't mean tomorrow I won't go straight out and lose everything I have on the toss of a coin," he added.

There was a noise at the door. They both looked up as Mei, leaning on her young attendant, shuffled slowly into the room. Cullen rose to his feet. As he had expected, Mei Fong was old, skin spotted, hair thinning, spine bowing under decades of burdens. But his strongest impression was that Mei's body seemed too fragile to contain life. He would not have been surprised to see her disappear between one blink and the next.

"Liana-ah," she said, her voice low and quavery. "Who have you brought to see me?"

"Auntie." Liana grasped Mei's hands and kissed her cheek. "Cullen...Matthew's father is here from Australia."

Mei turned, continuing to hold Liana's hands as she did. "Can it be?"

He moved closer, giving her time to get used to the idea that he really was in her sitting room, that after all these years of estrangement, he and Liana were standing before her together.

"This is a wonder," Mei said.

"Auntie, may I help you sit?"

Mei's eyes were unfocused, but he knew that she saw him clearly, if not precisely in the flesh, at least in her imagination. "Why?" She turned back to Liana. "This is a lucky thing, but why?"

"Let me make you comfortable first," Liana said.

The attendant, a Chinese-American woman in a bright flowered dress, helped Liana tuck Mei into an overstuffed chair and cover her legs with a white knitted afghan. Cullen noted a stunning sunburst spray of silver and onyx on the old woman's collar. He suspected it was one of Liana's first designs. He wondered, as he so often had, if Liana designed even the occasional hobby piece now. He'd seen no sign of a workspace in her apartment.

"Will you need me?" the attendant asked Liana, after Mei was settled. "I have errands I could do."

"Just don't be too long," Liana said. Cullen watched her signal the woman with a raised brow. "She may need your help to go back to bed."

The attendant seemed to realize that all might not be well after their visit. She nodded. "I'll be back in a few minutes." She checked Mei once more, squeezed her hands and spoke to her in rapid Cantonese, although Mei's English was excellent, then she disappeared out the apartment door.

For a moment the only sound in the stuffy room was the arrhythmic hiccuping of a clock that couldn't possibly keep accurate time. Cullen listened until he realized that his own heart was beating unevenly, too. He had pictured discussing Matthew's disappearance, but now he couldn't imagine this woman surviving the news.

"Auntie," Liana began, speaking louder than normal. "Do you remember that Matthew was supposed to fly to New York to be with Cullen this week?"

Mei's voice was barely audible. "I remember."

"I put him on the airplane yesterday, just as I'd planned. The airplane arrived in Denver safely, but Matthew didn't make the connecting flight. Right now we're not sure where he might have gone."

Cullen was surprised Liana hadn't eased into the truth a bit. "Nothing's happened to make us think he's in trouble, Mei. It's only that we can't seem to find out where he is."

Mei was silent, but her frail, knotted fingers kneaded the afghan.

"Matthew knows how to take care of himself. I think, wherever he is, he's perfectly safe. But we're searching for him, because he's too young to take off on his own this way," he said.

Mei still didn't answer.

"Auntie, do you know what we're saying?" Liana asked gently.

"He is a boy with much purpose," Mei said at last. "Matthew will do whatever he thinks he must."

Cullen couldn't have been less enlightened if Mei had printed her sentences in Chinese characters. "Can you tell us what you mean?" He leaned forward in order to hear her better. Each word she spoke was quieter than the one before.

"You cannot understand because you do not know all you should."

Liana exchanged glances with Cullen. He could see she was as mystified as he was. "What doesn't Cullen know?" she asked. "Is there something you should tell him?"

"Liana, you do not understand, as well. Your father never told you the truth. It did not suit him."

Cullen watched the curtain of Liana's hair swing across her cheek, hiding her expression, but he knew it would be puzzled and, perhaps, impatient. "Is there something you can tell us both?" he prodded.

"I have lived this long only to tell you. Do you think I am afraid to die?"

Cullen straightened and caught Liana's eye. She shrugged. He knew that she, too, was wondering about her aunt's state of mind.

Mei raised her chin and looked straight at Cullen. "Your father…he has told you of the way your family lost the Pearl of Great Price?"

"Mei," he addressed her respectfully, "how can that matter now?"

"Until you understand, you will not find your son."

Cullen could only humor her. "I know my great-grandfather Archer Llewellyn murdered your father, Tom Robeson, so that the Pearl of Great Price would belong to him."

"That much is true."

Although at one time in his life Cullen had tried to learn exactly what happened next, he had never been completely successful. And his own father had never seemed to know or care.

He told her the story he and Liana had put together years ago. "What was left of your family came here, and eventually your twin Thomas, Liana's father, paid a man to go to Australia and get the pearl from Archer. Somehow he was successful, and the pearl has remained in Liana's family ever since."

"This story is not true."

"Liana?" He raised his hands in supplication.

"Auntie, this is what my father told me," she admitted. "But please, what does this have to do with Matthew?"

"The child knows more than the parents."

Cullen and Liana exchanged glances again, oddly united in their confusion.

"A child who understands more than those who care for him is a child who *must* act. Bad luck for all if he doesn't."

Cullen shook his head. "Mei, please, if you know something, if Matthew told you he was running away, will you tell us? He's too young to be off on his own."

"Out of respect, Matthew would never tell me."

Cullen sat back, hope fading. He had begun to believe Mei had the answer to Matthew's disappearance, that his son had shared his plans. Now he suspected she was inventing explanations. "We're going to find him. You don't have to worry. But we felt you had to be told."

"No, you are the ones who must be told." Mei's eyelids drooped.

Liana rested her fingertips against her aunt's wrist. Cullen knew she was measuring Mei's pulse. Or searching for it.

"We'll go as soon as Betty comes back," Liana told him softly. "She has to rest."

Mei jerked, as if she were waking up, although Cullen doubted she had really fallen asleep. "You go, but come back tonight. I will tell you then."

"Auntie, I don't know if we can come back." Liana stroked her wrist. "We have to find Matthew."

"You come back. Then you will know...where to begin searching."

The door opened, and the attendant came back into the apartment. "How is she?"

"Tired," Liana said. She stood and took Betty aside to tell her about Matthew. Cullen heard Betty's sharply indrawn breath. Mei's eyes were closed; she was with Cullen and Liana in body, but not in any other way.

"How's she been the past several days?" Liana asked Betty. "She's upset about Matthew, but she's speaking in riddles. It's not like her."

"I haven't seen any changes." Betty eyed her patient with a frown. "She sleeps a lot, but she's alert when she's awake. Should I call her sons? Or the doctor?"

"She wants us to come back tonight." Liana looked at Cullen, as if asking his advice.

He wanted to discount everything the old woman had said, to write it off as Mei's way of coping with her own fear. But he knew better than to shake off any lead.

"I think we should come," he said. "Unless we're needed elsewhere."

"Just watch her carefully," Liana told Betty. "If she seems worse, call Sam. Otherwise, wait until we return. I'll decide then."

"Where is the pearl?" Mei said, her voice stronger than it had been at any time during their conversation.

"Auntie?" Liana went back to kneel beside Mei's chair.

"The Pearl of Great Price."

Liana hesitated, as if she preferred not to answer. Cullen wondered if that was because he was in the room. "You know I keep it locked away."

"And it is locked away now?"

Liana hesitated again. "Of course."

"Do you lie because you think I'm too old for the truth? Or because your husband is listening?"

Liana rose. "Auntie, you're very tired. We'll come back tonight." She started toward the door, but Mei's words followed.

"We will exchange the truth, you and I. This is as it should be." She closed her eyes again, but this time quite obviously to shut off the conversation.

Cullen followed Liana out into the narrow hallway, but when she tried to descend the stairs, he held her back. "What's going on? What does Mei know that I don't?"

"She's an old woman, Cullen, too old for this kind of stress. She's imagining things."

"Don't flaming hand me that!"

She faced him. "I don't have to hand you anything. You came on your own, and you can damned well leave the same way!"

"Has something happened to the Pearl of Great Price? Is there something you haven't told me?"

"The pearl is no concern of yours. It belongs to me."

He stepped closer. "Has something happened to the pearl, Liana?"

She was silent for so long that he didn't think she was going to answer. Then she looked away. "The Pearl of Great Price is missing, too. I discovered it at the same moment you told me Matthew didn't arrive in New York."

"The devil! And you were keeping this from me?"

Her eyes were defiant. "I've kept it from everybody, Cullen. Nobody knows but you and me and whoever stole it from the safe in my office. I thought it was better that way, and if Aunt Mei hadn't guessed the truth, I wouldn't have told you at all."

13

"What were you thinking, Lee?" Cullen shoved his hair off his forehead, a habit Liana remembered well. He had always done that when he was upset, so he had done it often. His moods had been reliably mercurial. He had been as impulsive with his emotions as with his money, frequently tossing both out into the universe to see what rewards they might bring.

But even she, Cullen's greatest critic, couldn't doubt his sincerity where Matthew was involved. Despite the things she had said since his arrival, Liana knew Cullen loved his son.

"I've never received a single lesson on how to act if my son is kidnapped." She glanced at the front of the limo to be certain their driver wasn't listening to their conversation through the barrier that separated them.

She lowered her voice. "I'm flying blind here. The pearl's gone. My son's gone. What was I supposed to think? Somebody stole that pearl from my safe, and somebody may very well have stolen our son. Exactly who am I supposed to trust?"

"Including me, of course. Don't you think I know what's going on inside your head? That pearl might as well be a tennis ball, the way it's bounced back and forth between our families."

"It doesn't bounce, Cullen. People steal it. And people have died for it."

"Yes, and I'd rather our son not be one of them!"

Liana fell silent. Matthew was Cullen's son, and the pearl's disappearance might well have something to do with him. No matter what fears she harbored, she realized he had a right to this information.

Finally he spoke again. "Do you have any theories who might have taken it? Does someone else have the combination?"

"No one but me."

"It's not your birth date or anything easy to figure out?"

"It's the same as in Thomas's day. And Thomas wasn't a sentimental man. The numbers are simply random."

"I suppose that has to mean someone broke into the safe."

"I'm not a detective, but there was no obvious sign of forced entry." Liana realized they were almost to her apartment. "Nothing else is missing—at least, not that I've heard about."

"Is anything else kept in the safe?"

"No. My office belonged to my father. He had the safe installed before he married my mother. It was state-of-the-art for that time. He took it into his head that the pearl couldn't be protected anywhere else."

"Or maybe he wanted to be reminded of the havoc it's wrought."

"It's a pearl. It can hardly be blamed for the acts surrounding it."

"And it disappeared right along with our son."

"Maybe not. I discovered it was missing almost at the instant you told me about Matthew. But I don't know how long it's been gone. I never remove it from the safe unless we need to show it off for some reason." She didn't add that she didn't like to touch or look at the pearl, or that its presence in the room made her uneasy.

"When did you last see it?"

"As near as I can remember, about two months ago."

The driver stopped and came around to open the door. Liana waited until she and Cullen were alone in the elevator before she spoke again. "Stanford doesn't know. I meant it when I said you were the only person I've told. I didn't even tell my cousin Frank Fong, though he's probably my closest friend.''

"Mei knows.''

She had to admit that was probably true.

"Are you going to tell Stanford now?'' he asked.

The elevator stopped. She got out, but she stayed just in front of it and spoke softly. "No. If he alerts his men, someone might tell Graham.''

"Can Stanford help find Matthew if he doesn't know everything?''

"If he knows about the pearl, will he divide his energy and his resources? Which will matter most?''

Cullen stared at her as if he couldn't believe she had asked, but she shook her head, trying to think how best to explain—without explaining everything. "Eventually the pearl will belong to me, but for a few more years it's still the property of Pacific International. That's the way my father's will was set up. Think, Cullen. Could we trust Graham to ignore it until Matthew's found? Can you imagine what it's worth?''

His silence was all the answer she needed. "Then do we agree we shouldn't mention the Pearl of Great Price to Stanford? At least not yet?''

"Not until we can come up with a connection.''

"Until or unless.''

"Your aunt thinks there's one.''

"My aunt is upset and confused.''

"I intend to go back there tonight.''

Liana knew she would go, too, out of respect for Mei and all she had meant in Liana's life.

She started toward the apartment door, but Cullen stopped her. "Lee, did Matthew have access to the Pearl of Great Price? Could he have nipped it, then sold it to pay for running away?''

She was appalled. "Matthew would *never* do something like that. He knows what the pearl means to our family.''

He spaced his words for emphasis. "Did he have access?''

She tried to think. "Matthew knows about the safe, but he doesn't have the combination, and I've never written it down.''

"Never?"

"I'd be a fool to put it in writing, wouldn't I?"

"Has he been in the room when you've opened the safe?"

"I don't think so."

"Has he been in the room alone?"

"Plenty of times. He works on his homework there while he's waiting for me to get out of meetings. But he doesn't know the combination." She hesitated, then shrugged. "It's six numbers, Cullen. It would take a millennium to figure it out."

"Is the room under surveillance?"

"No, I don't want to be watched. But there's a complicated alarm system on my office door. Anyone trying to get into the safe would have to disarm that first. And Stanford has security patrolling the building around the clock."

"Maybe that's another good reason not to tell him about the pearl just yet. He's the best candidate for bypassing those measures."

Liana liked Stanford, but right now she had to suspect everyone. "I don't see how Matthew could have taken the pearl, or why."

"If he's run off, he'll need money. Does he have a bank account?"

"Yes. And a bank card."

"Has anyone checked his account?"

"I gave Stanford the number this morning."

"Let's see if he discovered anything while we were gone."

She no longer loved this man. And trust and respect had disappeared long before love. But in the last few minutes, she and Cullen had worked together without animosity. Reluctantly, she realized she felt better because of that. She was not alone. For the first time in years, someone who cared as much about Matthew as she did could help her make decisions.

How frightening that after everything she had suffered at his hands, Cullen Llewellyn remained important in her life.

Cullen was a dinkum judge of character. And he bloody well ought to be, considering that he had been raised among characters—and now worked among some of the world's most colorful in Western Australia. Years ago he had learned to assess a man within seconds. It was a skill a gambler required, particularly if winning was all-important.

Winning had never been Cullen's primary joy. The moment a two-up coin twirled and glistened in the air, the moment a racehorse broke away and streaked toward the finish line, those had been the shining moments of Cullen's life. He had been addicted to possibilities, to the thrill of maybes. Winning had been almost incidental.

But this time, winning was everything.

Cullen watched Stanford as he subtly shifted his weight from one foot to the other, and he wondered what was bothering the man. Stanford was uneasy, and although he was deferential to Liana, his full attention was not on their conversation.

"No telephone calls," Stanford told her. "And nothing new from either airport. I have men making a slow sweep in both places, showing Matthew's photograph, talking to personnel. But so far, nothing."

"Nothing? Or nothing you want to talk about?" Cullen moved closer to include himself in the conversation.

Stanford hesitated just a fraction too long. "What do you mean?"

Cullen glanced at Liana. Today she had dressed in black, as if she were already mourning Matthew. She had always favored austerity, a look that suited her high cheekbones and cleanly sculpted features. But in the earliest days of their love affair, she had brightened her choices with beautiful fabrics or the occasional stunning piece of jewelry she had designed herself. Today the unrelieved black was merely a backdrop for her tortured face. With her hair swept back in a knot at her nape and not even a touch of makeup, the anguish in her eyes stood out in sharp relief.

"Stanford, you seem uncomfortable," Liana said.

Cullen had to give her credit. Like all artists she had always been attuned to nuances. And even in turmoil, her instincts were still sharp.

Stanford's shoulders slumped just enough to make Liana's point. "I don't have anything concrete to tell you."

"We'll settle for theoretical," Liana said.

"Well, we ran a check on Matthew's bank account this morning."

"And?"

"It's intact. Just one withdrawal in the past weeks. About fifty dollars three weeks ago. He still has over six hundred dollars."

"He bought you a present." Liana turned to Cullen. "A compass in a leather case. He thought you could use it on the camping trip."

"Have you looked in his room to see if it's still there?"

"No." She looked stricken. "Cullen, I should have. If it's here…"

He finished for her. "He had no intention of meeting me."

"I did a thorough search of the room, and I didn't see anything like that." Stanford shifted his weight again. "But a compass might be tempting to take along if he was running away. The thing is, before he left, he didn't touch the rest of the money in his account. We have a promise from the bank that they'll notify us if anyone tries to access it, but for the time being, we have nothing to go on."

"Did he have access to other accounts?" Cullen asked Liana.

"No, but he gets a healthy allowance. I wanted him to learn to manage money. He could have been saving it here at home."

Cullen could almost hear the way she was silently questioning her decision to give a child such financial independence. "Matthew's always been careful with his cash," he reassured her. "Now I know why."

For a moment she looked grateful, then he watched her question herself again. "I've given him my credit cards, just if he needed something big, but not recently. Not in months. I don't like the idea of him getting used to credit."

"Will you please check them and be sure you have them

all?'' Stanford asked. ''And do a quick inventory of your checks.''

Cullen saw she wanted to deny the possibility that her son might have stolen from her, but she nodded tersely. ''I'll do it now.'' She marched down the hall toward her room.

''She's a strong woman. She's holding up,'' Stanford said. ''But I know how hard this has to be.''

''What else did you find out?''

Stanford looked after Liana. ''I'm running a check on you. But I suppose you guessed as much.''

''No worries. My life's an open book.''

''You had a serious problem with gambling?''

''Still do.''

Stanford looked surprised. ''Oh? So far the reports say you've cleaned up your act.''

''Do they? That's gratifying, but I'm recovering, not recovered. The day I forget the difference is the day I'll lose my shirt again.''

''Twelve steps?''

Cullen twisted his mouth into a humorless grin. ''Too right. Although most of the time it feels like a thousand.''

''When was the last time you indulged?''

''What, in Gamblers Anonymous or the horses?''

''The horses were your game?''

''At my peak I'd bet on two blokes at a urinal.''

''How long ago was the peak?''

Cullen steeled himself. ''I'd say it was the day I gambled away my son's trust fund, wouldn't you?''

Stanford gave a low whistle. ''I haven't come across that bit of information yet.''

''Liana made certain no one ever would. A long-standing habit of covering up my failures.''

''And since then?''

''Since then it's been one day at a time. I finally lost count last year. Another milestone.'' Cullen's gaze was steady, but he saw something in the other man's eyes that wasn't. ''Look, you've skated over this a time or two. What's bothering you? What else did you discover today?''

Stanford didn't answer for a moment. Then he shook his head. ''I told you we'd checked with the bank. Well, somebody else checked first. It looks like somebody else might be trying to find your son, Mr. Llewellyn. And not necessarily because he or she wants to be a hero.''

Liana managed a nap in the afternoon, one filled with nightmares of Matthew bound and gagged in a car trunk. Even fretful sleep was better than nothing, and she awoke after an hour feeling slightly more rested. She dressed and went on a search. Stanford was gone, but she found Cullen in the living room, staring at the portrait of Matthew.

She watched him from the doorway. He was so wrapped up in his thoughts he didn't know she was there. The unadulterated longing on his face was evidence of that.

She had first been attracted to Cullen Llewellyn by his voice, then by the absence of pathos in his face. He wasn't a handsome man, but he was an immensely appealing one. And when a grin softened the square jut of his jaw, and broke up the lines that the unrelenting outback sun had engraved around his eyes, he was nothing short of magnetic.

She had been drawn to that grin, to the warmth in his blue eyes, to the way he used his body. He was comfortable with himself in a way that had seemed new to her. She'd been seeking security, and she had been sure Cullen had already found it.

Their relationship had been based on beautiful lies they had believed about each other.

He turned. ''It captures him completely, doesn't it?''

''I think so. Yes.''

''I don't know a lot of kids. But to me, Matthew seems unsophisticated—at least, as unsophisticated as any kid in the world can be today. He's interested in what's happening around him, and he doesn't pretend he's not. He doesn't try to hide what he's feeling.''

"I worry sometimes that he isn't growing up fast enough. Then I look at his classmates. We fight about his hair or the state of his jeans. Last year his best friend ended up in a detox center. It puts things in perspective."

"He's a wise kid, though, isn't he? He's perceptive, and he has good common sense. He knows how to take care of himself."

"If he's someplace where he can...."

"I made a reservation for a hotel near your aunt's apartment. I'll check in tonight after we visit Mei again."

She wondered how she would feel in Cullen's place. If Matthew had disappeared in Australia, and she had journeyed there to find him, how would she feel being at the edge of the investigation, lying awake in a hotel room while others discussed and decided her son's fate. She knew that if the tables were turned, Cullen would do anything in his power to include her. He had never been small-minded or mean-spirited. For all his faults, he had never set out to hurt her.

"I'd like you to stay." She watched his forehead pucker. "If I get a call or have to make a decision on the spot, I don't want to wait for you to get here. This is where everything is happening, and you deserve to be involved."

"You're certain you don't mind?"

"Who would have thought it, Cullen? As it turns out, after all these years, we have no choice but to work together."

"I was never good at working with anyone, was I?"

"No."

He didn't claim he had changed, and he didn't apologize. "Will we be leaving soon?"

"Stanford is sending a man to wait by the phone while we're gone. Did you have anything to eat?"

"Sue made me a sandwich. Will you at least try to force something down while I call the hotel?"

She had avoided lunch. Now the thought of dinner made her stomach clench. "I'll get something. We'll leave as soon as Stanford's man arrives."

In the car on the way to Mei's they hardly spoke. Many

times during their marriage she had sat beside him like this, bathing in the warmth of his grin and fending off his teasing overtures. She had been a different woman then, fearless, laughing and, most of all, enchanted by the young man with the musical accent and the irreverent perceptions of her world. They had believed that together they could conquer anything and that the distant past could not affect them.

"The Pearl of Great Price has never brought luck." She glanced at Cullen, who was sitting remote and unsmiling beside her. "If Matthew has it..."

"If you believe it's unlucky, why do you keep it in your office? Aren't you worried, having it so close?"

"My grandfather died for that pearl. I keep it there to honor him."

"Don't look now, Lee, but your ambivalence is showing."

She *was* ambivalent about the pearl, wildly ambivalent, as if her thoughts about it reflected two opposite sides of her personality. One side was bound up in duty, respect for her ancestors and honor, the other side was intuitive, yearning and emotional. That was the side that had fallen in love with Cullen Llewellyn.

"I'm grasping at straws," she said. "Next I'll be lighting incense and praying to gods with names I can't pronounce."

"Stories have meaning that logic can't explain away. The Pearl of Great Price has destroyed. How foolish can it be to wonder if it will destroy again?"

She shuddered.

Cullen put his hand on hers, a warm, strong hand with a callused palm. "He doesn't have the pearl, Lee. He couldn't. You said so yourself."

The driver stopped at the corner where he had left them earlier. Cullen squeezed her hand. "What can I do to help you get inside?"

For a moment she wanted to believe he could help, that for once she didn't have to carry the burdens of her fears alone, and that the warmth of his touch was a promise, not a lie. Then reality intruded.

She jerked her hand from his. "You can remember you're not here to make amends, Cullen. Stay on your side of this search, and don't make the mistake of crossing over to mine."

Once he would have lashed out at her. They would have fought, and, if the fates had decreed, eventually they would have gone to bed together—although nothing except sexual tension would have been settled. But this time Cullen said nothing. His eyes were steady, and his hand remained on the seat, as if hers were still beneath it. "There are no sides on this search. And I can only make amends if you'll allow it."

The driver opened her door, and she stepped out. The sidewalk rolled in tumultuous waves to her aunt's building. The ornamental streetlights flashed like the fiery breath of a dragon. She put one foot in front of the other, forcing herself not to gulp the poisoned air. She clenched her fists and took more steps, until she was inside.

When she had made the journey upstairs, Cullen joined her at the door of her aunt's apartment. They entered together, as if the scene downstairs had never occurred.

Mei opened the door herself. "Liana-ah. You are so pale."

Liana drew a deep cleansing breath. Here in the overheated cocoon of her aunt's life, the fear began to recede. "We can't stay long, Auntie. We have to be near the telephone."

"You will stay as long as you must." Mei took her arm, and they walked together to the tiny parlor. Liana wasn't sure which woman was supporting the other.

"Mei, where would you like me to sit?" Cullen asked, when Mei had laboriously settled herself in an armchair.

Liana saw that her aunt had spread photographs on the table beside her. As a girl, Liana had often pored over albums of Mei's family—pictures of her husband, Wo Fong, her sons and grandchildren, including Frank, who was Liana's age and now her ally at Pacific International. She had hoped that these pictures would make her feel that she belonged somewhere.

But these photographs were not familiar.

"You will sit beside me, Cullen," Mei said in her halting

voice. She pointed to the sofa angling to the right. "And Liana, you must sit here." She pointed to the chair at her left.

They settled themselves. Liana didn't look at Cullen. She was already growing ashamed of her outburst in the car.

"This story takes time, but we have no time," Mei said. She closed her eyes, and for a moment she was silent. Then she began. "I have been to Jimiramira, Cullen, to the place where you were born. And long ago, when he was young, I knew your grandfather, Bryce." She lifted a photograph and gave it to Cullen. "You see? As a girl, I was called by my full Chinese name, Měi-Zhěn. This means beautiful pearl, a name my mother chose carefully for me so that I would never forget my father's death. But your grandfather Bryce knew me only as May."

Liana felt Cullen's eyes on her. She clasped her hands, as if the appearance of self-control would trigger the real thing. But even as her aunt's words began to weave the spell of other times and lives, a part of her thought of Matthew. Where was her son? And how could memories of people he had never known and places he had never been bring him back to her?

She closed her eyes and saw Matthew's face. She held on to that vision like a talisman.

On a 747 over the Pacific, Matthew Llewellyn glanced shyly at the flight attendant with the pale blond hair and the gash of red lipstick outlining a professional smile. He had noticed her the moment he boarded the airplane. She wasn't exactly pretty, but she looked like someone who knew how to handle herself in any situation, something guaranteed to impress him at this particular juncture in his life. He could imagine her offering magazines to presidents or hijackers with that same cool smile, that same questioning lift of one eyebrow.

He wondered if her skin under the drab uniform was the same golden tan as her face. Then he looked away quickly, afraid that she might read that question in his eyes. If she did, it didn't stop her from pausing at his row to take his order. Her voice was matter-of-fact, but polite. "And what about you? Would you like something to drink?"

He pretended to examine his tray. "A Coke, thanks." His voice was reassuringly deep and mature.

"You look lonely up here all by yourself."

This time he met her eyes and lied with artistry. "My mother's in the back. She's taking a nap."

That seemed to make sense to her. The flight was only half full, and the experienced passengers had staked out rows all over the plane. "You ought to try for a good sleep, too. It's a long flight. You'll wish you had a nap by the time we get to Sydney."

"Good idea. Maybe I will after the movie."

She moved on to the next row, and he relaxed. He had intended to strike up an animated conversation with his seatmates so that the attendants, who might be questioned later, wouldn't think of him if they were asked about a young man traveling by himself. Now, since his row was empty, he supposed the lie about his mother would work just as well.

As well as his newly shorn hair, the cowboy shirt and boots he had bought in the Dallas airport, and the passport and driver's license he had borrowed from Simon Van Valkenburg, the one friend his mother would never know to question.

Now, until he was safely through Australian customs, he just had to remember to answer to the name of Simon.

The attendant returned with his drink and a package of smoked almonds. "Do you need something to read?"

"Oh, no, thanks. I have a book in my carry-on."

"Have you been to Australia before?"

"Twice," he said, although it was a lie. He had been born in Australia, but he'd only been back in his imagination.

"Have you, then? Where?"

He had prepared himself. Now he tried out his story. "South Australia. But I was only five the last time we were there. I don't remember anything."

"You'll certainly remember this trip, won't you?" She started down the aisle.

"No doubt about that," he said, although she was already out of earshot.

How would he ever forget it? Applying for a visa weeks ago under an assumed identity. Scheming and cheating. Lying and stealing. Ditching the Denver airport and traveling by cab to the bus station, by bus to the Dallas airport, by plane to Chicago. Cutting off his hair, stuffing his clothes into a cheap backpack and disposing of his suitcase. Avoiding cops, charming ticket agents, sweating buckets every time somebody compared him to the outdated photograph on Simon's passport and commented about how much a young man could change in five years.

No, he wouldn't forget this trip. Not in this lifetime. He downed the Coke in four swallows, then he leaned back in his seat and closed his eyes.

The attendant was right. It was a long flight to Sydney. And Sydney was only one more step toward Jimiramira.

Two points in the adventure of the diver,
One—when, a beggar, he prepares to plunge,
One—when, a prince, he rises with his pearl...

—Robert Browning,
Paracelsus, Part I

14

⟨⟨⟨⟨⟨⟨⟨⟨⟨⟨⟨

Northern Territory, Australia—1921

The trip to Jimiramira was arduous. Mei made the long voyage to Darwin first, on a pearling vessel belonging to John Garth. After her father's death, John had tried to offer assistance to her mother in small ways. He had never been one of the men who came late at night to the tiny bungalow to share Willow's bed so she could buy food for her twin daughter and son. He came in daylight, bearing practical gifts, or small misshapen pearls Willow could sell when life was bleakest. Sometimes he brought laundry, so his gifts wouldn't seem like charity.

John was the one who had diligently searched for relatives of Tom's who might help his children toward a better life. And months later, it was John who had written the letter to Tom's parents in San Francisco, enclosing photographs of Mei and her twin brother, Thomas, who had been lovingly named after his father.

Finally, it was John who had read the Robesons' response out loud in the sitting room of the bungalow, folded it neatly and soberly counseled a sobbing Willow.

"You must think about what will be best for the children, Willow. They have no life here. At least Tom's parents are willing to give little Thomas a home." John lifted the bewildered two-year-old to his lap, but he didn't smile as Thomas searched his pockets for the peppermint that was always waiting.

"Thomas is my son! I cannot send him across the sea alone. And Mei is the air he breathes. They cannot be separated."

"But the letter is very clear. They will take only Thomas."

"Because *he* does not look Chinese." Willow reached for her daughter, who began to cry, as well.

"It's unfortunate appearance has determined so much." John fidgeted in discomfort. "But they have promised to give the boy every luxury, and to give you money to help support and school her if you send Thomas to them. You and Mei can continue to live in this house, and, when she's older, perhaps she can go to California and find her brother. How could anyone stop her?"

"They are halves of a whole, my children. Can half a heart continue to beat?"

"Is the alternative to raise both children here?" He paused. "To sell your body more often? To men of lower quality and no discretion?"

She drew a startled breath.

He bowed his head. "I'm sorry. But yes, I know what you've been forced to do. Soon everyone will, if you continue. Is this the life you want for your children?"

"I cannot give up my son!"

But she had. In the end, when Thomas was four and the house nearly empty of food, Thomas, in the care of a woman who was paid to make the journey with him, was sent to live in San Francisco.

Now, after sixteen years without her brother, after her mother's lengthy illness and death, Mei was making a journey, too. Not as far as her brother's, but more dangerous than the oceans separating Australia from North America.

She was going to Jimiramira, to take back the pearl for which she had been named.

The decision to go had not come suddenly or easily. She

didn't even remember the first time she had heard the story of the magnificent pearl her father had lifted from the ocean floor or of his death at the hands of a faithless friend named Archer Llewellyn. She had absorbed the story along with tales of her ancestors in China and the rural village in the district of Kwangtung where Willow had been born in a wooden house with mud floors. She had learned about her father, his great kindness, his tender smile, his wish to marry her mother. And she had learned, from the catch in Willow's voice, of her mother's shame that he had not.

But the story of the pearl had stood out from the others. It was a legend, invested with power that went beyond simple history. It was a story of injustice crying out for retribution. Her mother told Mei of dreams where she held the Pearl of Great Price in the palm of her hand and gazed at it, and as she did Mei's father was reflected in its radiant glow. Tom Robeson was smiling, his gaze as warm as it had been when he was living.

Mei didn't know when she had realized she must go to the place called Jimiramira, where Archer Llewellyn was said to live now, and take back the pearl. The task would have been her brother's, if he had remained in Australia. But Thomas continued to live in California with the grandparents who also made minimal semiannual provision for Mei and paid for her education.

She knew little about Thomas's life. Once a bookkeeper who worked for the Robesons had slipped a photograph of ten-year-old Thomas into the envelope containing a bank note destined for Willow. It showed a boy who did not resemble Mei, a dark-haired boy with grave, round eyes and a small, unsmiling mouth. Mei herself had eyes that were shaped like the tapering oval of a mulga blossom and lips that seemed to curve, even when she wasn't smiling. Mei had stared at her brother's photograph for so many hours that eventually she had not needed to look at it again. It was burned into her heart, along with the memory of a younger Thomas wrenched from her childish arms and banished from her life.

Because her brother could not take back the family's honor, stealing the Pearl of Great Price had become Mei's destiny. She would take back what belonged to her family; then she would find Thomas in far-off America. Together they would use the pearl to establish a new life.

After Willow's death, she sold what furniture her mother had collected and gave Willow's clothing to the women who had helped nurse her through the final stages of consumption. For herself she kept only the jade bracelet Tom had presented to Willow and the last of Willow's savings. Then she set off for Darwin, chaperoned by John's wife, a proper English lady who, along with her husband, had always done what she could for Mei.

Mei's first glimpse of Darwin was reassuring. Feathery palms and sprawling banyans shaded houses with verandas that reminded her of home. Even the sultry air and the sunlit glare on sapphire water were the same.

The reasons for going to Darwin had been twofold. Like Broome, Darwin had a sizable Chinese community, and Mei's desire to begin anew there seemed sensible to the Garths. But, more important, Darwin was the only city of consequence in the Northern Territory. Jimiramira was many miles away, over horrifyingly bleak terrain, but the cattle stations sometimes sent to Darwin for whatever employees they couldn't recruit from among the local Aborigines. Mei hoped to find a job that would take her closer to Archer Llewellyn's homestead, then work her way to Jimiramira using whatever means she could.

She had not, in her most expansive dreams, hoped to go immediately to Jimiramira. As a child she had learned great patience. She had waited until there was money to buy fish to eat with their rice, and waited until her mother returned from long hours over a laundry tub so she could help Mei with her lessons. Later, Mei had waited and watched for books to teach her more than she had learned in school. During the Great War, when the pearling industry nearly ground to a halt and there was little work for anyone, she had waited for the cast-off clothing and household goods of others.

So Mei had been prepared to wait for years before she made her way to Jimiramira. Instead, the opportunity arose almost immediately. She had taken a job at a general store in Darwin's bustling Chinatown in exchange for room and board, and within a week she had been introduced to another young woman, who was on holiday from a cattle station near Katherine. The woman had taken her to see the man who had arranged her employment, a banker named Stuart Sayers.

Sayers was a small man with bandicoot eyes that examined Mei from head to toe as he questioned her. She told him her name was May Chun, anglicizing the spelling and pronunciation to further distance herself from her life in Broome. Although her name had been officially registered as Robeson, she kept that a secret.

He commented favorably on her English and listened silently to the fictitious story she told him about her childhood in Darwin. Finally, satisfied, he promised he would keep her in mind when positions became available.

"We've had only one request of late," he said, standing to announce that their brief interview had ended. "And I wouldn't send someone as young as you, not even a Chinese. You'd be back as fast as a blackboy's boomerang."

"You are most thoughtful, but I am both strong and clever."

Sayers lowered his voice. "The situation isn't impossible, mind you, but nearly so. Jimiramira's as remote as they get, and the missus there's a bit of a problem. Not a married couple we've sent has stayed longer than it takes to arrange transportation back. With the Wet coming, you might not be able to come home for months. I can't be bothered with the fuss you ladies make when things don't go just the way you want."

The mention of Jimiramira had sent Mei's heart thudding in her chest. She had known Jimiramira was her fate, but not that the fates would intervene to help her.

"I have no family left in Darwin to trouble you." Mei saw the way his tiny eyes brightened. "Perhaps my destiny waits at Jimiramira."

"Oriental folderol. A man makes his own destiny, and a

woman lets a man make one for her.'' Sayers swept her with another appraising glance. "I could find better work for you nearer to town."

"I am so sorry. But it seems I must try my luck there. Perhaps I will write the owner of Jimiramira on my own."

"You can't do that."

"I write well. Would you like me to show you?"

His eyes narrowed to slits. "I'm the one who told you about the job, missy, and I'll be the one to send you. Just don't say I didn't warn you."

Two weeks later she took the train to the north bank of the Katherine River, where the tracks ended. From there she traveled southwest to Jimiramira in a wagon drawn by mules, since the automobile, of which she'd seen several astonishing examples in Darwin, couldn't withstand the rigors of outback travel.

The voyage from Broome had been rough, and to her own shame she had been sick for some of it. Now, as the wagon rolled inch by tortured inch across the stifling, dusty nevernever, she longed for the tossing waves, the nightly creak of the chains, the stink of dead fish. The wagon she rode in was one of two, and both were crowded with supplies for stations along the way. In addition to the driver—who smelled worse than the pearling lugger's hold—and Rex, the Aboriginal youth who had charge of the second wagon, an aging English couple, bound for a station beyond Jimiramira, was also making the journey.

Nothing as official as a road had been cut through the wilderness. Some of the way was marked by the ruts of other wagon wheels, or the hooves of horses and even camels. Some ruts wound around swamps, over sandhills and into dry riverbeds that shifted with the winds, erasing all signs of previous travelers. They passed towering white ant castles, as complex and labor intensive as some of Europe's finest masterpieces. Dingoes howled in serenade, and at dusk kangaroos boxed on the horizon.

They traveled between waterholes and camped at night beside fires, boiling the billy for strong tea flavored with pungent gum leaves. The head driver, Bluey, slapped dough in a camp oven and buried it in the ashes for damper, and sometimes, to supplement the supply of salt beef and tinned vegetables, there was a treat of plum jam or fruit packed and padded carefully in crates.

Bluey, despite an aversion to soap, was kind enough. He didn't initiate conversation as they traveled, but at the day's end, when the fire had burned to embers, he would tell Mei of his days humping a swag through Queensland.

"When I was young I took three things with me everywhere I went," he told her. "Me mother's picture, a book of poems by Robert Burns and the finest little cattle dog in Queensland. Then the dog died, I learned all the poems by heart, and the picture just faded away. But I can still whistle the tune that dog liked best, and I can say the poems whenever I've a mind to. Someday I'll be seeing my mother's face again, when she comes to take me home. So now I don't need a thing but this wagon. And if that disappears, I've still got legs and feet, don't I?"

He was a grizzled old man, whose face was as empty of expression as his life was of possessions. But he had obviously found peace. He had no quest and few wants. He traveled from station to station, taking whatever came his way.

Sometimes after their talks, as Bluey snored in his swag across the campfire from hers, Mei wished her own life were as simple, that the Pearl of Great Price had never been plucked from the ocean and that her father had sailed back to harbor that fateful season to marry her mother and welcome his twin children into the world. Then, like Bluey, she would not have a quest. She would be content to take what life offered and to watch her brother make his way in the world. She would marry a good man and have children who would be content with their lives, too.

But the fates had made other plans.

The days passed, and she grew dizzy with the heat. They suffered two drenching rainstorms that disappeared as quickly as they blew in, but Bluey searched the skies each morning with the care of a man reading his daily newspaper. The English couple began to complain reliably as midday approached. The woman, fair-skinned and gaunt, grew brown under the relentless sun, and thinner. The man, who had been good-humored at first, spoke only if there was something to criticize.

They passed over stations so vast they were forced to camp beside rudimentary bores or billabongs with foul-tasting water. At others they stopped at ramshackle homesteads built of corrugated iron and stringybark, where bush hospitality made up for the lack of luxuries. Mei saw only two white women on her journey, both leather-skinned and old before their time. They were starved for news of Darwin and people met along the way, and content to gossip with Mei when they realized the Englishwoman was too dazed by the heat to keep up with them.

"Broome? You've come all this way?" And when they discovered where she was bound, the inevitable: "You're certain, dear?"

Even Mei questioned her decision as the days crept by. Bluey was trying to move faster now, muttering frequently about the approaching Wet. He planned to stay at the station where the couple was bound until the rainy season ended, but clearly he wasn't certain they would make it in time. At last, when they crossed an invisible boundary and he announced, "Jimiramira," Mei was too numb with fatigue to do anything except nod.

Most of four days passed before they spotted smoke from the homestead chimney. "There'll be a real boil-over if the boss isn't at home," Bluey muttered.

"Why?" Mei squinted into the distance.

"The missus set the place on fire once. No fires on the hearth now, not unless he's there himself, or maybe his boy. They got no help at the house but the blacks, and the blacks would just as soon let the place burn to the ground."

By now Mei knew Archer and Viola Llewellyn had one son, a boy named Bryce who was about her own age. She wanted to ask if Viola had set the fire on purpose, but she was afraid to know.

"So help me bob, the woman's off her nut," Bluey said, with no prompting. "You take care and watch her up close. Don't know why Sayers sent a young lass here, but I'll tell you this. I head up to Darwin after the Wet, but before I do, I'll be coming by here to take you back with me."

Mei hoped that in the intervening months she would discover whatever she needed to know about the pearl and take it for her own.

They didn't reach the homestead that night. A wheel came loose, and they were forced to camp several miles away to make the necessary repairs. They started a fire, and Mei made the damper and boiled the billy while Bluey tended to the wheel. She was just pulling the damper from the ashes when she heard the sound of approaching hoofbeats. The couple, who had sat mutely by as Mei did the work, stood and straightened their clothing. Mei dusted off her hands and rose as a horse appeared.

Her heart beat faster, fueled by thoughts of the father she had never known. She touched the jade bracelet securely tucked into the pocket of her skirt and watched without blinking as the horse, just one, came to a halt several yards away. The rider dismounted, holding the reins.

She faced the son of the man who had murdered her father.

"I'm Bryce Llewellyn." He nodded politely to Mei and the couple. Then his face lit in a wide grin as he spied Bluey by the wagon. "G'day, Bluey! Made it just in time, did you?"

"Bloody well did. In good nick, till now. You'd just get yourself a road out here, I'da made it sooner."

"Are you right there, mate?"

Mei watched as the young man walked over to Bluey and clapped him on the back. She had thought little about Archer and Viola's son except as an opponent in her quest to steal the pearl. Now she assessed her foe. He was tall and lean, brown-skinned from the sun and fit from a life that seemed to suit men and destroy all but the hardiest women. Under the cabbage palm hat shading his face, she saw hair just light enough to be called blond and pleasant features that were settling into maturity.

"I've about got it," Bluey said. "Still got six, seven days before we get down to Shadyside."

"Six or seven if you push hard." Bryce shoved his hands in the pockets of dusty moleskin trousers. "You'd better push hard, Bluey. Old Jake says the Wet's coming early this year."

"Too right."

"Why don't I take the girl back with me? You can leave from here in the morning. Save you a trip into the homestead."

"I got boxes, too."

"Leave them. I'll send a man in our wagon to get them first thing tomorrow."

Bluey looked relieved. "That's what we'll do, then."

"Will that suit you, miss?" Bryce asked Mei politely. His eyes flicked to Bluey. "She speak English?"

"As good as you, lad, and better than me."

Bryce grinned at Mei. "Do you have a name?"

"May." She wished Bluey hadn't extolled her English. In the days ahead she had intended to communicate as sparingly as possible, hoping that the Llewellyns would treat her like a piece of furniture, useful, but with no thoughts of her own.

Bluey wiped his hands on his trousers. "You'll stay for tea? We have damper to go with it."

"I should get back." Bryce hesitated. "My mum's alone at the house."

Bluey didn't insist. "May, you take your share."

Bryce started toward his horse. "You ought to do as he says, miss. The cook went walkabout, and the tucker's been sparse ever since." He paused. "Can you cook?"

"I can."

"Can you ride?"

She hesitated. "I'll learn."

He turned and grinned. "You'll learn right now, sorry to say."

"No matter."

"Good on ya."

Mei started toward him. She would ride the horse with the boy-man in front of her. She would wrap her arms around his waist as if he were not a stranger, and press her body against his to keep from falling to the ground.

But this was only a small sacrifice. Mei knew she could do anything to be reunited with Thomas. She would cook for these people, live in their house and make their life better in every way except one. When the right moment came, she would steal the pearl Archer Llewellyn had treasured more than the life of his best friend.

And then she would leave the Llewellyns to destroy each other.

15

Mei's first days at Jimiramira left her with a blur of impressions. Bryce Llewellyn had a purity of character that was foreign to his parents. Viola Llewellyn was quite mad.

And Archer Llewellyn was a man who had achieved his heart's desire and forsaken his soul.

Jimiramira itself reflected the emotional tumult of its inhabitants. The homestead was incongruously large, designed for a way of life that was impossible so far from civilization. At dawn on her first morning in residence, Mei wandered through the house, taking note of rooms that had little or no furniture, of walls with no plaster, of windows shuttered with rusting sheets of metal, of floors surfaced with dirt from white ant hills, smoothed and watered into a rock-hard surface.

In the rooms that were used by the family, a fine dust covered everything, and when she drew her finger across the rough surface of a table, dust filled in the spot as soon as her finger was lifted. A rosewood piano in the parlor was missing keys and badly out of tune. Old photographs in frames with broken glass sat on top of it like a profane altar to the departed.

In the sitting room, blackened stone and a charred fireplace mantel were testimony to the fire Bluey had mentioned the previous night. She ran her finger along the soot-streaked walls and wondered if Viola Llewellyn had wanted to kill herself and her family, or if she had merely forgotten to be careful.

Her next stop was the kitchen, erected to stand between the house and the men's dining room. It was awash in rotting vegetation and flies, and the window gauze, hung to eliminate the clouds of insects, had merely trapped them in solid, seething masses. She began her work there, fanning sticks into flame in the woodstove and scooping rusty water into a kettle to heat while she gathered garbage to be removed. By the time Bryce found her, she had cleared and scrubbed enough table space to begin breakfast preparations.

His "good morning" was tentative, as if he knew there was no way this morning would be anything of the kind. She prepared what little she could, coffee made from the boiling water, tinned tomatoes on bread so stale, mold would probably demand a better home. He said little until he had eaten, then he cleared off his own place and brought his tin plate and pannikin to her.

"My mother will be waking before long. I should warn you."

She wondered where Bryce's father was. Archer Llewellyn had not greeted her last night, as if one Chinese servant girl was unworthy of his attention.

"My mother," Bryce continued, "is not well. Sometimes she's quiet, and she won't answer if you speak to her." He paused, then he dropped cutlery into the bucket with a clatter. "I'm afraid those are the good times. They shouldn't have sent you here, you know. I can't imagine what they were thinking."

"What are the bad times?" Mei asked.

"The times she isn't quiet." Bryce rested against the table's edge. "She screams. She cries. She tries to tear out her hair. She can't be left alone then, and no matter how she acts, she can never be left in a room where a fire is burning. Not a lantern, not a fire on the hearth. She nearly burned the house to the ground once before."

"When she has these bad times, you would prefer I care for her and not the house?"

"I think we'll have another cook by tonight. The blacks have a camp down the road a bit. I'll ride down after tea and see what I can stir up there. I might put my hands on some help for the house, too, if I have a piece of luck. But even without that to worry about, you'll be tempted to tie a knot in your swag and move on. There's still too much to do.''

"And when there's too much, you will help me?''

"If I'm here. But my father needs me, too.''

"Your father is not well?''

He laughed, but he sobered quickly. "As a matter of fact, sometimes he's a bit crook himself. It's an odd place you've landed, May. I wish I could say it were different.''

"Odd for me, but odd for you, as well.'' She wished she could call back the words, but they had already flown away, like honeyeaters searching for the next perfumed flower.

Bryce didn't move, even though she had to walk around him to continue cleaning. "Why did you come here? You're young and strong. I should think anyone would hire you.''

"I am Chinese. Many people would not want me for that reason alone.''

"Foolish people.''

She was surprised he thought so, but she was also growing wary of this early-morning intimacy. Her upbringing had been untraditional, even for a Chinese girl born in Australia. Still, only rarely had she been in the presence of men her own age. As Willow's daughter she had been careful to avoid the attention of crewmen from the pearling vessels. With only a little effort she could have found a lover or even a husband, but she had seen what giving her heart might do. Her mother had never recovered from Tom Robeson's death. Willow had been glad to die.

"Foolish people, perhaps,'' she answered Bryce. "But real enough, too. Now I work for you, and work hard.''

"Do you think you could stir up something for tea, then? Most of the men won't be back to the homestead until nightfall, my dad among them. But some will be riding in before that. Maybe five people all together.''

She thought with distaste of cooking a full meal in this room before cleaning it thoroughly. "And your mother?''

"With luck, she'll entertain herself today once she's up."

"Will you spare a man to help me put this to rights?"

"I'll find someone. You're a goer, aren't you?"

She had been prepared to dislike everyone attached to Jimiramira, and although she hadn't spared a thought for Bryce, now she was dismayed to feel warmth at his simple praise.

He turned away. "I'll send Henry to see what he can do in here. He's a bit deaf, so you'll have to shout. And don't worry about Mum's breakfast. She won't eat until midday."

He slipped out the door, closing it carefully behind him, but a new generation of flies slipped inside in the brief moments the door was open. She set to work without having anything to eat, the small appetite she'd awakened with having gone for good.

Henry had a beard that almost hid a toothless mouth and a habit of spitting in dark corners. But even though he grumbled continuously, he hauled away trash before he settled in with soap and water to scrub the table and hearth and bring in wood. He took a broom to the gauze as his last contribution, and when he left, the room was nearly fit to cook in.

Mei was sorry the crates destined for Jimiramira hadn't been carried to the homestead last night, but she did what she could with the supplies on hand in a Condamine safe she found in deep shade on the porch. The safe was made of galvanized steel, with wire mesh sides overhung with bags anchored in a shallow reservoir at the top. Water in the reservoir soaked the fabric, so when a breeze blew, the food was cooled.

She soaked salted beef, then chopped it for a stew, adding onions and handfuls of rice, and while that bubbled convincingly, she kneaded damper for the oven.

By the time Bryce came back, the simple meal was ready. "I'll serve the men and eat with them," he offered. "Will you take a plate up to the house for my mum?"

She hadn't had time to meet Viola Llewellyn. She hadn't even had time to consider the purpose behind everything she was doing. But now she remembered that, for her, a job well done at Jimiramira had nothing to do with how clean the kitchen was or how savory the meal. It had to do with finding one flawless pearl.

"Is your mother feeling well this day?" She ladled stew into a quart pot to carry it to the house, and cut a thick slice of the steaming damper to go with it.

"She's docile." His voice didn't change, but his expression grew sad. "You'll find she has moments when she knows what's happening and moments when she doesn't." He shrugged. "Days, actually. Today's one of them. She thinks she's back in Broome."

"Broome?" she asked, as if she had never heard of it.

"A town in the west. A pearling town like Darwin, only my father claims pearling's the only thing they do there."

"Such a great distance." Mei forced herself to look mystified as she wrapped the damper for the short trip.

"Life there was easier for a woman," he added.

She thought of her own mother's life but said nothing.

On the trip to the house, she both dreaded and anticipated meeting Archer Llewellyn's wife. Rose Garth had told her how Viola had left Broome at Archer's side, despite her father's warnings. Viola's headstrong ways and disregard for others had been a favored source of gossip during Mei's childhood. She had imagined that Archer and Viola were well matched in their selfishness and hoped they were slowly destroying each other. Now, from the few things Bryce had told her, she realized that, at least in Viola's case, the job was already done.

She let herself into the house, set the table and ladled the stew onto a chipped plate before she went in search of Bryce's mother. She found her in a bedroom at the end of the longest hallway, sitting on a stool, gazing blankly into a hand mirror.

Mei took the opportunity to study the woman who owned what should have belonged—at least in part—to Willow. Viola Llewellyn had blond hair like her son, but there the resemblance ended abruptly. Bryce was in the full thrust of youth, tall and straight, clear-eyed and smooth-skinned. His mother was stoop-shouldered and bent, her complexion that of an old woman. She stared at herself out of red-rimmed, narrowed eyes.

The room itself contained an iron bedstead, shelves for clothing and pegs on the wall for the overflow. The crude table in front of Viola's stool held a tarnished dresser set and crystal jars that were the only adornments in the room. Mei guessed that the Somerset servants in faraway Broome had finer quarters than these.

Mei spoke. "Missus, I have dinner waiting for you."

Viola was unfazed by the unfamiliar voice.

Mei entered the room to stand beside her. "Would you like me to help you dress?"

"You're always bothering me. I tell *you* when to speak."

Mei ignored the criticism obviously meant for someone in Viola's past. "Let me brush your hair."

Viola finally looked up from her reflection. "I suppose." Her voice wavered with the cadence of age, as if all traces of youth had fled. Mei was stung with pity, which she immediately banished. No one had forced Viola to marry a murderer or come to this desolate prison in the Northern Territory.

Mei lifted the hairbrush from the table and removed the few pins holding Viola's hair. It fell to her shoulders, thin and lifeless. Mei remembered brushing her own mother's hair. Willow's hair had been silky and strong, even as her body weakened with illness.

Viola closed her eyes, as if she enjoyed this pampering. "What shall I wear, Susan?"

Mei wondered if, back in Broome, a stranger named Susan would relish knowing that Viola believed Susan was still with her. "You are already dressed for dinner, missus."

Viola ignored her. "The blue or the gold? My father dislikes me in gold. Perhaps I'll choose that."

Mei was learning quickly. "You are already wearing that dress, missus."

Viola looked down at the shapeless brown dress that badly needed washing and mending. "So I am."

Mei twisted Viola's hair on top of her head and anchored it

with hairpins, adding a mother-of-pearl comb she found on the table. "Much better."

Viola lifted her chin. "You're good with hair, if not with anything else."

Mei was feeling increasingly sorry for Susan. "Shall we find your shoes?"

"Don't be all day."

Mei found shoes beside the bed, scuffed leather shoes that had to be painstakingly fastened with a button hook. When Viola was ready, Mei helped her to her feet, and, arm in arm, as if Mei had now assumed the identity of some former suitor, they walked through the hallway to the dining room.

Mei took one look at the table and closed her eyes. The plate she had carefully filled was covered with flies. Even the damper was black with them.

Viola eyed the table with interest. "I like nothing better than a roast of lamb." She seated herself, gazing across the table as if she was at a dinner party. The flies lifted in a foul cloud and found homes on the ceiling. Viola picked up her fork and began to eat.

Viola napped in the afternoon, and Mei began the arduous task of putting the house to rights. An hour later Bryce appeared with two young Aboriginal women, Emma and Sally, whose real given names were something more musical and fitting.

"Emma will do the laundry," Bryce told Mei. "And Sally claims she's an ace cook. She's helped out here before, so I'm willing to give her a go if you are."

Mei realized she was now in charge. Although Viola should be the one to supervise everyone attached to the household, obviously that was impossible. The two women seemed affable enough, smiling shyly at Mei. "Thank you," she told them.

Together the three women stripped the beds, and Mei helped Emma carry the tattered bed linens to the billabong, which clearly served as the homestead laundry. Sally followed Mei out to the kitchen, and with a mixture of gestures and simple English, they communicated well enough to plan supper.

When Mei emerged, Bryce was lounging against a gum tree just outside the kitchen, idly stripping strings of bark and curling them around one finger. "When my father comes back, he'll be bringing Larry, the camp cook. If Sally can manage tonight, the two of them can work together when the men are here at the homestead."

She thought what a striking man Bryce was. Lithe and graceful in a wholly masculine way, he possessed all the virtues of youth. But while most men seemed anxious to parade their assets, Bryce did nothing to draw attention to himself. He wasn't ill at ease, but he seemed to have little sense of his own charm.

"She works hard," Mei said. "And Emma, too."

"I'd advise against having them in the house more often than necessary. Mum's not fond of the blacks. She went after one of the stockmen with a knife."

He looked up at his own words, as if he had just realized how frightening they sounded. "Usually we keep knives away from her, of course, only that time we missed it. She found the knife out in the yards somewhere, I suppose. She takes to prowling at night sometimes. I try to watch out for her, but I have a lot to see to." He paused. "And she's crafty. She'll pretend to be asleep...."

Mei nodded. "Has she always been like this?"

His face was shadowed. "Always? I don't know."

She knew better than to ask too many questions, but understanding the Llewellyn family was vital if she was going to steal back the pearl. She decided to invent a story to make her point. "There is a man in Darwin, a Chinese man. Very smart. Everyone goes to see him to get answers to questions. Then one day, his wife steps into the street and, as he watches, she is killed by a team of horses. And after that, he is much like your mother. He talks to her as if she is right there, not a spirit person, but real, like me, like you."

Bryce seemed fascinated. "Go on...."

"Well, it was seeing something so terrible that did this. Do you understand? I only wondered if perhaps the same was true for your mother."

He was quiet for a moment, as if he were turning this over in his mind. Finally he said, "She had a different sort of life in Broome."

"You've been to this place, Broome?"

"No. I don't know any place but this."

His world had been so narrow. How could he tell her what had turned his mother mad? To whom could he compare Viola? Perhaps he didn't even understand how strangely she behaved.

She began his education. "This life is hard for a woman."

"Jimiramira? I suppose it is."

"And what does she have to comfort her?" She hesitated, and when he didn't answer, she went on. "No pretty things here. Maybe she closes her eyes to things she does not want to see?"

"We have drought one year, floods the next. You can't fence land this vast, so duffers and roaming blacks pick off the cows that roam the boundaries. Malaria's a worry, barcoo picks off a man now and then." His lips twisted into a wry grin. "Those are the good times, I reckon. Those *are* the pretty things, but maybe Mum just doesn't see them."

Mei had to respect his sense of humor. Obviously he had retained it at great cost. She tried once more. "Maybe there is something she loves, something she looks at or hears or smells or tastes, so that she says, 'This is good. Life is not as bad as I thought'?"

His expression warmed. "It's right good of you to care so much already. Nobody has but me, you know, not in a long, long time."

She wondered if he realized how much that said about his father. "I must go back and see if she still sleeps."

"When it's cooler tonight, I'll take you for a stroll and show you all the things around the homestead you haven't seen."

She wondered about that as the afternoon progressed and she wiped furniture and floor with dampened strips of hessian to remove the layers of dust. She had not gone far beyond the kitchen, just down to the billabong with Emma, who had hung the newly washed bed linen on a line and removed herself once more, this time with a load of Viola's dresses and underthings and Bryce's shirts. Mei wanted to explore every square inch of the homestead proper and some of the land beyond, as well.

She was sweating before she had finished the parlor and dining room, and drenched by the time she started on the bedrooms. Her own room was tiny, airless and off to one side of the house, as if the space had been planned for storage. She ignored it, beginning with the rooms used by the family instead. Since Viola was still sleeping, she opened the door to Bryce's bedroom. Unlike anything else in the house, it was clean and in perfect order. There was nothing for her to do there, but she paused in this pristine oasis and inhaled. Bryce's smell, a mixture of worn leather, sweat and tobacco, pervaded the room. It was subtly masculine and oddly comforting.

She closed the door behind her and turned to find herself staring into the hard blue eyes of an older man. "I suppose you were the best Stuart Sayers could come up with? The man's a fucking idiot."

She needed no introduction. For one insane moment she wondered what Bryce's father would say if she told him who she really was. "I am sorry, but I was the only one who would come," she said evenly. "I will do my best to make you glad he sent me." She lowered her eyes as if in respect.

"Christ, a Chink. Just what we need. As if the blacks aren't bad enough."

She kept her eyes downcast and wondered how her father—at least, the saintly man portrayed by her mother—could ever have been friends with Archer Llewellyn.

"May's already worked miracles, Dad."

Mei looked up to see Bryce coming down the hall. He wasn't smiling, and he walked stiffly, like a man approaching a bucking horse. "She's worked harder in one day than the last couple did in weeks."

Archer ignored his son and questioned Mei. "What have you done? And I want it all, straight-up!"

She listed the chores she had completed.

"Where's your mother?" Archer snapped without turning his head to look at Bryce.

"Mrs. Llewellyn is sleeping," Mei answered for him. "I kept watch over her today."

Archer was silent. Mei felt no fear. Even if he sent her away, it would take time to make the arrangements. Finally he turned to his son. "You stay clear of this girl, do you understand me? I saw one good man ruined by a girl just like her. I won't tolerate another." He moved away, boot heels clacking sharply on the ant-bed floor.

Bryce's cheeks were flushed with embarrassment. His eyes sought Mei's forgiveness, but he had the presence of mind not to ask for it and humiliate them both.

She turned away, curiously exultant. She knew exactly who Archer had been talking about. She hadn't expected to remind Archer of her mother. She didn't really resemble Willow, whose beauty had been extraordinary, but Archer had seen Willow in her anyway. He did not suspect Mei's identity, but perhaps he knew, somewhere deep in whatever remained of his conscience, that she had come to Jimiramira to make his life intolerable.

She had done good work today. She had never been more certain that coming to Jimiramira was her destiny.

16

The stroll around the homestead did not materialize that evening, nor for the next week. Bryce was sent to carry mail and supplies to one of the mustering camps, and Archer stayed behind to keep an eye on both Mei and Viola.

Mei hoped this would be an opportunity to observe her father's murderer up close, but she saw little of him, since he seemed to detest his wife. She continued putting the house to rights, supervising Emma and her sister, Millie, who began, under Mei's tutelage, to put some of the outbuildings in order.

Mei and Millie discovered a chicken house with more roosters than hens and stoically wrung the necks of most of them to spare grain for a biddy, who was trying to hatch a much-needed flock. Surprisingly, Henry came up to the house every morning to ask for a list of chores for the day, and, with his help, the smokehouse was scrubbed clean.

Larry—a shortened version of "that old larrikin"—turned out to be an exacting cook and tolerant of Sally's assistance, so the meals improved as the week passed, particularly with the sudden influx of stewing chickens and the supplies that had been brought in from Darwin.

Mei spent much of her time tending Viola. After some difficulty they established a routine that included a bath and fresh clothes each day, and Mei even convinced her that taking a walk in the mornings was good for her health. On the afternoon of the first bone-jarring thunderstorm of the Wet, Viola watched from the veranda, her eyes flashing as the lightning did, as if, finally, something had broken through her imaginary world.

"I hate the Wet most of all.'·

Mei, who was startled at the surprising venom in Viola's voice, watched her. "Do the storms frighten you?"

"The thunder is God's voice."

Mei hadn't suspected God was a part of the Llewellyns' world.

"He's angry, of course," Viola continued. "As if I haven't paid dearly enough."

"Why is he angry?"

"I was supposed to marry poor little Freddy Colson. And now he's shouting at me."

"God is shouting?"

"No, you fool. My father."

Mei tried to put that together in her mind. The thunder. The deity. The father. "Perhaps the thunder is nothing more than nature, missus, and it has nothing to do with you at all."

Viola gave her a sharp glance. "Everything has to do with me."

The rain continued through the night, until Mei worried that Bryce might not return. The billabong, which had been at low ebb, rose quickly. And although the Victoria River was many miles away, Henry told her it was rising, too, overflowing into dry tributaries and isolating cattle that hadn't been moved to higher ground. The land was too parched to absorb water, so like a thirsty man whose tongue is too swollen to drink, the land rejected the rain, banishing it to basins and hollows, which overflowed in their turn to cut new channels through the land.

Archer found her the next morning before dawn, as she sat in the kitchen with Larry and Sally, having her breakfast. "You. Come out here." He stepped out to the narrow veranda facing the house.

She obeyed, brushing crumbs from her dark skirt as she joined him. He wore an unfastened oilskin coat over a blue shirt and ragged moleskins. His haggard face wore a frown. Archer's eyes were slits in a leathery face, and his mouth twisted cynically even in repose.

He didn't waste time. "Can you be trusted to look after my wife?"

She didn't point out that she had been doing exactly that since his return. To her knowledge, Archer hadn't even slept in the house, preferring a bed in the men's quarters and meals in their dining room. "I can."

"She's not right in her head."

Mei wondered if he thought she was such a galah she hadn't taken note of this.

He didn't wait for an answer. "I'm not crazy about leaving you here, but I don't have any choice. There's too much going on for me to stay home. I'm riding out this morning."

"I will see to things."

He narrowed his eyes still further. "That's why you're paid, isn't it?" Satisfied he'd made a point, he went on. "Your English is good. Where did you learn it?"

"I was born in Darwin. I speak English all my life."

"Are both your parents Chinese?"

She had wondered if Archer would ever look closely at her and ask this question, and she gave him the explanation she had invented. "Yes, but one of my grandmothers was an English missionary."

"Well, we won't have anything of that kind here. You want a husband, you can find a Chinese man in Darwin."

She searched for something good in him, something that would make sense of his friendship with her father. "I know you worry about your missus, and this is why you speak sharply to me."

He stared at her. "If you want the truth, girl, I'm worried about my missus burning down the house and starting a bushfire. I don't care one bit what happens to her. And I won't be responsible for what happens to *you* if you ever bat those pretty almond eyes at my son or any of my men. Or if you steal anything that belongs to me."

She did not avert her pretty almond eyes. "Do you have instructions for the days you are gone?"

"I just gave them to you." He wrapped his oilskin coat tightly around himself, pulled a battered leather hat lower over his forehead and stepped into the rain.

That morning she began her search for the pearl. She had already looked in the most obvious places. The pearl had never been mentioned by anyone, not even Viola, who revealed odd, disjointed bits of information in every conversation. Mei wasn't certain the Pearl of Great Price existed any longer. Even Archer hadn't mentioned it as a reason to keep his wife alive. But he *was* concerned about house fires. She wondered if at least part of his fear had to do with a valuable object secreted somewhere in the shabby rooms.

The search was not as easy as it might have been if the house were sound. As it was, there were a million potential hiding places between boards and ripple iron. There were cracks in plaster and beams under attack from white ants. She began in Viola's bedroom while Viola ate a solitary meal, painstakingly investigating every crevice, every suspicious projection. Later in the afternoon, she continued as Viola sat on the veranda, watching another storm blow in. She stripped the bed to wash the linen and used the opportunity to thoroughly examine the kapok mattress and the rusting springs that held it in place. None of the tears in the cover yielded a pearl.

By the end of the afternoon, no surface in the room was unexplored. She joined Viola as the storm waned, contemplating ways to hint at the subject of the pearl, but Viola's mind was like a ball of yarn that had slowly unraveled. Perhaps the core was still intact, but tugging at it might only tangle it further.

"It was raining when we first saw this place," Viola said out of nowhere. Her voice was a monotone, like a schoolchild doing her first recitation.

"Was it?"

"Torrents. The river had flooded its banks and crept nearly

this far. If we had been a week later, we might have drowned. I should have liked that better.''

Mei was afraid to speak, afraid she might disrupt Viola's reminiscences.

Viola went on without coaxing. ''There was no house, just a bark hut and a humpy made of tin for supplies. I had understood that things would be primitive at first, but I thought there would be a house, you see. And I hadn't understood about the insects or the blacks or how far we would be from civilization. By then, of course, I couldn't go back.''

''Couldn't you?''

''The land was all I had. I had even sold my jewelry to buy supplies.''

Mei stopped breathing. Viola had sold her jewelry. She had sold the pearl to buy blankets and tinned food and ammunition? She closed her eyes. She had come for nothing.

''Well, I did have something else,'' Viola said slyly. ''But, of course, I couldn't sell anything so fine.''

Mei didn't move. She waited, but Viola had finished.

Finally Mei took a breath. ''Some things are so fine we must keep them close to our hearts.''

''What would you know about that?'' Viola tossed her head. ''You have *never* owned anything as fine as my pearl.''

Mei didn't show any emotion. ''Of course I haven't, missus.''

''And close to my heart?'' Viola began to rock back and forth with a terrible cackling laughter. ''Now wouldn't that be the first place my husband searched for it?''

Mei was afraid Viola was sinking back into her imaginary world. The older woman's laughter rose in pitch, an eerie descant soaring high above the rain. ''No, of course you are more clever than that,'' Mei said desperately. ''You would have chosen a better place.''

''I...have...chosen...many!'' Viola rocked back and forth. ''So very, very many!''

''How can you ever remember where you put it last?''

But Viola only rocked, trapped by her own laughter until she was sobbing uncontrollably. Mei, torn between quieting her mistress and shaking the truth out of her, finally took Viola's hands in hers and led her back inside. On the bed that Mei had explored so thoroughly, Viola cried herself to sleep.

After two more days of futile searching and no further revelations by Viola, Bryce and Archer rode into the homestead together, along with a handful of muddy stockmen who looked as if they had camped for weeks in the middle of a stampede. Together, working with half a dozen cattle dogs, they drove their mob into the yard closest to the house, then headed to their quarters to wash and change for tea. Since no one had known to expect them, Mei left a sleeping Viola at the house and went down to the kitchen to lend a hand to Larry and Sally, who were about to reenact the biblical story of the loaves and fishes.

Bryce found her there. She was slicing fresh bread Larry had prepared that morning into wafer-thin slivers as Larry cursed colorfully in the background.

Bryce strolled in, spurs clanking, and removed his hat, a touchingly gentlemanly gesture under the circumstances. "How've you been, May?"

Mei gazed up at him, and her heart expanded in her chest. Bryce's hair was wet, his cheeks shaven and scrubbed clean. The glow of good health and high spirits seemed to light him from the inside. His smile was white and warm, and she found herself smiling back. "I am fine. And you?"

"Nothing to whine over, although if I'd a mind to, I could say a thing or two about the weather."

She wasn't really listening to his words, she was absorbing everything about him. The rumbling melody of his voice, the way his hair darkened to brown when it was wet, the glisten of water droplets on his eyelashes. He was wearing a clean plaid shirt, threadbare at the cuffs and collar, but stretched across his chest. She liked the way his tattered moleskins clung to his thighs and calves and tapered at his ankles, and the way he rested on the balls of his feet, as if he were set to fling himself at life.

She liked everything about him, this man who was the son of her father's murderer.

Immediately she averted her eyes. "We did not expect you. We have less food than we should."

"We couldn't spare a man to ride ahead. I'm sorry, May."

She continued slicing the bread without looking up again, but she knew Bryce remained there watching her.

"How was my mother?"

"We have good walks each morning, and she eats well." She wished she had more happy news to tell him. Viola was a sad, infuriating creature, but this young man loved her.

"She's still sleeping. I checked on her before I came down here," he said.

"Emma is ironing, and she promised to tell me if your mother awoke."

"You shouldn't have been left with the full burden."

She realized he was criticizing Archer. She wondered what Bryce really thought of his father. "We have rubbed along together, your mother and I, although the rain makes her sadder."

"You're like a gift that dropped out of the sky, May. I can't remember what we did when you weren't here to manage things." He turned and left, and she was sorry to see him go, although she wondered what he would think if he knew her real purpose for coming.

She finished helping Larry and Sally put together a meal, then she took a portion back up to the house. Bryce had already awakened his mother, and even Archer, who usually ate with the men, was waiting in the dining room.

She served them all silently, careful not to meet Bryce's eyes in his father's presence, then she took the pots back to the kitchen to be washed. By the time she returned, Viola was on the veranda with her son, and Archer had disappeared.

"I could stay with her," Mei offered. Viola was staring blankly at clouds forming overhead. The air around them seethed with the oncoming storm, and Mei could feel sweat beading on her brow and running along her spine.

"We never took that walk together, you and I," Bryce said.

She was sure Archer had given his son the same speech that he had given her, so there was no sense in reminding Bryce that his father disapproved of them spending time together. "I have seen every bit by now. I hardly need a tour."

"I bet there are things you haven't seen."

Viola closed her eyes and began to hum tunelessly.

"Tell me about Darwin," Bryce said. "Make me see it."

She heard a hunger for new sights and places in his voice. She wondered if Bryce stayed at Jimiramira because of Viola, or because the place was in his blood. She told him what she remembered, and because she had seen it through the eyes of a stranger, she could easily describe the most colorful sights.

"What about your family, May?"

She gave a carefully rehearsed reply. "My father died in the war, and my mother died when I was young. The old people in my family all went back to China, but I wanted to stay here."

"We're alike, you and me, aren't we? Trying to hold on to something when it would be easier by half just to grease our saddle straps and move on."

He thought she was trying to hang on to her citizenship, even though Australia had instituted a whites-only policy just after her birth. But she wondered what he was trying to hold on to. Jimiramira? His pathetic little family?

"We'll take that walk tonight." He rose. "It's a dead bird my dad won't like it, but no worries. I'll call for you when the moment's right."

He started off in the direction of the billabong. Viola stopped humming and began to speak, her voice low, as if she were sharing a secret. "Once I hid the pearl in Bryce's room, in a little tin cup with colored stones he'd taken from a trip to the river. We used to go down to the river, he and I, on horseback. When he was little. But not anymore." She shook her head in emphasis. "Now there are people waiting along the bank to push me in, but that would be wrong, wouldn't it? I'm to burn until I am nothing but ashes and cinders.''

Mei shuddered. Such talk was bad luck, as if Viola were asking for her own death. "Did Bryce discover the pearl in the cup?''

"Oh, it wasn't there for long." Viola began to hum again.

"Your husband found it?''

Viola stopped humming and faced Mei. "The pearl belongs to me.''

Mei nodded. She waited, not daring to breathe.

"And when I burn, it will burn with me." Viola stared at Mei for a long time; then, as if finally satisfied, she turned away and began to hum once more.

After the evening meal, Mei discovered why Bryce had felt confident enough to invite her for a walk. The skies had cleared, but the earlier storm had left the air steaming and fuming with insects, which multiplied with every drop of rain. The atmosphere at the house, always tense, heated with the air, and even the sun's slow departure did little to help. Archer began to drink, sprawling on a lone horsehair chair in the parlor as he stared at the piano with its recently dusted row of photographs.

He caught sight of Mei and called her in to face him. "D'ya see that piano?''

"Yes, boss.''

"Dragged it all the way from Katherine in a cart.''

"Did you?''

"Not me, stupid girl. I have better things to do.''

She knew there was nothing she could say that would please him tonight. "Yes, boss.''

"I had it brought here to please Mrs. Llewellyn. Do you think she was pleased?''

"I do not know.''

"Well, have you seen her pleased about anything since you arrived?''

"It is not for me to say what pleases Mrs. Llewellyn.''

"Do you have any idea what it was like trying to drag that piano through the bush?"

"No, boss."

He shook his head, as if, despite his disclaimer, he had inched the piano along what passed for a trail by himself. "All she could say was 'I don't want it.' Can you fancy that?"

This time Mei said nothing.

Archer rhythmically swung a bottle of rum in one hand, like the pendulum on a clock. She suspected the bottle had come with the supplies Bluey had delivered. It was already half empty. She wondered if a man could die from drinking too much too quickly. The possibility gave her pleasure.

"Do you play the piano?" He stopped brandishing the bottle long enough to gulp down another swallow.

"No, boss." She might have, of course, if he had not murdered her father. Certainly her life would have been very different.

"Do you sing?"

"No."

"Dance?"

"No, boss. May I go now?"

His eyes narrowed further, as if he were considering what to do with her. She wasn't frightened. For a moment she almost hoped he would try to grab her. He was strong and much larger than she was, but he was also drunk. If they struggled, she might be able to break the bottle and wound him with it. The fantasy gave her such pleasure that she found herself gazing about the room for other weapons so she could imagine attacking him with those, as well.

"Go on and get out of here." He leaned back in the chair and closed his eyes. "I wasn't the one who took a Chink to my bed. That was you, Tom. I told you not to, but you didn't listen, did you?"

Mei froze. She didn't even breathe.

"Why didn't you listen?" Archer's voice changed into something closer to a whine. "If you had listened...everything would have been different."

She felt as if she had fallen down a secret passage into the past. Archer was speaking to her father as if he were standing right there in front of him. Her gaze darted around the room, fearing, yet hoping, that in this strange moment, she too would see Tom Robeson.

Her own lapse in sanity brought her back to reality, and fury filled her. Archer Llewellyn had known her father, had slept in the same room with him, shared meals and stories. But he had not valued any of it, while she would give everything for one hour at her father's knee.

The father she had never seen or known. The father this man had murdered.

She felt hands on her shoulders, and she whirled around, startled. Bryce stood just inches away, and when she acknowledged him, he nodded toward the door. She followed him. Archer took no notice of either of them.

"Are you all right?" Bryce asked, when they were in the hallway nearest her room.

She swallowed. "He's had too much to drink. He began asking questions..."

Bryce looked distressed. "Please, it's not your fault. I should have warned you. He does this every time we get fresh supplies. Thank God they never send much. He knows better than to ask for more. He suffers the torment of the damned when he's drinking."

She wished she could lock Archer Llewellyn in a room with all the liquor in the Territory. She wished she could watch him suffer the torments of hell until the drink finally killed him and sent him there.

"He was speaking to someone named Tom."

"May, he's no good to gundy when he's drinking. It's the devil's own job to make sense of anything he says."

"He said everything would be different if Tom had just listened to him..."

Bryce plowed his fingers through his hair. "It's no one I know, but you're right, he talks to someone named Tom whenever he's in a bad way. They were friends, I think. Then Tom died. And Dad wishes he could have stopped it from happening."

He could have, of course. But Mei couldn't tell Bryce that.

"It gets worse," Bryce said, looking away. "Before long he'll start begging for forgiveness."

She was torn with conflicting feelings. She was elated Archer was tortured by guilt, that in some small way he suffered for what he had done. But she had no such feelings about Bryce. Two selfish, worthless people were all Bryce had in the world, and she wondered how he had turned into the man he was. Reluctantly, she felt compassion for the loveless life he had led.

"Let's take that walk now." Mei rested her hand on his arm. "Unless you think he will want you...?"

"No, he's fast reaching a place where he won't even know who I am."

"Will your mother be safe alone with him?"

"She's sound asleep. I looked in on her a moment ago. She'll be all right for a little while."

Mei led the way outside. She was certain they would be eaten by mosquitoes, but now that the darkness had deepened, the insects were not as fierce as she had expected. She was surprised to see that the moon was full, spreading light in silvery puddles on ground quickly growing lush in the Wet. Overhead, the Southern Cross was nearly lost in a sky filled with stars.

"We won't go far," Bryce said. "But there's something I've been waiting to show you. I think it's light enough to find it."

They left the cleared ground surrounding the house and started through the thicket of bush and trees that separated the house from the billabong. She knew they could not be going that far, since the denser the growth, the greater the possibility of snakes, which became more active at night.

"You'll have to trust me," Bryce said. "I know where I'm going."

They walked farther than she had expected. The trees grew sparser, then thicker once more. She stumbled over a fallen branch, and Bryce caught her arm. He tucked it under his. "You'll be safer this way."

She laughed, a sound that surprised them both. But she knew that when a man took a woman's arm, he usually had more than protection on his mind. "Exactly where are we going?"

"Just a little farther, I promise."

"Your father would not be pleased."

"My father is a poor judge of what's right."

She wished she could encourage him to elaborate on that. Bryce tucked her hand into his. "He's not a happy man. He'll never be happy, I reckon."

"And his son?"

"I have everything." He glanced at her and grinned. "Except a woman to make my own family with. I could be a better father than mine, you know. I know something about what children need."

She didn't know how to respond to that. She hadn't allowed herself to think about Bryce in that way, despite the feelings she experienced when he was near. But now she imagined being married to him and living as the mistress of this place.

What would it be like if Archer and Viola weren't here, and if Jimiramira belonged to her young, strong husband? Could she raise children with Llewellyn blood? Would that make her a traitor to her parents? Or would it be enough that at last the Pearl of Great Price belonged equally to the two families who claimed it?

The picture of a small boy came into her mind. Not Bryce, as he must have appeared as a child, but Thomas, the twin who had been torn from her childish arms and sent across the sea. Thomas, who must yearn for her as she yearned for him.

"All right. Stop now, and tell me what you see."

She had been so deep in thought that she hadn't realized they were at the edge of another thicket. She peered into the darkness, trying to make sense of the shapes. Ahead of her were tormented trunks of ironbark and mulga, their branches pleading with the skies for water. She shuddered, beset by ghosts.

"May, is something wrong?"

She tried to shake off her fears. "What am I supposed to see?"

"Well, do you notice anything over there? We can get a bit closer." He led her to the right about twenty yards, and they stopped again. "Now?"

She squinted, looking up and down. The only thing she saw was an odd structure at the base of two trees. It was several feet long and nearly as wide, constructed of odd bits of twig. She wondered if this was what the fuss was about. "What is it? The lair of an animal?"

"Not spot on. Do you know the bowerbird?"

She shook her head.

"You'll hear one singing around the homestead. A big spotted fellow with a bit of color at the back of his neck. He's a mimic, that one. He can low like the cattle, bark like a dog. I reckon I could teach him to talk if I wanted."

"Is this his nest?"

"No, it's better. This is where he entertains his lady friends."

She glanced at him to see if he was teasing.

"No, I swear. That's what he does. He builds this bower, then he decorates it with whatever he can find. I've seen bits of bone and snail shell, a length of ribbon. Once I found a button and even a piece of some poor bloke's comb. He'll use whatever he finds that might attract a mate."

She was enchanted with the bird's creativity. "And this is all? He lures a female here and shows her what he's done?"

"Well, he's just a bird, for all that. He can't rightly pledge eternal love, can he? This is the best he can do. But it's quite a lot for a scrawny mob of feathers, don't you think?"

She giggled. "Do they live here, then? Raise baby birds together?"

"If you want the truth, I think she builds a nest in a tree and raises the family alone."

"I suppose he is too busy flying off to look for pretty bits to add to his bower."

"It's his lifework, after all."

"This is the way of most families, isn't it?" She slipped her arm from his so she could face him. In the moonlight his expression was both watchful and somehow tender.

"What do you mean?"

"The man builds something to show a woman he has chosen. Then, when she marries him, he moves on with his life. She stays behind and raises the children alone." She thought of the little bungalow that her father had rented and furnished for her mother. Like the female bowerbird, Willow had been left alone to care for their children.

"That's not the way of things here in the Territory," Bryce said. "Here a woman and man can work together, if that's what they choose. They can build a life side by side. They have to, if anything is to come of it."

"This is not what your parents do."

"My father and mother haven't built a life, and they haven't made a home. The land is harsh. It destroyed Mum, and it's made my father bitter and old. But I know it would have been different if they had pulled together."

He looked as if he wanted to say more. She waited, leaning toward him as if she could pull the rest from him.

"Something came between them, right at the beginning," he said at last, as if the need to share his feelings was more important than caution. "I have a grandfather in Broome. He gave my mum a gift when she married my father, something valuable. My father wanted it. He planned to sell it, to make their life easier, to buy more cattle and hire more men. But my mother wouldn't allow it. She wanted to keep it. At first it was her security, in case things didn't work out here. So she hid it. Later, I think she wouldn't part with it because it was all she had of a better life."

"This was not something your father could take and sell without her permission?"

Bryce didn't object to the possibility his father would do such a thing. "No, it's something small, and that makes it easy to hide. She's always hidden it from him. I found it by mistake once, when I was a tiddler. She very nearly wrung my neck.''

Whatever compassion Mei had felt for Viola vanished. ''She keeps it still?'' The rest of her sentence went unfinished, but she was sure he heard it. *Despite the fact she's lost her mind?*

''I can't say. My father doesn't have it, that's a dead cert. If he did, I think he'd bloody well send her off to hospital somewhere, and that would be that, wouldn't it?''

There was bitterness in his voice, and a certain fatalism. He was so accustomed to the rift between Viola and Archer that he probably knew there was no hope for anything better.

If Mei had come to Jimiramira for revenge alone, it had just been handed to her. The Pearl of Great Price hadn't brought happiness to Archer. It had nearly destroyed him and the woman he'd married. The pearl had sought its own revenge. But she hadn't come for revenge alone. She had come because of Thomas.

''This is difficult for you,'' she said. ''You must worry that your father will find this thing of value.''

''He looks for it every chance he gets. I've seen him. But Mum was always clever in an odd sort of way. Despite…'' He shook his head. ''In the past, she always hid it well. Now I'm not certain even *she* knows where it is. She moved it and moved it, until she may not remember the last place she put it.''

''This is very sad for you.''

He reached out and took her hand. His was large and tanned. Hers was paler and delicate, despite the hard work she did. ''I've gone on and on, haven't I? I shouldn't have burdened you.''

''You have helped me know your mother.''

''Well, I brought you here to see the bower. If the sun was shining, you'd have a better view of all his decorations. I'll bring you back someday, and we can see what he's been up to.'' He squeezed her hand.

''Your father is not happy when I am in your company.''

''My father is not happy about anything, May.''

"He is your father, and you must do as he tells you."

He tugged at her hand, a faint but discernible pressure. "Do you really believe that?"

"In China, children do as their parents say."

"Have you ever been to China?"

She shook her head.

"Then you're not Chinese, are you? You're an Australian, just like me."

"Not just like you."

"No, and I'm glad. The things that are different are what I like best."

She could feel her cheeks growing warmer. Bryce was looking at her as if she was someone important. But he didn't see the woman who had come to steal from his family.

"Is there a man waiting for you in Darwin?" He tugged her a little closer.

She concocted wild stories in the seconds while he waited for an answer, but in the end, she couldn't lie. "It is not right for you to care about a Chinese woman."

"I don't. I care about an Australian."

"Others will not see it that way."

"What others? How many others do you see out here? How many women are willing to come out to this country and try their luck, May? You're one in a million. And does it matter where people's mothers and fathers came from when they're battling the plagues of fortune? Men out here take Aboriginal wives, and some of them even marry in Christian ceremonies. If you wanted me and I wanted you, who would stop us?"

"Your father."

"He can be damned."

"He might send you away."

"No, I'm the only son he has."

She thought long and well about her next words. "He is a man who will do anything to have his way."

"He might be angry, May, but he wouldn't harm either of us."

She knew better. Archer would kill her without thinking

twice if he realized Bryce was falling in love with her. "You must promise you will not tell your father any of what you have told me."

"You're afraid of him, aren't you?"

"He is your father. But he is not mine."

"I promise, but I'll keep you safe, May."

"We must go back to the house now."

"Must we?"

She knew she must go to preserve her own safety. No matter what Bryce said, if he continued feeling as he did, Archer would sense it. Nothing good could come of this.

But she couldn't insist that her own hands drop to her sides when what they wanted was to reach for Bryce, to flutter along his shoulders until they caressed the contours of his throat. And she couldn't insist that her lips speak the words that would free her from his attentions when they wanted only to kiss him.

This was the son of Archer Llewellyn, but his sad and lonely heart cried out to the sad and lonely heart of Tom Robeson's daughter.

She went into his arms and felt his lips warm and hard against hers. And for that brief ecstatic moment, she and Bryce were the only two people in the world.

17

The next morning, as if he suspected the attraction that had developed between Mei and Bryce, Archer sent his son with some of the other stockmen to ride the eastern boundaries. Archer said nothing of his suspicions, and she decided that his life was so much easier since she had come to Jimiramira that he was—temporarily, at least—reluctant to send her away.

Several days later Archer left, too, and she was alone with Viola and maddening swarms of insects that gloried in the sweat-drenched air. Dust was no longer a problem, but dampness seeped through every opening, and mold and mildew bloomed. She dragged herself through chores and used what energy was left to search unsuccessfully for the Pearl of Great Price.

The futility of her mission struck her on the third night after Archer's departure. She had draped a portion of the back veranda with netting and dragged mattresses outside so she and Viola could sleep where there might be a breeze. The nights, like the days, were sweltering, and although the veranda was better than the house, fear of the darkness kept Viola awake.

"The devil's calling me!" Viola bolted up, her eyes wide in the moonlight.

The devil was a boobook owl, screeching his haunting "mopoke" into the outback night.

"Hush," Mei murmured. "Go to sleep, missus."

Dogs barking at the men's quarters became the hounds of hell. Giant moths landing on the net turned into winged fiends coming to carry Viola away.

"I'm right here," Mei soothed over and over, like a lullaby. "I'll take care of you."

When at last Viola fell into a troubled sleep, Mei lay with her hands beneath her head and gazed at the Southern Cross. On their walk, Bryce had told her that late at night, the stockmen marked time by waiting for the cross to turn over. She suspected the hour when it would tilt from the east to the west was coming soon, but what did it matter? Like every other day, today she had learned nothing that would help her find the pearl.

The task was impossible. She could methodically search every inch of Jimiramira, but while she was searching, Viola might remove the pearl from its hiding place and hide it somewhere Mei had already looked. The game could continue forever, with Viola always one step ahead of her.

She closed her eyes and turned to her side, shutting out the stars. With eyes closed, she tried to pretend she was in cool San Francisco with Thomas, who told her he had never wanted anything but to be reunited with her. Together they would begin a new life that would bring honor to their parents.

The vision, which normally comforted her, wouldn't come tonight. Instead she pictured Bryce, just before he'd kissed her. His smile had been eager and worried, and when he had crushed her in his arms, she had never wanted to leave them.

She berated herself for losing sight of her goal, for preferring a murderer's son to her brother, but Bryce was real, and Thomas was a shadow. She opened her eyes, and that was when she saw Viola slowly, noiselessly sitting up.

Mei said nothing, hoping that Viola would lie down and fall back asleep without making another fuss. But if Viola had any lingering fears of the darkness, now they didn't matter. She peered over the railing, then in Mei's direction. Mei quickly closed her eyes and didn't open them again until she heard Viola move away from the mattress. Then she peeked through her lashes to see Viola moving stealthily toward a corner of the netting.

Viola lifted the net and, with surprising grace, slithered under it. Mei waited until Viola had entered the house before she followed, showing the same care Viola had not to make noise or give herself away.

The interior of the house was hot enough to make Mei catch her breath. She could see little, the contours of chairs, the length of a table, the outline of last year's calendar on one unplastered wall. She waited, hardly daring to ease her body into a better position, as she listened and watched for Viola.

A minute passed, then two. Just when she was beginning to think she would be forced to search, she heard a noise in the hall. She crept across the room to stand beside the doorway, just in time to see Viola slipping into Bryce's bedroom. She followed her and watched as Viola, oblivious to her presence, tilted a small table in the corner and felt along one leg.

Apparently the search was successful. Viola found something and held it close to her chest, crooning tunelessly for a moment before she righted the table.

Mei's heart beat faster. Whatever Viola had retrieved was small enough to have been easily hidden somewhere between the table leg and primitive claw foot, but the object could be as large as the Pearl of Great Price. She told herself Viola was crazy and might have retrieved nothing more than a nail or a splinter. But hope climbed inside her, wild ecstatic hope that her journey to Jimiramira had been for something after all.

When Viola started toward the door, Mei melted into an empty room across the hall, praying Viola had a different destination in mind. She watched as Viola started back the way she had come, and when it was safe, she trailed her. For a moment she was afraid Viola would return to the rear veranda and see she was missing. But Viola turned toward the front of the house and quietly slipped out the door.

Mei watched from a window until Viola stepped off the veranda. With her pale hair and white gown she was a ghostlike vision in the sultry darkness. Mei headed toward the door and

followed, trying desperately to stay in the shadows as she kept
Viola in sight. Somewhere in the distance thunder rattled softly
like the initial warning growl of a watchdog, but Viola ignored
it, moving steadily farther away.

Mei hid as best she could, but all the trees had been cleared
from the vicinity of the house for fear of bushfires. She stayed
in the shadow of the veranda until she was forced to dart to
the first row of trees. Viola was far ahead of her and paid no
attention to anything except her own quest. At last she slowed,
then stopped.

Mei slipped closer when it was apparent Viola wasn't going
any farther. She could hear Viola crooning again, loudly
enough to drown out the crunching of leaves under Mei's bare
feet.

She had been too busy trailing Viola to notice where they
had ended up. Now she realized the small patch of trees was
the same one where she and Viola had stopped to catch their
breath that morning on their walk. The adventure had been
memorable because Viola had whined continuously about the
heat and shrieked curses when a wedgetail eagle circled above
them.

In contrast, she seemed happy now. She held out her carefully cupped hand, palm up, and waved it from side to side.
Then she bent low and placed whatever she was holding beside
a protruding tree root. She straightened, stripped off her night-
gown in one fluid motion, then, naked, stood swaying and gazing at the branches above her.

Viola's body was paler than the eucalpyt's bark, and for that
moment she no longer seemed prematurely old or hollowed out
by misfortune. She seemed like a girl, a wood nymph fanned
by the whispering branches, dancing in the moonlight.

But she wasn't young. She was a sad, bitter woman with a
hopelessly distorted vision of the world. Just as Mei had decided that everything Viola had done tonight was simply mad-
ness, Viola picked up whatever she had placed on the ground
and popped it in her mouth. Then stepping on the highest root,

she shimmied against the tree until she could reach the lowest branch.

And Viola began to climb.

Mei forgot to breathe. The sight of the naked woman climbing the tree, perhaps with the Pearl of Great Price in her mouth, was the strangest of her life. Viola was surprisingly fit. She climbed until she reached a limb about twelve feet from the ground, then she edged along it until Mei was certain it couldn't bear her weight.

Only then did she realize what Viola was going to do. A nest the size of a dinner plate lay balanced between two smaller branches and Viola stopped just short of it. She reclined along the limb until her fingers could touch the nest. Mei couldn't see well enough to know for certain what happened next, but she could picture what she didn't see.

Viola removed the object from her mouth and dropped it into the nest; then, satisfied that the job was well done, she began a backwards journey.

Mei lingered just long enough to be sure Viola reached the ground safely. Then she fled, determined to reach the veranda before her mistress discovered she had been followed.

Mei couldn't return immediately to search the nest. Viola was restless for the remainder of the night, never falling so soundly asleep that Mei could take the risk. In the morning Viola was flushed and feverish, perhaps from the unaccustomed exertion of her midnight romp, but Mei was obliged to stay beside her, sponging her neck, face and arms with rags she soaked in water placed in the shade of the veranda to cool it.

When the humidity came to a head, then broke in a raging storm, Mei watched the torrential downpour and pictured the Pearl of Great Price washed from a flimsy nest of sticks and mud to be carried by rising waters into the heart of the Victoria River. And where did the Victoria empty? Did it flow out to sea? Would the pearl be returned to the setting that had created it?

Her thoughts were fanciful, but her fear was not. Viola

seemed oblivious, as if by placing the pearl in a bird's nest, she had guaranteed its safety. But Mei knew that the nest and its contents might not survive the drenching. Just as certainly, she knew that going outside to rescue it would be lunacy.

Viola worsened by midafternoon, growing steadily hotter and more contentious. Mei fed her sips of boiled water and fanned her with the rain-dewed branch of a palm tree until Viola fell into a troubled sleep. When Mei had been sick as a child, her mother had visited Sheba Lane to consult an herbalist, who questioned her carefully about the illness. Then he had given Willow instructions and herbs to help Mei's body heal itself.

Now Mei had no instructions. Larry suggested a mixture of sulfur and treacle to make Viola vomit, but Mei saw no purpose in that. In the men's quarters there were quinine tablets for bush fever, but neither Larry nor Mei were sure that they were called for, and they were far too precious to waste.

"Save 'em," Larry said. "We'll know by tomorrow if she needs 'em or no."

He brought the evening meal to the house himself, but Viola, who was awake again, was too sick to eat, and Mei too busy to do more than swallow a few bites. There was no hope now that she could sneak out to the scrub and look for the pearl. Viola moaned and thrashed as her fever climbed, and it was all Mei could do to keep her in bed.

By midnight, when the sky was cloud-covered and starless, Viola's fever broke. For an hour she sweated so heavily that Mei was afraid she would melt away. Mei sponged and dried her and, when the worst was over, helped her into a clean gown. Finally Viola closed her eyes and fell into a deep sleep. Exhausted, all Mei could do was wash herself and fall into bed.

She was feeding Viola breakfast the next morning when Archer and several of his men rode in. She waited until he came up to the house to tell him of Viola's illness.

"She was very sick, boss. I was afraid she might die."

Archer, mud-stained and unshaven, motioned for her to move out of the doorway. "Well, she didn't, did she?"

Once again, she wondered about the intelligence or integrity of any man who had called this one friend. She folded her arms and didn't move. "I know little about how to take care of a person as sick as this."

"Then learn." He pushed past her, but he didn't stop by Viola's room to visit. He stayed at the homestead just long enough to change horses and have a meal; then he headed off again with a curt warning that he would be back that evening.

Mei saw her chances of retrieving the pearl—if it was the pearl—fading away. She couldn't risk being seen climbing the tree, most particularly not by Viola, who insisted on recuperating on the front veranda. At night, when Viola was finally in bed, Archer would be at home. And unless he had another bottle of rum hidden away, he would be alert and watchful. If he stayed at the house, she had no hope of eluding him.

For the next two days she watched for an opportunity to search the nest, and when she wasn't watching for a lucky moment, she was watching for Bryce's return. She didn't want to think about the future he envisioned here at Jimiramira. Despite nearly intolerable living conditions, she saw potential in the Territory for anyone willing to make sacrifices. Someday there would be sealed roads and modern conveniences. But she didn't want to imagine herself with Bryce beside her, wresting a living from the land and raising a family. That vision had no place for Thomas.

Still, she watched for him.

On the third day, Bryce rode into the homestead just before the evening meal. Early that morning, Archer had ridden out without word of his plans. When he didn't return at his usual time, she had hoped that he planned to sleep away from the homestead. When he still didn't return in time to eat, she made plans to search the nest once Viola fell asleep.

Excitement had built inside her until the ring of horses' hooves destroyed it. Bryce and three of the stockmen were back, and now there were four new people to catch her in the act.

She waited for Bryce to come up to the house. That afternoon, as Viola napped, Mei had washed her own hair and left it loose to dry. Now, torn between braiding it or changing into a clean dress, she chose the dress and tied her hair back hastily with a pale blue ribbon. She knew what she would see if she had a mirror. A plain face, with features that were not quite Chinese, not quite European, and a slender, almost boyish, body.

But what did Bryce see when he gazed at her?

Whatever he saw pleased him. A slow smile lit his face when he found her in the parlor polishing piano keys. He rested his hands on her shoulders for a long look. "Your hair is beautiful that way."

Color rose in her cheeks. "Your mother has been sick. You should see her now."

"Is she better?"

"Yes. Much better."

"And I'll wager you nursed her through it, didn't you?" He smiled tenderly. "You're a real dinky-di bushie, May. You do whatever has to be done, don't you?"

"Perhaps you can help her eat? She is not well enough to be out of bed yet."

He continued to smile, but he dropped his hands. "Is my father expected?"

"He told me nothing of his plans."

"Has he helped with Mum?"

"No." She saw no reason to protect Archer.

"Later, will you take a walk with me?"

She thought of the pearl hidden in the nest. Bryce would be tired from his time away, and he would sleep soundly tonight. If the skies stayed clear, if Viola slept soundly, too, if Archer didn't come home, perhaps she still had a chance.

"A small walk," she told him. "But then you must rest. Your mother is better, but who will be next?"

"No worries. Nothing puts me crook." He touched a long lock of hair draped over her shoulder. "Nothing except not being with you."

* * *

Archer rode in about an hour after Bryce. He was flushed and irritable, and Mei suspected that whatever had stricken his wife was nibbling at him. He waved her away when she offered to bring food from the kitchen.

"Just let me sleep."

He headed for a room in the back of the house, next to Bryce's. She couldn't believe her good fortune. Now Bryce would not feel as free to leave his own room with his father in the one beside his. With Archer ill and Bryce trapped, no one would know she wasn't asleep. If she waited until midnight, she could sneak outside and climb the tree.

If the pearl was there, it would be hers.

She had carefully thought out the rest of her plan. She would shred the nest, as if the rain had destroyed it and washed away its contents. Then she would hide the pearl somewhere other than her room, in case Viola discovered it was missing and suspected her. Archer and Bryce would be convinced Viola had truly lost her mind, particularly if she admitted she had hidden the pearl high in a tree.

Then, when Bluey came back at the end of the Wet, Mei would retrieve the pearl and leave with him. She would go back to Darwin and find work until she had saved enough to buy passage on a ship to California. At last she and Thomas would be reunited.

And Bryce would remain here at Jimiramira with his hateful parents and faded dreams of a better future.

Her heart was heavy. She could tell herself that Bryce was falling in love with her because he was ready for a woman and she was simply here in his house. But did that somehow explain the yearning she felt, too? They had been thrown together, but from their first meeting, she had felt that his heart was open to her, that she could see into it and read the sadness there.

She had not seen her enemy's son. She had seen a man worthy of love.

"May?"

She opened her eyes to find him standing before her.

"Your father is home," she said softly. "No walk tonight."

"I'll come and get you when they're both asleep."

For a moment she was tempted. Then she realized that if he came, her resolve would lessen. Each time she was with Bryce, he mattered more. How long before the Pearl of Great Price became merely a curiosity and not the means of her family's salvation?

"No." She stepped back. "Your father and mother disapprove. You must honor their wishes."

"Did he say something to you?"

"He has said many things."

"But I told you I'd protect you. You have nothing to worry about."

"You are not here always. He sends you away. I cannot take a chance."

"You *will* not."

She turned away.

"My dad's a hard man, but he wouldn't hurt you, May. He's not capable of that."

Archer was capable of so much more, but how could she tell Bryce what she knew? "Please, we cannot speak of this any more tonight."

She heard a sigh behind her. "I'll see you in the morning."

She waited until his footsteps had died away before she went to help ready Viola for bed.

It was dark by the time she finished her chores and put out the lanterns. Her room was unbearable, and she sat on her bed without undressing. The heat was so fierce, she was afraid that if she fell asleep, she wouldn't wake until morning.

She waited for what seemed like hours before she got up and changed into a dress that was a blue as dark as midnight, and she made sure to turn under the white collar. She braided her hair and pinned it high, then removed her shoes, despite fears of snakes and brambles. When she was ready, she edged open her door and stepped out into the hallway, listening carefully.

The house was quiet. Once before, she had sneaked outside,

hardly daring to breathe. Tonight she didn't have to follow Viola, she only had to leave without attracting attention. With great care, stopping every few feet to listen, she did so.

The night was windy, as if another storm was building. Welcoming the breeze, she followed the shadows again, until she could cross to the trees. She rested for a long time, watching the house and the grounds around it in case anyone had spotted her. When she was finally satisfied she was alone, she started through the trees to find the nest.

She hadn't been to this place since the night she had trailed Viola. Because of Viola's illness, there hadn't been any more walks. But she had no trouble finding the right tree. When it loomed above her, she gazed up into the lightly swaying branches, willing the nest to be there.

The night was too cloudy for her to see more than a few feet up into the lowest branches. She would have to climb to discover the fate of the nest. Unlike Viola, she had no plan to strip off her clothes, although she risked catching her skirt on a branch. But she knotted the skirt so that it rose above her knees and rolled back her sleeves.

Then, just as Viola had done, she stepped on top of the highest root and used it as a boost to reach the lowest branch. And slowly, carefully, she pulled herself up to the first limb.

Minutes passed before she reached her destination. The dress was clumsy, and although she was strong, she discovered that the height made her dizzy. Twice she closed her eyes and held on to the tree as if it were a bucking horse, until the world stopped whirling below her.

She reached the limb at last and stretched carefully along it, peering through the cover of fragrant gum leaves until she thought she saw the nest. But she wasn't as tall as Viola, and she saw she would have to edge out farther. She did so with the ground undulating in drunken waves below her. The limb drooped as she inched farther along its length, and when it swayed dangerously, she flailed her arms in terror.

And felt the nest.

She lay still, hardly daring to breathe until the limb stopped its protest. Then she tugged at the nest, moving it slowly and carefully toward her. When her grip was firm and the nest was freed from its home, she started back until she and the nest were safe in a crook of the tree.

She realized that her long journey to reclaim the Pearl of Great Price ended here. If the pearl was lodged at the bottom of the nest, from this moment forward it belonged to her. Everything still to come was insignificant.

But if the pearl was not here, if a stone or a shell lay at the nest's bottom, then her journey had been for nothing. She would never find the pearl. She would have to make a life without it.

Oddly, she wasn't sure which ending to hope for.

Above the ground in the swaying branches, she was cooler than she'd been in days. But her hands were sweating so badly that she had to take turns wiping them on her skirt. Finally, when there were no reasons to wait, she reached inside the nest and began her exploration.

The nest was rough inside as well as out, as if it had never been softened by the down of a baby bird or smoothed by the flutter of tiny wings. She moved her fingers slowly, feeling below twigs and under shreds of moss. But nothing was there.

She had seen Viola place something in the nest, hadn't she? She had *almost* seen it. Mei closed her eyes. Had her imagination run wild that night? She had been standing nearby, but not close enough to see everything. Had she been wrong?

She felt the contours of the nest again, this time tearing away the fragile inner lining as she progressed around the rim. But again she turned up nothing. The nest was empty and intact. She felt for holes. Was the pearl on the ground after all? Or had it washed into a nearby crevice?

But the nest, though rough, seemed secure. And what bird would build a home with a gap a tiny egg could slip through? If the storm had destroyed it, that would be different, but the storm had not.

She shook the nest angrily, then, methodically, carefully, she began to shred it, inch by inch, until it was a heap of broken twigs in the lap of her skirt.

She leaned back against the trunk and closed her eyes. There was no pearl here. There had never been a pearl in the nest, and she was as much a fool as Viola Llewellyn.

18

Hours passed before Mei was able to sleep. When she finally closed her eyes, she dreamed she had fallen into a fiery pit. Something tugged at the edges of slumber, but she was so tired and the heat so paralyzing that she couldn't pull herself awake.

Then a scream split the darkness, and she bolted upright.

"You did this! You stole it!"

Precious seconds elapsed before Mei remembered where she was and the events of the night. She couldn't move or think clearly. Viola's screams were coming from outside, although Mei thought it was hours before dawn.

"You...did...this!"

Mei folded her arms over her chest and began to tremble. She wondered if Viola had seen her searching the nest. Had she watched, then waited for the opportunity to check it herself? Did she believe Mei had stolen the pearl?

She realized that the screams weren't coming closer. Then she heard a man's angry voice.

"Shut up, you bitch! I didn't steal anything!"

Mei recognized Archer's snarls, followed by Bryce's calmer tones. "Dad, she's not right, you know she isn't. Leave her alone. Please..."

"It's gone! You took it!"

Mei knew better than to join the fray in front of the homestead. Somewhere nearby a dog was howling in protest, and she thought she heard a shout from the direction of the men's quarters. She hastily slipped on her dressing gown and went into the parlor, where she could watch through a window, unseen.

The Llewellyns stood in a clump some yards from the house. Bryce had his hand on his father's arm, and Viola stood away from the men, but she was brandishing her fists like weapons.

"I want it back!"

"She's completely out of her mind. I'm going in." Archer turned his back on his wife and started toward the veranda, but Viola launched herself at him. Before Bryce could stop her, she had thrown Archer off balance. He tripped and fell to one knee.

He whirled and grabbed Viola's arm and threw her to the ground beside him. Then he slapped her across the face. "Attack me, will you?"

"Dad!" Bryce grabbed Archer's hand before he could hit Viola again. The two men struggled, but Archer's desire to hit Viola seemed to fade.

Archer shoved his son away and got to his feet. "See to your mother."

"I put it in a bird's nest. The nest is gone. It's nothing but sticks. Sticks." Viola's voice dropped and she sat up. "You did this. I know you did."

"You don't know *where* you put the fucking thing," Archer shouted. "You haven't known for months, maybe even longer. You've gone and lost our future, you stupid cow. You'll never find it again."

Viola covered her face. "The nest is gone."

Archer looked at his son, dismissing his wife as if she wasn't there. "When the Dry comes, I'm sending her away. Nothing you can do will stop it from happening. She's no use to anyone here."

"Send her away and I'll go, too."

"You'll stay right here. There's nothing you can do to help her. Damn it to hell, Bryce, most of the time she doesn't even know who you are!"

"I know who she is. She's my mum."

"Would to God it weren't true." Archer started toward the house. Mei knew she couldn't let him catch her watching. She went back to her room and quietly closed her door.

Minutes later she heard the sound of Bryce helping a sobbing Viola inside. She rose to light a lantern and went out, as if she had just awakened. "Is she ill?"

"At heart." Bryce helped Viola into her room, and Mei followed. In the dim light, she could see that Viola's cheek was beginning to swell.

"He took it. He climbed the tree, and he stole it!" Viola's head swivelled back and forth. "He took it, and now he's going to send me away. I put it in the nest. He took it."

Mei frowned at Bryce, as if she didn't know what Viola meant. He shook his head, as if to say it didn't matter.

"It's *my* pearl." Viola gazed up at Mei, who was pouring water from a pitcher into the bowl on the bedside table. "My father gave it to me!"

Mei caught Bryce's eye. He shrugged.

"In the morning," Mei told her, "you will find it again. We will help you look."

"Start with his pockets, then! That's where you'll find it."

Mei bathed Viola's cheek and helped her into bed. "Maybe you only had a dream? Maybe you dreamed about a nest? Tomorrow you will remember better."

Viola curled into a pathetic ball on the mattress and covered her face with her arm.

"Maybe we should leave the lantern for her?" Mei said without thinking.

Bryce shook his head. "No, we can't."

If Mei had found the pearl, she would have stolen it herself. Despite that, she felt compassion for Viola, who was curled as tightly as a baby in its mother's womb. Wherever Archer sent his wife could not be worse than Jimiramira, but at the heart of Viola's sadness was the loss of what little power she had wielded. The pearl had stood between her and utter impotence. She had nothing to take its place.

Bryce took the lantern before they went into the hall. She followed him to the parlor, where he set it down.

"You will leave Jimiramira as you told your father?" Mei asked softly, no longer pretending that she hadn't heard it all.

"Too right. I should have left years ago."

"This is your home."

"Home's supposed to be more than a peg to hang your trousers and a billabong to fill your billy, isn't it? The people who live there are supposed to love you, aren't they, and love each other?"

She thought about her own home, gone now. But the warm memories of Willow stayed with her. "That is not always the way of things." She touched his arm. "But this is your home."

"Any station in the Territory would be glad to have me. I'll be off when she goes." He lowered his voice. "Come with me."

"I could not stay at Jimiramira if your mother was gone, and if you—"

"I mean, come with *me*. Come wherever I do. It won't be much of a life at first, but we can make something of it. I know cattle." His voice grew softer, but more intense. "Someone will hire me, and you can work at the homestead. Maybe later we could find a place of our own to manage. You'd be the boss's wife. You'd like that, wouldn't you? I could take care of you, May."

She saw the evening's events in his eyes. He had suffered, and now he needed her. No one had ever loved him, not the way he deserved, and now he was asking her to be the first.

"Bryce..." She tried not to imagine Archer lying in a bed not far away, straining to hear them. "Go to bed now. This is not the time to think of the future. You need to sleep, to—"

He put his arms around her waist and hauled her up against him. If their first kiss had been sweet exploration, this one was raw need. She didn't have time to protect herself, to remember why she had come to this place or what a failure her mission had been. She was enveloped by sensations as old as their island continent.

She let him draw her so close that she could feel his body changing through the thin cotton of her gown. He was muscle and sinew, and his lips were as demanding as the life he had led. She molded herself to him, and for a moment she was part of something beyond herself, beyond thought and plan and mission. She was simply, gloriously, a woman.

Then Bryce was sprawling on the floor and Archer had his hands at her throat. "You slant-eyed bitch! I told you to leave my son alone!"

She couldn't even scream. She gasped and struggled, but Archer squeezed tighter. A strong wind swept through the room and everything suddenly went dark as Bryce leapt from the floor and grabbed his father's arms. Archer was strong, but his son was younger and more determined. He wrenched Archer's hands from her throat and dragged him away. Mei gulped air as if she would never have enough again.

The two men rolled on the floor, trading punches. She screamed at last, but there was no one to hear and help. The station hands and stockmen were too far away, and the woman curled on her bed in the next room was as powerless as she was.

"Stop!" She moved away as they crashed toward her, aware that she didn't have the strength to separate them. "You must stop!"

She could see that Bryce was on top of his father now, his hands gripping Archer's shoulders. He lifted and slammed his father against the floor, once, twice, before Archer threw him to the ground. They traded punches, but Bryce's were more precise. Archer faltered, his next punch aimed wildly into space.

"Stop!" Mei danced around them, and when the opportunity arose, she grabbed Bryce's arm. "Enough! Stop, Bryce."

He seemed to hear her for the first time. He went rigid, although he easily deflected Archer's next blow. Then he moved out of his father's range and got to his feet.

Archer sat up. "You little bastard! You're...not my son...."

"Too bad it's not true!" Bryce opened his mouth and brushed his fingertips across his jaw.

Archer spat blood on the floor. "First your mother, now you."

"Yeah, and you know what we've got in common, Dad? Have a good look in the mirror sometime."

"I told you to stay away from this girl!"

"And why should I listen to you?" Bryce went to Mei's side. He was still breathing hard. "I'm going to marry May, and you can't stop it. I don't want you or this property or anything about it. I'll make my way without you."

Archer stared at him. "I did this...everything...I did everything for you."

"Everything?" Bryce laughed bitterly. "What have you done, Dad? Built this bloody awful house? Raised some cattle? Do you think any of that matters now?"

Mei stepped forward, shaking off Bryce's arm. She had come to Jimiramira for the pearl and revenge against the Llewellyns. But now she realized how little she wanted the latter. There was nothing she could take from Archer and Viola, because they possessed nothing of importance. No love, no character, no honor. She couldn't take the pearl, because it had disappeared. And now she couldn't bear to take their son. Not this way. Because Bryce was not a means to an end. He was so much more.

She loved him.

The revelation startled and strengthened her. She drew herself to her full height. "You must stop. Please, go to bed. Both of you. These words shame you." She didn't look at Bryce, because she was afraid if she did, she would begin to cry.

"This is my house." Archer got to his feet. "Don't tell me what to do."

She turned away, and Bryce caught her hand, but she shook him off. "Then *I* will go to bed. And I will think about tomorrow and the things that should be said only then!" She started through the house, but neither man followed her. Once she reached her room, she closed the door and pushed her trunk against it for protection from Archer. Then she began to cry.

She was still crying minutes later when she heard a soft tapping. "May? Please, open the door."

She shook her head, as if Bryce could see her.

"May...please?"

"Go away."

"There's nothing we can say tomorrow that will change a thing. Tell me you'll come away with me then. May..."

She was silent, stuffing her fist against her mouth to resist temptation.

He went away at last.

The room was unbearable, but she lay on the bed without stirring. Not everything that had transpired tonight was her fault, but she *was* responsible for some of it. She had not taken the pearl, but she had stolen the real treasure of Jimiramira from Archer and Viola. She had stolen their son.

Whatever the reason, Bryce loved her, and while part of her exulted that this young man, straight and strong and brimming with vitality, wanted her, another part knew how unlucky this was, how doomed for misfortune.

The Northern Territory was vast and largely unpopulated by Europeans. But despite its size and isolation, gossip was lovingly tended and broadcast by every passing swagman and cattle drover, every supply wagon and camel caravan, every lonely settler who crossed desert or gibber plain to attend a far-flung race meeting. How long before someone who had known her in Broome discovered that Měi-Zhěn Robeson had traveled to the Territory? How quickly would the story of Tom Robeson's murder make its way to Bryce? How many moments before he realized it was not a coincidence she had found her way to Jimiramira?

How many heartbeats before he understood she had come here to steal the pearl?

And would he believe her when she told her that she had never found it? That she had not taken it from the nest where his mother claimed to have hidden it? She imagined the betrayal Bryce would feel, and at last, with tears on her cheeks, she fell into a restless, anguished sleep.

She dreamed she stood beside the billabong as smoke plumes rose into an outback dawn. The sky was streaked with fingers of light; the homestead was a candle blazing brightly to ward off the terrors of night.

She wasn't frightened. The homestead had never been a home, and between the fire break and the Wet, the blaze would be contained. As flames shot from windows and the veranda crumpled in a shower of sparks, she thought of vast stretches of wilderness she had seen on the trip to Jimiramira, burned to the ground by the local Aborigines so that richer possibilities could emerge. This ancient people had tended the earth with fire since the beginning of the Dreamtime. New growth emerging from the seeds of old, life emerging from death.

As the smoke billowed higher, she felt a profound sense of peace. She drew a breath, the preliminary to a contented sigh. Instead her lungs filled with smoke, and as her eyes widened in horror, ashes stung her cheeks.

"May!"

She was losing consciousness. The blaze before her began to fade; the dawn turned into blackest night. She fought to keep her eyes fixed on the fire, to will herself to stay awake.

"May!"

She forced her eyes open and saw that she was in her tiny, airless room at Jimiramira. It was filled with smoke. As she watched, horrified, the trunk she had placed in front of the door slid drunkenly, then crashed against her narrow bed. In a moment Bryce loomed over her. He grabbed her shoulders.

"May! Get up. House is—" He coughed, hacking uncontrollably, as if he had swallowed live coals.

She was not standing beside the billabong. Terror engulfed her. She swung her feet to the floor, and Bryce, still coughing, grabbed her hand to pull her toward the door.

"Get out," he managed. "My mum...can't find..."

She understood. He wanted her to escape, but he was going back to find his mother.

"No! Bryce!"

He pulled her along the hallway into a storage room at the back. The smoke was so thick she couldn't see, and she would not have found her way without him. He flung open the door and pushed her toward it. "Go!"

She held on to his hand. "No! You can't!"

He shook her off. "Get out. Now!"

He disappeared the way they had come. She would have followed, but he was swallowed up immediately, and she knew she would not find him without risking both their lives. She screamed for him to come back, but he didn't return. At last she stumbled out of the house.

Fifty yards away, she stumbled into Larry's arms. "Who else is out?" he demanded. "Where's the boss and the missus?"

She shook her head, coughing now. "Bry—"

"G'down to the billabong. We'll get buckets. Start a chain...." He disappeared into the night.

She understood what the men were trying to do, but it was too late. The house would burn to the ground, and everyone left inside would perish. She fell to her knees sobbing. She remembered the fight last night, and the lantern. The room had gone dark, and in the confusion she had blamed a gust of wind for blowing out the flame. But she had never gone back to check.

Now she knew what she would have seen if she had. In the midst of the fight, the lantern had been spirited away, its flame husbanded lovingly by the woman who had tried once before to burn Jimiramira to the ground. Mei had no proof, but she knew that at the end of her life, Viola had not been as powerless or pitiful as any of them had believed.

She heard shouts and running feet. In the distance horses whinnied frantically, and the station dogs set up a howl. She stopped the first man to run by. "Bryce! Inside."

"No one can get back in now, miss."

She stumbled to her feet and started toward the billabong, stopping another man along the way, old Henry, the station hand who had helped her put the homestead to rights. "Bryce… Please…"

"Nothing we can do but put out the fire." He slung his arm over her shoulders and propelled her along beside him until they were only a hundred yards away. "C'mon, May. The blacks'll be here to help as soon as they see the smoke. We can get it out."

"Let…it…burn." She began to sob.

Henry disappeared, leaving her alone to grieve. She turned and faced the homestead, and it was exactly the way she had dreamed it. As she watched dawn light the sky, the veranda collapsed in a shower of sparks.

But this time she felt only an unrelenting sense of dread.

The sky was nearly light before she heard Henry calling for her.

"May? You out there?"

She couldn't seem to answer. She opened her lips to reassure him, and something obscene rasped from her throat.

"May?" Henry moved into view, then, when he saw her, he came to her side.

She pointed to her throat, and he understood. "Too much smoke," he said. "Bugger it. You'll be crook a while, but it'll come out all right in the end. Seen this before."

She didn't care how it came out. She stared at the homestead. The ruins were merely smoldering now, and the human chain was beginning to break up.

Henry spoke calmly, as if he were discussing which cattle to send north to market. "Boss and missus are both dead, burned nearly to cinders. Fire started in one of the back rooms. They was together. She probably set the poor bastard on fire."

"Bryce?" She managed the word with difficulty.

"Don't you know?" He looked surprised. "Didn't nobody tell you?"

She stumbled to her feet. His expression changed to dismay. "I sent Sally to find you. Didn't she?"

"Bryce?" she croaked.

"Larry found him passed out by the front door. Dragged

him out just in time and carried him down to the kitchen, to his room. Emma's with him.''

She pushed past him and started around the ruins toward the kitchen. The building was far enough from the house that it hadn't been touched. Every step she took was harder than the one before. The ground sucked at her feet, but she kept going.

The sun was up now, balancing on the horizon as if weighing its decision to rise. Some of the men were already picking through the ruins, their mouths screened with handkerchiefs, and in front, two sad mounds carefully covered by an array of saddle blankets testified to the fire's deadly force.

She averted her eyes from the shrouded bodies and saw the skeleton of the piano surrounded by charred timber. She remembered the night Archer had complained that Viola hadn't wanted it. The night he'd drunk too much and seen her father in the room.

She wondered if in some world beyond this one Archer still complained of all the things that hadn't gone right. Had her father and mother met him at the instant of his death to damn or forgive him? Had Viola, beautiful and sane once again, taken her place beside him?

Mei's vision of that other world was foggy, composed of Bible illustrations and stories and legends her mother had brought from China. Willow had prayed to Kuan Yin, the goddess of Mercy, and sometimes to the Virgin Mary. She had not believed in anything, so much as hoped.

Now hope filled Willow's daughter. Archer and Viola were dead, and her father had been avenged. The pearl was gone from all their lives, but Bryce was not gone from hers.

She and Bryce had one chance. When she could speak clearly again, she could tell him the truth, starting at the very beginning. She could tell him of her change of heart, of the way her love for him had grown. He might hate her. He might be unable to forgive. But she had to know.

Thomas lived on the other side of the world, and now she had nothing to take to him to start a new life together. Bryce was only a few feet away, and she had everything to give him.

Inside the kitchen she saw Emma sitting at the table, her hands neatly folded, as if she was waiting for instructions.

"Emma?"

The girl stood.

"Bryce?"

Emma frowned at Mei's rough whisper. "He been sleep."

Mei motioned for Emma to leave. The girl shot her a grateful smile. Mei paused at the door to the room where Larry slept, then she opened it slowly. Bryce lay on his back on Larry's bed, staring at the ceiling. One arm was credibly bandaged, and his trousers had been cut away at one knee so a portion of his calf could be bandaged, too.

"Bryce?"

His gaze settled slowly on her, as if she were pulling him back from someplace far away. "May?"

He sounded only slightly better than she did. He pushed himself to a sitting position, coughing as he inched forward. "You're all...right?"

She nodded.

"Sally said you disappeared, that no one knew where you'd gone."

"No one...told me." She moved closer so he could hear her better. "About—"

He tried to smile, but his face was a study of warring emotions. "I made it. Larry—"

She reached out and touched his lips to silence him, but he spoke anyway. "They're...dead." He closed his eyes.

She didn't know what to say. She couldn't tell him she was sorry. Viola was better off, and Archer had deserved to die. *Her* father by water, *his* by fire. The cycle was complete.

He sat on the bed, struggling not to cry. She wanted to comfort him. She eased down and put her arms around him. He winced when she touched his chest, but when she tried to withdraw, he pulled her closer. "May..." The tears he wouldn't cry were in his voice.

"Maybe...they have peace now?" She rested her head under his chin, even though she knew her hair smelled of smoke.

His arms tightened. "That would be new, wouldn't it?" His voice broke.

She lifted her face and kissed him. It was the only way she knew to comfort him. He returned the kiss, as if he hoped that small intimacy might be able to heal a broken heart. The kiss deepened. She could think only of what she had to tell him. She wanted him to know she loved him. When she told him the truth, she wanted him to remember this, to remember that now, when she had no reason to kiss him, she had kissed him anyway. Not for the pearl. Not for revenge. But for love.

"Oh, May..." He kissed her cheeks, her chin, her forehead. He loosened the braid that fell untidily down her back and spread her hair over her shoulders. "Promise me you won't leave me, too."

She thought he might want her to leave very soon, but she murmured her promise. She would not leave unless he asked. If he could forgive her, she would stay beside him and help build a new home from the ashes of a home that had never been.

He eased her down beside him, turning so that he could kiss her better. His arms were boyishly awkward and trembling, but she embraced him. He cupped her cheek; then his fingers tangled in her hair. "Stay with me...."

She touched his chest, his shoulder, the slender plane of his hip. She didn't know when sympathy and love became something else. By then she was floating on a flood tide of hope for the future. They could overcome the past. If she could forgive him for being Archer and Viola's son, then he could forgive her. They could start over together.

She let him undress her, and she moaned when he touched her breast. Then, slowly, she forgot about the past, about revenge and regret. She forgot about the future and the hurdles they still faced. She gave herself to him, and for those moments there were no ghosts between them.

Mei lay beside Bryce, who was breathing heavily. He had been sleeping for a while now, and she suspected he would sleep for most of the day. She knew she should rise and find Larry to help her make breakfast for the men. But she was drained of everything, content to lie beside the man she loved.

From somewhere nearby she heard the peculiar call of a bird. For a moment she wondered how it could so perfectly imitate the barking of a dog. Then she remembered walking with Bryce to see the lovingly constructed bower. The bowerbird was near, perhaps investigating to see if the fire had left any shiny bits of glass or stone.

"You'll hear one singing around the homestead from time to time. A big spotted fellow with a bit of color at the back of his neck. He's a mimic, that one. He can low like the cattle, bark like a dog. I reckon I could teach him to talk if I wanted."

She sat up suddenly, remembering the other things Bryce had told her about the bowerbird. The male built his bower, then adorned it with anything bright or shiny that he could find. Shells, pieces of bone.

A pearl?

For an instant she wondered if she was as crazy as Viola. If she stayed at Jimiramira, would she always look, always hope that someday she would find the Pearl of Great Price? And what would she do if she found it?

What about Thomas?

She told herself to go back to sleep. She told herself to get up and begin breakfast preparations. But when she rose and dressed, she didn't pretend she was going to look for Larry.

She told herself the truth.

Outside, several of the Aboriginal stockmen were picking through the ruins, and they took no notice of her. Larry was coming from the direction of the quarters, and he paused as she passed. "Henry'll be riding over to the telegraph station to tell them what happened."

Mei knew that the telegraph station was many days away, a particularly difficult trip in the Wet. But the authorities had to be notified.

"There's no house for you to see to anymore," Larry said. "If you want to leave, he can take you that far. When he's able to, the man there can help you get back to Darwin." He didn't wait for an answer.

She started toward the billabong, as if that was her destination. But when she reached the trees, she followed the route she had covered with Bryce, taunting herself as she walked. No pearl waited in the bower. The pearl was gone forever. If she didn't guard her sanity, she would become like Bryce's mother.

"Bryce." She didn't smile as she said his name. In her own way she knew she was preparing to leave him.

She reached the patch of scrub, and she stood just outside the trees, her mind whirling. She didn't know what to hope for.

At last she stepped into the scrub and found her way to the bower. In the daylight it was larger and more complex than she had remembered. But even as a part of her marveled at the bird's extraordinary talent, another part screamed at her to turn around and run away.

Instead, she slowly stooped, and when she had taken a deep breath, she peered inside. The pearl for which her father had died glowed at the entrance.

The bird had known that no female could resist its temptation.

"Of course, I took the pearl," Mei told Liana and Cullen, in the sitting room of her small apartment in San Francisco. "I held it in my palm, and I saw Thomas's face reflected on its surface. I knew I could not keep it for myself, that I must bring it to him in California. This is what my mother would expect of me. Your grandfather was still sleeping, Cullen, as I rode away with Henry later that morning. I never saw him again."

Liana blinked back tears, but Cullen, who seemed less affected, spoke. "You chose your brother over my grandfather?"

"I came to America three months later. There was much flooding in the week after the fire, and even if Bryce had wanted to find me and take me back to Jimiramira, he could not have. I was able to make my way to Darwin, where I found a family traveling to the United States. I agreed to help care for their children in exchange for my passage. I was an Australian citizen because my father was white. And I was able to emigrate to California because of it. In those days, Chinese were not wanted in America, either.''

"Was it worth it, Mei?''

Liana watched her aunt's face. Mei smiled sadly. ''I found your father with little trouble, Liana, just as I had so many times before in my dreams. Thomas was tall and strong, as I had imagined, but he looked nothing like me, not Chinese at all. We met in secret. He told me he did not want our grandparents to know I had come, because they would try to send me back.''

Even the sad smile disappeared. "I was so glad to see him. He was the other half of my soul, and I clung to that, because I had lost everything else that mattered. I held out the pearl for Thomas to see, and I told him about our father and Archer, and all I had done to bring it to him. He reached for it and rolled it in his palm, fingers caressing it. And then he told me to go back to my boardinghouse. He would come for me the next day to start our new life together.''

Mei shook her head sadly. She didn't go on.

"He didn't come, did he?'' Liana whispered.

"The next morning the police came to put me in jail. They said that Thomas had accused me of stealing his watch, and one of the policemen pretended to find it in my clothes. They kept me there for two days. Then one of them came to my cell and told me that Thomas would not press charges, but if I bothered him again, he would have me sent back to Australia. He could have, of course. Our grandfather was a powerful man, and Thomas was to inherit everything.''

Liana looked at Cullen and saw he was gazing at her.

Mei finished. "When I returned to the boardinghouse, a letter was waiting. Thomas said that I was never to tell a soul who I was or anything about the pearl. And if I was silent, he would not have me sent away. This was his favor to me. Because I was his twin sister.''

a family traveling to the United States. I agreed to help care
for their children in exchange for my passage. I was an Asian-
Italian citizen because my father was white. And I was able to
emigrate to California because of it. In those days, Chinese
were not wanted in America, either.

"Was it worth it, Mei?"

I once watched her son's face, Mei smiled sadly. "I found
your father was little humble. I hate. Just as I had so many
times before in my dreams. Thomas was tall and grown. He
had imagined. And he looked nothing like the one Chinese at
all. We met in secret. He said you he did not want our second
parents to know. I had come, because they would try to send
me back.

"Even the sad smile disappeared. "I could no longer see him.
He was the other half of my soul, and I clung to that because
I had lost everything else that mattered. I held on the bee. For
Thomas to say, and I had him, seeing together, and As her
and m—I had come to bring it. By now, the second one I slid
rolled it in his palm, began pressing it. And then he told me
to go back to my home harbor. He would make that for the
next day to wait proven to go agree some is no they...

Mei shook her head sadly. She didn't go on.

"Why didn't you, did no?" Liang was good.

"The next morning, the police came to our inn in jail. They
said that Thomas had accused me of stealing his words, and
some of the baggage amounted to find it in my clothes. They
kept me there for two days. They got of them came to our cell
and told me that Thomas would get pass charges, but if I
battered him again, he would have me sent back to wash to.
He could have it of course. Our grandfather was a powerful man,
and Thomas had no interest everything.

Liana looked at Celiia, and saw he was gazing at her.

Mei finished. "When I returned to the boardinghouse, it for-
tress was waiting. Thomas said that I was never to tell a soul
what I saw or anything about the past. At last, it was clear to
would me have me sent away. This was his love for me. Because I was his twin sister.

The love of my life came not,
As love unto others is cast;
For mine was a secret wound—
But the wound grew a pearl, at last.

—Edith Matilda Thomas
The Deep-Sea Pearl, Stanza I

19

Sydney, Australia—Present Day

Matthew wasn't sure when his wallet had disappeared. He had paid the taxi driver, paid the reception clerk for the first night at his hotel in King's Cross, paid cash for the worst spaghetti dinner he'd ever eaten. Then he had stumbled back to his room and slept for nineteen hours straight.

And when he had finally opened his eyes again, he had discovered that his wallet was missing.

Fading sunlight filtered through the greasy shade covering the only window in his room. Matthew jerked the cord, and the shade wrapped around itself with a loud explosion. Three stories below, he could see two men in front of an open-air vegetable stall gesturing and shouting soundlessly at each other as the owner began to shift the displays inside.

"Shit." Matthew closed his eyes. Simon had chosen this hotel for him. They had pored over sites on the Internet, and Simon had found the hotel on a travel board for college students. Cheap, easy to find and not the least bit particular. He hadn't planned to stay in Sydney any longer than it took to book a flight to Jimiramira. He had intended to stay two nights. One to recover from jet lag, another to finalize his travel plans.

Now the second night was about to begin, only he had no money to pay for it.

"Shit," he said again, but he didn't feel a bit better—which he'd thought was the whole point of cursing.

He was in the Southern Hemisphere, as far from San Francisco as he could get without heading back. He had someone else's passport, an empty stomach, a hotel room he couldn't pay for, and no clue where he had lost his wallet.

He sank to the only chair in the room and tried to piece together the minutes between slurping his final strand of spaghetti and falling asleep fully clothed.

He had paid for his meal in cash, Australian cash. He had exchanged all his money at the airport, even though he knew he might get a better rate somewhere else. But the airport had been crowded and the clerks forced to work without socializing. Since the same wouldn't necessarily be true elsewhere, he had resigned himself to losing a few cents on the dollar.

He had expected to be confused, but except for adjusting to dollars in coins, he had caught on quickly. With relative ease he had counted out the money for the taxi, counted out more for the desk clerk and later for the cashier at the café. He had tucked what was left of the eight hundred dollars in his wallet. He remembered, because he hadn't been sure where to put all that heavy change. He had slipped the wallet inside the back pocket of his jeans and the change in the front.

Now his wallet was gone.

His alarm grew as he went over the next minutes out loud.

"I put the wallet in my pocket. I said good-night to the guy at the cash register. He asked if I was an American...."

He remembered feeling chagrined. For years he had practiced his father's accent, drawing out vowels, dropping "r's" in the middle of some words and adding them to the end of others. As Cullen's son he had felt secure in his ability to pretend he was Australian, but apparently he wasn't as adept as he'd thought.

"I told him I'd lived in the States for a few years. I walked outside...." Matthew pictured the street in front of the restaurant. It wasn't far from the hotel, but the restaurant was on a seedier street, one that reminded him of the least appealing sections of San Francisco's North Beach, with window displays that both interested and repelled him, and neon signs advertising entertainment he wasn't old enough to see—but wished he could.

By the time he left the restaurant the sky was fully dark, but more than stars had come out. The street teemed with people strolling and staring in shop windows. Music drifted on the air, something loud and rhythmic playing over speakers that screeched on the high notes. He stopped in front of a shop labeled Chemist and peered inside, half expecting smoking vials and foaming beakers. Instead the store was exactly like the pharmacy near his school, only here the condoms were prominently displayed.

And that was when the girl had approached him.

"Got a smoke, mate?"

He had turned quickly to face her, shoving his hands in his pockets. She'd seemed to be at least twenty, and she was a full head shorter than his six foot, with long brown hair and dark eyes. Or at first he'd thought they were dark, until he realized he was staring into pupils so enlarged they were just barely ringed with vivid green.

"I don't smoke." He cleared his throat and wished for the first time that he did.

"No? That's crook. I need one."

"Do they sell them in there?" He inclined his head toward the chemist shop.

"I don't buy smokes. Blokes give 'em to me." She moved close enough to make him acutely aware of the short length of her skirt and the unfastened buttons of her blouse.

"Wrong bloke here, I guess." He didn't know what to do. He noticed the exotic way she smelled. She wore too much eyeliner, with her eyes as heavily rimmed as a racoon's, but she was pretty, just the same.

"Maybe not the wrong bloke." When she smiled, her front teeth were just crooked enough to interest him. The girls at his school were all on their way to perfect teeth, and their fathers had the orthodontist bills to prove it.

Exhaustion was beginning to claim him, but Matthew wasn't ready to end the conversation. This was the most exciting thing that had happened to him since he got off the plane. "Do you live around here?"

"Here and there. I move around a bit." She reached out to straighten his shirt collar. Just reached out, as if touching him was an entirely normal thing to do. He hadn't heard that Australian girls were more forward than Americans, and he wondered why this hadn't been trumpeted up and down every travel board in cyberspace.

She slowly dropped her hand. "Where in America do you live?"

"How do you know I live in America?"

"I dunno. The way you talk. And this shirt." Her eyes traveled down. "And those boots. Are you from Texas?"

"I'm from here. I was visiting the U.S. For a long time," he added.

She shrugged. "Is that right? I like the shirt. Turn a bit and let me see the back."

And that was exactly what he had done.

Now Matthew put his head in his hands as the truth settled over him. He had been so tired he hadn't even suspected that the girl had lifted his wallet. While his back had been turned, she had bumped up against him. Accidentally, he guessed at the time. The only thing he had really noticed was the way his body betrayed him. He'd been exhausted, but not *that* exhausted.

When he turned around again, she looked perfectly innocent. They exchanged a few more sentences—with him mumbling and wishing he could adjust his jeans—then she wandered off, and he headed back to the hotel. If she had stolen his key, too, he would have noticed right then that the wallet was missing. But he had shoved the key in his front pocket, along with his passport, change and return ticket.

The girl had stolen his wallet.

He had grown up in San Francisco, and even though his home and school were in parts of the city best known for sweeping views and noteworthy architecture, he had still learned street smarts. Smart guys watched themselves with strangers. They kept their wallets in their front pockets, no matter what else had to go there. After dark, they stayed out of places they didn't know.

Smart guys didn't travel halfway around the world and lose their wallets to the first girl they met.

He had to get it back.

For a second Matthew discarded that as impossible. The girl was probably long gone by now. Why would she stay around King's Cross and wait to be caught? She must have realized he would figure out what had happened and probably call the police. Of course, she wouldn't know that, for him, calling the police was totally out of the question.

But what if she wasn't gone? And what if she hadn't spent all the money? He had to retrieve what he could. He still had a long way to go, and he couldn't do it without cash. Even if he slept outside, he still had to eat. He had a stash of Mounds bars and half a bag of potato chips he had bought in Dallas. But that wasn't going to get him very far.

Of course, he could always call his mother.

Matthew rose and grabbed his backpack. If he found the girl and his money, he would come back, finish his stay and pay for the room. If he didn't, he would spend the night in a park. Some day he would send the hotel money to make up for leaving.

In the hallway, he walked quietly down the worn carpet, trying not to attract attention. Thankfully, the clerk was not at the desk when Matthew crossed the lobby and let himself out into the King's Cross twilight.

By midnight Matthew gave up searching for the girl and started searching for a place to sleep. He had combed the neighborhood near the café one street at a time, peering into shadows, entering shops and restaurants, scouting alleys and the hallways of apartment buildings. By ten he had begun to ask strangers if they'd seen the girl, describing her with the details he so vividly remembered. People were surprisingly friendly, but no one knew a thing. No one but one old woman who manned a musty book shop just a block from where the girl had approached him.

"What is it you'd want with a girl like that?" The woman seemed nearly as old as his beloved aunt Mei. Her accent wasn't Australian. She spoke as if she were repeating lines from *Braveheart*, his favorite movie. He guessed since she was a stranger herself, maybe she was more willing to help him.

"She has something of mine." Matthew picked up a novel with a torn paper jacket sporting a cartoonish Canadian Mountie. "I need to find her and get it back."

"You'll be better off without the likes of her. Didn't your mum teach you right from wrong?"

Matthew looked up. "You know the girl I'm talking about?"

"Aye. I know her, sure as you're born. Tried to help her, I did, but she wanted none of it."

"Help her?"

The woman looked him over. "How old are you, lad?"

"Eighteen."

If she knew he was lying, she didn't let on. "That's old enough to know better, isn't it, now?"

"How were you trying to help her?"

"I tried to get her off the street, but she wasn't having any of that. She didn't want to shelve books and mind the counter here. No, she'd rather stand on street corners and pick up men."

The image was too vivid to mistake. Matthew might be just fourteen, but he understood exactly what the old woman meant. For the first time he realized what a fool he'd been. The girl was a prostitute, and he hadn't even realized it.

"Do you know where she is now?" He stammered out the words, embarrassed by what he had discovered—but more embarrassed that it had taken him so long to figure it out.

"Had a room nearby somewhere, I suppose. But I haven't

seen her for a while. She comes and goes, that one does. I wish
she'd go back where she came from. Maybe then she'd find a
real life.''

He had left the bookshop without another word, and when
the door closed behind him, the old woman flipped the "Open"
sign to "Closed" and pulled down the shade.

He had stayed in the immediate neighborhood, but after that,
he stopped asking about the girl. She was a prostitute, and no
one would willingly admit to knowing her. He tried to imagine
where prostitutes went at this time of night, and how they spent
their time, but those images sent his entire body into panic.

By midnight, when he gave up the search, he resigned himself to sleeping outside. He had come too far to turn back now.
Tomorrow he would have to consider his options, but only after
he'd had more sleep.

His stomach rumbled, and he began to look for a place where
he could open his backpack and dig out the potato chips. He
had already decided that shrubbery would be his best choice
for sleeping. If he could find an overgrown hedge along the
side of a building, it might provide decent shelter. He just
needed to be out of sight to stay safe.

He found exactly what he was looking for about a quarter
of a mile from the bookshop. A stone church stood on a street
more notable for its relative quiet than anything else. Surrounded by rundown apartments and parking lots, the church
was away from the worst hustle of commercial King's Cross.
Best of all, it was rimmed with tall evergreen bushes that gently
arched into a thick canopy along the front facing the street. A
chest-high iron fence with ornamental spikes ringed the lot, but
there appeared to be a gate in the back. If the gate was locked,
it would be easy enough to get over.

Matthew scanned the street, which at the moment appeared
to be deserted. Then he took the long way around, since the
shortest route was illuminated by lampposts. The gate was pad-
locked, but easy enough to climb. He tossed his backpack over
first, wincing as it hit the pavement with a loud thump. Then
he hauled himself over to retrieve it. Keeping to the darkest

part of the lot, he made his way to the front of the building and the sheltering evergreens.

He couldn't have asked for a better place to sleep. The ground was sandy and free of debris. The building blocked what little wind there was, and the branches drooped enough to render him invisible. He opened his pack and took out the potato chips, regretfully denying himself a candy bar, since he didn't know when he would be able to afford a real meal again.

Potato chips had never tasted so good.

At first, when Matthew awoke, he didn't know where he was. He was cold, and his pillow scratched his cheek. The voice he heard didn't belong to his mother or Sue Lo, their housekeeper. Those women had gentle voices. The voice that awakened him was younger and more abrasive. And the girl was speaking to a man.

"What do you mean, no worries, Charlie? I gotta have some money to pay off my room. The old cow told me she'd change the lock on the door and sell my stuff if I don't pay her tonight."

The man's reply was deep and rumbling, but too low for Matthew to understand.

The girl raised her voice. "It's my money. I earned it. I don't want it all, just—"

The rest of her sentence was interrupted by a cracking noise and a screech.

Matthew sat bolt upright and peered through the trunks of the evergreens. In the dim glow of the streetlight he saw a man shaking a slight young woman by the shoulders. This time he understood the man's words.

"You think you know what's best? Well, you're a silly bitch, aren't you? I got ten just like you, and not a one of me others whines all the time. I told you, tell the old lady I'll pay her tomorrow. She makes trouble, tell her the next time I see her, I'll give her more than a couple of quid!"

He shoved the girl away, but she recovered quickly and came

at him, striking out with both hands. "It's my money! And you were supposed to take care of me if I gave it to you!"

If the man had ever had patience, it was exhausted now. He grabbed her arms and twisted them over her head. Then, in a lightning quick maneuver, he slammed her in the belly with his knee. The girl shrieked and crumpled, but the man held her up and repeated the blow.

Matthew had seen enough. He sprang from the bushes and ran toward the street. "Hey, you! Leave her alone."

The man dropped the girl's arms, and she fell to the sidewalk like a rag doll.

"Just who are you ordering around?" The man grabbed the iron bars in front of Matthew and rattled them. Then he tilted his head back and howled with demented laughter.

Matthew didn't think. He had never seen another human being abused. He grabbed one of the man's wrists and pulled it through the bars, then he twisted the man's arm over his own shoulder and slammed it back and forth from bar to bar.

The man wasn't laughing now. He scrambled for Matthew's hair with his free hand, but Matthew ducked and tugged harder, bending the man's arm backwards as he did. His only intention was to give the girl a chance to escape, but as he pulled the man's arm back toward the rail, he heard a loud snap. Horrified, he released it immediately. The man screamed and fell to the ground.

Matthew didn't know what to do next. He was stunned at his own strength, his rage and its aftermath. He was more stunned when the girl lifted herself to her knees, grabbed a rock from a garden edging the sidewalk and hit the writhing man in the side of his head.

He stopped writhing and lay perfectly still.

The girl looked up. The face was familiar, but not the triumph in her green eyes. "We've got to get out of here. Somebody'll call the cops."

Matthew looked down at the man. "You killed him."

"Nah, I don't have that kind of luck." She leaned over. "See? His chest's still moving. Are you coming?"

Matthew tried to think. Somebody had to stay with the injured man, didn't they? But even if he wasn't dead, Matthew
had probably broken his arm. How could he explain that to the
police? How could he explain who he was and what he was
doing in Australia? Why he was sleeping in bushes? How he
knew this girl? The police would put him in jail and take all
the time they needed to investigate.

And he would never finish what he had come so far to do.

He peered at the girl through the bars. "You stole my wallet."

"Right-o. And I'm about to pinch it again. You want it back,
you'd better come with me."

From somewhere in the distance Matthew heard sirens. "But
my backpack's in the bushes."

"There's no time!"

She was right. The sirens were rapidly getting closer, and he
heard voices from one of the apartment buildings up the street.
He climbed the fence as she searched the man's pockets. The
wallet she retrieved was Matthew's.

"Got it, let's go."

He grabbed the wallet from her hand and shoved it in his
front pocket. "Are you all right? Can you run?"

"Me? No worries. I've been running since the day I was
born."

"Name's Tricia." The girl offered Matthew the last bite of
fish he'd bought her at a kiosk at Sydney harbor. He wolfed it
hungrily. His own order had disappeared in record time.

"Matthew," he mumbled, swallowing the last of her fish in
one gulp.

"That's not what it says in your wallet."

He was learning to think fast. "Simon Matthew Van Valkenburg. My friends call me Matt."

"Hmmm…" Tricia leaned back against the bench and
closed her eyes.

"You don't think they'll find us here?"

"They won't even know who to look for. When Charlie

wakes up, he won't tell them anything. Even if he did, they know him at the cop shop, and they wouldn't believe a thing he said anyway.''

Matthew was beginning to feel more like himself. He had his wallet back, even if most of the money was gone. But there was still seventy dollars inside, minus what they'd spent on dinner. That was something, anyway.

"Why'd you steal from me?" he asked.

"Because I could."

"No, I mean why did you choose me instead of somebody else?"

"You were an easy mark."

He squirmed, but he could hardly refute that. "How could you tell?"

"You had that look. Like somebody who can't figure out where he is and what he's doing."

That was true enough. He silently vowed to be more careful.

Tricia shrugged. "I thought you'd go back to your mum and dad and they'd take care of you. I didn't know you'd end up on the street."

Anger flicked through him. "And I didn't know you were a hooker."

She giggled, a surprisingly innocent sound. "I could tell that. And here I thought I was pretty good at it."

"Why do you do that, anyway? The lady at the bookstore said she offered you a real job."

"Old Mrs. Duff?"

"I was trying to find my wallet."

"Oh, she offered me a job, she did. If I wanted that kind of job, I could have found one back in Humpty Doo."

"Well, it sure sounds better than what you do."

"Most blokes like what I do just fine."

"You're too young to do it." He was surprised at his own tone. He sounded the way his mother did when she lectured him about picking up his dirty socks.

She didn't seem offended. Just curious. "How old do you think I am?"

"I don't know. Twenty?"

She giggled again. "Har-dly."

"Well, if you're older, you're still too young to—"

"I'm sixteen."

He wanted to ponder that, but he didn't know where to start. "How long…?"

"Last year. I got tired of the Territ'ry. Nothing there except flies and cows and willy-willies. You ever been there?"

"No, but I'm going."

"Beyond the black stump?" She sounded incredulous. "Why?"

"I'm going to see my grandfather. Roman Llewellyn. He has a ranch there…" He remembered that his father and Aunt Mei had always referred to his grandfather's land as a station. "A station called Jimiramira."

"Yeah, I know Jimiramira."

"You do?" For the first time since he'd broken Charlie's arm, his mind moved solidly to something else. "How?"

"No reason."

"Do you live nearby?"

"Nothing's near anything else in the Territ'ry. Don't you know that?"

"What did you call the place you lived?"

"Humpty Doo. And don't look at me like I'm blathering. I didn't just think it up. It's a real place. My mum and dad have a bit of land there. Mango trees. We lived on a station when I was younger. They saved everything they could to buy their bloody mangoes. Said they were doing it for me."

Matthew thought of his own mother, who claimed *everything* she did was for him. He supposed this was one of those things that had nothing to do with international boundaries. "Don't you miss your parents?" Tricia was silent, but he persisted. "Come on, don't they worry about you?"

"It's too late to think about that, isn't it? Besides, you don't think they'd want me back the way I am now." It wasn't a question.

Matthew thought about Liana. There would be hell to pay

when he returned home, but never any question that he was wanted.

Tricia folded her arms. "Besides, I don't want to go back. I'm never going to live in the Territ'ry again."

"Can you live here, with Charlie looking for you?"

"I can stay out of his way."

"Doing what you do? You can't do that just anywhere, can you? And next time he might kill you. Why'd you hook up with him, anyway?"

"The bastard told me he'd keep me safe. He told me if I made good money, I could have anything I wanted."

Matthew was trying to understand. "If you made good money and kept it all, you would have been further ahead."

"Too right. But then I would have been alone, wouldn't I?"

Matthew was aware of Tricia's hip, warm and solid against his. Until he'd seen Charlie beating her, he'd been sure that if he caught up with this girl, he would feel nothing but anger. Now, incongruously, he was trying to convince her that there was more to life than standing on street corners earning money for Charlie. It was as unlikely a scenario as he could imagine, considering that right now he couldn't manage his own life.

"What's your story?" she said at last. "And don't tell me you're not a Yank. I saw your driver's license. San Francisco, it said."

He considered what to tell her. "That's where I live. But my father lives in Australia, so that makes me half-Australian."

"Which half? Top or bottom?" She flashed the smile he remembered from their first encounter.

He could feel his cheeks heating. "I came over to visit my grandfather. I've never met him, and I wanted to. That's all."

"Why didn't you ring him and ask for money so you didn't have to go bush last night?"

"He doesn't know I'm here. It's a surprise."

"Then why didn't you ring your father?"

"He's in the States right now." Matthew had tried not to dwell on the way Cullen must have felt when he didn't show up in New York, or about the accusations that were probably still bouncing from coast to coast. He just hoped that by now his mother had found the message he had left for her.

Tricia was still gazing at him. "Your father's there. You're here. Your grandfather doesn't know you're on your way to meet him. Does anybody know where you are?"

"Sure," he said too quickly. "How else would I have gotten here?"

She left it at that. "Well, what are you going to do now? You can't get to the Territ'ry without money."

"I guess I'm going to find a ride."

"How will you do that?"

"I guess I'll take the bus or train as far as I can, then start walking and see if anybody stops."

"You've really gone off your brain. There's nothing in the heart of this country but roos and dingoes and heaps of flies. I reckon you'd die by the side of the road and nobody would ever find more than a bone and a tooth."

"I'm going to my grandfather's."

"You don't know a thing about how to survive out there."

Matthew waited. She seemed poised on the brink of something.

She finished after a long pause. "Well, I'm not going back to the Territ'ry. Not ever."

"That's too bad. You need to get out of here so Charlie won't find you. And I bet you could show me a lot of tricks." His cheeks flamed brighter as he realized what he'd said.

She didn't seem to notice. "What would I do when I got there, anyway? I couldn't stay. I'd have to come back here alone. And it was hard enough getting out the first time."

"After we got there, my grandfather would buy you a ticket if I asked him. A ticket to someplace where Charlie wouldn't look for you."

"You don't even know your grandfather."

"Maybe not. But he'd help. My father says..." He cleared his throat. "He says he's a man of high principle."

"High principle? Maybe it would be worth the trip just to meet a man with *any* principles." She rolled her eyes like the girls back home always did, and for the first time in days he didn't feel far from San Francisco.

Matthew didn't know why he wanted Tricia to come with him. The desire was mixed up with his fear that Charlie would find her and beat or kill her. But there was more to it. He was lonely and unsure of himself after everything that had happened.

"I don't suppose I have anything better to do in Sydney until Charlie settles down." She swatted at the crumbs dotting her skirt. "Maybe I'll give it a go. But I'm not going home. Just to Jimiramira. Not one kilometer closer to Humpty Doo."

Matthew knew he was good at figuring out what people were really saying. Both his mother and father struggled to be honest, but too often he sensed emotions they wouldn't admit to. Now he suspected Tricia meant something else, too.

"Not one kilometer," he agreed. "But this time, keep your hands off my wallet."

She grinned. "Too right. We'll be mates."

His heart lurched. It seemed to have something to do with the way her lips curled over her crooked front teeth.

She got to her feet and finished brushing the crumbs away. "I know a place we can sleep for the rest of the night. Then we'll figure out what to do next. I have a couple of ideas."

"Not your place…"

"No. I can't go back there. And that's crook, too, because now Charlie will pinch all my stuff."

"Did you have much?"

"No worries."

He got to his feet, although he was rapidly growing too tired to move. "Looks like we'll both be starting off with nothing."

She shook her brown hair back over her shoulders and straightened her skirt. "I'll be happy to share my half of it. How about you, mate?"

Matthew found that he wasn't too tired to smile.

20

San Francisco

"You didn't know any of this?" Cullen combed his fingers through his hair. He had been silent all the way back to Liana's apartment, but he'd begun questioning her the moment they dismissed the security associate who had been manning the silent telephone.

"I knew Aunt Mei and my father were estranged. But until I was thirteen, I didn't even know she existed." Liana strode through the hallway to the bar between the living and dining rooms. Ordinarily a glass or two of wine with dinner was her limit. But tonight she needed something that would get right to the root of her pain and dull it quickly.

She threw open a cabinet door, pulled out the first bottle she came to, an aged, unblended Scotch, and poured herself a generous shot. Then, wordlessly, she offered the bottle to Cullen.

He shook his head.

"Since when did you refuse a drink?" She tossed down half the contents of her tumbler and marveled that the liquor found its way past the lump in her throat.

"So you never knew Mei was the one who stole the pearl from my family?"

"Well, by rights it didn't belong to your family, did it?"

He leaned over the bar. "That's hardly my point."

She finished her drink before she answered. "You already know some of this story."

"Don't leave anything out."

She poured another drink, but she didn't gulp this one, because it had to be her last. She took it into the living room and lowered herself to a corner of the sofa. The portrait of their son loomed in front of them as Cullen joined her.

"When I was thirteen, my class went on a field trip to Chinatown. We were probably doing one of those rah-rah 'We Are the World' units in social studies. But while we were there, I noticed an old woman watching me. We were standing on the sidewalk on Grant Avenue, and our teacher was lecturing. As we moved away, the woman came over and gave me a piece of paper. She said, 'Call me.'"

"The woman was Mei."

Liana nodded. "It wasn't a coincidence, of course. She'd known about me since I'd come to live with my father, and I think she'd been watching me, or had me watched. Maybe she knew I was a rebellious teenager and miserable living with my father and stepmother. Maybe Mei guessed I would call just because I was hungry to be recognized by somebody...."

"She's a sharp old girl."

"Until we met, I didn't know my grandmother had been born in China and that I didn't get my black hair from some roguish Irishman in the Robeson past. Once, when I was a child, I was walking with my father, and an old Chinese man spoke to us in Chinese, as if he expected us to understand. My father was furious. But how unusual was that? He was always furious about something."

Cullen was silent. Liana stared at her son's portrait. "When I called Aunt Mei, she asked me to meet her at a restaurant in Chinatown. I didn't know why she wanted to see me, but I knew my father wouldn't like it, so, of course, I went. I remember she ate with a fork. I ate with chopsticks. I guess I'd learned that in social studies, too."

Liana glanced at Cullen. She had forgotten how intently he

could concentrate, how thoroughly he could immerse himself in something if it interested him. She felt an unexpected stab of longing. Once she had interested him the way her story did now. She had been the focus of everything he was and did. She had tried to forget the way that felt, too.

"What did Mei tell you that day?" he said.

"Well, she didn't say why she wanted to see me. At least, not right away. The waiter came over to take our order. He chatted and laughed with her, and I could see they were talking about me. When he left, I asked what they'd said. Aunt Mei said, 'He wanted to know if you were my granddaughter.' I laughed, because that seemed funny to me. Then she said, 'I told him no, of course not. You are my niece.'"

"And you were completely surprised?"

"I thought she was crazy. Then she told me that she and my father were twins who had been raised apart and that later, when they found each other again, there had been a terrible fight. Since that day they had never spoken. She wouldn't tell me what they fought about—she never told me until tonight. But she did say that if I asked my father, he would deny her story because he didn't want anyone to know he was Chinese."

"Was she trying to get back at him, do you suppose, by telling his secret?"

"Maybe. But I thought, even then, that she wanted to see if I was like my father. I think she hoped there might be more to me than Robeson pretensions. In some strange way, I think she thought she had to help me, that her mother would have expected her to. Despite everything Thomas had done to her."

"And she's never, by word or deed, indicated that she harbors any ill feelings toward you?"

For a moment Liana couldn't imagine what he meant. Then she realized he was talking about Matthew's disappearance. "Cullen, you think she's involved in this somehow?"

"Do you understand why she told us that story tonight?"

"No. Do you?"

He shook his head.

"After our lunch, I knew better than to go back to my father and tell him what I'd learned. Aunt Mei suggested I do a little digging on my own if I wanted to be sure of the truth. So I did. I told one of my teachers I was going to write a paper about my family tree, and I asked her to help me get a copy of an Australian birth certificate. Two months later, I discovered that without a doubt a woman named Lian Sing was my grandmother.''

"Lian?''

"Yes. Willow's Chinese name was Lian. When I saw that, I realized something even more startling. My own mother had named *me* Liana, after my grandmother. Somehow she had discovered my father's secret, and she had named me Liana either to spite him or just as a silent salute to another woman who had suffered at his hands. Another woman Thomas had tried to render invisible.''

"Your mother never told you that you had Chinese heritage?''

Liana's mother was another story entirely. "Remember, my mother left my father before I was born. He didn't even know she was pregnant. So she had a huge investment in keeping everything about him a secret. And I was only eight when she died. I didn't know I *had* a father until the social services agency where we were living traced him.''

"And from all this, you determined Mei was telling the truth, and that she really was your aunt?''

"Aunt Mei had her own birth certificate. Of course everything matched.''

"So from that point on, she took you into her family?''

"From that point on, she took me under her wing. Despite what they must have known about the pearl, her sons and their families were always kind to me. Frank, Mei's grandson by her youngest son John, even works for me now that Thomas is dead. Hiring him was something I could do for Mei.''

"Your father never suspected you knew her?''

"Not for years. By the time he did, he realized it was too late to deny who she was, but he gave me an ultimatum. It was simple, really. The Fongs, or Thomas and everything that went with him, like Pacific International, the Robeson personal fortune, everything right down to my good name and identity as a white Anglo-Saxon Protestant. It wasn't a hard choice. I was young and idealistic, and I was nursing a boatload of resentment. I had money from my mother's estate, so I took off."

She looked up at him. "Along the way, of course, I met and married you."

His gaze was warm. "Yeah, I remember that part."

Liana felt her cheeks flush. She looked away and tried to think what might be important about all of this. Was Mei's story just an old woman's ramblings? Had she seen an opportunity to tell Cullen the truth about her relationship with Bryce Llewellyn as a sort of "deathbed" confession?

Or did this story have something to do with Matthew's disappearance? Did Mei know something more, something she hadn't told them?

"Lee, what are you thinking?"

"Right after she arrived in America, Mei married a man named Wo Fong. Think about it, Cullen. She was only twenty. She had journeyed across the world to bring my father the pearl. She had given up the man she loved, only to have her own brother cast her out empty-handed. She was alone in America. No family. No friends. No job. She only had one thing in her favor. Most Chinese men had been forced by law to leave their families in China. So an unattached Chinese woman was a rare commodity. Mei must have had her pick of suitors. She told me once that she chose Wo Fong because he was a kind man, a hard worker with good business prospects. But she didn't marry for love."

"So she married a stranger and raised a family. While my grandfather wondered for the rest of his days why she left him."

"What was your grandfather like, Cullen? Tell me what you know about him."

"I don't know what bloody difference it makes, Lee."

She shared his frustration. It seemed only natural to put her hand on his. She did so before she realized it, then looked down with something akin to horror.

If Cullen felt anything of the sort, he didn't indicate it, but he didn't try to stop her when she pulled away. "I hardly remember my grandfather. I was barely four when he died. I don't remember him paying attention to me. He was a quiet man. Stern. Remote. He married my grandmother because their lands were connected, and she was as determined to make a go of her place as he was of Jimiramira. She was one of those Australian women bred to live in the back of beyond. Strong as a man and better with a horse. My father was an only child because she needed one son to leave the place to when she died and she didn't want to be bothered with more."

"Neither of them married for love, then. Not Mei and not Bryce."

"I don't know that my grandfather was unhappy. But I don't think my father ever had much of a family life. His parents were always off at one end of the station or the other, rarely together. He was raised by couples who came in to take care of the homestead. Some were good and some weren't."

During their marriage Cullen had talked as little as possible about his father, Roman. Liana knew they had been estranged for many years, and nothing Matthew had told her indicated that the estrangement had ended since the divorce. "From what Aunt Mei told us, I'd guess Bryce never had an opportunity to learn how to be a good father," she coached.

"Well, he passed that much on to my dad. Dad tried, I think. He wanted to be a good father. But he didn't know how, either. I was only ten when my mother died, and from that time on, he just got worse and worse." Cullen took a deep breath. "I've wondered all these years if I've done the same poor job of it with Matthew."

Liana had been so immersed in her own unhappiness that she had given little thought to Cullen's. Some small part of her had been glad that for once Cullen was finding out that parenting was more than a month of camping trips and baseball games.

Some terrible, hurtful part of her.

Cullen was suffering as much as she was, and she had done nothing to help him, as if by pushing him further away she could bring Matthew closer.

"Matthew adores you," she said softly. "And sometimes I've gotten so angry about that, Cullen. Because I'm the one who sits by his bed when he's sick, and you're the one he worships." She paused. "But I'm sorry. I wish he were here right now, worshiping at your feet."

"I'd give up my month each year with him just to have him here with us."

They stared at each other in mute misery. She felt tears slide down her cheeks. Until then, she hadn't been aware she was crying. He put his arm around her and pulled her to rest against his shoulder. She resisted, but not long enough. She was tired and frightened, and Cullen was the only person who could understand exactly what she was feeling.

He stroked her hair, pushing it behind her ear and smoothing it with his fingertips. "I've been angry, too, Lee. Because I want to be the one sitting by his bed. You're the one he can count on, and if he worships me, he has to do it from afar."

She believed him. For the first time since his arrival, she believed what he was saying without examining every little part of it. In the years since they had been apart, Cullen had turned into the father she had wanted for her son.

"How did it all go so wrong, Cullen? Where's our boy?"

"I think I know what Mei was trying to tell us. We haven't listened to Matthew. Not the way we should have. No one ever listened to Bryce. No one understood his feelings. He tried to protect his parents from each other...." His voice trailed off. "The way Matthew tried to protect each of us."

"And you think that's why he left?"

He laid his cheek against her hair, and she felt a shudder pass, lightning-quick, through his body. "I don't know. It's not like Matthew to frighten us. Even if he ran away, he'd be sure to let us know he's all right."

She wanted to believe otherwise. "Maybe he's just afraid to

call. Maybe he knows we'd put a trace on the line." She took a deep, ragged breath and willed the tears to stop.

"There hasn't been a letter, either."

"Maybe he was worried about postmarks. Or maybe it hasn't arrived."

Cullen sat up straighter, pulling her with him. "The devil." He didn't push her away as much as he positioned her to face him. "Lee, is Matthew's computer still on?"

She was choking back sobs. "I'm sure it is."

"Come on." He stood and held out his hand. She let him help her up; then she followed him to Matthew's room. He sat down at the computer. "I've got to E-mail Sarah."

"Your girlfriend?"

"She's not my girlfriend, Lee."

"Then what's the point?"

"I haven't told Sarah about Matthew. I need to, because someone in Broome needs to know what's taking place here. But that's not all. If I give her my password, she can access my E-mail. Don't you see? She can check to see if Matthew has sent me anything."

Liana felt a pinch of hope. "Phone her, Cullen. Get her to do it right now."

He consulted his watch. "Most likely that won't be any faster. It's about noon there. She'll be off around the farm somewhere—down at the canteen, most likely. But she'll check her mail as soon as she gets back. She always does. And I'll have her ring me the moment she checks mine."

As he spoke, he composed a quick letter to Sarah. Liana read it over his shoulder. "But she won't know this is from you, will she? You'll be using Matthew's account, so won't it look like it's from him?"

"Just in the heading. I'll sign the letter. You don't spend much time at the computer, do you?"

He activated the program and waited as it went through the steps to connect. Then, just as quickly, the computer logged off.

"That's odd." Cullen leaned over, as if being closer would help him understand what he saw.

"What is it?"

"It says the account is already signed on."

"That has to be a mistake, doesn't it?"

"Does Matthew share this account with anyone?"

"What do you mean?"

"Whose name is on the account, Lee?"

She heard the impatience in his voice. "Mine. It's billed to my credit card."

"Well, you're bloody well not surfing the net at another computer, are you?" He activated the program again. The same thing happened once more.

Cullen slapped his hand on the desk in frustration. "Did you give Stanford Matthew's password? Or yours?"

"I don't know Matthew's password. And no one asked for mine."

"So by rights, unless Matthew's given his password to a friend, this computer is the only place anyone besides him should be able to access his account. But right now someone is using it."

"Matthew?"

"Maybe."

She waited for an explosion of joy, but Cullen's tone was anything except relieved. "What's the other possibility?"

He spun the chair to face her. "It might be someone else."

"Someone else? But how? Why?"

"How? I don't know for certain. Someone may have figured out his password through trial and error. Kids like to use descriptions or nicknames, so they'll remember. Someone who knows him might have made a lucky guess. Maybe his password is something obvious like his birth date, although I've warned him that's not a good idea. Or maybe he stored it somewhere and somebody found it."

Her tears had long since dried, but now a shudder snaked up her spine. "That leaves why, doesn't it?"

He said nothing.

"Why, Cullen? If Matthew's not using his own account, why would someone else want to use it?"

"It could simply be a friend trying to get free Internet access while Matthew's gone."

"And?"

"It could be someone looking for him, Lee. Someone searching for clues from his E-mail, just the way we are."

"Why would anyone...?" She stared at Cullen and saw he knew something she didn't. "What do you know?"

"When Stanford rang Matthew's bank to see about his account, he discovered he wasn't the first person to check it."

"He didn't tell me that."

"He didn't want to worry you unnecessarily."

"Maybe it was the police."

"Maybe, but I think we have to face the possibility that someone else might be trying to find Matthew."

"Someone who wants to hurt him? But why?"

"If Matthew has the pearl, Lee—"

"Matthew doesn't have the pearl! He wouldn't steal from me."

"Then who would benefit most if Matthew never came back home?"

"I don't know what you mean."

"Your father left almost everything he owned to Matthew, didn't he?"

She tried to think how best to explain it. "It's a tricky will. Graham and I have use of a reasonable share of the money as long as we're working for Pacific International. But yes, after all's said and done, Matthew stands to inherit everything."

"And if he doesn't live that long? Who gets it?"

"Graham..." She breathed the word as if it were cyanide she was expelling from her lungs.

Cullen fell silent again.

Liana shook her head. "No, Cullen. I just won't believe it. Graham and I are hardly best friends, but he wouldn't hurt Matthew. As long as he stays at Pacific International, he's a rich man, anyway. What could he want that he can't have now?"

"Control over his life?"

She stared at him. Thomas had set up his will to bind his family to Pacific International forever. Even Matthew had to dance to a dead man's tune in order to inherit what should rightfully have been his without strings. In death, as in life, Thomas had insisted on having his way.

But if Matthew died, Graham's power increased a hundredfold.

"I'm not saying Graham kidnapped our son," Cullen said. "But it seems that someone's looking for him as hard as we are, Lee. Maybe Graham's only trying to take advantage of a golden opportunity."

She knew she couldn't afford to dismiss any theories, that Matthew's survival might depend on questioning her loyalties. But the possibility that Graham might want Matthew dead made her sick.

"Just think about it." Cullen turned his chair and tried once more to access Matthew's account. This time he logged on without difficulty. Whoever had been using the account had logged off.

"Check his mail, too," she said.

"If someone read it just now, they may have deleted it."

"We have to tell Stanford about this."

Cullen didn't turn. He was too intent on the screen. "How closely does Stanford work with Graham?"

She realized Cullen was asking if Stanford could be trusted. "I can't stand this, Cullen."

"Lee…" He pointed to a box he'd just opened. "These are the people who can access this account. Just you and Matthew."

"I told you that. No one else is authorized to use the account. Just us."

"Have you checked your E-mail?"

"I never use the account. I've never even given anyone my screen name. I never—"

He cut her off. "Who set this up, then?"

"Matthew did, of course. He wanted me to learn.... Oh." She realized what Cullen was saying.

Cullen exited, went back and selected Liana's screen name, and began the process again. "I'm assuming he programmed in your password."

She tried to think. "I don't know. It's Cruella. He was mad at me for something the day he set it up. We had a good laugh afterwards."

"It's stored in the computer. It's working. It's logging on."

"Why didn't I think of this?" She leaned forward, praying she would see mail from her son. A man's voice announced that she had mail. She watched as one letter was retrieved and the program shut down.

Cullen clicked the mouse on Incoming Mail and the letter was listed. "SEZ. That's not Matthew's screen name," Cullen said.

"Matthew had mail from someone named SEZ, Cullen. I picked up something from him the first time I checked his mail."

"Him?"

"A figure of speech. It wasn't signed." She watched as Cullen opened the letter.

Cullen read out loud as she followed the letter silently. "Mom, I'm all right. I promise you don't have to worry. I can take care of myself, and I won't be gone long. I guess when I get back I'll have to stay in my room for the rest of my life. Please tell Dad I'm sorry. I really wanted to go on that camping trip more than anything."

"Love, Matthew." Liana read the last two words aloud, and her voice broke.

This time she didn't resist when Cullen rose and took her in his arms.

21

"Lee, he's all right."

Cullen could feel Liana trying to compose herself, but her voice was muffled against his shoulder. "What if he didn't write this? Or what if he wrote it under duress? Maybe he was fine when he sent it, but he isn't now."

He held her close and stroked her hair. Her body was subtly feminine, but like everything else about her, the promise of what lay just out of his reach was most powerful. It was the elusive lure of her mind and heart that had always drawn him.

"Lee." He lifted her chin with his fingertips. Her eyes were red-rimmed and haunted. "We have to believe he's all right. What's the point in believing anything else?"

"How can you say that? He's only fourteen!"

"We have to keep looking for him. But this is the first good news we've had since he disappeared. Now we have to find a bit of faith. In Matthew. In our ability to find him."

He watched her struggle. He had given her little or no reason to have faith in him. Life had given her little reason to have faith in happy endings. But life had also given her Matthew, and Cullen reminded her of that now.

"I know you've had a hard shake of it, but no matter what else has happened in your life, Matthew's a gift. We're going to bring him home. You have to believe it."

"Why are you so strong?"

"I'm not as strong as you think. Tell me we're going to find him. That'll make me stronger."

"Nothing I ever said or did changed anything about you."

"You're wrong."

"I can't..." She shook her head.

"We're going to find him. Tell me we're going to do this together. Whatever it takes. Tell me."

He watched her weigh a lifetime of disappointment against the flicker of faith that had refused to be extinguished.

"You love him. As much as I do," she said. It wasn't a question.

"Enough to bring him home. But only if you're with me."

"Yes. Okay."

"Lee..." He managed a smile, but it faded at the expression in her eyes. She was terrified, as if by telling him she trusted him she had opened herself up to a lifetime of sorrow.

"I'm not going to hurt you. I'll cut out my heart before I hurt you again."

"I'll sharpen the knife."

He didn't think about what he did next. Impulsiveness had been his trademark, and he hadn't eradicated it completely. Her lips trembled, and he touched them with his own as a promise. But at the first warm whisper of flesh against flesh, he knew what a mistake he had made.

He lifted his head, and in her eyes he saw the same emotions he felt. Shock. Discovery. Resurrection.

He knew that anything he could say was inadequate or dangerous. He stepped back, as if what had happened was the most natural thing in the world, and spoke about the one thing guaranteed to deflect her attention.

"Then we have a bargain. We'll bring Matthew home, no matter what it takes. And the first thing we have to do is find out who SEZ is. He or she plays a part in all this. At the least, he sent on a message from our son."

"I E-mailed SEZ after I got the message addressed to Matthew. I never got a reply."

"Did you check member profiles?"

"Stanford tried to get profiles for everyone, but he said registration was voluntary. I'm fairly sure SEZ wasn't listed."

Cullen turned away to log back on. He was glad to have a moment to compose himself. A quick check of the provider's membership directory showed she was right. "We might be able to force them to turn over SEZ's name and address, but I reckon it would take a battle, and we don't have time."

"Stanford might know how to shortcut the process."

"Let's leave him out of it for the moment. I think we should tell him we're going to pursue a few things on our own."

"He'll suspect something's up. And besides, he'll wonder why we're not hovering beside the phone."

"Then let him know you're convinced Matthew ran away, and we want to try our luck looking for him without the police in tow. Tell him Sue's agreed to field telephone calls and that you'll have your cell phone with you. But right now, I think our time will be best spent talking to Matthew's friends. One of them may know who SEZ is. What about schoolmates? If we're lucky, SEZ is local."

"And easily intimidated…"

"I'm going to send a message to everyone in Matthew's Internet address book. It's time we started being straight-up about what's happening. After you've talked to Stanford, start ringing Matthew's friends. By the time we go to bed tonight, we'll know exactly what we have to do next."

She brushed her fingertips against his shoulder, an unexpected and bittersweet affirmation.

He closed his eyes and wished he could begin his life all over again.

Alicia Rivera had boy-short black hair, distinctive features she hadn't quite grown into, and a gold spike in her nose that she touched frequently for reassurance.

"Alicia, you tell these people what they want to know, you understand me?" Mrs. Rivera, a less flamboyant version of her daughter, sat forward on the sofa in her Daly City apartment and stared daggers at Alicia. "I've got a shipment of Carole Little coming in any minute. I've got no time to waste."

Liana glanced at Cullen. She doubted he had slept well last night, but he was completely focused on Alicia, his gaze understanding, his Akubra twisting with masculine grace in his hands. If the teenager didn't respond to Cullen's warmth or her mother's threats, it wasn't because either of them hadn't pulled out all the stops.

Inside the apartment, dust motes danced in a shaft of morning sunshine. Outside on the busy avenue, the harsh squeal of brakes was followed by angry shouts and horns, and in the dress shop below, someone turned up a soft-rock radio station to drown out the noise.

"Carole Little," Mrs. Rivera repeated. "And if we're still here waiting for you to say something, I'm not going to be happy. You understand me, Alicia?"

"I don't know any SEZ." Alicia's nose spike wobbled as her pout deepened. "I told them."

Cullen leaned closer. "As a matter of fact, what you told Matthew's mother last night was that you didn't rat out your friends. That's just a bit different, wouldn't you say?"

The teenager's expression was poised somewhere between sullen and scared. Liana could see they were going to lose her. "Alicia, I know Matthew only chooses good friends. Loyal kids who would never do anything to hurt him. But sometimes you can hurt somebody by doing what they ask you to. You'd stop a friend if he was drinking and wanted to drive, wouldn't you? Don't you see? Matthew has disappeared. And he could be in danger."

"Car-ole Lit-tle…" Mrs. Rivera looked at her watch.

Liana forced patience into her voice. "Mrs. Rivera, we can talk to Alicia alone, if that's better for you. We'll be finished in a few minutes anyway."

Mrs. Rivera stood and pointed a finger at Alicia. "You tell them what they want to know." In a moment she had disappeared down the stairs.

"Car-ole Lit-tle," Alicia singsonged, in perfect imitation, once her mother was out of earshot.

"Will you help us, Alicia?" Liana said.

"What'll you do to Matthew when you find him?"

"Hug him to death."

Alicia sighed. "I don't know where he went or anything. He didn't tell *me* he was running away."

Liana nodded, as if she had all the time in the world.

"But Simon might know," Alicia said at last.

"Simon?"

"Simon Van Valkenburg."

"Does Simon go to school with you and Matthew?" Cullen said.

"No. He doesn't go to school anywhere. He's a genius. But maybe…like he's a friend of a friend of mine. Like, maybe I introduced them."

"Is Simon SEZ?" The moment she said it, Liana knew. "Simon SEZ. Of course."

Alicia didn't answer, but Cullen was frowning.

"Simon Says," Liana explained. "It's a children's game. I used to play it with Matthew when he was little. That's probably where Simon got his screen name."

"Sometimes he's pretty stupid for a genius," Alicia said, attempting to toss her short locks.

"Are Simon and Matthew good friends?" Liana asked.

"Maybe."

Liana knew she needed one thing more. She said a silent prayer that Alicia wouldn't refuse her. "Alicia, please. Will you give me Simon's address? If you prefer, I won't tell him where I got it."

"Are the cops going to talk to him?"

"Just us. I promise."

Alicia considered, then she shrugged. "I guess I can give it to you. But don't tell Matthew what I did. Okay? I really like him. I don't want him to be mad at me."

"The future Mrs. Matthew Llewellyn?" Cullen opened the car door for Liana. He had flatly refused to be driven here in the company car, preferring to brave the San Francisco traffic in hers. But Cullen was driving. In the past year Liana's terror of open spaces had spread to getting behind the wheel of her own Miata.

Liana snapped her seat belt in place. ''She's not a bad kid, but she'll have to lose the nose spike.''

Cullen got in on the driver's side and started the engine. ''Are you doing okay?''

''Fine.'' Liana was doing better than she had expected. She had braved the walk to and from the Riveras' apartment with little more than trembling knees.

He flashed her the same grin he'd used on Alicia, and something tugged inside her. For too many years Cullen's smiles had reduced her good sense and multiplied her flaws. She had allowed that questionable equation to rule her life. And when he'd kissed her last night, she had seen how little that had changed.

''Can you get us there, Lee?''

Alicia had told them that Simon lived in a condo on Green Street in Russian Hill, and Liana was familiar with the block of bay-windowed buildings juxtaposed with sixties concrete high-rises. She gave Cullen instructions, and he set off, weaving in and out of traffic.

''I wish we could have talked to Aunt Mei.'' Liana had phoned her aunt twice that morning, but both times Betty had insisted Mei wasn't feeling well and needed to rest. Liana had hoped to question her some more about her story and its relevance to Matthew. But clearly Mei had said all she was going to.

Cullen pulled into the right lane and slowed as he neared a freeway entrance ramp. ''It would be like her to make us work this out by ourselves, wouldn't it? She's told her story, now it's up to us.''

''I suppose. Maybe there's something in the Robeson blood that makes us exasperating.''

''Matthew's never mentioned this Simon to you?'' Cullen

said when they were on the Junipero Serra Freeway heading east.

"Alicia, yes. Simon, no." He drove the red Miata like a devil-may-care foreigner used to the other side of the road, but she felt safe enough. "And he hasn't mentioned Simon to you?"

"No."

"Graham says I baby him. Maybe Simon was Matthew's way of breaking free. Maybe having a friend I didn't know about made him feel grown up."

"Or maybe he knew you wouldn't approve."

"I don't restrict his friends, Cullen. Not any more than you would."

"I believe you. But maybe he'd never presented anyone quite like Simon to you."

"Maybe not, but he collects oddballs. He gets that from you. He's never met a stranger."

"Is that how you saw me?"

"I envied you for it. I wanted to be that way. But I was always afraid I'd trust the wrong people."

"And then you did. You trusted me."

"Maybe we ought to stop right there."

"I've thought a lot about our marriage in the years since it ended. I think when we met, we saw each other clearly. But what we saw were the real people hiding under the trappings. And when two people marry, the trappings come with them."

Scenery sped by. Glimpses of oddly sculptured hills, tile roofs gleaming in sunlight, gray lengths of freeway that set each image apart like the sashing between colorful quilt blocks. Somewhere deep inside her imagination, Liana saw semiprecious gems set beside flowing pewter rivers. She pushed the vision away as she always did now, an idea unborn and unwelcomed.

Cullen fell silent.

"All right. You've hooked me," she said at last. "Go on. What did we see and what were the trappings?"

"What did you want when you married me, Lee?"

She thought a while. "A strong man. Someone I could count on. Someone I could make a life with."

"That man was there, only I buried him so deeply it took years to find him."

How could she dispute that without causing another argument? Besides, the mere fact that they were discussing their relationship was an example of how much Cullen *had* changed.

"What did you want when you married me?" she asked in return.

"A free spirit. Someone who didn't make demands. A woman so confident that I didn't have to offer anything I didn't want to give."

Something tightened in her chest. "Boy, you can really pick 'em, can't you?"

"You were that woman, Lee. You followed me to the wilds of Australia. You cocked a snook at every blighter who tried to stand in your way. You made do with nothing and never whined or fretted."

"I was scared to death."

"But you had a bash at it anyway."

"Because I thought we were building something together."

"And that scared me to death."

"Damned from the start, huh?"

"Maybe. Or maybe if we'd looked beyond the trappings, maybe if we'd had the courage to be the people we wanted to be, we could have made it."

"Courage? I think looking backwards has skewed your vision. Mine has always been in short supply. And now I can't even cross a street without feeling like the universe is caving in."

"But you keep going, don't you? You don't give in and you don't give up. In my book, that's what courage looks like, Lee."

Her eyes misted. She wasn't used to receiving praise for her worst flaw.

He didn't take his eyes off the road, but he reached over and covered her hand.

* * *

Simon Van Valkenburg lived on the ground floor of a Russian Hill apartment building that had nothing to recommend it except the address. Despite that, Liana knew someone had anted up big time for the unrenovated space.

The young man who greeted them had shoulder-length brown hair, murky brown eyes and a beard that barely covered his chin. Obviously Simon's genius did not extend to personal presentation.

Cullen introduced himself, standing close enough to the door to stop Simon from closing it in their faces. "We're here to talk about Matthew."

"He's back from camping?"

Liana stepped forward to discourage Cullen from answering. "May we come in?"

Simon was still trying to decide when Cullen took matters into his own hands and moved past him. Liana smiled and murmured thanks, as if their entry had been Simon's idea.

"I guess we can go in the living room," Simon said.

"Do you live with your parents?" Liana asked.

"My dad. When he's home."

The living room was sparsely furnished in sixties avocado green. Balls of fur dotting the wood floor announced the presence of a dog even before Liana got to the sofa and found it occupied by a snoozing Border collie.

She took a chair in the corner, first setting the books that covered it on the floor. She read the top title out loud. *"The Computer Revolution—How to Bring the World to its Knees on Your Lunch Break."* She looked up. "Pretty scary stuff."

"It's stupid. Anybody with a catchy title gets published."

"You're interested in computers?"

Simon shrugged. "Some."

"We hear you and Matthew are Internet mates," Cullen said. He seated himself beside Simon on a fading loveseat, slinging his arm over the back with his hand parallel to Simon's collar.

"We chat sometimes. Yeah."

"Are you good enough mates to trade your passwords?"

"I'd never give anybody my password. Do you know what could happen?"

"Did he give you his?"

"Why would he? I don't need it."

Liana was glad Cullen had checked with the boy to see if he might have logged on to Matthew's account last night. "Matthew's missing, and we found several messages with your screen name. One of them was addressed to me." She leaned forward. "We have to know where he is, Simon. And obviously you know something."

"If Matthew wanted you to know, he'd tell you, wouldn't he?"

"Fourteen-year-old boys don't always make the best decisions. How much older than him are you?"

"A little."

"Tell the lady how old you are," Cullen said quietly.

Simon glanced at Cullen; then he wriggled back farther into the corner of his seat. "Eighteen."

"That could be a problem for you." Liana shook her head as if she were concerned for him. "Matthew's a minor. There are laws about contributing to the delinquency of a minor."

"Delinquency?" Simon gave a nervous laugh. "Matthew's not a delinquent. And he'll be back. Then you can find out where he's been."

"We're going to find out now," Cullen said, in the same quiet voice.

Simon looked uncomfortable. "I let him use my computer to write an E-mail. And I posted it for him. That's all."

"Where is he?" Cullen asked.

Simon was silent.

"Look," Liana said, "is this worth going to jail over, Simon? Matthew made a mistake by involving you. You don't owe him anything. And we think he might be in some danger. You don't want that on your conscience, do you?"

"Matthew can take care of himself. He's a lot older than

fourteen inside." He touched his narrow chest. "Matthew's an old soul."

"We don't bloody care if he was King Tut in a former life," Cullen said. "We're going to find our son, and you're going to help us."

"Please." Liana pleaded with Simon with her eyes, good cop to Cullen's bad. "He's all we have."

"If you cared about him, why did you make it so hard for him to love you both? You divided him up like a Thanksgiving turkey." He looked at Liana. "You get the drumstick..." He inclined his head toward Cullen. "He gets the wing. Maybe Matthew was just tired of it."

Liana frowned. Had they really made the divorce so difficult that Matthew had finally given up and run away? Guilt, which was as much the aftermath of divorce as alimony and child support, stabbed at her.

But Cullen shook his head. "Good on ya. You're fast on your feet, I'll give you that, though I haven't seen any signs of genius yet. But think about this, mate. In one minute I'm going to show you bang on how we carve a turkey where I come from."

"Oh, come on! This is my house. You can't threaten me."

Liana stood and moved closer. "Now look, we don't have time to linger over the niceties. I'm sorry we're meeting this way. When this is over, you can come to my apartment and we'll start again. But for now, you'd better tell us where our son is."

Since he appeared to be considering, she stopped just in front of him and folded her arms.

"Matthew's going to be furious at me," he said at last.

"He'll get over it."

Cullen edged closer to the boy and touched his collar. Simon sighed. "Matthew's been participating in an on-line chat room. I'm the one who told him about it. He spends a lot of time there, and he met a girl."

"Go on...." Cullen said.

"Well, she's in some trouble. Matthew's been trying to help

her, but he got worried because he was leaving for a month. He knew you wouldn't let him go and see her, and he was afraid if he didn't, she might do something to herself.''

''Like what?'' Liana asked.

Simon shrugged. ''She was talking crazy.''

''And that's where he went? To see her?''

Liana was skeptical. Simon was the kind of kid who enjoyed outsmarting adults. Still, the pieces fit. If Matthew thought someone needed him, he would risk almost anything. And she knew he participated in several chat rooms. They had talked about standards and rules, but she had trusted him to enforce them.

''Matthew felt like he didn't have much of a choice, you know? He was afraid if he didn't go...'' Simon let the sentence hang.

''Where does this girl live?'' Cullen said.

''He'll be okay. Can't you just leave him alone?''

''We can't,'' Liana said.

Simon released a long breath. ''Her name is Brittany Saunders. She lives in a place called Tillman, in Arizona. He planned to get off the plane in Denver and take a bus or another plane to see her.''

''Can you E-mail Brittany to see if he made it?''

''She doesn't have her own computer. Her family's like poor white trash or something. She uses a friend's whenever she can.''

''Obviously Matthew had her address.''

''Maybe, but he never gave it to me. The town's not much more than a gas station. It wouldn't be hard to find her.''

Cullen and Liana locked gazes. There had been a time when they were so close that often words had been unnecessary. Apparently it was still true, because she saw her own thoughts mirrored in Cullen's eyes.

Neither of them trusted Simon, but the story was plausible. Too plausible to ignore.

''How far is this Tillman?'' Cullen asked her.

"We're going to have to look at the map. I've never heard of it."

His lips twisted in a half smile. He didn't take his eyes off hers. "Simon, lad, if you're pissing in my pocket, you won't like the consequences. Understand? We're going to have you watched, and if we come back without our son, we'll know exactly where to find you. Do you want to have a go at changing your story?"

Simon looked sad. "No, but when you find Matthew, please tell him I'm sorry."

22

"**Lee**, I can go without you. I'll bring him back to San Francisco. We'll confront him together before we make any decisions about what happens next." Cullen glanced at Liana's chalk white cheeks. He could only imagine what she was feeling.

"We don't have any reason to believe Simon. We don't know Matthew's really there."

"If he's not there, I'll come back. We'll decide what to do next."

"No, I have to go with you."

Cullen debated. They could drive to Tillman, which had turned out to be a speck of desert just over the Arizona border, but if Matthew was there, he might vanish again by the time they arrived. Their best bet was to fly into the closest airport and take a rental car to Tillman as fast as possible.

But flying terrified Liana.

"You can do this?" Cullen didn't look at her again. The fear in her eyes made his stomach roil. She had looked like a doe in the crosshairs of a rifle since they'd called the airlines to arrange this flight to Yuma.

"I *will* do this."

He knew men and women who weren't afraid of anything. But who was more courageous? The person who never experienced fear? Or the one who faced it, eyeball to eyeball?

"I'll be right beside you," he promised.

She didn't answer. He supposed his presence was less a prize than a curse, but, in the last hours, her attitude toward him *had* changed. They were working together. Over the years, he had learned to be grateful for every victory.

He turned into the airport parking lot, following signs until he was able to turn off the ignition. "You can sit on my lap. We can kiss and cuddle."

"You really know how to make things worse, don't you?"

He laid his palm against her cheek and turned her face to his. "Would a good stiff drink help? A blow to the head?"

Despite everything, she smiled weakly. "You always teased me when you didn't know what else to do."

"Every bloke's born with a gaping hole where his good sense ought to be. He needs a smart woman to fill it."

"I did my best."

"I reckon at the time my hole was more like a crater."

"And now?"

"Now, I'd give my right arm if I could just make this easier on you."

"Why do you care? Do you see this as some sort of opportunity to make up to me for everything that happened all those years ago? Are you really wallowing in guilt?"

"I don't know." For a moment, anyway, he had succeeded in his intention. He had managed to divert her attention from the impending flight. Her frown had deepened, but it wasn't aimed at him.

"There were two of us in that marriage," she said. "I made mistakes, too."

"We had some good times, though, didn't we?"

"You're just trying to take my mind off flying, aren't you?"

He opened his door and came around to open hers. "Is it working?"

She looked up from her seat, but she made no move to get out. "Do you know how many times Matthew pleaded with me to get on a plane? We never went on a vacation unless it

was some place in easy range. He wanted to go to Hawaii.''
She shook her head in disgust. ''We ended up in Malibu.''

''Put your hand on my arm and stand up.''

''Let me apologize in advance. I'm going to embarrass
you.''

''As much as I embarrassed you at the race meeting when I
bet our ute on the wrong horse and we had no way to get
home?''

''Not that much.''

He wondered that she could still think. From the pallor of
her cheeks, he guessed all the blood had drained from the top
half of her body. He squatted in front of her. ''Let me take
care of you, Lee. Bugger it, I can't wait for you to embarrass
me. It'll be a brand-new memory.''

''Let's do it, then.'' She got to her feet, but she swayed. He
grabbed her hand and found it was ice-cold. He tucked it into
his and put his other arm around her waist. ''We're going to
find our son.''

''We'd better,'' she said through clenched teeth. ''I'm not
doing this for the scenery.''

Liana hadn't opened her eyes since settling in her seat. She
could feel Cullen beside her, the long length of his thigh warm
and secure against hers. Under any circumstance but this, she
would have pushed him away, but now she was pathetically
grateful for his support.

She knew where her fear of flying had originated. Her first
panic attack had sent her running to therapists—of which there
were an overabundance in the Bay Area. She'd had her pick
of Rolfers, EST enthusiasts, Gestalt gurus, as well as every
casual acquaintance who had ever read a self-help tome. One
hypnotherapist had suggested regression to the moment she
emerged from her mother's womb. Another wanted to begin
even earlier, with a hypothetical past life, most probably on
Atlantis.

She had gotten her first real help from a kind old man who
took few patients and made no promises except that he would

listen. He had done more, of course. Skillfully, he had guided her to the source of her fear, to the memories that were the hardest to bear. One of those was with her now. She felt Cullen's hand steal over hers, warm and strong.

And as the airplane began to taxi down the runway and her heart skidded with terror, she remembered.

Thomas Robeson hadn't married until he was fifty-seven. Now, of course, Liana understood why. Thomas's entire life had been a lie. He had denied Willow's heritage until it had become a festering sore inside him, and the possibility that an heir's Asian eyes might give away his secret had forced him to remain a bachelor.

But aging bachelors suffered their own forms of prejudice. Faced with rumors that he preferred men in his bed, Thomas had taken a frosty-eyed survey of the young women in his social class, and his gaze had fallen on Hope Lynch, the daughter of a senior partner in one of the city's oldest law firms.

Hope was nineteen, with a pale blond beauty that needed years and confidence to bring it into focus. She had no particular direction for her life, no career she wanted to pursue, no strong opinions. She had been a surprise gift to aging parents who had given up hope of having children, and they had been busy with other things by the time she made her appearance. Hope was a fairy child who could stare out a window for hours. She was happiest in the shadows of life, and that made her perfect for Thomas.

Hope's quiet ways had never made her popular with men, and Thomas's interest gave the young woman a new status with her mother and father. Although Thomas was certainly too old, the Lynches saw him as her savior. An older man could guide and mold their daughter as a younger man might not. And if Hope could not be molded, at least she would be well taken care of.

On their wedding day, Thomas presented Hope with the Pearl of Great Price, set just for that event in a sheer golden web that wouldn't mar its beauty. Afterwards she noted that the photographer had not taken any pictures of her that did not feature the pearl. As she changed into a pink suit after the hotel reception, Thomas retrieved the pearl and personally escorted it back to his office to be locked in his safe.

A year after the elaborate society wedding and three months after her parents' death in an automobile accident, Hope attempted to take her own life. She botched her death, as she had botched her future, and after four weeks in a plush psychiatric hospital, she returned to the Pacific Heights mansion to take her place behind the husband she had grown to fear and despise.

But her four weeks' escape away from Thomas's demands had given her new strength, and for the next year Hope nurtured that tiny flicker and waited for the moment when she could leave him. She knew she wasn't strong enough to live by her wits, but at age twenty-one she was to inherit her parents' estate, which had been put in trust. And that was the moment when she would never look back.

On the day she signed the papers to receive the trust, Hope vanished. The young woman, whose intelligence had never been noted or appreciated, had worked out a complex scheme guaranteed to thwart Thomas's best efforts at finding her. She took nothing from his home. She changed her appearance, cutting and dyeing her hair an attractive strawberry blond and affecting a more casual manner of dress. She converted a portion of her trust into cash and bought a used car and a fake driver's license. Then she set off to hide herself in the burgeoning counterculture, a still innocent, idealistic world of folk music and coffeehouses.

Two months later, on the other side of the country, she saw a doctor to confirm what she strongly suspected. She had left Thomas Robeson, but Thomas had not exactly left her. She was pregnant with his child.

Thomas hadn't wanted children. Hope's first moment of marital disillusionment had come on their wedding night, when he had rigorously protected himself before making love to her. She had always liked babies, and she had assumed Thomas liked them, too. But this was just one of many assumptions that were wrong.

Now she had a new life to consider. If she had harbored any thoughts of going back to San Francisco to obtain a divorce, they disappeared forever. Although Thomas had been adamant about not wanting a child, the child, whose will was stronger than Thomas's condom, existed anyway. Thomas was equally capable of insisting on an immediate abortion, or later, when that was impossible, insisting that the child belonged to him alone. Better than anyone, Hope knew he was a coldhearted, calculating man who was capable of turning every hand into a winner.

But Hope had a trump card. She could not imagine a life spent looking over her shoulder, wondering if Thomas would find her, wondering if he would steal their child out of spite or some new scheme that required an heir. She wrote him one letter, a short one with all the necessary punch.

"Dear Thomas, as I made my plans to leave you, I searched through all your papers to find a weapon. Your birth certificate was all I needed. Please eliminate me from your life as thoroughly as you have eliminated your Chinese mother. Like her, my only shame is that I once loved you. I will keep your secret, Thomas, unless you try to find me or contest a divorce."

By then, Hope was living in Ann Arbor with a houseful of college students. Although she didn't need the income, she took a job at a bookstore to fill her days. The baby inside her grew, and so did the new circle of friends who haunted the bookshelves. The shy young woman who called herself Nancy Starke was always good for a loan or a listening ear, and for the first time in her life, Hope felt accepted.

The birth of her daughter was a cause for celebration. Perhaps if the baby had been a boy Hope might have seen Thomas in him. But the tiny girl with the mop of black hair looked like neither of her parents. She was a product of her Eurasian heritage, the best of everyone who had come before her. Hope named her Liana after Thomas's mother, whose very existence had given Hope a way to keep her daughter safe.

Liana grew up surrounded by Hope's friends, who played with her, then left her to fend for herself when they tired. The fresh new start that had energized Hope had not turned out the way she had imagined. Students graduated or dropped out, and the small world she had created for herself and her daughter was constantly changing. The times grew increasingly more difficult, too, as drugs took up space in the life of her friends and eventually in her own.

By the time Liana was old enough to remember what she saw, Hope was tripping frequently. The woman who had always been a little fey was now decidedly so. She had quit the bookstore when Liana was still in diapers to travel through New England with friends who wanted to find land for a commune. "Nancy" had promised to pay the bills if everyone would plow the fields. But the city kids, with nothing but idealism binding them, quickly tired of the chores that were necessary to make a minimal living off the rocky Vermont acres. They drifted away, one by one, as other disillusioned youths drifted in. Only Hope, tied to the land by a mortgage and a debilitating drug habit, stayed on.

By the time she was three, Liana had learned to take care of herself. By the time she was four, she was caring for Hope. By the time she was five, Liana and her mother were back on the road. One evening Hope had surfaced from a drug-induced haze long enough to notice that there wasn't any food in the house or one adult capable of replenishing supplies. She had taken a sober look at Liana's thin frame and pinched cheeks and realized that if anyone reported her, she would lose her daughter.

Over the next years, Hope did her best to make a life for Liana. The little girl knew her mother adored her, but it was rare for her to wake up two mornings in the same place or to find the same man in Hope's bed. They lived in motels or with people they met along the way. Hope promised they would find a place to settle, but the search for the right location never ended. Liana started school in so many towns that she felt uneasy if a teacher remembered her name.

By the time Liana was seven, Hope had given up again. They moved into a furnished room in a small town in western New York, a village of small white houses and emerald green pastures. Lakes dotted the countryside, and children rode bicycles along winding country roads. The old woman who owned the rambling Victorian was as friendly as a grandmother, and she baked sugar cookies and helped with Liana's homework while Hope slept away the nights and days.

Then, one day, Hope never woke up.

In later years Liana learned that her mother had taken too many pills, and they had quietly eased her from a world she hadn't been suited for. She doubted Hope had set out to kill herself, but the result was the same. The grandmotherly landlord helped Liana lay her mother to rest and cared for her as the local social services agency attempted to trace her closest relative. Then, one day nearly a month later, Thomas Robeson came to town.

Liana had just turned eight when Thomas entered her life. He was sixty-nine, and the years hadn't mellowed him. While other men his age were spending hours at the golf course or building furniture in their garage workshops, Thomas was working on his next million. Two years after his divorce from Hope, he had married a woman nearly as ruthless as he, and with Sammy Wesley beside him, his wealth and status had increased.

Thomas didn't need a child, particularly not one from his marriage to Hope. He especially didn't need a child whose appearance might give away his long-held secret. But Thomas knew that if he refused to see Liana, the story would follow him. At the first phone call, he flew to Buffalo, then drove the necessary miles to face and examine his daughter for the first time.

When Thomas strode in, Liana was drawing at a mahogany table in a dining room cluttered with ceramic knickknacks and crocheted doilies. She looked up and found a strange man examining her. To her childish eyes, he seemed very tall and old.

"Stand up," he ordered. "Let me look at you."

She really didn't know why she ought to. On the rare occasions when someone had told her what to do, she'd ignored it, since she knew people always moved on. And "Nancy," for all the love she showered on her daughter, had trod the path of least resistance, allowing Liana to do nearly anything she pleased.

After a moment of indecision she decided to stand anyway, so she could get a better look at the stranger. He had thick silver hair and round black eyes, and the deep wrinkles on his cheeks made him look like a piece of unwashed clothing. "Who are you?" she asked, when he didn't say anything else.

"I'll ask the questions."

"That's not fair."

Thomas moved closer. "Be quiet."

She fell silent, but only because she had already lost interest. Nothing much interested her since her mother had died. Not school, where the other children whispered about her, and not the landlady, who tried too hard to make her feel better.

Thomas stopped just in front of her, lifting her chin to stare into her eyes. "What's your name?"

"I can't tell you. I'm supposed to be quiet, remember?"

He tightened his hand around her chin, squeezing until she yelped with pain. "I said, what's your name?"

"Liana." She tossed her head, and his hand fell away.

"Liana what?"

"Starke!"

"Well, it's not. It's Robeson. And I'm your father."

Sometimes Liana had wondered if she had a father. So many men had drifted in and out of her mother's life, she had thought maybe she was a product of all of them. When she'd asked, Nancy had gotten upset, an occurrence Liana always tried to avoid, since Nancy sometimes wept for days once she started.

Now, for the first time, Nancy's reaction made sense. If this man was her father, there was every reason to be unhappy.

She narrowed her eyes as he narrowed his. "So?"

"I should have known Hope would raise a brat."

"My mother's name was Nancy."

"Before she married me, your mother's name was Hope Lynch. Nancy Starke is something she invented."

Liana considered that. She wished she could invent her name. It would not be Robeson.

Thomas grimaced, as if he didn't like what he saw. "You'll be coming to California with me. And you'd better learn some manners, young lady, and fast."

"I'm not going." That seemed simple enough to Liana. She had never had a real home, but she already knew enough about Thomas to see that living with him wouldn't be the same as having a home anyway.

"Well, you have no choice. As a matter of fact, you'll have very few choices in the coming years. You'll live with me, and you'll behave. If you don't do exactly as you're told, you'll be punished."

"If you touch me, old man, you'll be sorry."

His dark eyes gleamed. "Do you think so?"

Liana had never really been a child. She had fended for herself for so long that she had all the survival skills of an adult, with none of the safeguards. When Thomas attempted to clamp his hand on her shoulder, she sank her teeth into it. When he screeched and tried to slap her with his free hand, she kicked him.

She had never drawn blood before. She had never realized that victory had a sickening salty tang. She kicked him again, and he backed away, waving his injured hand in the air. She listened to him curse, all words she had heard a million times from her mother's friends.

"Fuck you," she said when he quieted. "I told you not to touch me."

"So it's to be a battle, is it?"

"Don't worry. I'm not going with you."

But she did. Kicking and screaming, she was carried onto her father's jet by two burly men who had made the trip to New York with him. Liana took her very first airplane ride on the floor of the tiny galley, bound and gagged like a hostage.

* * *

Cullen knew Liana wasn't sleeping. Her chest rose and fell erratically, and her eyelids fluttered, as if she was struggling to keep them closed.

"It won't be long, Lee." He took her hand and rubbed it. Then, as if it was the most natural thing in the world, he raised it to his lips and kissed it.

"What do you think you're doing?" she said through clenched teeth.

"If I make you mad enough, maybe you'll forget to be scared."

"It didn't work the first time."

He was puzzled. "First time?"

"Yeah, the first time I flew. I was furious." She released a deep breath. "I was also so frightened I wet my pants."

"You won't be doing a replay, will you?"

"No!"

He kissed her hand again. "What were you furious about?"

"That I was too little to fight back."

He listened as she explained in a few terse sentences, and he wished Thomas Robeson were still alive so that he could kill him himself. "You never told me."

"I didn't want to remember."

He supposed not. For many years he had pushed away his own bleak childhood. For too many more, he had pushed away everything that had come afterwards.

"What made him such a bastard?" he said. "Do you know?"

Her tone was clipped and rapid, but talking seemed to help. "When he was four, Thomas was sent away from his mother and the only home he'd ever known. The ship he sailed on barely made it into port on the morning of the San Francisco earthquake. No one came down to the harbor to pick him up, of course, because the city was in flames. The woman who had escorted him abandoned him. Days later, a fireman found him in the ashes of a burned out building. No one really knows what happened to him during that time. I doubt he remembered himself."

"It was a bad trot, certainly, but no excuse for what he did to you."

"For years I told myself he wasn't to blame for being the kind of man he was. It was weeks of chaos before his grand-parents located and claimed him. And he might have been bet-ter off if they hadn't, because they were cold, rigid people who probably made him ashamed of who he was. But none of that was my fault. And people have choices, don't they? Archer didn't have to kill my grandfather. Aunt Mei could have stayed with Bryce and built a life in Australia. And Thomas Robeson could have loved his only daughter."

Cullen rubbed her knuckles along his cheek. "It was worse at home than you ever let on, wasn't it?"

"Oh, I'm a quick study. I learned how to give Thomas the minimum without letting it touch me." She gave a bitter laugh. "Only I guess it did after all. Because one day I woke up, and I was scared to death of everything. It got worse after I left you, because I had to crawl back to him, and for a while I had to face him every day. When Thomas died, he left me the pearl and a boatload of insecurities. Interesting legacies."

"He didn't defeat you. We're on a plane. You're taking the tiger by the tail."

"I'm dying inside! The tiger's trying to claw his way out."

A bell tinkled, and the seatbelt sign flashed. Cullen knew they would be landing soon. "It's almost over. If we find Mat-thew, we'll drive back to the city. You won't have to do this again."

"If we don't find him, I'll get back on this plane or any other plane until we do." She opened her eyes. He wasn't sure which was stronger, the fear or the determination. "I won't let this defeat me."

He didn't drop her hand. Instead, as she watched, he raised it to his lips once more.

By the time they picked up their rental car and bought food for the road, the sun was sinking. Liana felt as if every nerve ending in her body was exposed. She was bruised and bloody, but somehow, healing. She would never get on an airplane with joy. But next time, if she was lucky, the fear might not be as great.

Cullen was responsible, of course, as much as she hated to admit it. He had helped in every way. She had sensed...what? Compassion? Understanding? No, it had been deeper. Empathy, as if her suffering was familiar because he had suffered, too.

And he had. She realized it now. She had left Cullen to start over with nothing, knowing that he had made a complete failure of everything in his life up to that moment. She didn't feel guilty for leaving. She could not and should not have stayed with him. But she had never allowed herself to feel his desolation.

"When this is over," she said tightly, "we'll talk about visiting arrangements, Cullen. Matthew needs to spend more than a month every year with you."

She saw his knuckles tighten on the steering wheel. "Are you saying that because you got through the flight alive?"

"It needs to be said."

"Will you be all right without him?"

"Are you all right without him?"

"Never. We should have had a bloody houseful of kids, Lee."

"You didn't want even one." She remembered what he had said about that. "I'm sorry."

"I'm ready now."

"Is Sarah going to be the lucky woman?"

He gave her a side glance and raised an eyebrow. "I meant I'm ready to spend more time with Matthew."

She analyzed her own reasons for bringing up Sarah again. She was in no state to lie to herself, but she didn't like the truth. The thought of Cullen with another woman upset her. Why should he succeed with someone else when they had failed?

Miles of gently sloping plains dotted with burro weed and creosote bush passed for scenery along the uncrowded interstate. Washes, outlined with ironwood and mesquite, and small settlements of trailers or concrete-block houses broke the monotony until the sun touched the horizon and a breathtaking variegated sky stole the spotlight.

She closed her eyes and saw carnelian and coral, hematite and lapis lazuli. She opened them again and concentrated on the road in front of her.

They stopped for gas and toiletries about forty-five minutes from Tillman. Liana leaned against the side of the pale blue Pontiac while Cullen filled the tank under the glare of artificial light. "What did the clerk say?"

"He doesn't know any place to stay, but he claims he's never paid much attention. And he thinks we'll have a problem finding Brittany tonight."

"He knows her?"

"Nothing like that. But there's not much to Tillman. And the petrol station closes early in the evening, so he doubts there'll be anyone to give directions. There's a pub a bit up the road, but he advised us to stay away. He doesn't think the blokes will be much help."

"You're planning to go anyway, aren't you?"

"Too right."

She felt something old, something rancid that should have rotted a long time ago, rising inside her. "Maybe you'll find a good game of craps while you're at it."

He looked up, still balancing the gas nozzle. "Maybe."

"Not that dice was ever your best game."

"Not if there was something better."

"And now?"

He pulled the nozzle away from the car, shaking it carefully before he hooked it back on the pump. "Well, I run a book with myself that you'll bring this up every chance you can, Lee. But that's it for gambling, from go to whoa."

"You don't gamble at all anymore?"

"I take it a day at a time. I don't use words like 'all' and 'anymore.'"

"Why? Are you afraid to make the commitment?"

"No, I'm afraid to sound like a whacking idiot."

"How long, Cullen?"

He shoved his hands in the pockets of jeans that clung to his slender hips. "Long enough and not long enough."

"Days? Months? Years?"

The line of his jaw hardened. "It doesn't matter. What I do today? That's what matters. I'm not betting I'll get a pay-off somewhere down the track. This isn't a two-up game. It's my life."

"What about the rest of it? The drinking? The running around?"

"I *never* ran around. When we were married, I never had another woman. I never wanted one."

She was silent. She knew she ought to be ashamed she had pushed him. She ought to be more ashamed that she'd cared.

"And since we're having a bash at clearing the air, I'll tell you this," he continued. "I don't have a problem with drinking, but I figured out that it does make it harder not to put paid to my gambling. So most of the time I'm a real wowser, a dinky-di teetotaler. But my mates like me anyway."

Since coming to California, Cullen had held her hand as she faced her worst fears. For the first time since the dissolution of their marriage, she was sorry she hadn't been there to help him.

She tried to put that into words. "I know this is probably the wrong thing to say and the wrong time, but I'm proud of you. I know this can't be easy."

He didn't answer.

"And I know it shouldn't matter to me so many years later, but...I'm glad you weren't...that there wasn't another woman. But you were gone so often, and I was alone, and I didn't..."

He smiled sadly. "I always loved you. Even a fucked-up bastard could see what he had, Lee. I didn't want another woman. I just wanted to be the man you deserved."

23

Tillman, Arizona

If there were any locals at the Shady Lady Bar, they didn't own up to it. Four eighteen-wheelers took up half the parking lot, and the license tags of the remaining cars and pickups were equally divided between California and Arizona. One of the truckers—better-humored than his cohorts—told Cullen that the "Lady" was the only bar for thirty miles. But either Brittany and her whereabouts were a mystery to the men who had driven the distance, or they were suspicious of this foreigner who was asking questions about her.

Back in the Pontiac, Cullen flexed his fingers and reclined in his seat, closing his eyes. "Unless some bloke lifted my wallet, I still have every cent I went in with."

Liana made a face he couldn't see. "I'm sorry I grilled you, Cullen. It was none of my business."

"There's a tourist camp not far away. Sounds like a right scenic spot. Somebody built it during the thirties, for migrants on their way to California. My mate at the Lady claims it hasn't changed much since Steinbeck's day. We could keep driving until we find something better, but I reckon the camp will put us closest to Tillman."

"It can't be worse than the house at Pikuwa Creek."

"You'd have a surprise if you saw it now."

"Would I?"

"I've tinkered with it a bit."

Like most of his countrymen, Cullen rarely bragged about his accomplishments. She guessed that the fact he'd even mentioned the house was like announcing it had won first place awards for design. "I hope you didn't tinker with the view."

"You liked that, did you?"

"That was one of the things I liked, yes."

"There was more?"

"Not the heat, and not the mozzies," she said, unconsciously choosing the Australian slang for mosquitoes.

"Shall it be the tourist camp, Lee? Or shall we drive the back roads and hope we find someone who can lead us to Matthew?"

She had already resigned herself to not catching up with Matthew tonight. It would be better to casually question people tomorrow at the service station that was the heart of Tillman.

"Tourist camp," she said. "And who knows, maybe the people there can tell us where to find Brittany."

They drove in silence, turning off the highway on to a road marked only by a small wooden sign. Half a mile down, Cullen slowed, and Liana got her first glimpse of their accommodations.

She whistled softly. "Ma Joad probably told old Pa to turn around right about here."

"Have a look at the cars."

He was right. The tourist camp, a ramshackle collection of camping sites and cottages, was bustling. She lowered her window to get a better look. "Just don't sign us up for horseshoes."

Cullen pulled into a gravel driveway and turned off the engine in front of a cabin with a sign designating it as the office. "Coming in?"

She measured the space that separated them from the door. Even though she was in a place she had never been, her heartbeat was as sedate and regular as the ticking of the clock in the tower at Ghirardelli Square. She supposed the flight had used up her panic quota for at least the next few hours. "Sure."

He grinned. "That's my missus." The grin faded, and he grimaced. "Sorry. Old habit."

Once "that's my missus" had been his highest praise. She knew better than to make anything of it now. She shrugged, as if it hadn't meant a thing. "I may have to be your missus tonight. We may not be able to get separate accommodations."

As it turned out, they weren't. The overweight woman in a fifties housedress and foam rubber slippers fiddled with keys on a pegboard, turning each one to peer at the number on the back. Liana glanced at Cullen. She could tell he was preparing to charm the woman into offering them a broom closet.

"Got one cabin left. Not our best, so I'll give you a discount." The woman shuffled forward and set a key on the peeling laminate counter.

"We'll take whatever you have," Cullen assured her.

"We're remodeling. Haven't gotten to yours yet. It's clean, but that's all I can say."

"It'll do." Liana watched as the woman shuffled off to get the registration book. "By the way, we're looking for a local girl. Brittany Saunders. She's a friend of our son's, and we told him we'd try to see her on the way through Tillman. But we don't have her address."

"Can't say as that sounds familiar." The woman brought the book back with her and opened it. "Darn shame I can't leave this on the counter, but people try to make off with it."

Cullen gave his warmest grin. "So you don't know Brittany?"

"Used to be some Saunders over in Yuma. No, they was Sanders, I think."

"And you know most of the people in Tillman?"

"Used to. Last few years, though, I don't get around much. Check at the post office in the morning. It's over at the store—that's over at the station. She's around here, they'll know."

Cullen thanked her and took the key. The woman gave instructions on how to find their cabin and warned them again.

"Plumbing's kind of touchy. You have to flush a couple of times. And the hot water don't last long."

Outside, Cullen held the car door for her. "Just like our honeymoon, Lee."

She felt surprisingly optimistic, and she allowed herself a smile. "We didn't have a honeymoon."

He started the car and pulled it along a narrow dirt path, stopping frequently as children darted back and forth in front of them. "Funny, I thought that was you."

This was forbidden territory. She changed the subject. "How many beds does the cabin have?" She realized she hadn't changed the subject enough.

"The lady didn't say."

She raised a brow. "Will you be comfortable in the car?"

"Why? At the end of our marriage we had a fair go at sleeping in the same bed without touching each other. We could do it again."

She winced. "Ouch."

"It's true enough, I reckon."

She wondered if he was challenging her. "Well, I'm used to having a bed all to myself these days."

"Is that right?" He grinned at her.

"Let's just see what the cabin looks like. I'll stop borrowing trouble."

"I should think the real trouble is waking up every morning in a bed by yourself."

"Why? It beats waking up with somebody who makes my life miserable."

"What about somebody who doesn't?"

"Is there a man like that?"

"You hate men, Lee?"

She didn't, but sometimes she wished she could. "I'd have to love somebody passionately to try again, Cullen."

"The first time was that bad?"

"For both of us."

He examined the faded number on the last cabin before a

stand of evergreens, then he parked in a space just in front of it. He faced her. "No. Not for both of us."

"Our marriage didn't sour you on the institution forever?"

He didn't answer. He leaned across her to open her door. Then he got out and walked up the path to the cabin. He was jiggling the key in the lock when she joined him, carrying the plastic bag from the convenience store.

The door swung open, and they stared inside. She was the first to hoot. "I'd say a little renovation's not a bad idea."

They had been warned for good reason. The cabin was a shambles. And there was only one bed. Any additional furniture had been removed. "It has a roof. I guess we can't complain."

Cullen strode inside and pointed to a space where a window had once resided. It was now covered by planks with wide spaces between them over which some thoughtful carpenter had nailed a rotting screen. But the narrow spaces between the planks in the wall were open to the elements, as if someone had stripped away the inside paneling.

He stuck his finger through one of the cracks. "If you don't like enclosed places, this is the spot for you. I've thrown my swag under the stars where there was less fresh air."

"And where there's fresh air, can the spiders and centipedes and scorpions be far behind?"

"You're certain you want me to sleep in the car?"

He sounded dubious. She tried to summon some backbone, but she was wilting fast. "Maybe I'll sleep in the car. At least I can roll up the windows."

"And suffocate. Look, I'll stay on my side of the mattress, Lee. But I'm not leaving you alone in here."

She really didn't want to be alone. She was melting into a warm puddle of emotion.

He took her silence as assent. "Do you mind if I take my turn in the loo first?" He disappeared through the only possible door and closed it behind him. "As charming as an outback dunny," he called.

"I've got the picture, Cullen. Australian desert is better than

American desert. Well, you've got a hell of a lot more of it than we do, so you've had more practice!''

He stuck out his head. "That's my missus." He winked at her, then disappeared back into the bathroom.

"Not anymore!"

"Don't tell the lady at the desk."

She had forgotten how splendidly Cullen could make roses out of rat tails. His charm was a magic wand he waved over everything, and when he was finished, everything always looked better.

She turned down the comforter and sheets, and grimaced at the mattress. But it seemed solid enough, and there was nothing crawling on the bottom sheet to give her pause. She measured the distance with her eyes. The bed was queen-sized and large enough for two. But unless Cullen had changed, he was a sprawler and a cuddler. She sat on the edge, and it didn't sag. She bounced, and it didn't creak.

She heard the sound of a shower, then, a moment later, Cullen's howl. "The hot water's gone!" he shouted.

"You were warned," she muttered, trying not to smile.

He emerged a few minutes later. He had slipped back into his jeans, but he carried the shirt he'd worn that day over his arm, and his T-shirt was nowhere in sight. "My shirt's hanging in the shower. I reckon you'd like me better in the morning if I washed it tonight."

"And I'll bet you wore it into the shower and soaped it before you took it off, outback style."

"It got the job done," he said with a grin.

"My turn, I guess."

"I'd wait a bit for the hot water."

"I'll take my shower in the morning, thanks." She wanted to be done with this intimacy, to get under the covers and turn her back to Cullen. She shut the bathroom door behind her and brushed her teeth with her new toothbrush. Then she washed her face with cold water, brushed her hair and then, although she hated herself for it, took a good look at the woman in the mirror in the harsh glare of a fifty-watt bulb.

She had dark circles under her eyes, but that was no surprise. Her hair was lank, and the few strands of silver seemed especially prominent tonight. In the yellowish cast of the bulb, her skin seemed sallow and unhealthy.

"He wouldn't want you anyway," she mouthed silently, but somehow that only made her feel worse. She grimaced; then she stripped off her wrinkled linen shirt and pants, followed by her underwear. She washed that and the shirt in the sink, hanging them next to Cullen's shirt to dry by morning. Finally she donned the extra-large Arizona Cardinals T-shirt that she'd bought in the aisle devoted to Native American artifacts—made in Taiwan. It fell nearly to her knees, but she wished she had been able to buy panties to go with it.

When there was absolutely nothing else to do, she pulled the chain on the light bulb and opened the door. Cullen was under the covers, his back turned. She doubted he was asleep, but she wasn't going to ask. She crossed the room in her bare feet and slipped in beside him.

"Just a couple of rules," he said without turning. "You can't hog the covers, and you can't snore. And no nookie tonight, no matter how badly you want me."

"You are such a jerk."

"I've moved up that far in your estimation, have I?"

She punched her pillow, which whooshed in defiance. "You always did that, you know. Resorted to humor or charm to get what you wanted."

"Too right. And have a look how far it's gotten me."

She thought about that as she lay in the surprisingly comfortable bed with Cullen, careful inches away, trying to fall asleep beside her. There had been a time when she had thought that nothing they did together could fail. She had been twenty-one to his twenty-two, and she had loved him with a single-minded intensity that eclipsed all reason.

Everything that had come afterwards, even this moment, had begun such a long time ago. She thought about those days now, as she hadn't allowed herself to think about them for many years. She wondered if Cullen was thinking about them, too.

* * *

Liana had been born into a world of total acceptance and no security. Her life with Thomas had been exactly the opposite. But she was an intelligent child who had realized after the terrifying flight to California that silent rebellion was the only kind that would not turn her new world upside down. So she settled into the monotony of toeing the line, while inside she plotted revolution.

Liana learned quickly that her stepmother, Sammy, and Graham, a chubby preadolescent with stress-induced asthma, would never be on her side. Until Mei came into her life, Liana quietly resigned herself to battling the world alone. But with Mei as a refuge, more endearing qualities took root inside her. Mei was the first person who recognized her artistic ability. And in her adolescence, when a course in jewelry-making turned into a passion, it was Mei who encouraged her to follow her muse.

The counterculture movement that had nourished Liana's childhood had peaked early in the Bay Area—perpetual well-spring of the untried and truly weird. By the time she was sixteen, nearly all that was left was a crass commercialization of the Age of Aquarius. Street vendors in tie-dyed T-shirts still sold crafts from the backs of aging VW buses, and the smell of marijuana at Golden Gate Park remained as commonplace as cypress and eucalyptus. But California cuisine was fast replacing macrobiotic diets, and disco was replacing acid rock.

One regional characteristic that hadn't wavered, however, was a belief that following one's own heart was most important. No matter how many threats Thomas made, Liana knew it was just a matter of time until she would be free to do just that.

Thomas wanted her to earn a degree in business so that someday she could take her place at Pacific International. But Liana had decided immediately that this was something she would never do. She was disillusioned enough with the life Hope had led not to strike out on her own before she was ready, but she was also determined to reject everything about Thomas as soon as the time was right.

At Mei's urging she signed up for more jewelry classes and used her allowance to buy supplies. She found a designer at a local craft show who agreed to trade lessons in lost-wax casting for baby-sitting and simple chores. She fired clay beads in a raku kiln and wove delicate strands of hand-dyed silk on a Chinese loom.

The day she turned seventeen, Thomas came to her room when she was experimenting with colorful rhinestones she had pried from thrift-store costume jewelry. She often worked on simple designs at home, twisting wire for decorative borders for rings or bracelets or attaching findings to pieces she had made in class.

Today as always, she did nothing to hide her latest attempt at design. Her father stood in the hallway and eyed her coldly. While she had grown, Thomas had shrunk with age. At seventy-eight he was neither robust nor frail, but while he had once thought nothing of slapping her if she displeased him, now he never raised a hand in her presence. She was sure he was afraid that this time, if she fought back, she would win.

"I've come to show you your birthday present," he told her.

Since birthdays were only nominally celebrated in the Robeson house, she was surprised. "Right now?"

He looked past her to the project on her desk. "It doesn't look like you're doing anything important."

"Of course not." She smiled sweetly.

"Your study time would be better spent practicing your languages."

Years before, Thomas had ordained that Liana would become fluent in German and French while she was still in high school, so that later she would be an asset to the corporation's negotiations in other counties.

Her temper flared, and for once she forgot to be cautious. "My Cantonese is improving rapidly."

He narrowed his eyes. "Cantonese?"

She didn't know what motivated her to go on. "Yes, I've

met a woman who's teaching me privately. That only makes sense, don't you think? With the Chinese population here in the Bay Area and all the opportunities for development abroad, someone in management at Pacific will need to be fluent. I did it to surprise you.''

"Who is this woman? Where did you meet her?"

Liana wondered what had possessed her to bait Thomas. She hadn't planned to flaunt Mei in front of her father until she was ready to leave home.

It was too late now. "Her name is Mei Fong. She's wonderful. Witty, intelligent and warm. I've learned so much from her.''

He didn't ask *what* she had learned. He stepped into her room, pushing her farther inside. "How did you meet this woman?''

"One of my teachers introduced us. We had an introductory class in Chinese, and I liked it. I thought you'd be pleased if I learned a little more.'' She favored him with another beatific smile.

Thomas's expression had dipped from cold to frozen. "What do you know about her?''

"Let's see…she's a widow. Her husband owned an import business, and her sons run it now. I think she's well off. She only tutors me as a favor.''

He glared at her, assessing her expression in his all-too-familiar way. "What else do you know?''

She pretended to consider. "She has lots of grandchildren and great-grandchildren, mostly boys. One of them, Frank, is almost exactly my age. He's going to Harvard next fall.''

He wanted to prod. She could see it in his eyes. But the question he really wanted to ask couldn't be spoken. If she didn't know everything about Mei, the wrong question could give him away. "You're not to see her anymore.''

"Why not?''

"I know of this woman. Her family has a bad reputation.''

"You're probably thinking of the wrong person. Mei's family is highly regarded.''

"You will *not* see her again."

She wanted to tell him everything. Nothing would have pleased her more than to see real emotion cross Thomas's face. But she wasn't ready. She had a plan for her life, and this was not the time for confrontation.

She shrugged, as if none of it mattered. "If you say so. I don't have much free time, anyway. I was just doing it as a surprise. I live to make you happy."

He moved closer, but she didn't budge. "You live to make me angry. I've offered you the world, and you throw it back into my face." He waved at the rhinestones on her desk. "Do you think I don't know about this 'interest' of yours? That I don't know you take classes behind my back? That I don't know you've studied with some hippy pothead who's as maladjusted as your mother? I watch you. I have you watched. I know what you do."

She didn't flinch. "Then I'm surprised you didn't know about Mei."

He raised his hand. She raised an eyebrow. "I really wouldn't do that," she said. "It could ruin my birthday."

"You're a disgrace."

"I thought I was exactly what you'd made me."

He dropped his hand. He rarely did anything without thinking of all the consequences. "You'll stop this little hobby, too."

"I don't think so. Not unless it begins to interfere with my studies. Most girls my age have a hobby, Thomas. Think of all the things I could have chosen."

"Your future is not assured, Liana. I can write you out of my will. I don't even have to give you a job in my steno pool."

There was so much she couldn't say. That she would never darken the door of Pacific International whether he gave her a job or not. That his threats were meaningless, since she knew that at eighteen she would inherit a substantial amount of money from her mother's estate. That he would never have a real hold over her, because she knew his secret. There had never been any shame in Thomas's heritage, but the fact that he had hidden it for so long was unforgivable.

The time wasn't right, so she simply smiled. "Well, I sure hope you don't offer me a job in your steno pool. My secretarial skills are abysmal."

His breathing was labored, the only sign that she had gotten to him. He didn't respond, and he didn't move away. He stood absolutely still for a moment, composing himself. Then he shook his head. "Change your clothes. I'm taking you to see your gift."

She was surprised. "Okay." She couldn't resist. "We'll have fun. Real father-and-daughter stuff."

He spun on his heel and left her room. She closed the door and leaned against it. She wondered if she could bear to live with Thomas Robeson and all he represented for one more year.

She wondered if she could bear the loneliness that was always with her.

24

Thomas's birthday gift was the Pearl of Great Price. Not that he had any real intention of giving it to her. Thomas took Liana to the Robeson Building, past guards who bowed and scraped as if he were royalty. In his office, he unlocked the safe and removed the pearl, displaying it in the palm of his hand.

Liana felt a painful squeeze in her chest as she eyed the magnificent gem. She knew about the pearl, of course. In her quest to acquaint Liana with family history, Mei had told her the story of Tom and Archer, along with stories about Willow and her own childhood in Broome. And Liana had seen photographs of the pearl that accompanied articles about Pacific International Growth and Development. For decades "Pigged Out" had exploited the pearl as a symbol of purity and perfection: Pacific International Growth and Development, Pearl of the Pacific.

"Would you like to hold it?" Thomas asked.

Liana knew better than to answer yes, since Thomas would then refuse. On the other hand, if she said no, he would rail at her for not appreciating his generosity.

"It looks wonderful right where it is," she said in a rare moment of compromise.

"There's nothing you could create that would be half as beautiful. I don't know why you try."

"The oyster gave its life for the pearl. I'm not that dedicated."

"My father died for this."

She pretended to be surprised, as if Mei had never told her the pearl's story. "How?"

He searched her face, as if he was weighing the honesty of her response. Then he related the story of Tom Robeson and Archer Llewellyn.

As her father spoke, Liana listened carefully, almost surprised that Thomas's story so closely matched her aunt's.

"But how did *you* get it?" she asked. Mei had never been clear on this point, only explaining that someone had reclaimed the pearl from the Llewellyns and brought it to America.

"We Robesons take back what's ours. When I learned about the pearl, I made certain it would belong to our family again."

"And the Llewellyns?"

"Stupid people, and easy to fool."

She suspected there was more to *that* story than she would ever hear. "Don't they want it back?"

He sniffed. "I doubt the Llewellyn descendants even know it's here. They live in Australia on a worthless cattle ranch. But be wary of every stranger who shows an interest in the pearl, Liana. The Llewellyns could come after it someday. Once it belongs to you, it will be yours to protect."

"Once it belongs to me?" Her palm itched to hold the pearl.

"Did you think I was really going to present it to you now?"

She rolled her eyes. "Thomas, if nothing else, give me credit for knowing you better."

For years he had insisted she call him Father—and for years she had declined. He shook his head, and his lips thinned into a grimace. "It won't belong to you if you continue to defy me."

She felt the chains that were binding her tighten, but only a little. She didn't want the pearl that badly. "You don't want obedience, you want total control."

"I'm too old to have another child. I didn't want one in the first place, but your mother defied me."

"'There's a pattern here,'' she pointed out. ''Mother defied you. I defy you. Do you detect a message?''

He continued as if she hadn't spoken. ''I will never have another child, and Graham doesn't have Robeson blood.''

Silently she placed Graham a rung higher on the evolutionary ladder.

''This pearl should remain in our family,'' he finished.

''Sounds like I'm the Great White Hope for the Great White Pearl.''

''Well, I can have it sold or locked away for future generations if I have to. I can secure it legally for decades, even a century.''

''Why this sudden sentimental attachment to family? Why should you care whether someone with your bloodlines gets it or not?''

He closed his fingers around the pearl, and it vanished. He didn't speak.

She wondered if this man, who had never shown her any real kindness, had a flicker of warmth in his icy soul. Could Thomas feel some attachment to the father he'd never known? Some attachment to future generations? It seemed so human, and so unlike him.

''I really don't set out to defy you,'' she said, when they had stood in silence long enough to make her uncomfortable. ''It's just that we don't have anything to offer each other. I wish things between us were easier.''

''When I was a boy, I didn't think what my grandparents could offer me. I was grateful for whatever they chose to do.''

She tried to think of something she was grateful for, just to let him know she was trying. But she was afraid the moment she told him something pleased her, he would take it away.

''What about the things your grandparents didn't do?'' she asked at last. ''Didn't you ever wish there was somebody who loved you just because you'd been born?''

For just the briefest moment there was something faraway in his eyes, something almost childlike. Then it vanished before she could be certain it had ever been there. ''This can be yours someday, Liana. But only if you live the way I want you to. Study and learn. Perfect yourself. Curb your tongue. Above everything, show me that you're worthy of this legacy."

Any possibility of understanding vanished. A knot formed in her stomach. It was so much worse to believe in possibilities, no matter how briefly. "I can't show you what you don't want to see," she said.

He turned away and strode to the safe. She had not even held the pearl. As he placed it back inside, she suspected she had seen the Pearl of Great Price for the first and last time.

One year later, with her high school diploma in hand and her inheritance from her mother safely transferred to her name, Liana packed her suitcases and, in the dead of night, slipped away from the red sandstone mansion in Pacific Heights. She had never felt closer to Hope than she did at that moment. She supposed her father would discover the news of her disappearance, only to say "like mother, like daughter," and go about his business.

She had been preparing for her departure for a year, although part of her had hoped it wouldn't be necessary. But on the day of her graduation, their troubled relationship had erupted irrevocably. For the past year she had been doubly careful to hide every encounter with Mei. This had meant less contact and rigorous planning, but Thomas had never again mentioned Mei. Liana hoped she had fooled him. She was proud to be Mei's niece and sorry to be Thomas's daughter, but until she was eighteen, Thomas controlled her life.

On graduation morning Thomas announced he would not be attending the festivities, nor would Sammy, who would be accompanying him to a business dinner. This meant that no family member would be present to mark the occasion, since Graham was still at Princeton, finishing his sophomore year. Liana couldn't believe even Thomas would be so unfeeling. She was sure she would be the only graduate with no one to cheer for her. Until she thought of Mei.

Mei questioned her about the wisdom of attending the ceremony, but Liana assured her that Thomas wouldn't be there. "And besides," Liana said, "I'm nearly eighteen. Until now I didn't have any choice about this, but now I don't care what Thomas knows. Pretty soon he won't be able to hurt me anymore. But if you're afraid he'll come after you…"

Mei didn't smile. "I have strong sons, and influence of my own."

So Liana graduated that night under a bower of ivy and white roses, knowing that the one person in the world who really loved her was sitting proudly in the audience. The euphoria lasted as long as the ceremony. Afterwards, as Mei came to hug her wayward niece, Liana looked up to see Thomas and Sammy standing at the edge of the crowd.

Liana turned her attention back to Mei. "Auntie Mei, my father's here."

"Is he?" Mei seemed unconcerned. "Perhaps he hoped to trap you?"

Liana rejected that. Thomas would never want this scene to be played out in public. "I won't let him hurt you," she promised.

Mei touched her cheek fondly. "He can't hurt me. But I'll say goodbye now."

"I'm going to tell him I know who you are."

"I think he knows already, Liana." Mei kissed her, then disappeared into the crowd. The small auditorium was filled with members of San Francisco's most successful families. Ironically they represented a rainbow of nationalities and races, and Mei melted in, unremarkable and unnoted. Thomas's Chinese heritage might have been a professional asset in this rapidly transforming, multicultural world, but even the national fascination with genealogy, inspired by the bestselling *Roots,* had never moved him to tell his secret.

"I've sent Sammy home," Thomas said, taking Liana's elbow with no preamble. "We'll start back on foot until the car returns."

She shook off his hand. "I have two better invitations tonight. Why did you come? You said you couldn't."

In an unusual absence of self-control, a muscle jumped in his jaw. "There will be no parties for you."

"Try to stop me and I'll jump back up on that stage and tell everyone who Mei is." She kept her voice low and a smile on her face. "But just for the record, *Daddy,* I'm proud to be Chinese. The only thing you've *ever* had to be ashamed of is your puny little heart. Luckily your sister's is larger."

"You won't see her. You won't mention her. Never again. If you do, you'll lose everything. Choose her family or mine, Liana. But don't make the mistake of believing you can have both." He turned on his heel and disappeared into the crowd, but Thomas didn't blend in the way his twin had. His stiff carriage and cold expression set him apart.

The next morning they didn't speak of Mei. Liana stayed on in Thomas's house only long enough to sign the papers that transferred control of her mother's estate and to buy a used Rabbit convertible. That night, she escaped. She made just one stop on her way out of town. She drove to the apartment on Waverly Place and climbed the stairs as she had so many times before. But now she didn't watch over her shoulder. She climbed proudly and boldly. Already she could feel the shackles falling away. She was free. She had made it through her childhood.

She knocked on her aunt's door, and in a rare display of emotion, she threw her arms around the sleepy woman the moment she answered.

"I'm off, Auntie Mei. At last! Wish me luck."

Mei didn't ask where Liana was going. She knew her niece and how badly she needed freedom to try her wings. "You will write? You will call?"

"Oh, you know I will! I'll miss you so much."

Mei clasped her close. Then she held her away. "I have regretted only two things in my life. The second was not having a daughter. Until I found you."

Liana felt tears running down her cheeks. "You got me through this, Auntie. You're the only person in the world I love."

"That will change soon enough." Mei hugged her again, then she pushed Liana away. "Go, but be warned." She spoke in Cantonese, then smiled when Liana looked bewildered. "This is something your grandmother often said to me. You are like her, of course. In appearance and in your heart."

"What does it mean?"

"It's a common saying. Once you climb on the back of a tiger, you cannot climb down."

"I don't understand."

"You have chosen a new and daring path, Liana. Once you commit yourself, you must see it through."

"I have to see it through. I sure can't go home again."

"This is the time for you to go forward." Mei stepped back. "I will be waiting to hear from you."

Liana opened the door and stepped out into the hallway and her brand-new life.

She spent the summer as an apprentice to a craftswoman in Nevada who taught her mokume gane, the Japanese art of metalworking. In the fall she traveled across the country to begin school at the Pratt Institute in Brooklyn. She wrote and called Mei often, and informed Thomas of her whereabouts, too, although she knew he had surely excised her from his life forever.

From her first day on campus, Liana remained open to other avenues for her life. She loved jewelry. She loved the cool feel of precious metals, the incomparable sparkle of gems. She loved to manipulate materials, both mundane and priceless, to create beauty that would, by its very existence, enhance the allure of a woman or the attractions of a man.

She had expected her new world to offer limitless possibilities. Instead, with each class, with each new, unrelated adventure, her desire to focus on jewelry expanded. By the time she entered her senior year, she had won prizes for her designs and interest from the giants on New York's Fifth Avenue, as well as smaller manufacturers and retailers on Forty-seventh.

After graduation, on a trip to Manhattan to meet with an art director at Tiffany who had attended her senior exhibition, Liana met Cullen.

In her years away from San Francisco, Liana had attempted to shed the opposing philosophies of her parents and develop her own style and opinions. She had proceeded carefully in relationships, ever mindful of the many worthless men who had inhabited Hope's life. She was terrified that, like her mother, she wouldn't be able to see men clearly, and so she had kept them at a distance, losing her virginity but never her heart.

She had developed a polished but exotic exterior, symbolized by dramatic clothing of her own design, which was always a showcase for her newest pieces of jewelry. She framed the austere oval of her face by twisting and pinning up her long black hair with ivory or jade combs, or braiding it with silken cords and beads. That day in Manhattan, she wore a princess-style dress of deepest plum and her favorite gold brooch, cast and chased with amethysts and pearls. She had entwined her chignon with a rope of seed pearls and left her earlobes and arms bare, so not to subtract from the effect.

She wasn't nervous, despite being in the sacred palace of designers like Donald Claflin, Angela Cummings, Elsa Peretti and Paloma Picasso. She wasn't even sure if she wanted a job with Tiffany, where she would probably spend years translating the designs of others. She knew the risks of going out on her own. She had chosen a career that demanded intensive, exacting craftsmanship in a world that valued mass production. But she had worked the craft-fair circuit the previous summer with a lover who made mandolins and banjos, and she had relished the freedom, if not—by summer's end—the man.

Since she had an independent income, she was considering her own shop in some wealthy tourist town in New England, and she had prepared herself by taking every relevant business course. After four years of study she was ready for an adventure.

The reception area where she waited was as classy as the jewelry Tiffany produced. The receptionist might have been a model. The gray leather furniture was comfortable enough to be welcoming, but not enough to encourage a casual posture.

Liana was wishing she had a magazine to pass the time when a young man strode in and gave his name to the receptionist. Liana watched the woman's eyes light. A smile curved on her artistically painted lips, and her layered blond hair bounced as she gestured to the area where Liana was sitting.

Liana watched him approach. He was tall, lean-hipped and broad-shouldered. His clothes, a navy sports coat and dark trousers, weren't expensive, but he wore them with the casual flair of a man who was more interested in comfort than show. That alone set him apart here.

"Mind if I join you?"

She moved over, making room for him. "Australian, right?"

He grinned. "And you're a Yank."

"More or less."

"Looks like I'll be here for a bit. My clock's all turned around. It feels like midnight. I thought it was one-thirty."

"It's one."

"The flash gal at the desk told me. I could go for a walk, but I doubt I'd find my way back."

"You're finding New York confusing?"

"Naw. Fascinating. I've only been here a day or two. I keep wandering off to see something and forget what I'm here for." He held out his hand. She took it for a brief handshake. "Cullen," he said.

"Liana."

"You live here?"

"Brooklyn."

His gaze flicked to the portfolio she'd set on the table. "Not hocking the family jewels, are you?"

She laughed. "I design jewelry. They want to see my portfolio."

"You're too young to be this close to the big time."

There was no sting in his words. His blue eyes were dancing with good humor, and, in response, she felt something warming inside her. Cullen wasn't exactly good-looking, not in a New

York kind of way, at least. But his rugged masculine features were allied with the most charismatic grin she had ever seen.

"How about you?" she asked, despite the fact that examining the lives of strangers wasn't her style.

"First, tell me about the pearls on your brooch. No, I'll tell you. The one in the middle's a dazzler. But it's not one of ours. Probably Japanese, an Akoya. The nacre layer on our pearls is sixty, maybe a hundred, times thicker than theirs. Our pearls grow twice as fast, too, two years to their four. Of course, we learned something of what we know from the Japanese, so we give them a bit of credit."

"I'll bet this isn't a hobby."

He fished in his pocket and pulled out a business card. "I have a pearl farm in Western Australia, Southern Cross Pearls. I don't produce heaps. Not yet, anyway. But what I produce is top quality. I'm trying to develop some interest here in the Big Smoke. If I don't, the crocs can have the farm."

She closed her fingers around his card without looking at it. "You farm pearls? Like people farm soybeans?"

He settled back and crossed his legs, as if he were there for the long haul. "I fell into it. A great-great-grandfather of mine was a pearler, successful by half, too. When old Somerset carked it, he didn't leave anything to my side of the family. The company passed down through a son by a second marriage, and nobody on my side knew a bloody thing about it. Times changed. The relatives scraped through, growing pearls instead of fishing for them, but before long there wasn't much left except some land on Pikuwa Creek in Western Australia and a couple of rotting luggers."

If anyone else had been telling it, the long personal story might have seemed odd, but Cullen carried if off with brash charm. Liana nodded, hoping for the next installment. "And that's where you live now?"

"Right-o. The last descendant died off, but before he did, he traced my side of the family. The whole thing passed to my father. Dad didn't want anything to do with it—or me, for that matter—so he handed it over and told me to go stuff up something new.'' He grinned. ''I changed the name to Southern Cross. And that's how I came to farming pearls. More than you wanted to know, huh?''

She was fascinated, both by the story and the man. ''Do you like what you do?''

''I reckon. I was raised where the crow flies backwards, so the isolation doesn't bother me. Everything rises and falls by my hand, and I like that, too.''

''My father was born in Australia. In Broome. Is that anywhere near your creek?''

He whistled softly. ''Broome's the big city in my part of the world. Pikuwa Creek's about thirty miles north, an hour or so when the roads aren't washed away.''

She tried to remember if she had ever met anyone else from Broome. ''My grandfather was a pearler. Well, just for a short time. His best friend murdered him over a pearl they found.''

''More common than some think.''

She smiled at him. Her entire future might depend on the results of her upcoming interview. But she wasn't thinking about that. Cullen's life intrigued her. She was drawn to the man and the rough-and-tumble world he lived in. ''So you like being your own boss?''

He rested his arm along the back of the sofa. His fingertips nearly touched her shoulder. ''I'm the only man who could stand to have me work for him.''

She laughed. ''You're not so bad, are you?''

''I take more risks than most blokes could tolerate.''

''Are they paying off?''

''You wouldn't think so if you saw the way I live.''

''Then how did you get to New York? It's an expensive trip.''

''I took a few that worked out.''

They were silent, but neither of them looked away. She had tried to ignore the immediate chemistry between them, telling herself that she was attracted to this Australian stranger because he was different and refreshing—as well as a hunk. But suddenly explanations seemed irrelevant. She felt giddy. Her pulse was speeding out of control. His grin deepened into something subtler—and even sexier. Then he reached over and cupped her brooch, and the heel of his hand rested against her breast.

"The little pearls in this? Hardly worth mentioning, are they? But you've done something important with them. I pay attention to my pearls, not what happens to them. But every pearl should be set like this." His hand brushed lightly across her chest as he withdrew it. "I'd like to see what you could do with mine."

She tried to sound natural. "So would I." Her voice emerged as something just above a whisper.

"Miss Robeson?"

For a moment she didn't, couldn't, move. Then she looked up and saw that the receptionist was standing.

"Liana Robeson." Cullen seemed to be trying the name to see how it felt on his tongue. "I'll still be in town this evening. Will you?"

She had promised herself a real life when she left San Francisco. Maybe it was time to make that happen. She answered before she could change her mind. "I might wait for you."

He favored her with a sexy grin. "I'd like nothing better."

She nodded and stood. Only then did she realize she was still clasping his business card in her hand. She glanced at it, and for a moment she stared at the words, rearranging them. But the result was the same.

She looked up. "Cullen Llewellyn?"

"That's right."

"From Broome…"

He frowned. "Nearly."

"Are you related, even distantly, to a man named Archer Llewellyn?"

He cocked a brow in surprise. "My great-grandfather's name was Archer. How did you know?"

"A lucky guess."

"Why? Does it matter?"

She slipped the card inside her purse. Then she looked up at him again. "No reason, really. Except that Archer Llewellyn was the man who murdered my grandfather."

25

Somewhere in the evergreens near their cabin, a bird—a crow, perhaps—squawked a greeting to dawn. Cullen stirred until he felt Liana's bottom warm and lush against the small of his back. By forbidding himself to sleep deeply, he had managed to stay on his own side of the bed. But Liana had inched steadily closer, a heat-seeking missile guaranteed to find and destroy its target.

He suspected he could turn and wrap his arms around her and she wouldn't wake. But if she did, he was certain she would blame their intimacy on him. And his protests would go unheeded.

He smiled, thinking of the early days of their marriage, when arguments had merely been an excuse to reconcile. The smile disappeared as he thought about all the things between them now that could not be cured by sex.

He was wrong about how deeply she'd been sleeping, because she spoke. "You're awake, aren't you?"

"Before you get angry, measure the mattress and divide it by two."

She moved, but only a little, as if she were only removing the worst of temptations. "Did you ever think we'd end up in bed together again?"

"After I found out who you were, I didn't think we'd *ever*

end up in bed together." He turned over and rested his arms behind his head so that moving closer would be harder.

Her voice was sleepy. "It hardly seemed possible, did it? We were doomed from the start."

They *had* been doomed, of course, but Cullen realized now that at the time he had seen that as a plus. He had been a gambler who was far too cocky to bet on a sure thing. He was the champion of lost causes, the no-hoper who put all his money on the horse least likely to finish the course. He had taken a good look at this woman whose history was in direct conflict with his, and he had known that he had to have her.

"We made a go of it for a while," he said. "Do you remember that first year?"

"Doesn't it frighten you to think that Matthew might grow up to be as crazy as we were?" She didn't sound angry. She sounded wistful, as if, despite her words, she yearned a little for that exhilarating dizziness of youth.

"I hope someday Matthew falls in love as totally as we did. I just hope he can handle it better."

"Totally?"

"Right."

She faced him, stretching unconsciously as she did and shooting his libido into outer space. "From this side of the bed the percentages don't look that good. If it was total, how could we have failed?"

He had never forgotten the fragrance of Liana's skin, the musky woman smell of early morning, the floral essence of her hair. He had awakened with other women since their divorce, reached for them and felt a jolt of disappointment, even years after he had last held Liana. Now his body pleaded for the reunion it had been denied.

She sighed and sat up, pushing her hair back from her face with both hands. "I think I'll start on my shower. The way yours went last night, I might have to take mine in stages."

He watched her walk to the bathroom door, her legs bare and beautiful as the T-shirt brushed the tops of her thighs. "Our failure didn't have anything to do with love, Lee."

She paused with her hand on the doorknob. "I wish it had. If we hadn't loved each other so much, everything would have been easier, wouldn't it?"

The door closed behind her, and he heard the water running. He remembered that first night together in New York. After their conversation at Tiffany, he had expected her to change her mind, but when he emerged from his appointment, she had been waiting. They had talked late into the night in his hotel room, piecing together what they could of their own lives, of Archer and Tom's story, of the years in between.

He could barely force himself to remember what had come after their conversation—her dark, seductive gaze, and the way she had unbound her hair and combed it with her fingers until it was a midnight river flowing over her shoulders and down her back. He had extended his hand, afraid that if he did anything more, she would refuse him. But she had come to him easily, her body fitting perfectly against his, her breasts flattening enticingly against his chest.

No, the failure of their marriage hadn't had anything to do with love. They had fallen in love so quickly that there hadn't been time for thought, for dreaming together, for learning the smallest things about each other. That next morning, as the sun rose and the honks and beeps of Manhattan crescendoed into an overture to daylight, he had asked Liana to come back to Australia with him, to take his pearls and make them come alive in her creations. Foolishly, he had believed that finding each other was a victory born from the tragedy of their ancestors. It was ordained that they take something so wrong and make it right.

And she had said yes.

He remembered too well their first morning together, the way the shower beat against glass doors as he lay in bed and thought about the commitment he had made. He hadn't asked Liana to marry him, only to come to Australia, to see the place where her family had lived and to give their relationship a try. As the water splashed and the sun rose, he had been torn, even then, by his need to love and protect her and his need to be unfettered. He had been so young, too young to understood that loneliness and regret were the heaviest chains a man could wear.

But he understood that now.

"I look like a madwoman. Nobody will answer any question I ask. You do the talking."

Cullen glanced at her and liked what he saw, wrinkles and all. "You look lovely. Not as lovely as you did in the T-shirt, but lovely enough."

"My clothes look like I slept in them. So much for natural fibers."

"You just need a piece of your own jewelry to pull it together." When she didn't answer, he went on. "That brooch Mei was wearing was one of yours, wasn't it? An early piece?"

"Yes."

"Matthew's never said what you're designing these days."

"I suspect he's as uncomfortable talking about me with you as he is you with me."

From the tone of her voice, he knew a change of subject was in order. He turned the rental car onto the highway leading back to Tillman. "What will we say to him if we find him?"

"I don't know. We haven't had to deal with him together, have we? Not for a long time."

"I vote we let him tell us exactly why he did this."

"That's a good first step," Liana agreed. "Then we kill him."

Cullen pulled into the fast lane, although there was no traffic. "Dinkum follow-up."

"We should tell him we're going to discuss what to do. Maybe letting him hang a little wouldn't hurt."

"He's going to find it odd enough that we're looking for him together. Won't he find it doubly odd if we consult each other?"

"Maybe it'll be a good lead-in for the future. Nothing's going to be the way it used to be. It's doubtful we'll be able to trust Matthew the way we once did. But we'll trust each other more. Everything's been shaken up, hasn't it?''

She was silent so long he thought she'd finished. But she spoke again. "I'm so sorry it took Matthew's disappearance to make it possible for us to begin talking."

"It's in the past now."

"I said something when you first arrived, something I've regretted. I threatened you. I told you I'd tell Matthew what you did all those years ago, and why I couldn't stay married to you. You said you knew I'd never hurt Matthew that way. Well, you were right. I would never tell him.''

He glanced at her. "Lee, it doesn't matter. He knows."

Her eyes widened; his hands tightened on the wheel. "What do you mean, he knows?"

"I told Matthew that when he was four, I took all the money from the trust fund you'd set up for him. I told him you'd been forced to set it up because you were afraid I might get hold of the money you had inherited from your mother and lose it. And I told him that even though it was illegal, I found a way to tap the money, because I believed if I just had a stake, I could win enough to save Southern Cross from going under.''

He turned into the parking lot of the petrol station where they would start their questioning. He cut the engine and faced her. "I explained that Southern Cross was in trouble because I'd already gambled away everything I could, but I was so terrified, that the only answer I could see was gambling more. So I stole my own son's inheritance.''

Her eyes filled with tears. "Why did you tell him?"

"I owed it to him. How could I tell him how sorry I was unless he knew what I had done?"

"When, Cullen?"

"Two years ago."

She was silent.

"I asked him not to tell you," he explained. "That's the only reason he didn't.''

"But why?"

"Because I knew it would frighten you too much. You've

lways believed that the only reason I let you keep full custody
f Matthew was your promise not to tell him what I'd done.
Once you realized that had changed, I knew you'd be afraid I
vas planning to take him away from you."

She shook her head, as if she didn't know what to say.

"I knew you wouldn't believe me if I told you I would never
urt you or Matthew by battling for him in court," he finished.

"All this time."

"Since you know that much, there's something else you
hould know, too. Through the years, I've reinvested more than
took. He'll have a nest egg when he comes of age. I wanted
Matthew to have what you tried to give him."

"But how? Southern Cross was in disarray when I left. I've
ever understood how you kept it going. Did you get a lucky
oreak after all? Make a lucky bet?"

"I haven't made a bet since you left Australia. The bank
ound an investor who was willing to put up enough money to
lelp me hold on, some anonymous adventurer in the east who
hought Australian pearls had a future and was willing to pull
ne out of the worst of it. I've done the rest a bit at a time."

Tears glistened on her cheeks. "You should have told me."

"I didn't do any of this to prove myself to you."

Their gazes caught and held. He had never expected to tell
er this story or allowed himself to imagine what that might
eel like. He wasn't prepared for the vulnerability in her eyes
or something closely following it that looked like respect. He
adn't done any of this for her, and certainly not to win her
oack. That, he had known, was impossible.

But for the first time, he allowed himself that fantasy. Liana
nd Matthew waiting for him at night, instead of an empty
louse. Liana returning to the creative work that was so much
a part of who she was. Southern Cross a family enterprise they
could build together, that they could pass on to their children.

He looked away, because the pain of those images cut too
leeply. "We're here, Lee."

"Here's a long way from there, isn't it, Cullen? How did
vou come so far?"

He managed a weak grin. "One bloody step at a time. The same way you got yourself on that plane yesterday."

"But yesterday I had you."

He looked at her. "And years ago I *lost* you. Don't underestimate what a powerful motivation reality can be."

She leaned over and kissed his cheek. Her lips lingered, and for just a moment, her fingertips touched the back of his neck. Then she sat back. "Let's go find our son, Cullen."

Brittany Saunders didn't live in Tillman. She lived in what the teenage clerk at the station called "the country."

"I didn't know Brittany *had* friends," she said, when they told her their cover story.

Liana pretended alarm. "Oh, dear. Do you know something we don't?"

"I'm not saying anything." The girl, brown-haired and stick-thin, clamped her lips. Liana fully expected her to run her fingers across them as if she were zipping them shut.

"I'm sorry." Liana offered her warmest smile. "I just don't want to walk into trouble."

The girl rolled her eyes. "Oh, you won't have any trouble. She keeps to herself, that's all. Brittany thinks she's better than anybody else. Smarter, you know?"

"You're a smart girl yourself," Cullen said. "You've got a job already. You're on your way somewhere, aren't you?"

The girl preened for him. "I'm on my way out of here, that's for sure."

"Well, I guess we'd better see Brittany, anyway, or our son will be mad. Can you give us directions?"

The girl gave detailed instructions, right down to the rock formation in the field just before Brittany's driveway. "There's not much out that way," she said, when she'd finished. "She lives with her aunt. You can't miss it."

They thanked her and left. Cullen had the car out on the road before Liana's seat belt was fastened.

The trip took most of twenty minutes, even as fast as Cullen drove. They hardly spoke, caught up in their own thoughts.

Liana was the first to spot the formation the clerk had described. For an instant the colors became beads on a thin golden chain. *Agate and jasper, cat's-eye and cordierite.*

"Slow down," she told him. "Looks like we're there."

He made the turn without fishtailing, a feat she couldn't have accomplished at half the speed. "He could be gone already," Liana said.

"Let's wait and see."

She knew she was borrowing trouble, or perhaps just preparing herself. "Or maybe she won't let us in to see if he's there."

"Lee..."

"All right."

"That's my missus."

She couldn't bring herself to complain.

Brittany lived in a wide mobile home parked in the shadow of a small, vegetation-dotted hillside. On either side of it, twisted silver-barked trees formed sculptures against the brilliant blue sky. The site was neatly laid out, with a cactus garden planted in a tractor-trailer tire, just beside the awning-draped entrance.

They parked ten yards away, but theirs was the only car. "What if no one's home?" Liana said.

"Let's find out." Cullen opened his door.

Liana winced at the first blast of desert heat, but she waited for Cullen to join her before starting up a walkway lined with colorful rocks. Her anxiety had nothing to do with fear of open spaces and unfamiliar surroundings. "Will you do the talking?" she said. "I'm inclined to go straight for her throat."

He put his hand against the small of her back. "Just hang on a few minutes more."

At the door, Cullen tapped sharply, then stepped back. A dog began to yap, a toy poodle or something equally miniature. Somewhere in the rear, a girl issued a sharp command, and the dog quieted. Finally the main door swung open.

The girl behind the screen door was blond and fragile, with

wispy shoulder-length hair and blue eyes that were too large for her face. She looked like a shriveling English wildflower.

"Brittany Saunders?" Cullen said.

The girl looked suspicious, but she nodded.

"I'm Cullen Llewellyn, and this is Liana Robeson. We're trying to find our son, Matthew. Simon Van Valkenburg tells us Matthew was headed here."

Liana watched the girl's expression closely. Brittany didn't look like someone who could hide her thoughts or edit them for viewing. As Cullen's words penetrated, the look of confusion that crossed her face was utterly genuine.

"What? What are you talking about?"

"Do you know our son? Matthew Llewellyn? Simon tells us you're on-line together, that you visit the same chat room."

"What's his screen name?"

Liana spoke for the first time. "DoubleL."

"I..." Brittany shook her head. "Have you ever been in a chat room?"

"No, I haven't."

"People come and go. I don't get on-line very often. I don't have a computer, but when I use my friend's..." She shrugged. "I just remember a few names, and that's not one of them."

"How about SEZ?" Cullen said.

"SEZ? Sure. Kid with a big mouth. He's kinda funny sometimes, though. I guess he's all right."

"Brittany, are you in trouble of some sort?"

Again the girl looked confused. "Trouble?"

"Simon told us that Matthew was on his way to see you because you were in trouble and needed a friend."

"Look, I just finished high school, and I got a scholarship to Prescott College. I've never been better. I'm leaving next week to get a job and spend the summer there."

"Have you ever told Simon where you live?"

Brittany appeared to consider. "You know, maybe I did. Before I realized you weren't supposed to do that. I guess that was stupid, huh? But a couple of months ago we were talking

about our hometowns, and I was trying to describe this place.''
She grimaced. ''Pretty hard to do.''

''The phoney little bastard,'' Cullen said. ''I'll bet he knows
where Matthew really is.''

''Simon,'' Liana clarified for the girl.

''Simon sent you all this way for nothing?''

''You're sure DoubleL isn't familiar?''

Brittany looked sympathetic. ''This Matthew, has he done
something wrong?''

Liana's throat felt tight. ''Nothing. Except disappear.''

26

The Northern Territory, Australia

Matthew wondered what day it was at home and what his parents were doing. But he didn't wonder for long, since that required concentration. Right now he was so tired he could hardly keep his eyes open and, unfortunately, there wasn't any place to sleep.

"Well, *I* thought he was nice." Tricia said the words around a piece of hard candy that was passing for supper.

Matthew forced his eyes open. "You judge men the way I judge distances. The road-train guy wasn't nice, and Jimiramira isn't right around the corner."

They were at one of the few outposts of civilization for hundreds of miles, deep in the heart of the Northern Territory. The building was low-slung and might be gray, except that red dust was so embedded in every crevice and knothole that it looked like the welcome station for hell. There was a dining room off to one side for use by tour groups, a bar with stools for everyone else, and a store, of sorts, that sold disintegrating paperback novels and basic toiletries with unfamiliar brand names.

Matthew knew the aging woman behind the bar was suspicious of him and Tricia, but he wasn't sure what to do about it. Half an hour ago they had arrived with the driver of a small—by Australian standards—road train. And when both he and Tricia had gone to the "loo," the man had left them behind.

"Well, he would have been nicer if I'd given him what he wanted," Tricia pointed out.

Matthew flinched. "Are you kidding?"

"Sure. That's why he left us. You didn't figure that out?"

"When did all that happen?"

"While you were asleep sitting straight up in the seat. Kinky tastes, that one. I told him I had my period. I guess he thought we weren't such good company anymore."

"You should have told me."

Tricia giggled. "Why? Would you have broken *his* arm, too?"

"How did he know...ummm...what you do?"

"Do girls in America dress like this?" She held out the short, tight skirt, as if she was about to curtsy.

"Not the nice ones..."

"Well, they don't in Australia, either." She giggled again. "You're a bit of a mopoke sometimes, aren't you?"

"People can just look at you and tell?"

"That's the point, mate."

He was so tired his head was spinning. He couldn't remember exactly how they had gotten this far. Over the past days and nights they had ridden in a variety of vehicles. They had never had to wait for a ride. For the most part people had been helpful, particularly when they realized he was a stranger. Now he wondered how many of the men had been hoping for some time alone with Tricia.

"The woman at the bar has it figured out," he said, understanding for the first time why the woman stared with such disapproval.

Tricia looked serious, as if she was trying to concentrate but finding it difficult, too. "I don't know if anyone else will come along tonight. The deeper into the Territ'ry we go, the harder it's going to be to find rides."

"Do they have rooms here, do you think?"

"Not that we can afford. I guess we have to find out how far we are from Jimiramira and see if we can figure out something from that."

Matthew ran his tongue over his teeth and swallowed. He tried to remember when they had last eaten. The driver who had picked them up in Broken Hill had divided a stale ham sandwich between them. But that had been at least a couple of rides ago.

"I'd better do the talking," he said, when the woman shot them another glare. He reached in his front pocket for his wallet, having learned his lesson. He counted what little money he had left. "We've got enough for something to eat," he said, returning the wallet. "If we split chicken and chips."

"No. Meat pies. They're cheap enough we can each have a whole one."

He had a vague memory of going into town with his father as a boy and receiving a meat pie as a special treat. He doubted he'd had one since, but the memory made him eager to repeat the experience.

"Get some crisps, too," she continued. "And Passiona, if they have it."

"Passiona? Is that some kind of Aussie dirty joke?"

"You really are a bit of a mopoke." She wandered off to thumb through the desiccated paperbacks.

When he got to the counter he waited patiently until the woman had finished with a bearded old man who looked like an extra in a silent cowboy movie. When she finally stopped in front of Matthew, she scowled and folded her arms.

For a moment he couldn't think of anything that might break the ice. Certainly not, "You've got a great little place here." He swallowed. "We were so glad to see your sign. We've been traveling a long time."

She was dark-haired and sturdy enough to sling him across the room with her pinky. "Where are you from?"

It wasn't a question. It was a command. "The States." He saw that this wasn't enough. "California."

"They don't have enough girls like that one in California that you had to find one here?"

"Tricia?" He feigned surprise. "She's a nice girl. Somebody's got to teach her to dress though."

"Hmm...."

"We're on our way to a place called Jimiramira. Have you heard of it?"

The woman didn't even blink.

"My grandfather lives there. Could you tell me how much farther we have to go?"

"I suppose you left your map in your ute?"

He debated whether to tell her the truth. What if someone hauled them away when they were so close to their goal? "Never mind," he said. "You're busy. I won't bother you. Could we just have two meat pies and some crisps? And, um...some Passiona if you have it."

She turned her back, swinging ample hips as she walked to a refrigerator and took out two packaged pies. She flung them in a microwave and pushed buttons until it started, then she came back with two bags of potato chips and two cans of Coke. "Do you have money?"

He reached for his wallet. "What do I owe you?"

"Lad, I asked if you have money?"

"Enough to pay you, thanks."

She waved away the bills he offered. "What do you want at Jimiramira? And don't lie to me."

He suspected *no one* ever lied to this woman. Besides, he was so close now, he guessed there was no point in continuing his charade. "My name is Matthew Llewellyn. Roman Llewellyn is my grandfather. I'm on my way to see him."

"That so? I didn't know Roman had a grandson."

"He and my dad, they aren't close." Matthew looked down at the counter. "Do you know him?"

"Your grandfather? Maybe I do."

"He doesn't know I'm coming. I don't know what he'll think." Matthew didn't know why he was going into such detail, but he was too tired to screen his comments.

"He'll probably think it's strange, you having been invisible until now."

"Well, I'm a kid. I don't have a lot of choice about what I do and where I go."

Something close to a smile disturbed the sour lines of her face. "Sounds like you might finally have taken matters into your own hands."

He knew he'd said too much. He stood, reluctantly leaving the food on the counter. "I've got to go. I can't take your food. Thanks, but that wouldn't be right."

"Sit down. No, get your friend, and both of you come and sit. It's my shout. And don't worry. I'm not about to ring somebody to carry you off. We'll figure out what you should do. But first I reckon you'd better eat."

He weighed their conversation. He was too tired to know whether he could trust her or not. Hungry. Exhausted. Afraid that coming to Australia had been the biggest mistake he would ever make.

She reached over the counter and touched his arm. Gently, as a mother soothes a toddler. For a moment he missed Liana so much his chest ached.

"Come on, lad." She patted his arm. "She'll be right."

The expression was one his father always used to encourage him. *She'll be right.* He nodded. "Okay."

This time her smile was definite. "Good lad."

He hoped he was being a smart lad, too. He motioned to Tricia, who looked as if she might be propositioning a middle-aged man in dusty moleskins who was standing beside her at the book rack.

"We've got to find that girl some clothes," the woman said. "Or find you different company."

For the first time since spaghetti in Sydney, Matthew was full. He was also as tired as a teenage boy could get. Every time the old ute hit one of the road's considerable ruts, he slammed against the side of the truckbed. But he was fast reaching the point where even that wasn't enough to keep him awake.

"Charlie wouldn't have banged me up this bad," Tricia said. She sounded philosophical. No matter what happened to her, she never whined. Matthew had to give her a lot of credit. Her expectations were low, but even when those weren't met, she didn't complain.

"It wouldn't be bad if the roads weren't so rough," he said.

"Well, Yank, you're in the backblocks, now. We think it's good luck just to have any road at all."

"I know," he said grumpily. "And lucky to have a ride." The woman behind the bar, Mrs. Myrtle, had really come through for them. First she'd fed them. Then she had found jeans, sneakers and a plaid shirt for Tricia, and a clean T-shirt for him. Finally she had let them shower one at a time in a guest room. And when they emerged, she had introduced them to Noel, the old man at the bar who looked like he ought to be leading packhorses for Gene Autry.

"I won't be turning off to Jimiramira," Noel told them. "You can spread out your swags at the crossroads and walk in tomorrow."

Matthew had been about to point out that they had no swags, when Mrs. Myrtle interrupted. "I'll put something together for you. Just tell Roman to bring them back next time he comes this way."

They had climbed into the bed of the battered ute, and Mrs. Myrtle had followed a few moments later with patched sleeping bags and pieces of canvas to tuck beneath them. She had wrapped sandwiches, too, and added bottles of spring water and a flashlight.

"You be sure to point out the way so they don't wander off," she instructed Noel. "And you two," she warned Tricia and Matthew, "stay on the road. Don't take shortcuts. Just use the torch tonight, and follow the road straight along in the morning. You'll be at the homestead soon enough if somebody doesn't pick you up first. Just in case, I'll ring up Roman and have him keep an eye out."

Matthew hated to lose the element of surprise. In a matter of minutes a man could come up with a thousand excuses why he didn't want to meet a grandson he had never acknowledged.

He thanked her as profusely as she would allow. Then he added casually, "Maybe you could wait until afternoon to call my grandfather?"

She gave a brisk nod. Then she turned to Tricia. "And you. Go back home soon as you can. Somebody's looking for you, that's for certain."

Tricia had just shrugged. Now, bouncing in the back of the ute, Matthew wondered if she would comply. He had no idea what his grandfather was going to say about him, much less her. He had practically promised that Roman would buy her a ticket wherever she wanted to go. But in his heart Matthew suspected Roman would send her back home to her parents.

Maybe she had known that all along.

"Can you see why I got out of the Territ'ry when I could?" Tricia asked sleepily.

"Is Humpty Dumpty like this?"

She giggled. "Humpty Doo. No, it's a bloomin' paradise in comparison. Darwin's too far down the road for my tastes, but it's a pretty enough town."

He thought it was a good sign she was defending her roots. "Then what's your point? Why did you leave?"

"Doesn't matter if it's Jimiramira or Darwin. It's not Sydney, is it? It's hard work, all the time, and heat and flies. I just had enough of it, that's all."

"You fought with your parents, didn't you? That's why you left."

She was silent.

"What about?" he asked after a while.

"Doesn't matter."

"It matters to you."

"My dad was always after me. Work harder in school. Work harder at home. We're doing this for you. We want you to be somebody. It made me crook, that's all."

Matthew felt like he was swimming in deep water—with

crocodiles. But he felt obliged to continue. "Did he, you know, hit you and stuff?"

She shook her head. "Not my dad. Not ever. Nobody ever bashed me, till Charlie."

"Then he yelled?"

"No. My dad doesn't shout."

"You know, I'm having trouble understanding this."

"Why? You ran away, too, didn't you? You've been lying all this time about why you're here and who you are. I heard what you told old Myrtle. Matthew Llewellyn. But you're carrying somebody else's wallet now, aren't you?"

"I didn't run away, not like you mean. I just had to come here and do something."

"What?"

"Meet my grandfather." It wasn't a lie. It just wasn't the whole truth.

"Well, I had to do something, too. I had to get away from my parents. Because I was never going to be anybody, only they just couldn't see it. I'm as useless as an ashtray on a motorbike. I could have worked day and night for the rest of my life, and I never would have been what they wanted. I'm not good in school. I don't want to help them grow their bloody mangoes, I got tired of disappointing them, so I left. And now they'd be really disappointed, wouldn't they? If they knew what I've been doing."

Matthew didn't know what to say. Tricia's problems were a lot greater than his ability to solve them. He only knew one thing for sure. "If we were talking about my parents, I know they'd take me back, whatever I'd done."

"Yeah? Well, mine might take me back, I guess. But I'm a drongo. Still and always. Nothing's changed."

He had to guess what a drongo was. "You're not. You're funny and clever, and you have a good heart. You make the best out of things, whatever they are. And you stand up for yourself when you have to. Anybody who wants to be successful has to learn that."

She seemed surprised he could find anything good to say about her. "Think so?"

"Yeah. And you're smart enough to do anything you want. You could be good in school, if you thought it mattered."

"Not good enough to make Mum and Dad happy."

"Maybe that changed while you were away. Maybe they've done some thinking. You have, haven't you?"

She didn't nod, but in the pale light of a canopy of stars, she looked pensive.

The ute slowed to a halt, and Noel opened his door. The two blue heelers riding on the seat beside him began to yelp as he came around to the back and pointed down a dirt track. He was a man of few words. "Jimiramira."

Matthew swung himself over the side and reached for Tricia to help her to the ground. Then he grabbed the canvas covered sleeping bags and handed one to her. "About how far, do you think?"

Noel scratched his head. Then he shrugged.

"Six hours by foot?" Tricia asked.

"About."

Matthew held out his hand. "Thanks, Noel. We really appreciate the ride."

Noel shook his hand, but dropped it quickly. "Don't wander." Without another word he got back in his ute. The dogs quieted and the engine roared. In a moment he was a cloud of dust. In two he was gone.

Matthew couldn't remember ever experiencing a world that was so completely still. If Tricia hadn't been there beside him, he would have been sure he was the only person left alive.

She plopped her swag on the ground and dropped to sit on it, head in hands. "I'm knackered. Don't tell me we're going to knock about the old backblocks tonight."

"Let's get down the road a little. Then we can find a place to camp."

"We don't have to go way off in the bush. No worries someone's going to run us down out here."

He turned on the flashlight, and they started along the track, picking their way carefully in the darkness. Despite his exhaustion, Matthew felt excitement rising. "Do you suppose we're on Jimiramira? I mean, it's a big place, right?"

"Mopoke. We've probably been on the station for miles and miles."

"Why didn't you say something?"

"I figured you knew."

"This is where my dad was raised." Matthew tried to imagine that. This was where his grandfather had been raised, too. And his great-grandfather. He was a Llewellyn, and this was Llewellyn land. An apartment in the city was one thing. But the apartment building only had streetlights. Jimiramira had stars, galaxies, an entire universe, shimmering above it.

"I'm not going a step farther." Tricia stopped in the middle of the track. "This is it."

Matthew looked off in the distance. He had been born in Australia, and since he was old enough to read he had devoured every book about the country he could find. But he wasn't sure what to call anything. Plants were different here. He recognized eucalyptus trees, because they were common enough in California, but the landscape was so alien he almost felt as if he were exploring another planet.

The land stretched back from the track in low, undulating waves—not hills, exactly, but products of wind, water and erosion. Somehow he had expected grass. It was a ranch, after all, a station. But no grass was in evidence as far as he could make out. Only tufts of vegetation and odd desert shrubs. There were trees, too. A few towered high in the distance, but most seemed stunted and forlorn.

"I've camped a lot," Matthew said. "How about you?"

"More than I wanted."

"Mrs. Myrtle gave us some matches." Matthew shone the flashlight in a circle around them. "Let's figure out where we want to sleep, then we can find some sticks and start a campfire."

"A regular Boy Scout." Tricia shook her head, but she didn't argue.

They settled on a wide bare patch about fifteen yards from the track. Tricia spread the canvas and untied their sleeping bags, while Matthew took the flashlight and searched for wood. He found enough within a hundred yards to start a good-sized blaze. It seemed as dry as the landscape, and he was glad they had chosen a spot away from trees. He didn't think his grandfather would be impressed with him if he started a bushfire.

Just to be safe, he collected stones, an easy enough task, and made a ring before he piled the wood in the middle. For some reason he remembered a Jack London story he'd read in English class about a freezing man with only a match or two between himself and death. He wondered if his own fire would catch. Suddenly he didn't want to be here, in this silent, desolate place a million miles from San Francisco, without a fire. "I wish we had some paper...."

"No worries. We've got something better." Tricia stripped dried leaves from some of the branches he had brought back with him. "Gum leaves are so full of oil, the trees explode like bombs in a bushfire."

"You've seen it?"

"Nah. But my dad has. He's not a reader, Dad isn't, but he loves to tell stories. At night, when I was a little girl, he'd put me to bed if my mum was busy, and he'd tell me about growing up here and the things he saw."

Matthew knew that Tricia must be as tired as he was, because she sounded wistful, as if it was just too exhausting to hide her feelings. "My dad tells me stories, too. That was the only way I could find out what it's like to be here."

"You never came to visit him?"

"No." Matthew piled the leaves in the middle of his circle and lit a match. They caught quickly, and soon enough the twigs had caught, too. When the fire was burning brightly and he was satisfied it was going to continue, he took the flashlight and went in search of more wood. Three trips later he was sure they had enough for the night.

Matthew crawled into his sleeping bag, which Tricia had laid out right next to hers so they could share the biggest piece of canvas. The temperature had dropped as darkness fell, and he was grateful for the fire as well as warm covers. The ground beneath him was hard, but he didn't think that was going to matter.

He was all set to sleep. He was exhausted.

And he was still wide-awake.

Beside him, Tricia tossed and turned, as if she couldn't get comfortable in any position. "Are you okay?" he asked.

"I'm not used to sleeping when it's dark."

He thought about that, and his cheeks flamed. "Are you going to get used to it?"

"I don't know."

"Did you like that...you know...so much you want to keep doing it?"

"You mean having sex for money?"

That was exactly what he'd meant. "Uh-huh."

"I never did it 'cause I liked it. I didn't plan to do it when I left home. I thought I'd get a real job at a bank. I'm good with figures, that's one thing I can do. But I couldn't find anything, and then I met Charlie. He made me feel special, like I was important. At first I didn't know what he wanted. Then, well, it seemed like the only thing to do. I thought I could just save some money, you know, and then I could find something better."

"Why didn't you take the job that lady at the bookstore offered you?"

She was silent for so long he didn't think she was going to answer. "Mrs. Duff knew what I'd been doing, you see. I knew she'd be watching me all the time and wondering if I was up to no good. She was trying to save me from myself, only I didn't think I needed it. I'm not a bad person."

"Well, you stole my wallet."

"But I thought you'd be okay. I always picked people who looked like they'd be okay." She paused. "I guess that part *was* bad, though. I didn't much like stealing, but I had to give Charlie money every night, whether I'd been with men or not. And sometimes that was the only way I could do it."

Matthew closed his eyes. The stars were so brilliant the sight of them made his chest hurt.

"I'm sorry," Tricia said. "If I hadn't nicked it, you'd be with your grandfather right now. You wouldn't be hungry—"

"I'm not hungry."

"Well, you wouldn't be out here on the ground now, would you?"

"Neither would you. You'd be back in Sydney, stealing somebody else's wallet or—kissing men."

"Not a lot of kissing goes on."

His cheeks flamed again. "I know what goes on. That was just a nice way of saying it."

"*Do* you know what goes on?"

He was silent.

"Have you ever done it?" she asked.

He remained silent, growing warm in new and distant places.

"I guess not," she said, humor in her voice.

"I'm only fourteen. Almost fifteen."

"No. Really?"

He was gratified she sounded surprised. She wasn't an easy girl to fool. "Really."

"Do you want to do it?"

He stiffened. A touch had accompanied her words. Now her hand rested lightly on his shoulder.

Did he want to do it? Was he a healthy teenage boy who had reached puberty early? Did he have a rich fantasy life that couldn't possibly be as satisfying as the real thing?

"I mean, if that's what you want," Tricia said, "I could show you how."

No one would ever know whether she showed him or not. In fact, Matthew guessed that anyone who had seen them together just assumed they had been…that they'd done…

He couldn't even say the words to himself.

"I didn't ask you to come with me for that." He choked out his response.

"Oh, I reckon I know. I thought American boys were sophisticated, but you're not. You're shy, aren't you?"

"No. I just don't think this is right."

"You're a Bible-basher, are you?"

"No! I just don't think it should be this easy for you."

"You don't want me selling it, but I'm not supposed to give it away, either?"

"You're doing it because I've been nice to you, that's all. It's not supposed to be a reward. You're supposed to be in love. Or something."

She giggled. "You don't have to love somebody for all your parts to work right. That's a dead bird."

"Maybe not. But it's better if you do, isn't it? Haven't you ever done it with somebody you cared about? Wasn't it better?"

She pulled her hand away. For a moment he thought he had hurt her feelings. "I never have," she said at last. "But I thought maybe I was going to have the chance tonight."

He turned toward her. In the flickering firelight her face seemed innocent and vulnerable. He reached out and touched her cheek. "I like you, too."

"Don't you think I'm pretty?"

He remembered one of his father's favorite expressions. "Abso-bloody-lutely."

She giggled. "Maybe you'll come back to Australia when you're older. Maybe I'll be somebody else by then, somebody better."

"I like you the way you are."

"Well, if you do come back, you won't know where to find me. I'm not going home to Humpty Doo."

"Right."

"But I'm not going back to Sydney, either."

"Good on ya."

"You're sure about tonight?"

He was sure, but he knew it would take some time for his body to cooperate. He settled for taking her hand and threading his fingers through hers. Slowly they fell asleep under the gleaming canopy of stars.

27

Roman Llewellyn kept to himself. His men understood and honored that, and so did the owners of the neighboring stations, who had long since given up inviting him to socialize. He attended the local yearly race meeting, participated in the occasional charity fund-raiser, and opened the homestead for an old-fashioned bush barbecue at the end of each year's muster, inviting all his employees and anyone else who cared to come.

But Roman's hospitality was governed by the calendar. He would no more consider attending an impromptu gathering than he would casually shoot Jimiramira's prize Brahman bulls. He preferred solitude, craved it, in fact, and vastly preferred the company of a horse to any man he knew.

He was a stern taskmaster, whipcord lean and even now, at sixty-three, as strong as any man half his age. He drank whatever and whenever he pleased, ate a diet rich in station beef, and until a year ago—when he'd finally given up the habit—rolled his own cigarettes. He had never been inside a health club, but he still rode for hours each day and did every job he asked of others. He was ''Boss'' to his men and ''Mr. Llewellyn'' to his housekeeper and cook. He could hardly remember the last time anybody had called him Roman.

Or Dad.

''Boss, someone on the phone, back at the house.''

Roman looked up to see Luke, one of the aboriginal station

hands, standing at the stable door. He couldn't imagine who might try to reach him. Jimiramira's staff was large. He had a pastoral superintendent, a commercial manager, a bookkeeper, a housekeeper. Although his word was final, there was always someone more suited to answer inquiries than he was.

He looked down and continued picking the hoof of the thoroughbred gelding in the first stall. "Bloody shoe. Never did fit to start with," he muttered. "Told Sandy to have it fixed. He'll hear about this."

"Boss, you want I tell Mrs. Myrtle to ring you some other time?"

He looked up again and frowned. "Helen Myrtle?"

"That's who it is, yeah."

Roman dropped the horse's hoof and dusted his hands on his trousers. "I'll take it here."

Luke jammed his felt hat deeper over his ears and strode off toward the house. Roman headed for the tack room, where he'd had a radiotelephone installed when the technology had become available. He picked up the receiver and punched a button. "Helen?"

He listened for a moment. "You're certain?" he said, when Helen Myrtle had finished. He listened again, thanked her and hung up the receiver.

"Bloody hell." He shoved his hands in his pockets and rocked back on his heels.

Roman Llewellyn might keep to himself and prefer it that way. But apparently a young man named Matthew Llewellyn did not.

"It's winter here, right? It's not supposed to be hot." Matthew trudged along the road next to Tricia, his sleeping bag under his arm. He wasn't sure what time it was. At some point on the trip to Jimiramira, the battery in his watch had died. He didn't know when they had awakened and eaten their sandwiches, and he didn't know how long they had been walking. He only knew that the next time they stopped to rest, they would finish their water.

What if they weren't on the right road? What if somehow they had gotten turned around?

"This isn't hot," Tricia informed him. "You don't know hot, do you?"

"It never gets cooler than this?"

"At night."

He had been cold as he slept. He remembered waking to a great, brooding silence and wishing that he and Tricia could share their sleeping bags. He'd lain awake for a while, fantasizing about that, but eventually he'd piled more wood on the fire instead.

"How long do you think we've been walking?" Matthew said.

"It doesn't matter, does it? We have to walk until we get there."

"You don't think we got turned around?"

"No, Yank, I don't!"

He settled into stride again. He was surprised there wasn't more to see, but the uniformity of their surroundings was something he could count on. He had expected exotic marsupials of all shapes and sizes. Instead he'd seen a cow or two in the distance, but nothing like the herds he'd imagined when Cullen told him stories of his childhood.

"I thought we'd see cowboys on horseback by now. Stuff like that," he said after a while.

"More likely you'll see men in helicopters these days. They still use horses, only not as often for mustering. A station like this is so large it would take weeks to cover it any other way."

"My dad said when he lived here they went out for weeks at a time on their horses and camped at night."

"Still do, to work the beasts once they're in the yards. Only they use whatever's handiest to bring them in now. They probably still have men who ride the boundaries to keep an eye on the fences. Maybe your grandfather will give you a job."

Matthew knew she was teasing, but he wondered what his grandfather would say if he asked to live here with him. He didn't want to, not really. He knew his mother would never come to visit, and his father hadn't been back in years. But even though the terrain was alien, even though he knew so little about how a station like this one was run, even though his grandfather was a stranger, Jimiramira still felt special to him.

They fell into a long silence. He ached from nights of sleeping in trucks. Even with a sleeping bag, the ground last night had been hard and unyielding. The sandwiches had already worn off, and his thirst was bigger than the remaining water. But all that seemed minor in comparison to the real question of the hour.

"You know," he said at last, "my grandfather might not let us stay."

"That'd be a cow of a thing, wouldn't it?"

"He and my dad go their separate ways. I'm not even sure he knows I exist."

"Happy little family, huh?"

They crested a hill. Matthew hadn't minded the climb because he'd hoped that when they reached the top, the homestead might be in view. Instead he saw another long stretch and another low rise in the distance. "Crap." He shook his head.

"Suppose he doesn't let you stay. What'll you do next?"

Matthew hadn't wanted to think about that. It had taken every bit of planning and energy just to come this far. "Oh, I'll just move on. I have to go somewhere else, too."

"Where?"

"Western Australia."

"You planning to walk?"

He moved the sleeping bag into a more comfortable position. "I don't have a plan. Not yet. Right now my plan is to see my grandfather."

"Why do you have to go to Western Australia?"

"I just do, that's all."

"I'm not going with you. Not this time."

"At least *I* know where I have to go. You don't even know that."

"Well, I know something you don't."

"Like?"

"Somebody's coming."

Matthew peered down the hill at the road beyond. At first he didn't see anything. Then, at the edge of the horizon, he saw dust clouds rising in puffs. His throat closed, and for a moment he was speechless.

Tricia filled in the gap. "I reckon we could keep walking, but it hardly seems wise, does it? Whoever it is will be here in a few minutes." Tricia pulled the bottled water from inside the waistband of her shirt and held it out to him. "Drink up, mate. You'll need all your strength, won't you?"

The homestead was not at all the way he had pictured it. Matthew felt the way he had on his first trip to Disneyland. Then he had expected nothing more than a pumped-up amusement park. This time he had expected the Jimiramira of Aunt Mei's description, with a few updates. His father had spoken only rarely of his boyhood home, preferring to tell stories of people he'd known and colorful trips into the outback. When questioned, Cullen had been evasive, as if he didn't want to think too much about what he'd lost.

Now, for the first time, Matthew understood. Cullen hadn't lost a house and a father. He had lost a village, an entire way of life, an identity.

"The boss, he's waiting up at the house." The dark-skinned man named Luke got out of the ute and slammed the door behind him. Matthew opened his door and got out, motioning to Tricia to follow him.

She slid across the seat and down to the ground. "Right pretty place, don't you think?"

He did think. The main house where his grandfather was waiting was sparkling white and shaded by huge old gum trees with smooth, mottled bark and feathery leaves. A wide veranda with a dark red floor surrounded the house on the three sides he could see, shaded by an expansive corrugated metal roof. The veranda was surrounded by shrubs and flower borders, and the flourishing lawn was bordered by a green metal fence with an ornate gate.

He spoke his thoughts out loud. "I guess when the house burned down, they decided to build something better."

"When did it burn?" Tricia asked.

He thought about Mei, whose age, to him, was indeterminate. "I don't know. A long time ago."

"Didn't your father live here?"

"He doesn't talk much about it."

"Uh-oh."

He cleared his throat. Luke had disappeared, but other people moved around the periphery of his vision. The house was only one of many low-slung white buildings, and beyond the house was a wide stableyard, fenced and divided into paddocks. He glimpsed men on horseback, as well as a flotilla of vehicles. Far off to one side was an airstrip with a small plane at one edge and a helicopter at the other.

"Looks huge to you, doesn't it?" Tricia said. "It's not one of the biggest, though. Coolibah Downs, now there's a station. My dad was a stockman there. Jimiramira's an infant in comparison."

"Is it?" He couldn't imagine. He suspected Jimiramira might be larger than some states in New England.

"Big enough, though," Tricia conceded.

"We should go right in." Matthew straightened his clothes, although there wasn't much he could do with a T-shirt and jeans. He had combed his hair with one of Mrs. Myrtle's donations, but he hadn't had water or toothpaste to brush his teeth, even though a new toothbrush resided in his pocket. He was meeting his grandfather looking exactly like a runaway instead of a man with a mission.

"I think I'll wait on the porch," Tricia said.

"You're sure?"

"It's your frigging reunion, not mine."

He wondered if she meant her own would come later. He hoped so.

He opened the gate and ushered her through. Then they

walked along a stone pathway to the porch. Tricia split off to take a seat on a green wooden bench nestled beneath a shuttered window. "Luck to you," she said. Then she settled herself on the bench, thrust her feet in front of her and her back against the shutters, and closed her eyes.

Matthew knocked. A gray-haired woman in a plaid dress came to the screen door, a feather duster in one hand and a rag in the other. She seemed surprised. *He* was surprised no one had told her to expect him.

"Umm...I'm Matthew Llewellyn. I'm here to see my grandfather."

For a moment she just stared at him, as if he had said he was there to burn down the house with everyone inside it. "Matthew?"

"That's right." He sent her a shaky smile. When she didn't move, he cleared his throat. "I'm Cullen's son."

She frowned. "Cullen?"

"Cullen Llewellyn. Roman Llewellyn's son."

She muttered something under her breath, either a curse or a prayer. Then she opened the door and peered outside. "You've brought someone?"

"Yes, but she'd rather wait on the porch. If you don't mind," he added quickly.

"Does your grandfather—"

"I'll see to him, Winnie," a man said.

Matthew found an older man staring at him, his eyes narrowed in contemplation. Matthew's heart seemed to move in his chest. Winnie melted into the cool shadows of the house, and the man didn't speak again. Matthew knew it was up to him.

"Hello, sir. My name is Matthew Llewellyn. I'm Cullen's son. Are you...?" Suddenly he couldn't say the word. At school he had been surrounded by friends with family at their fingertips. He had ached for more time with his father, and for years he had imagined knowing this man and coming to this place.

But in his imagination, this man had smiled and welcomed him.

"I'm Roman Llewellyn."

Matthew stood taller. "Then you're my grandfather."

"I suppose."

"I know you weren't expecting me."

"An understatement."

They stood quietly, taking each other's measure. Roman seemed both older and younger than Matthew had imagined. The boy could see traces of his father in Roman's weathered features, but the scowl, which seemed permanently etched in his face, was so unlike Cullen that Roman seemed even more a stranger.

Roman continued to scrutinize him. Matthew could feel his cheeks growing warm, but he refused to look away. "Where are your parents?" Roman asked at last.

"I don't know, sir. I haven't spoken to them since I left."

"Left?"

Matthew tried to think how he could tell his story in the few words he sensed this man might give him. "My mother put me on a plane to New York to meet my dad, only I got off in Denver and made my way here, instead. I'd planned it that way."

Roman nodded.

Matthew realized he was supposed to continue. "Well, you see, I knew I could never come here, to Australia, any other way. I left them a message and told them I'm safe, of course. But, it's just, well, they don't know where I am exactly."

"Exactly?"

Matthew smiled wryly. "At all."

"You've left out a thing or two."

"Or three," Matthew admitted.

"Why did you come to Jimiramira?"

"You're my grandfather."

"So I'm told."

"I just thought if I didn't take the bull by the horns, I'd never meet you."

Roman's scowl lines deepened. "Did you stop to think I might not want to meet you?"

"Sure. That seemed likely, as a matter of fact."

"But you made the trip anyway? You lied and ran away and made the trip anyway?"

"I'm not a troublemaker. You can ask anybody. It's just that sometimes things are too important to leave up to other people."

"How did you get here?"

"I'm not proud of this part." Matthew squirmed a little under Roman's gaze.

"Go on."

"Well, I used a credit card of my mother's to buy the ticket. I'll pay her back every cent—and interest, too—I swear. She canceled the card, or thought she did, but I found the letter before it went out. I bought the ticket on the Internet. She won't check that card until her—"

Roman's eyes narrowed to slits. "I have the picture."

"I used a friend's passport, and got my visa in his name."

"You lied, cheated, robbed your own mum. You're a disgrace."

"Maybe. And maybe I'm just a kid who's tired of grownups who ignore me and decide what's best without asking how I feel about it. I have a family, only I hardly get to see my dad, and I've *never* seen you. I was born in Australia. I want to know who I am and where I come from. And—" He stopped himself just in time. He wasn't ready to finish this explanation.

"You're going to ring your mum right now. And then I'm sending you straight back. With an escort, if I have to."

"You can do that." Matthew looked his grandfather straight in the eye. "Or you can let me spend a day here. What's one day, sir? I've waited my whole life to meet you. I'll call and leave word for my mother that I'm still all right. I've never wanted to worry her. But I came for another reason, and if you send me away, I'll never be able to tell you what it is."

"You're like your father, aren't you? You think you can talk your way out of anything."

Matthew was slow to anger, but now he could feel it building inside him. "I hope I'm like him. He's the finest man in the world. Of course, you'd hardly know, would you, since you don't speak to him anymore."

Roman's hand slashed through the air in disgust. "You don't know what you're talking about."

Matthew stepped closer, anger flaming faster. "Oh yes I do. I know it all. I know my dad had a gambling problem. I know he made serious mistakes. I just hope I take after *him* when I grow up and not you, because I'm going to make plenty of mistakes in my life. And when I do, I want to be as sorry about them as he is and work just as hard to make them right!"

"You've made a big mistake coming here."

"No, I haven't. Because I had to find out where I came from. And who I came from. And now I know."

Roman stepped closer, too. For a moment Matthew wondered if his grandfather would hit him. They faced off like opponents in a boxing ring. Then Roman shook his head. He turned and walked back the way he had come. At the end of the hallway he turned.

"Come inside. And bring the girl. Winnie will feed you, then you can shower. When you've finished, come to my office." He turned away.

Matthew spoke before his grandfather could disappear. "Sir, my parents will never let me go anywhere again after this. This may be the only chance we'll ever have together."

"It's one more chance than I wanted, boy." Roman disappeared, and Matthew was alone.

28

Roman had a framed mirror in his office for those rare occasions when he had to comb his hair before greeting visitors. He'd had government officials at Jimiramira, politicians, men from the police and armed forces. For all practical purposes he was the mayor of a small town, and no matter how many people hired on to help him, there were some things other men couldn't do.

Like be Matthew Llewellyn's grandfather.

He stared at his own reflection and saw exactly what Matthew had seen. Bitterness. Cynicism. Detachment.

The brass mirror had been his wife's, and he had kept it on this wall for the nearly thirty years since her death. Joan had been a Darwin girl, a city she'd loved so well she had named their only child after Cullen Bay, where she had picnicked as a girl. And although she had never whined about the hardships of the never-never, Joan had cherished pretty things. He had kept other mementos. Her silver comb and brush, the odd piece of jewelry, the wildflowers—paper and poached egg daisies, running postman, Sturt's desert pea—she had carefully dried and framed after the Wet.

But God help him, he had not kept their son, Joan's most beloved possession. After the cancer had taken her, Roman had abandoned Cullen as surely as if he had trotted him off to an orphanage. Immersed in his own sorrow, beyond consolation, he had sunk further into himself until eventually he hadn't been able to find his way back.

He knew these things now. Almost twenty years had passed since he had seen Cullen. No day went by that he didn't think of his son, or the mess the boy had made of his life because he hadn't had a father to guide him. No day passed that Roman didn't feel the deepest regret. Yet he didn't know what he could do about any of it. He was like the land he tended, remote and arid. Like Jimiramira, he did not recover easily from injury, and he suffered change with deep, abiding hostility.

Where was Cullen now? Was he frantic that Matthew had gone missing? The boy imagined his parents had been satisfied with a message that he was fine, but Roman knew better. He was a father, too. He knew how it felt to lose a son.

A knock sounded on his door, although it was too soon for the intruder to be Matthew. He growled a reply, and the door swung open. Winnie, hands on hips, stood on the threshold, staring daggers at him.

"If you send this boy away, I will go with him." She took one hand off her hip long enough to shake a finger at him. "Do you hear me, Roman Llewellyn? I will leave, and I'll take my Harold with me. Then what will you do? Who'll put up with you, I ask you?"

"Woman, this is none of your affair."

She wasn't cowed. "I run this house and everyone inside it. And my Harold's your manager. We come as close to knowing you as anyone. You have a chance to set things right at last. And I'll be damned if I'll let you waste it."

No other human being could have talked to Roman that way, but Winnie had been with him long enough to think she was safe. Routine was everything to him, and she knew he would do nearly anything to keep her from leaving.

He felt unsuccessfully in his pockets for tobacco. "What's the boy doing now?"

"He and that girl tucked into a plate of sausages like they hadn't eaten in a week. Did you ask how he got here?"

"No."

"Did you ask who *she* is?"

"No—I—didn't."

"Well, I think I know."

Roman didn't care. He had enough trouble just thinking about his grandson. "What does it matter, anyhow?"

"You know Robby Simmons, don't you?"

"Robby Simmons from over at Coolibah Downs? Damned fine stockman."

"The same, only that was years ago, which shows how much you know. Presently he and his missus have a small property over at Humpty Doo. Orchards, I believe."

"What does Robby have to do with the girl?"

Winnie had deep lines in her leathery skin. Now they fanned out from her pursed lips like the rays of a spider web. "Daughter of Robby's disappeared around Christmas last year. I heard all about it when I was in Darwin visiting my family."

Roman's growl could have meant anything.

"I saw a photograph in the newspaper while I was there, and this girl seems familiar to me," Winnie said, unperturbed. "Better yet, the Simmons girl was named Patricia, but her family called her Patty. This girl calls herself Tricia. I'm fair certain it's her."

"What do you plan to do about it?"

"What should I do?"

Roman didn't want her to do anything. He understood horses and cattle and working dogs. He could drill a bore, yard a mob, build a fence guaranteed to frustrate dingoes or cattle duffers. He understood international finance and veterinary medicine. But he didn't understand kids.

"I suppose you'd best ring up Robby," he said at last. "He'd expect it."

"I suppose I'd best." She hesitated. "And the boy?"

Roman was silent.

"Didn't he come far enough to suit you?"

"You're overstepping yourself, Winnie."

"No, I'm not, *Roman.*"

He glared at her. Until today he had always been Mr. Llewellyn. Unperturbed, she pointed her finger at him. "Act like the boss, then I'll treat you as such."

"You've turned a bit cheeky, haven't you?"

"Not soon enough." She turned on her heel and strode away.

Roman didn't know what to make of the change in Winnie, but the change in himself was more upsetting. He had learned to live with Joan's death and Cullen's estrangement. He cushioned his emotions by creeping carefully along the same paths, never daring to venture into forbidden territory. And just as he'd always feared, in this new, unexplored wilderness he was reminded of everything he had tried so hard to forget.

Half an hour later he was staring at papers on his desk when someone knocked on his door. He knew without asking who was there. At his shouted acknowledgment the door opened. Matthew, hair wet from the shower, strolled in as if he were as comfortable here as he was in bloody California.

"Well, I feel better. How about you?"

Roman looked down at his papers again, pretending Matthew had interrupted something other than soul-searching. "I'm not the one who ate lashings of sausages."

"They're different from the ones we have at home. But they taste familiar. Maybe I had them when I was a kid."

"You are a kid."

"A little kid. When I lived in Australia. Did you ever visit me? Is that something I've forgotten, too?"

"No." Roman fully expected him to ask why not. The boy seemed to have little patience with tact. Roman supposed he had inherited that from Cullen.

"That's a shame," Matthew said. "I'm told I wasn't too bad, as little kids go. But not everyone likes kids. Some people like teenagers better."

Roman couldn't pretend any longer. Every word the boy uttered went straight through his heart. "I didn't visit because your dad and I pugged up our relationship so thoroughly there was no turning back. He wouldn't have wanted me."

"You asked him?"

"I don't have to. I'm his father."

"Do you know how much he misses you?"

"He knows where I live."

"But he doesn't know you want to see him again."

"I don't."

The boy walked to the window and stared outside. "I know about Jimiramira. About Archer and Bryce. I know more about them than I do about you."

Roman was surprised. He hadn't been much for telling Cullen stories, particularly not about his family. He wondered exactly where Cullen had gotten information. "Your father told you?"

"Well, no."

"Your mother?"

"No, she doesn't know all the parts I do, and my dad probably doesn't, either. It was my aunt. Mei Fong. She lived here once, when your father was still a young man, and Archer and Viola were alive. She was here when Jimiramira burned to the ground."

Roman was caught off guard. He had expected something different from the boy. A lecture, perhaps, on his duty as grandfather. Or anger. An attempt to shame him. But never a discussion of family history.

"You have me thoroughly confused," Roman said. "Why would an aunt of yours live here?"

"Great-aunt. She's my grandfather's sister. Grandfather Robeson, that is. But I don't remember him very well. He didn't like kids, either. That's one reason I had to come here and meet you. You're the only grandfather I have left."

"One reason?"

"There *is* another," Matthew said.

Roman could feel his carefully orchestrated life falling apart. An abyss was opening at his feet, and he was certain that if he commented on anything Matthew had said, or asked even a single question, he would plummet straight to the bottom.

"It's time you rang your mother, boy, and told her you're coming straight home. If you're trying to find a way to stay longer..."

"I'll call her. Only I'm not going home. Not yet. I have something I have to do first. Then I'll go home, and they probably won't let me leave again until I'm twenty-one. They'll hire a guard. Chain me to the bed." He flashed a grin that reminded Roman so strongly of Cullen that for a moment he was dizzied by it. "My dad will have to come to California to see me." Matthew sobered. "That won't be much fun."

"Why not?" The words were out before Roman could stop them.

"He and my mother barely speak. Lots of my friends have divorced parents. Some of them scream and yell at each other, so I guess Mom and Dad are better than that. But I don't know what would happen if they had to be in the same house for very long."

Roman decided to put one theory to the test. "You didn't run away because you hoped they'd get back together?"

Matthew looked genuinely surprised. "Are you joking?"

"No, I'm trying to find out why you showed up on my doorstep."

"I guess that's easy enough, Granddad. Because you never showed up on mine."

Matthew was surprised when his grandfather left him alone in the office to make the phone call to his mother. Roman set up the radiophone to make the call, dialed the number Matthew gave him, then disappeared when the phone began to ring. But the door was left ajar, and Matthew knew his grandfather was making sure he went through with it.

He listened for the familiar voice-mail message, then he

spoke. "Hi, Mom. This is Matthew. I'm safe, and I'm doing fine."

He saw a shadow lengthen just outside the door and knew he would be required to do better than that or his grandfather would quickly reappear. "I'm in Australia. I know I'm not supposed to be here, and I knew if I came when Dad was here you'd think that he'd put me up to it. So that's why I left while he was in America. I had to come. I had to see where I came from. I'm flying back home in a couple of days...."

At that he wondered if his grandfather was going to come charging back into the room, and he hurried on. "And I'm going to pay you back every cent the ticket cost with interest. You can take what I have in the bank as a start. I'm really sorry, but nobody seems to understand how important this is." He hesitated. "I'm sorry you aren't there, Mom. But maybe it's better if we don't talk until I come back. Then you'll have all the time in the world to tell me what you think, because I doubt I'll be leaving the house for a long, long time."

Matthew imagined Liana, her head bent low over the telephone as she listened, her eyes glistening with tears. His own throat felt tight. "I love you." His voice deepened. "Mom, if you talk to Dad anytime soon, tell him I love him, too."

He wondered why he felt so sentimental when his mother wouldn't even be the one—at least, not the first—to hear the call. He had given his grandfather the Pacific International number and left the message there because he was afraid if he left it at home the call might be easier to trace. Tomorrow a secretary or assistant would get the call at the beginning of a harried business day. If he was really lucky, it might be misdirected or even ignored for a while. Someone might even assume it was just a wrong number. He had been careful not to give his mother's name. He hung up, just as his grandfather came back into the room.

Matthew stood. "She wasn't there, but I left her a message."

"And you told her where you were?"

"I told her I was in Australia." He waited for his grandfather to question him further, but Roman just looked stern.

"Have you met Tricia?" Matthew hoped a change of subject would be good for both of them.

"I'll ring up your mother myself later in the day. You haven't got away with anything, boy."

Matthew was sorry to hear it.

"Now, suppose you tell me about this girl you've brought along."

Matthew had mulled over what he should say about Tricia. He wanted her to go home. He was afraid that if she didn't, he would regret not telling his grandfather the whole story. But after everything they had been through, he also felt a certain loyalty.

"Just tell me the straight-up truth of it," Roman prompted.

"I don't know everything," Matthew said carefully. "I met her in Sydney. I...lost the money I had with me, and she had just lost her place to live. So we...decided to travel together. She knows the Territory, and I knew she'd be a help."

"Lost the money?"

Matthew tried not to squirm. Any moment now he might have to choose between lies and betrayal. "Somebody took my wallet. I got it back, but most of the money was gone."

Roman grimaced. "The girl have something to do with that?"

"Tricia's okay. You don't have to worry about her." Matthew hoped it was true.

"Does she have a surname?"

"She must, but she's never mentioned it."

"Is she *from* the Territory, boy?"

Matthew felt like a trout being reeled slowly toward shore, then an idea occurred to him. "I know, let's ask her." He grinned. He had just slipped the hook.

"Is she from Humpty Doo?"

"We could ask her that, too."

"The pair of you belong together." Roman started toward his desk. "I have work to do."

"Granddad?"

Roman flinched. "What is it?"

"I'd like to see Jimiramira. Is there someone who could show me around? I might not...you know, be back. At least, not soon."

"You want me to take you on a tour, do you?"

"It doesn't have to be you, although that would be great."

Roman sighed, a deep rasping sound that seemed to come from the center of his being. "I suppose since you won't be dropping by often I can take some time with you now."

"Really?"

"You look like your father when you do that, you know. Like my father, too, for that matter. I have some photos. Would you like to see them tonight?"

Matthew was stunned. "Of my dad? Or yours?"

"Both."

"Awesome."

"That's American for yes, I take it?"

"Can Tricia come with us while you show me around?"

"By all means. Maybe the girl won't be as slippery about answering questions as you are."

"I wouldn't count on it."

Roman reached for his hat, a sweat-stained Akubra that reminded Matthew of the one his father wore. "We'll see, boy."

Jimiramira was more than Matthew had hoped. He had known he didn't have a prayer of seeing all of it in the short time he had here, but the first thing Roman had done was take him and Tricia out to a stableyard fenced in coolibah rails to choose horses.

"You can ride?" he asked, as if the possibility that a grandson of his could not was unimaginable.

"Sure. My dad always takes me riding in the summer. And I had lessons when I was little."

Roman harrumphed to show what he thought of lessons. "How about you?" he asked Tricia.

"Like a ringer at a race meeting."

"You sound like a Territory girl."

"Oh, I've been around."

Matthew hoped she wouldn't explain how much.

Roman lectured a little about Australian stockhorses. "We breed our own horses. A stockhorse ought to be sweet-natured and trustworthy. Smart, too, with a good eye. He has to out-think a cow or a mob of them. You can choose most any horse here and he'll give a good ride."

Matthew chose a chestnut with a white blaze streaking from nostrils to forelock. Roman gave him an approving look. Tricia's choice, a gray mare, was met with less enthusiasm. "You're certain you can handle her? She wasn't bred here. She needs some proper training."

"She'll be right, thanks."

They mounted, and it took Matthew some time to accustom himself to the saddle, which had a Johnny strap for mounting, instead of a horn. Tricia's horse performed a series of stiff-legged leaps as soon as Tricia lowered herself into the saddle, but the girl had the mare under control in a matter of seconds.

"A Territ'ry girl," Roman muttered.

They rode out of the yard and up toward the house. "You know about the fire?" Roman asked Matthew. "Well, my father was hardly more than a boy, but afterwards he had the station hands build another house. It wasn't much, but I was raised in it. He always promised my mother he'd build something better, but she was content with a roof and four walls. When I brought your grandmother here, I wanted something that would make her proud."

"Was she?"

He cleared his throat. "She loved this house. Yes."

"Is she buried over there?" Matthew pointed toward a graveyard on a slope not more than fifty yards away. The fence

surrounding it was painted iron, like the one ringing the house.
The site was shaded by giant gums, too.

"She is."

"I'd like to visit later."

Roman turned his horse away from the house in answer.

Matthew would always remember the remainder of the afternoon. They rode past the other buildings in the homestead
complex, and his grandfather explained what each was used
for. "That's the store." He pointed to a squat stone building
the size of a suburban convenience store. "We can't run off
for something when we need it here. If we don't have it, we
do without."

Next he pointed out the cool house, packed with spinifex
between the walls and regularly hosed down to lower the temperature inside. They rode past the men's quarters and dining
room, an office building with a narrow front porch and small,
high windows, even a swimming pool, which for the moment
was empty.

At the stockyards—vast, interlocking paddocks fenced in tu-
bular steel—Roman gave them a quick lecture on cattle and
the introduction of the Brahman and Santa Gertrudis breeds to
increase body weight in the herd.

Matthew watched men on horseback riding among the cattle
"yarded" here, turning them, gentling them. Dust flew, and
the noise of the assembled herd—or "mob" as his grandfather
called it—was raucous.

"We have two other camps on the property," Roman said.
"We have the odd hut or two along the boundaries, too, for
our riders. Each man has to keep the fences repaired along
seven, eight hundred kilometers. We grade the road after the
Wet, but it's never easy to make a go of it, even then. And it's
a lonely job. It takes a hardy sort of bloke to sign on."

Matthew had watched his grandfather drop his guard as the
afternoon progressed. Roman liked to talk about Jimiramira.
Matthew supposed that if this was all they needed to discuss,
things would be fine between them. But he was surprised when

Roman led them through a gate below the house to a sheltered sanctuary, a watering hole fed by a murky creek and shaded by bloodwood and stringybark trees. As they rode in, a flock of birds rose screeching into the bright afternoon sky.

"Galahs," Roman said. "And cockatoos. A ruddy nuisance."

Matthew thought he had never seen anything as beautiful as the birds, which were a rainbow oasis against the austere landscape.

Roman swung himself to the ground; then he held Tricia's horse so she could dismount, too. "Does this remind you of the billabong over at Coolibah Downs? Smaller, I know, but I'm always struck by the similarity when I'm visiting there."

"It's smaller, all right." The girl clamped her lips shut, and her posture stiffened, as if the cells in her body had frozen in alarm. "How did you know?"

"Winnie recognized you. She saw your photograph when she was in Darwin. Your father's well remembered here."

Matthew recalled that Tricia had talked about Coolibah Downs yesterday.

"I'm not going back to Humpty Doo," Tricia said. "So don't get your knickers in a knot. I just needed a holiday from me job in Sydney."

"What sort of job, girl?"

"The sort that would curl an old man's hair," Tricia said defiantly.

To Matthew's surprise, Roman simply nodded. "You wouldn't be looking for something better, would you?"

"Why? Do you want me to move my business north?"

"Speak to me the way your father taught you, girl! I remember your mother, too. Good people, both of them. And they would be ashamed of you."

"Don't you think I know that?"

"And I suppose that's why you're not going home?"

She thrust her chin out, but Matthew thought her eyes sparkled with unshed tears.

"We could use you here." Roman dropped his reins and started toward the water's edge, as if Tricia's answer meant little to him. "At the moment Winnie and my bookkeeper's wife share responsibility for the store, but neither of them has the time. You'd be in charge. Are you good with figures?"

"Good enough."

"It's a proper job, no bludging tolerated. You'd work hard. And at the first sign of trouble or old habits, you'll have your notice."

"You'll be watching me, waiting for me to do something I shouldn't."

"No more than I watch anyone. And no one here need know where you've been and what you've done."

"Why should you give me a job?"

"Because I know when I mate a prize bull with a prize heifer, the calf is worth looking after, even if it strays a time or two. In the end, it always comes 'round. You think about it." He squatted at the water's edge and scooped some up in his hands to wash his face.

Matthew looked at Tricia, who was staring into space, and he was surprised at how much he envied her.

"So what do you think of the place? Did you see enough of the outback to suit you?" Tricia motioned for Matthew to join her on a bench in a shady spot next to the house. Winnie had told them to get some fresh air and that she would call them when dinner—or "tea," as she called it—was on the table.

Matthew didn't think he could ever see enough of Jimira-mira. He knew better than to wish that the past had been different, but since returning from their ride, he had found himself thinking about the way his life might have been if Roman and Cullen had never had their falling out, or if his mother and Cullen...

Tricia didn't wait for his answer. "Your grandfather's a right enough bloke. What do you think about his offer? Do you think I should stay?"

He settled himself beside her, all too aware of the way her hip pressed snugly against his. "Sure I do. It's a good place to start over."

"I went to the store, just to have a look. It could do with a good tidying, but I've seen worse."

"Could you be happy back in the Territory? You said you hated it here."

"Maybe I hated it because I didn't know what else was out there."

"And now?"

The bench was so narrow and they were so close that the side of her breast brushed his arm. "Now I do."

"And this is better?"

"Safer." She sighed, her breath warm against his cheek. "In the Big Smoke, I saw heaps of things I wish I hadn't. If I ever want to be a city girl again, I guess I'll wait until I can get the right kind of job. Maybe I'll see about getting more education."

"When we came to Jimiramira, I didn't think I'd be leaving you here."

"Are you leaving?"

"I have to. My grandfather's going to call my mother. He may be calling right now. I have to get out of here before she sends somebody to bring me home."

She didn't ask for details, as if she understood that he didn't want to tell her. She had never pried. She had never argued or lectured. She had, in fact, been the best company he could imagine.

"I'll miss you," he said. And he meant it. Not just because he had found being with her exciting, but because he liked her. She was courageous and straightforward. She had an odd sort of confidence that brought her through the worst, and an odd sort of faith that made her hope for the best.

"Well, I suppose I'll miss you, too, Yank. But maybe we'll meet again."

They stared at each other. They were so close, mere inches

apart. He had been proud of himself for not taking her up on her offer to make love. Now he faced the truth. He hadn't done it for many reasons, but one of them was because he was afraid.

Tricia leaned closer. "Are you going to kiss me goodbye?"

He had kissed girls before, but never one he had wanted the way he'd wanted Tricia. He wondered how a man kept his head and his self-respect when other parts of his anatomy were screaming for mercy.

It was up to him. She didn't move closer, as if she knew the next move had to be his. He leaned toward her and cupped the back of her head with his hand. Her hair was sleek and soft against his fingers. He didn't close his eyes, because if he was going to do this, he didn't want to miss a thing. He touched her lips with his, then pressed them harder, until she was kissing him back. She slid her arms around his back and snuggled her chest against his. And in the sunlit outback afternoon, Matthew saw stars.

Tricia's parents arrived about an hour before sundown. The pilot of the single-engine plane that touched down at the Jimiramira airstrip was a friend of Robby's from Coolibah Downs, and he had been easily persuaded to pick up the Simmonses in Darwin and fly them in. Tricia's father was a tall, wiry man without an ounce of flesh to spare. Her mother had a sweet face with green eyes like her daughter's, and square, sturdy hands that twisted against her own vain attempts to keep them still.

Tricia, who hadn't been told her parents were coming—but who surely had guessed—hesitated in the sitting-room doorway until her mother opened her arms.

Matthew, who had come in with Tricia, beat a hasty retreat. He found his grandfather on the porch, talking to the pilot. "Jim here tells me he'll take us up for a few minutes if you're game, boy. I thought you might want to see the run from the air."

Matthew barely smothered a whoop.

Ten minutes later they were in the sky over Jimiramira. Matthew's heart felt as if it had begun to float at take-off and was now pressing against his lungs. The world was too bright, the air too thin, so that he was forced to gulp it in frantic bursts. He wasn't afraid. He just wished that he could hold on to each glittering moment.

"That's one of the camps I told you about," Roman shouted over the engine. He pointed below them to what looked like the village of a toy train set. "Mirror Hill. Just a house, stockyards, an outbuilding or two. The road's good enough. We ship to market from there when we can get the road trains in." He pointed out each landmark below them. A range of hills that defined Jimiramira's northern border; the feathery tracings of a dry riverbed; the second camp, which was even more primitive than Mirror Hill.

By the time they landed back at the homestead, the sky was galah pink, a limitless expanse that seemed to be the only barrier between Jimiramira and forever.

On the ground they thanked Jim, who headed off to the men's quarters to look up an old friend. Matthew hadn't discussed Tricia with his grandfather, but as they walked back toward the house, he broached the subject. "Now that you've brought her parents here, do you think she'll stay or go home with them?"

"I suspect she might go home for a holiday, but she'll be back here before too long. They can visit her here and edge back into being a family."

Matthew wondered how possible that last part was. He needed it to be possible. Better than possible. He needed this grandfather, who until this very day had never acknowledged his presence.

"Could we walk up to the cemetery?" he asked, as they neared the house.

Roman stopped. "What for?"

"Well, it's my family."

"You can go up by yourself."

"But I'd rather go with you. You can tell me about the people buried there."

"You want a lot, don't you, boy? Your father was never satisfied, either. Nothing was ever enough for him."

Matthew knew Cullen wasn't perfect, but he didn't want to hear about his father's faults from this man. "Well, you know, maybe he didn't get anything to start with. That would leave him wanting more, wouldn't it?"

Roman started down the path, and after a moment Matthew caught up with him. They had nearly reached the tiny grave-yard before Roman spoke again. "When your father was still a boy, I'd catch him up here sometimes, sitting on his mother's grave, yammering away like she was right there listening. He'd tell her what he'd done that day, which horse he'd ridden, if he'd gone down to the billabong and caught a fish." He shook his head. "They were always close, those two. When Joan was alive she held the three of us togeth—"

He cut off the last word, as if he wished he hadn't spoken. Matthew felt the same scratchy lump in his throat that had been there after his call to California. He had never thought of his father that way, as a lonely little boy with no one to talk to except the mother who had gone away.

"And so I don't come up here anymore." Roman stopped at the gate. "When I do, I see them both." He stood as rigid as a soldier, and his face was immobile, as if one twitch of emotion would shatter him.

Matthew felt tears welling, unmanly, little-boy tears he knew his grandfather would despise. He blinked them back and put one hand on the fence. He knew the time had arrived to tell his grandfather why he had come.

"Sir, I told you that meeting you, seeing Jimiramira, was one of the reasons I came to Australia."

Roman's response was guttural, noncommittal.

Matthew looked away, and as he did, a flock of sulfur-crested cockatoos rose from the billabong and spread their wings to the dusk-tinged sky. He was transfixed, not forgetting so much as adjusting what he had planned to say.

"Get on with it, boy," Roman said at last.

Matthew turned to him. "It's simpler than I thought. Simpler than I was going to make it. A long time ago, two of my ancestors found a pearl. And this pearl, well, it's so flawless, so perfect, that everyone who touches it, everyone who owns it, can't, well, they can't measure up. That's the only way I know to explain it. The pearl brings out the worst in everybody who has it or wants it or—"

"What are you talking about, boy?"

"The Pearl of Great Price." Matthew spoke quickly, words tumbling out faster and faster. "My great-grandfather, Tom Robeson, found it in the Indian Ocean. Your grandfather, Archer Llewellyn, killed him so they wouldn't have to share it. My great-aunt Mei came here to Jimiramira and stole it from Archer and your father, Bryce. Then she took it to San Francisco, and her brother Thomas, my grandfather, stole it from her. Now my mother has it. And it's destroying her. The pearl's flawless, but it brings out everybody's greatest flaw. Don't you see?"

Roman looked confused.

Matthew tried harder to explain. "Archer was selfish, so he killed Tom for the pearl. Tom trusted the people he loved, but he trusted them blindly, no matter what they did. Because of that, Archer was able to kill him. Your father and my aunt Mei fell in love, but the pearl destroyed that. My mother and father were happy together, but they ended up getting a divorce.

"And now my mother can't even walk down the street. See, that's her greatest flaw. She wants to be free, but she needs to feel secure. So she's always fighting with herself. And my father, well, his greatest flaw is fear that somebody will take away his freedom."

He stopped. He was breathing hard. He knew there was a good chance he hadn't explained any of it well enough. "There were Viola and Willow, too, and my grandmother Hope, who wore the pearl on her wedding day. I forgot them, but the pearl destroyed them, too. And Thomas, my grandfather. His flaw was being ashamed of who he was and trying to prove himself to his own grandparents and everybody else. He spent his life trying to prove he was good enough, even if he was half-Chinese. He never even realized, not ever in his life, that being Chinese was something to be proud of. So he stole the pearl from the sister who had given up everything just for him and used it to try to make himself important. At least, that's what I think happened. I've had a lot of time to think about this.''

Roman leaned against the fence and studied his grandson. ''Why did you really come here? What does any of this have to do with me, boy? I've never seen this pearl, though I've heard tales. But I don't know half of what you're talking about.''

''But it *has* affected you, don't you see? Your father loved Aunt Mei, but after she took the pearl and left him, he was probably afraid to love anybody again. Even you. And isn't that some of the reason you didn't know how to love *my* father the way you should?''

Roman stepped forward, as if to silence him. ''This is bloody nonsense.''

Matthew knew the time had come. Either he had to leave Jimiramira right now, before Roman figured out exactly why he had told him this story, or he had to trust that Roman would help him.

The cockatoos floated back toward the billabong, probably to settle in the treetops for the night. Even from a distance, he could hear them squawking and screeching. Suddenly he felt calm, as if his life, his decision, was as simple as the flow of air under their outstretched wings.

He pulled up his shirt and pulled down the waistband of his jeans. A large round Band-Aid covered his navel. He teased it loose as his grandfather eyed him with suspicion; then he cupped a hand below it and let the Pearl of Great Price roll into his palm. He held it out for his grandfather to see.

"*This* is why I came here," he said. "I want you to come to Broome with me, Granddad. I'm not old enough to rent a boat by myself, and I wouldn't know how to sail one if I did. I was born to do this, only nobody else understands it. I want to put this pearl back where my great-grandfather found it. I'm the only one who can do it, because I'm both Robeson and Llewellyn."

"You've gone mad!"

Matthew shook his head sadly. "No, I haven't. It's just that I'm the only one who sees that throwing this pearl back into the ocean is the only way *any* of us will ever be free of it."

29

San Francisco

In the end, after one look at the murderous expression on Cullen's face, Simon Van Valkenburg told them everything.

"He's gone to Australia." He stood in his Russian Hill doorway and focused on Liana, as if facing Cullen might be dangerous. "To meet his grandfather."

"Australia?" For a moment she couldn't comprehend it.

"Yeah. Matthew knew you'd never let him go, so he took the initiative." He sneaked a glance at Cullen. "He wanted to do it while you were here, so she—" he nodded his head toward Liana "—wouldn't think you'd put him up to it or something."

"Does my father know he's coming?" Cullen moved closer, and Simon shrank backwards into the hallway.

"Nobody knows. Just me. I—" Simon stopped.

"You what?"

"I, ummm…helped him work out the plans."

"*What* plans?"

"He flew to Sydney. He was going to see if he could find a mail plane to get to Jimiramira or something. That's all I know. Matthew thought if he flew to Sydney, then made his way to the ranch, he'd be harder to trace."

"Why did you send us to Arizona?" Liana said, still trying to make sense of it all.

"To give our son a bang-up head start. Or *something*," Cullen said. "He probably had his strategy planned, just in case we showed up on his doorstep. But what I want to know is how Matthew pulled this off. He'd need a passport. Since he was born in Oz, I'm not sure he needs a visa, but he might."

Simon looked uncomfortable. "I can tell you a little."

"Why should we believe anything you say?" Liana demanded.

"Because it's the truth," Simon said. "He made all the arrangements on my computer. He used an old credit card of yours, one you canceled—or thought you did. You can check if you want. I think it was from a bank in Nevada or someth—" He turned red. "Matthew's not the kind of kid who would do this stuff without a really good reason. He just thought it was important."

"This is my fault," Liana said.

"This is Matthew's fault," Cullen said firmly. "And I'm going to tell him so, when I catch up with him."

"Why don't you just leave him alone?" Simon said with surprising courage. "He risked a lot, you know. Let him come back on his own. Can't you deal with him then, instead of going after him like a naughty little boy?"

"I'm going after him, Simon," Cullen said in measured tones, "because Matthew may not be *able* to come back unless we find him soon. It seems someone else may be looking for him, and if they find him first, none of us might see him again. So do you know anything more that will help us?"

Simon couldn't tell them anything else useful. At the end he said he was sorry they had been worried. "But Matthew's all right," he insisted. "He can take care of himself."

On the way back to her apartment, Liana leaned against the Miata's headrest. She was exhausted from the trip to Arizona. She was angry. She was terrified. "Australia…"

"Do you believe Simon?"

She didn't want to. Some teens ran off to the big city. Her son, their son, had hopped a plane to the other side of the planet. Short of hitching a ride on the space shuttle, how much farther could Matthew have run?

"Lee?" Cullen sounded frustrated.

She swallowed tears. "I did have a credit card from a Nevada bank. And I thought I'd canceled it."

"Not bloody likely Simon made a wild guess about that."

"Have you told Matthew so much about your dad that he'd lie and steal to visit him?"

"I've told him stories, but he knows I haven't been to Jimiramira in years." Cullen thumped the steering wheel with his palm. "What possessed Matthew? I've never given him any reason to believe Dad wanted to see him. We've talked about the things we'd do in Australia when he was finally able to visit me there, but we can't do them now, can we? I'm here and he's there!"

Liana shared Cullen's frustration, but her mind was already whirling. "We have to go and bring him home, Cullen. We can't depend on your father or anybody in Australia to send him back."

"*We?* It's at least a fifteen-hour flight. And that doesn't include the leg to Jimiramira. You'd need a visa and a passport—"

"I have a passport. I've kept it current, even though I never use it. And visas are practically instant these days."

"Don't you trust me to do this alone? After everything that's been said, are you still afraid I'll keep him once I get there?"

As she searched his face, she searched her own heart. "No," she said at last. "Not one little bit. Don't make the mistake of thinking I don't trust you. Because I do."

"The devil. I wish I had time to enjoy it."

"When we get home, I'll get on the telephone. I'll make the arrangements."

"What about Stanford? And what about your brother?"

She didn't know what to tell them. Or anyone, for that matter. She had called Sue for messages on every leg of the Arizona trip, and every message had been from Graham or the security chief. Both men were upset that she and Cullen had gone off without informing anybody.

"We can't tell them the truth." She shook her head, emphasizing her own words. "We *can't* trust Graham. Not now. Not when we're so close to finding Matthew. There's no point in telling anyone he's down under. And if—" She stopped. There were more reasons than Cullen knew for keeping Matthew's journey a secret.

"If Graham's looking for Matthew for reasons of his own, and if Stanford's helping him..." Cullen supplied, when she didn't go on.

She composed herself. "They'll look for me if I just disappear off the face of the earth. They'll trace us to Australia."

"Then we need to mislead them." Cullen pulled into Liana's parking space. "But before we do anything, you have to confirm Simon's story about the credit card. And I have to call my dad."

She was glad one of them was thinking clearly. She followed him to the garage elevator and punched in the code. He said nothing on the trip to the penthouse, although she knew from his expression that he was sorting through the possibilities and making plans.

At the door she fished for her key while Cullen waited beside her. When she couldn't find it immediately, she rang the bell. "Sue probably heard the elevator anyway."

"I reckon she's nearly as worried about Matthew as we are."

Liana frowned when Sue didn't come to the door. "We must have caught her at a bad moment."

"Maybe she's gone out."

"Not a chance. She promised she would stay glued to the telephone." Liana located her key, which she had zipped into an inside pocket in her handbag. She unlocked the door and stepped into the dark hallway. She tried the switch, but the light didn't come on. "Sue?"

The silence didn't even twitch in response.

Liana frowned. "I'll go look for—"

Cullen put his hand on her forearm to stop her. "Let me," he said softly.

She was about to protest when she realized his fingers had tightened like a vise. "Why?"

He dropped her arm, but he put his finger to his lips. She understood, suddenly, that he was afraid of what—or who— she might find. He motioned for her to stay by the door, but she followed anyway. It was her apartment, her haven. And the thought that someone might have breached it or harmed Sue made her furious. Fear—for once the intelligent response—deserted her.

Their footsteps sounded like bricks dropping. The living room was empty and dark, and so was the dining area.

The kitchen was occupied. "Sue!" Liana shot forward and knelt beside the housekeeper, who was sprawled facedown on the terra-cotta floor.

Cullen knelt beside her and lifted Sue's wrist. "Heart's beating steady and strong," he said after a moment.

"Can we turn her over?"

"Better not. Do you have an emergency number?"

Sue moaned, and the problem of whether to turn her over or call for help was solved. She pushed herself up with one hand and stared at them as if she were swimming through fog. With another moan she turned and pushed herself into a sitting position. Then she hung her head.

Liana put her hands on Sue's shoulders to help hold her erect. "Cullen, dial 911. Tell them we need an ambulance."

He stood, but Sue protested. "No...I think...I'm fine."

"You're not fine," Liana argued. "You must have fainted."

"I heard a noise. I turned to see who. Then everything..." She shook her head, but moaned at the movement.

Liana gently explored the back of the housekeeper's neck and head, spreading Sue's short black hair.

Protesting, Sue pushed her hands away.

Liana stood. "She's got a knot bigger then the Pearl of Great Price on the back of her head. Somebody hit her."

"You call 911." He hiked a thumb toward the telephone. Then he disappeared.

Liana knew he was going to make sure there was no one else in the apartment. Her heart beat faster. She didn't want him to face an intruder alone. She grabbed the receiver and punched in the numbers, giving a cursory explanation before she hung up. "Sue, will you be all right for a moment by yourself?"

At a faint "yes," Liana followed Cullen's path, walking as quietly as she could and wishing with every step that she had a gun. She had nearly bought one when she returned to the city, but in the end she had been more afraid of Matthew finding it than of a break-in. Instead she had chosen her condo carefully, with security uppermost in her mind. And until now, she hadn't regretted her decision.

Cullen wasn't in the hallway, her room or the master bath. She continued on, following the photographs of Matthew's childhood until she reached his room.

"Oh, God…"

Matthew's room had been trashed. The mattress was half off the bed; the floor was covered with papers and beloved possessions that had been on his desk and shelves. One glance told her that his computer was gone, and some of the stereo equipment was missing, too.

Cullen stood perfectly still in the center of the room, making mental notes. "Don't touch anything. Wait for the police."

"What about the guest room?"

"Don't worry. Whoever did this is gone."

She had only peeked into her room, but she hadn't noticed that anything had been disturbed. "Is anything else missing?"

"You'll need to check your jewelry, I reckon, or anything else of value."

She heard sirens. It helped, she supposed, to have a prestigious address. "But even if something else is gone, it's Matthew's room that got the worst of it, Cullen."

"Yeah, it is."

"That isn't a coincidence, is it?"

His face was serious. "I think the same person who logged on to his account the other night wasn't satisfied reading his E-mail. I think he wanted to get inside Matthew's head. The computer was as close as he could come."

"There's stereo equipment missing, too."

"A decoy."

"He's trying to find Matthew."

"Yeah. He's looking for our son, Lee. Now we have to find him first. And we have to do it without anyone knowing where we've gone."

The police were sympathetic, but little help. They took a statement and left, and the paramedics left without Sue, who promised she would have a friend take her to see her own physician.

"She's not sure how long she was unconscious," Liana told Cullen after Sue had gone. "She remembers she'd just put chicken in the microwave to defrost, which is probably the reason she didn't hear the intruder until it was too late. The microwave was finished by the time we arrived, and she thinks she'd set it for about twenty minutes."

"So she was unconscious at least that long."

"She's lucky she didn't hurt herself worse when she fell. She may have grabbed the counter for support before she passed out. She insists on coming back as soon as she sees her doctor."

"There was no sign of forced entry, Lee."

"I've already called the locksmith."

"Who has keys to the apartment?"

"Sue, Matthew and me. But workmen are in and out. And Matthew loses his key about once a month."

"So it's possible somebody stole one from him, and he just thought it was lost."

"I'm going to look for that credit card, Cullen."

While she rummaged through papers in her office, Cullen went into the living room and called his father at Jimiramira. He was finished with the telephone by the time she joined him, waving a paper in her hand.

Cullen got to his feet. "The housekeeper claims Dad's off at the other end of the property for a few days, and I didn't want to leave my name or a message. It's better if we have the element of surprise. If Dad knows I'm the one who rang him, he might not take the next call."

"He's that angry at you? After all these years?"

"I'm fair afraid to take a chance."

Her search had come close to confirming Simon's story about the credit card. At one time she had possessed a Mastercard from a bank in Nevada, but some months before, when the rate increased she had canceled it—or thought she had. A quick check had turned up a new statement, which included a second request for payment on a balance of over two thousand dollars. Apparently Matthew had gotten to the first statement before she could. Now a call to the bank confirmed that the bill in question was payment for an airline ticket on Qantas airlines.

"Well, at least this time Simon wasn't lying," Liana told him after she hung up.

"We have plans to make."

She pictured herself on an airplane again, but this time for hours and hours. Her heart began to pound, but she nodded. "Then that's what we have to do," emerged from a mouth suddenly gone dry.

"You're sure you want to make this trip?"

"I'm going with you, Cullen. Just try and stop me."

Early the next morning, Cullen parked the Miata in front of Graham's house, and Liana left him to wait while she went in search of her stepbrother.

Graham was an early riser. He had equipped a room in the back of the house with weights and treadmills, stationary bikes and ab rollers. He worked out religiously, then ate a breakfast guaranteed to undo any good he'd accomplished. Graham's weight had always been his weak spot, one Thomas had exploited ruthlessly. Liana suspected her stepbrother still heard Thomas's taunts every time he picked up a fork.

"Liana?" Graham emerged from a bout with the treadmill, wiping sweat off his rounded cheeks with a hand towel. "What are you doing here? Have you heard something?"

"We found Matthew." And because the truth was more upsetting than the lie, her acting skills weren't taxed. "He's in Arizona."

"Arizona?" Graham frowned. "What in hell is he doing there?"

"He's upset, Graham. Confused." She lifted her hands in defeat. "He made a friend on-line, and he went to visit her. He wanted some time away from Cullen and me. He's never rebelled against anything. I guess it's just his turn."

"So he's coming home?"

"No, but we've seen him. Cullen and I got a tip from a friend of his. That's where we've been."

She thought of the hours she and Cullen had spent choosing their lie. After long debate, Simon's story had seemed their best choice. If Graham or Stanford investigated, their trip to Arizona was on record. And if Graham really *was* searching for Matthew, the Sonoran Desert country was as good a place as any for a wild-goose chase—as she and Cullen had already learned.

Graham mopped his forehead. "You mean you left him there?"

She embroidered, since she couldn't produce her son. "We were afraid if we insisted Matthew come straight back with us, he'd just take off again at the first opportunity."

"Don't you think leaving him with strangers is dangerous?"

"We checked them out thoroughly, Graham. The girl's family lives on a ranch, and there are plenty of chores for Matthew to do to earn his keep for a few more days. He's living in a bunkhouse with her brothers, and they're willing to let him stay. Then Cullen's going to pick him up and take him east for a couple of weeks. Matthew promised to come home in July and try to work things out here."

"I can't believe this," Graham said. "You act like the boy's off on a little vacation!"

She mustered up some indignation, although of course Graham was right. "Are you a parent?"

"You know I'm not."

"Then since when did you get so damned good at it?"

"This isn't like you. You've always made him toe the line."

"Well, he hasn't been a teenager for long. And a week ago you suggested I might be smothering him, remember? I don't like what he did, but this is the only way I can handle it right now."

"We've spent a fortune looking for him, and he's off forking hay and riding horses?"

"I'm afraid that's what it comes down to."

He stood in the hallway staring at her, his eyes narrowing into slits. "Look, I know what I said before, but I don't like this. Pacific's spent a lot of money. Stanford's put everything else on hold for days now. I want Matthew's phone number so I can check out these people or have Stanford do it."

She had expected this reaction, but her blood chilled as she thought of all the reasons why Graham might be interested in Matthew's whereabouts. Was he really so concerned about her son's welfare? Graham, who had little reason to love anyone descended from Thomas Robeson? Or did he have his own reasons for wanting to find Matthew? Despite her stepbrother's pleasant exterior, she knew he could be utterly ruthless when representing Pacific International.

No one had more to gain if Matthew never came back home.

"Liana?"

"I don't want you to interfere," she said, although, of course, there was no number in Arizona to give him.

"I just want to call and be sure he's all right. He might need an uncle right now. Someone to talk some sense into him."

"He's all right. Take my word for it."

"This kid is not a stable hand. This is the Pacific International heir."

Liana drew herself up to her full height. " 'This kid' is also my son."

In the end, there was nothing Graham could do except let her go. She promised regular reports and announced that she was taking some vacation time at a Southern California spa to try to put herself together again; then she and Cullen drove to the office building on California Street so she could speak directly with Stanford.

Compared to Graham, Stanford was less upset, more assessing. Unlike Graham, he didn't try to change her mind. But Liana wondered how long it would take him to dial her stepbrother after she left his office. And how long after that before the two of them began to retrace the trip she and Cullen had made? At least, if they got as far as a mobile home in the Arizona countryside, Brittany Saunders wouldn't be there to help them. She had moved to an undisclosed location. In the fall the young woman would head for Prescott College with a healthy bank account, earned by vanishing for the summer so that no one else could question her.

The final stop was Frank's condo in Pacifica. Since he was scheduled for a business trip to Seattle over the weekend, he had taken a morning at home. Frank lived just two mudslides away from oceanfront property. At the moment he lived alone, although it was more common for him to have a lover in residence. Over the years Liana had watched women wax and wane through Frank's life with the regularity of the tides that nibbled at the city's cliffs. He was handsome and personable.

Women rarely left him because they were disenchanted. But Frank was easily bored.

"My view's better," Cullen said.

"The view from that condo is worth half a million easily." Liana cracked her door. "You'd better stay in the car again."

"Maybe I ought to build a condo or two at Pikuwa Creek and forget the pearls." Cullen was still shaking his head over the price of California real estate when she got out of the car.

She found Frank practicing golf swings on a terrace landscaped with evergreens in shiny brass pots. A stone Buddha smiled from a corner, an orange foam ball resting like a flower in the crook of one granite arm.

"Fine use you've made of poor old Gautama," Liana said from the terrace doorway. She had found his front door unlocked.

"Hey, what are you doing here?" Frank grinned, then sobered quickly. "You've heard something, haven't you?"

She told the now familiar lie.

Frank set down his driver and dusted his hands on his denim cutoffs. "The little bastard."

"I know. We're not happy with him, either, but at least we know he's safe."

"How are you?"

She wished she could tell Frank the truth. Next to his grandmother, he was the closest thing to a confidant she had allowed herself since her return to San Francisco. He was the grandchild who most resembled Mei, and the similarity had drawn her from the beginning, that and his sense of humor, which now made her hours at Pacific International more bearable.

She smiled a carefully tempered smile. "I'm okay, I guess. But the whole thing's thrown me for a loop. I need to get away and do some thinking."

"Your ex have anything to do with that?"

She threaded her way through that obstacle course with care. "Just that now I realize how badly Matthew needs the guidance of a man."

"I wish I could do more."

Frank hadn't been a constant presence in Matthew's life, but over the years he had stepped in as surrogate father on the occasional Cub Scout and Webelo campout. Mei, who had always had a special place in her heart for Frank, had asked him to look out for Matthew, and Frank had done his best.

Liana reassured him. "He's been lucky to have you. But right now I'm going away for a couple of days. I need some space."

"So Matthew's off with his dad?"

She repeated the rest of the lie. "No, Matthew's staying in Arizona a little longer. He needed space, too. Then he and Cullen will have their time together."

"Where are you going?"

"I thought I'd stay at a spa down in Monterey. I could use about a week of massage to get over this."

He flashed a warm smile. "You'll be all right?"

Frank was the only person at Pacific International who knew the scope of her agoraphobia. "Thanks, but I've been there before. It's small and familiar. I'll be okay. And there's nothing hanging fire at work that can't wait until I come back."

"You've told Grandmother?"

"Every time I call, Betty says she's sleeping and shouldn't be disturbed. Will you do it? I don't want her to worry." Liana pictured Mei's fragile features. "Tell her I'll bring Matthew to visit just as soon as he comes home."

"I'll tell her."

She gave him a brief hug, then turned to go.

Behind her Frank's voice was bright with relief. "I'm really glad everything's okay. I was a teenage boy once. I know what a mess they can make of things."

She told Cullen about the conversation as they drove to the airport. He had booked seats on the first available flight into Cairns through L.A., since Cairns was closer to the station than Sydney.

They boarded together and found their seats. "By the time

you get off the plane in Australia, you'll never be afraid to fly anywhere again,'' Cullen promised her.

"I flew home from Australia when I left you. That's when the trouble erupted."

He squeezed her hand. "But you didn't have me with you that time, did you?"

She glanced at him, or at least that was all she'd intended. But their gazes held. She thought about all they'd been through, and all that was still to come. She was afraid, but not as afraid as she had expected. If her life ended in the next hours, at least she and Cullen had made a sort of peace with their past.

As she watched, he leaned toward her and, without apology, kissed her. Not a lingering kiss, but not a brief one, either. He kissed her as if it were one in a series, neither preamble nor postscript. Then he sat back, still holding her hand. "Close your eyes," he said. "And go to sleep. When we get to Los Angeles, I'll let you know."

30

Queensland, Australia

It was evening, Cairns time, when they arrived. During the interminable flight Liana had slept nearly as much as Cullen. He was convinced she hadn't been pretending. Her breathing had slowed gradually, and her eyelids had drooped, despite a determined attempt to keep them open. Eventually she slumped in her seat—slumped against him, in fact—and pillowed her head against his shoulder. Even when the cabin grew light, Liana slept on.

He had reserved rooms at a hotel. There were no connecting flights to the vicinity of Jimiramira that evening, and he'd known they would be too exhausted to make another trip, anyway. He tried his father's number from the lobby, but this time there was no response.

"Odd," Cullen told Liana. "But not that odd. No one sits beside the telephone at night. We'll try again in the morning."

Liana was pale with fatigue and worry. He could only guess what the trip had taken out of her. It was a balmy Queensland winter, and the air felt unnaturally warm after San Francisco. He wondered if the humidity reminded her of the better days at Pikuwa Creek.

"I wanted to bring you here when we were married," he told her. "But we didn't have many holidays, did we? I wanted to take you out to the Reef, maybe off to one of the islands."

"You spend enough time on the water, don't you?"

"There's no place in the world like the Reef." He lifted her bag—she had only packed a small one. "Let's get you settled."

The hotel was small but charming, with tan wicker furniture and tropical prints. Aquariums graced corners and hallways as previews of the wonders that guests had come to explore. They had been given adjoining rooms. Liana unlocked hers, and he followed her inside. The draperies covering a wall of French doors were open, and he saw that the room overlooked a terrace with a small pool resembling a jungle grotto. The pool was subtly lit with colored floodlights, a step too artificial for his taste, but romantic, he supposed.

Liana didn't speak. He felt sure something was required of him, but he didn't know what. "Better than the motor court in Arizona, wouldn't you say?"

"Do you think Matthew's all right, Cullen? Why didn't someone answer the telephone?"

He forced reassurance into his voice. "If he's with Dad, he's fine. And there's no reason to think he didn't get to Jimiramira safely. He's a smart kid, our Matthew. He knows how to watch out for himself."

She faced the French doors, looking out at the view. "How do you make that trip back and forth to the States, year in and year out? Even if you like to fly, it must still be horrible."

"It has to be done to have time with Matthew."

"I should have realized how much that said about you. You were always there, no matter how hard it was to get to him or how inconvenient for your work schedule."

"It doesn't matter now, Lee."

She turned. "It matters to me."

He saw that her eyes were filled with tears. "Come on. She'll be right. You're done in by the flight. You're worried sick. You need a good rest and you'll feel better."

"Can you forgive me for refusing to see what a good father you are?"

He didn't rush to answer as he might have once. He considered his response, as now he considered all things. He had not conquered the impulsive Cullen, but he had learned to channel his own bursts of spontaneity and the high energy that still coursed through him. He had, in short, grown up.

"I do," he said at last. "Everything you've done, you've done to survive. And God knows, Lee, I gave you cause to hate me."

"No. I knew, even all those years ago, that you were driven by forces you couldn't control. But I taught myself to hate you, because it was the only way I could leave. I loved you so much." She shook her head, and the tears spilled down her cheeks.

"It's over now," he told her. He had gathered her against his chest before he realized what he was doing. "Let go of it."

She clung to him. He stroked her hair and told himself what he had told her. She was exhausted, fearful, shaken to the core. Her body trembling against his was not an invitation.

"Go to bed," he told her at last. He held her away. "Take a shower. Order something to eat. Then go to bed and sleep. Don't say anything you might regret."

Her eyes were wide and vulnerable. The brittle angry woman who had greeted him in San Francisco was gone. This softer one seemed almost like a stranger. Except this softer one was the one he had loved.

He started for the door. She didn't try to stop him. In the doorway, he faced her again. "I'll see you in the morning." Before she could reply, he stepped over the threshold and closed the door behind him.

In his own room, he switched on the lights and closed the curtains. Then he stumbled into the shower and stood under the hot spray for minutes. He shaved and brushed his teeth, but when he had finished, he didn't feel any better. For a man suffering jet lag, he was hopelessly wide-awake and sexually frustrated.

A knock sounded at his door, and he searched for a towel to wrap around his waist. He supposed Liana had ordered a meal to be delivered to his room. He opened the door a crack, expecting to see a hotel employee, but she stood there instead. Like his, her hair was damp. Like his, he supposed, her eyes were haunted.

"I ordered food for both of us." She shrugged. "You're not a detail person. I knew you'd shower first, and you'd be starving. So I just—" She cut off her explanation. "Do you mind too much? I don't want to be alone."

Mind? She was barefoot, wearing a lavender sundress that hung halfway down her calves. She no longer looked as sad, just soft and utterly feminine. With her face scrubbed clean and her hair loose around her shoulders, she looked young enough to bring the newborn Matthew home from hospital.

"It might not be a good idea." He folded his arms over his bare chest.

She didn't pretend not to understand. "I have no ideas, Cullen. Not a one, good or bad. Come with me. Eat something. Be with me."

The last set his heart pounding. He wasn't sure what she meant, and she didn't withdraw her words or elaborate. "Please?" was all she added.

How could he say no? Only in his deepest, most uncontrolled dreams did she come to him this way. And every time, he was unable to refuse himself.

He nodded. "I'll put on some clothes."

"Don't be too long. The tea is steeping." She turned away.

He heard the click of her door, but for a long moment he couldn't make himself move. Because this might be a dream, after all. And he didn't want to risk waking.

Cullen was wearing shorts and a white cotton shirt when he went back to Liana's room. He looked none the worse for wear.

She, on the other hand, knew she looked like a wet dishrag.

Twice, as he was dressing to join her, she had nearly gone back to tell him to forget her offer. She had considered taking food to his door and holding out a plate as if nothing much had changed. "Here," she would say. "I know you're pooped. It was selfish of me to demand company at a time like this. Get some rest, and I'll see you in the morning."

But she hadn't. She wanted Cullen with her. She was beset by demons. Hers. Mei's. Tom Robeson's. Willow's. The worst, of course, were the demons that might yet pursue her son. In the years of their marriage, she hadn't been able to lean on Cullen. In the years since, she hadn't allowed herself to lean on anyone. Now, having him near, having him care, made her stronger.

"I didn't know what you'd want." Her hands fluttered as she spoke. "I ordered too much. Scones. Tea. Sandwiches. A vegetable platter. Cake. You'd probably prefer steak and eggs, wouldn't you?"

"It's all right, Lee. I could tuck into a sand hill about now."

"I liked to cook for you. You were the perfect audience."

"You made flowers out of beetroot and tomatoes. They were too lovely to eat."

"I don't recall that stopping you." She waved him to the table in the corner, where the food had been served. "Maybe you don't want tea. Maybe you'd rather have a soft drink or coffee?"

"Not want tea? A bushie like me?"

She felt herself smile. "We had fun at first, didn't we?" The smile lingered only a moment. She wondered if he was thinking of the same things she was, of nights when sunset made up for the unbearable Western Australian summers and for the menacing saltwater crocodiles that sunned themselves too close to the house. They would sit together on the old front porch, looking over the water, and the sky would streak with color. Sometime during the heavenly spectacle he would pull her to his lap. His hand would brush her breast, tentatively, in question. She would brush his hair—longer then—off his forehead and kiss the space between his brows, tickling it, perhaps, with her tongue.

He would slowly unbutton her blouse, or lift it by the hem to slip it over her head. One of them would have the presence of mind to look around and be certain that none of Southern Cross's employees were about. Her lips would be sweet and willing, wicked sometimes, pliant at others. His callused palms would be gentle—at least at first—against the soft flesh of her breasts.

"I was always sorry we had to marry," she said, pulling herself from that memory. "Perhaps if I hadn't gotten pregnant, if we had gone on being lovers…"

"It was nothing we said in front of a minister, Lee. And it was never Matthew. It was you and me and what I felt about that." He motioned her to join him. She felt the need to flutter, to stir pots or fill glasses with ice. But there was no stove or refrigerator here. Someone else had done the work, and she was forced to sit.

"I loved you. It frightened me. It was love that did it. Not marriage."

As she considered that, she felt relief rising inside her. "Then it wasn't my fault."

"Fault?"

"Matthew's birth didn't drive you to gambling. Because I didn't get pregnant on purpose, Cullen. Not really. But the night Matthew was conceived, I was tired and hot, and I convinced myself I didn't need to fuss with birth control. I told myself it was the wrong time of the month to get pregnant. I should have known better."

He broke open a scone with his fingers, but he didn't bring it to his lips. "The devil. I'm glad you didn't. What would I do without him?"

Relief was rising higher. "You really don't blame me?"

He leaned toward her, elbows on the table. "Of course I

blame you. Loving you forced me to see myself two different ways. The way I was, and the way I needed to be. And I didn't know how to be that second man. So you're to blame. But how can I hate you for that?''

"I was a million miles from perfect. I whined—''

"Spot on, you did. About little things like man-eating salties, and weeks of being alone, and a house that was falling down around you. You whined constantly, didn't you? At least once every month or two. And there were those cheeky bits, like 'Cullen, do you suppose you might fix the leak in Matthew's bedroom?' or 'Cullen, I think the snake living under the porch is a death adder.' ''

"Well, it wasn't, as it turned out.''

He grimaced. "No, it was a Western brown, every bit as dangerous.''

"I loved Pikuwa Creek.'' She surprised herself. She stopped and considered. Cullen looked mystified. "I did,'' she confirmed. "The sunsets and the birds. The tides most of all. Nothing subtle there. And going out on the water with you. Sometimes I still dream we're on that old lugger of yours....'' She stopped.

"You dream of me, then?'' he asked.

"I dream about your lugger.''

"But I'm on it, of course.''

"Maybe.''

"You don't have me strapped to the mast, do you?''

"Your imagination is better than mine.''

He smiled at her, a tender smile that filled her chest. "We could have made a go of it, couldn't we? We had the chance. We weren't crazy when we took off together.''

"We could have, if we'd done our growing up first.''

"If I had struggled with my addiction...''

"If I had struggled with my fears.'' She held up her hand when he started to deny it. "Oh yes, Cullen. If I'd made a life for myself that was independent of yours. But I left too much of my self-confidence in New York. Right from the start, I was overwhelmed by Australia. All my insecurities came bobbing to the surface.''

''We should be meeting now. For the first time. With no history.''

''Not Archer and Tom, not Mei and Bryce...''

''Not Liana and Cullen. Just two people so powerfully attracted to each other that everything else seems unimportant.''

''Isn't that what got us into trouble the first time?'' Her voice was soft; her gaze was locked with his.

''No. That's what nearly got us through it.''

She knew they had run out of words. The future loomed before them.

He reached across the table and took her hand. His palm brushed the top of hers slowly, then crept beneath. He raised her hand to his lips and kissed her knuckles.

She felt the kiss in every part of her. She wanted him. She could tell herself it was a need for comfort from the one person who understood what it meant to worry about Matthew. She could pretend it was only a need for closure, that making love would be proof they had forgiven each other. And perhaps it *was* those things, but it was also more. More even than profound sexual attraction. She wanted him, as she always had, even in the worst of times. Because he was the one man who could truly touch her.

His blue eyes were smoky with invitation. He clasped her hand against his freshly shaven cheek and kissed her palm. But his lips were gentle, a temptation, not a demand. When he lowered her hand, he covered it with his own. Her gaze fell as he wove his fingers through hers. She saw their entwined hands and remembered the many times their bodies had entwined, too. The memory was powerful and primitive, and tempting. So terribly tempting...

Panic rose inside her, swift and familiar. ''Look, this is a bad idea.'' She got to her feet and pulled her hand away.

He continued to sit. ''Is it?''

''We're tired. I don't know what I'm doing.''

"I think you know exactly."

"Okay, I know. Or I knew. But, Cullen, wanting you is one thing, having you is another. My God, Matthew's missing, and we're sitting here reminiscing."

"You know it's more than that."

"Maybe. And maybe that's the problem." She pushed her hair behind her ears with trembling hands. "Are you ready for this to start up again?"

"This?"

Her voice rose. "This. Us. Everything. We've almost forgiven each other. Could we ever do it again if things got out of hand? We're further ahead than I ever thought we could be. I don't want to destroy that."

"What's life without risks, Lee? Can you say that keeping yourself safe all these years made you feel alive?"

"Keeping myself safe?"

"Isn't that what all your fears are about?"

"Maybe I don't feel alive, but I don't feel like I'm dangling from a precipice, either!"

"Is that how you feel with me?"

"That's how I felt. And you felt like I'd chained you and thrown away the key. We're no good for each other. Lord, didn't we learn anything?"

He stood, too. "I did. Here's what it was. Loving someone is not the same as climbing a mountain without safety gear. It's giving up some things and getting others in return. It's risk and heartache, but take it from a gambler, it's still worth taking a chance on."

She could feel panic continuing to rise, as if Cullen was throwing open the door to a whole terrifying world she didn't know. "Well, not for me."

He nodded, but the heat in his gaze turned cold as she watched. "All right, then."

"I'm sorry."

"I know." He moved around her, careful not to touch her.

She didn't turn or follow him. "Please, we've still got to work together. For Matthew's sake."

"Nothing will keep us from finding our son." The door closed quietly behind him. For one long moment she stared at the table filled with food they had nearly shared. Then she swept her empty plate to the floor with a crash.

They flew out of Cairns at ten the next morning. Liana had avoided breakfast with Cullen, and they'd had only a brief conversation on the terrace when he announced their schedule. A morning flight to Darwin, then a friend of Cullen's would meet them in his plane and fly them directly to the station.

She hadn't really spoken to him until they were in the hotel van heading to the airport. "Did you get some rest?" she asked.

"Some. How about you?"

"I'm okay."

"We've nearly caught up with him."

Silently she thanked him for the reassurance. If he was angry after last night's about-face, he wasn't going to take it out on her. "What's the first thing you're going to say to him?"

"Words will fail me. I'm going to kiss him, then I'm going to shake him."

"Words never fail you."

He glanced at her, and he nearly smiled. "They did last night."

She could feel herself blush. But it had been the perfect thing to say. She thought of all the times when his sense of humor had saved face for one of them. This, too, she had forced herself to forget.

She changed the subject. "Tell me about the plane to Jimiramira, so I'll know what to expect."

"You know that fear of flying you claim to have?"

"Uh-huh."

"This will bloody well kill or cure you."

She rolled her eyes. "Tell me!"

"Small plane. You'll have to pedal to keep us airborne. I'll jump over the side when we get close to the ground, so John can land."

"Cullen!"

"John's a stunt flyer. We'll have to remind him a time or two to fly right side up."

"You're not going to be any help, are you?"

"You can't practice everything in advance, Lee. John's the best pilot I know. Do you think I'd trust your life to just anyone?"

She forgot about the plane. "You're not angry at me, are you?"

"Because we didn't want the same thing at the same moment?"

"It wasn't about wanting or not wanting."

"I know what it was about." He opened the newspaper he'd bought at the hotel to signal that the subject was closed.

The flight to Darwin was blessedly short. When she descended the metal stairway and walked across the tarmac with Cullen beside her, her legs were surprisingly steady.

"John's going to meet us inside." Cullen checked his watch. "He's probably here already."

She knew Cullen had tried to call Jimiramira that morning from their hotel, and again there had been no answer. "Are you going to phone your father and let him know we're coming?"

"I don't see the point now. I'd rather look him in the eye, wouldn't you? And if Matthew gets wind that we're on our way, he might take off again."

"You don't really think so? Why would he? He got what he wanted. A trip to Australia. A chance to meet his grandfather."

"That's what he told Simon. How do we know that's what this trip was really about? Have you forgotten the pearl?"

"I'm genetically programmed to remember it always."

"Well, the bloody thing's in my genes, as well."

"That means Matthew was born with a double dose."

"Which might mean he has it with him, Lee."

She had denied that possibility long enough. She had let her heart proclaim her son's innocence. But this was a boy who had lied, stolen and schemed to get this far, a boy with secrets. "He might have it," she admitted. "But why? I can't think of any reasonable explanation."

"Take 'reasonable' out of the equation. If he has it, the reason is purely emotional. He's fallen prey to superstition."

"I don't see…"

"He's bringing it back here to Australia. I'll bet he thinks it belongs at Jimiramira. That's what Mei was trying to tell us. Maybe she even put him up to it."

Liana contemplated that as they moved off the field into the airport. It was a small enough building, with a colorful souvenir shop filled with Aboriginal art and T-shirts with wallabies and kangaroos bounding across them.

Cullen left her in the waiting area as he went to look for their pilot. Cairns, though beautiful, had resembled other tropical resorts, and it had been different enough from Broome and Pikuwa Creek that she hadn't felt the sting of past memories. But here, surrounded by both the commercial clutter and the twang of Australian accents, she could not pretend any longer. She had journeyed halfway across the earth again. Again, as she had once before. That time for love, and this time, too.

Had Matthew sat in this very airport, drinking in the culture she had denied him? Had he found a flight to Jimiramira from Darwin, or had he taken one directly from Sydney? When one alternative was closed, he always seemed to find another. His resilience was one of his finest traits. Had he used it to his advantage here?

Cullen came back. "John's out on the field waiting for us. Are you ready?"

She looked up at her ex-husband, the man she had sent from her room last night. The man she still wanted, despite a hair-raising past. "Let's go get Matthew, Cullen."

He held out his hand.

The trip neither killed nor cured her. She was frightened, but not as much as she'd expected. The plane, a four-seater Cessna, rode every air current, soaring like an eagle. She found she could gaze at the ground below and make out riverbeds and tiny settlements. When Cullen realized her eyes were open, he pointed out the occasional sight.

"Lost my first bet on a horse race at that station."

"You won a few, too, as I recall."

"Too few."

Actually, he had won many, but memories of the times when he'd been on a streak of good luck were something Cullen would battle for the rest of his life.

"Is your father a gambling man?" she asked.

"Dad likes to bet on the horses, but he knows when to stop. The only thing he's addicted to is Jimiramira."

"What does it mean? Jimiramira."

"It's a word used by the local Aboriginal people. It means big."

"That's all?"

"Apparently there wasn't much poetry in Archer Llewellyn's soul. He wanted big. He got big, although there are properties in the Territory that are bigger."

"Are you worried about seeing your father?"

"I should have done this a long time ago. He's not a young man. We have things we should say to each other."

She searched his serious face and wondered what he was feeling. "Why didn't you come before this?" she asked gently.

"I wanted to set Southern Cross on its feet first. I didn't want Dad to think I was coming to him for help."

"You wanted to prove something?"

"That, too, I suppose. But I wanted him to know I was coming back because I wanted to put things right, not because I wanted something. He paid off more than one of my debts when I was living at home. I didn't want him to have any fears he'd have to do it again.''

"He paid off your debts. Doesn't that show some affection for you, Cullen?''

"I always thought he did it because he didn't want me to drag down the station. He knew the men I owed money to. He couldn't risk his own reputation.''

She sat back. She couldn't dispute that, since Roman Llewellyn was a stranger to her. But it seemed sad that both she and Cullen had been blessed with heartless fathers. She hoped Roman was at least a kind enough person to take care of Matthew.

"It looks like we're coming in now," Cullen said, leaning over to peer through the small window. He shouted up to John and had his suspicion confirmed. "Okay, Lee. Now we find out what's going on.''

"I pray to heaven Matthew's here.''

"Heaven would be the right address.''

The landing was unexpectedly smooth, even though the station runway didn't resemble the one at the airport. There was no one to meet them, since no one had been notified they were coming. "We'll wait a few minutes," Cullen told her. "I'm certain someone saw us land. But if they don't send a car, we'll walk. It's not far.''

She didn't know what she had expected. There had been cattle stations inland from Pikuwa Creek, but none she had visited. They had been minimally staffed, and the owners had lived in other places. The homesteads had been so far off the beaten path—which, in the case of Pikuwa Creek, hadn't been very beaten at all—that she had never even glimpsed them.

Jimiramira was both less and more than she had imagined. They had flown over a variety of buildings, and even from the airstrip she could see that they were well cared for and architecturally varied. A spot of green lawn identified the house, whose metal roof had gleamed from the air.

Emeralds and sterling, and the sapphire sweep of a limitless sky.

She had expected cattle and horses, working cowboys, perhaps, despite knowing that Australia had none of the rich grasslands of Texas. The land was more arid than she had envisioned. The Australia she had known so well, a country of craggy coastline and tropical foliage, did not exist here.

"What do you think?" Cullen asked.

"It has its own sort of beauty." She waved away bush flies seeking sustenance. "How does it feel to be home?"

"Home is the house I shared with you."

Her heart made a funny leap in her chest. "How does it feel to be here?"

"Odd."

She let it go at that. Cullen had his own set of demons.

A dust cloud mushroomed on the horizon and drew consistently closer. "They've sent someone," Cullen said. He went to talk to John, who was examining the airplane's nose. He was a quiet young man with a shy smile that had buoyed Liana's confidence immediately. Cullen returned as a battered station wagon pulled up next to the airstrip and the driver cut the motor. "John's making an adjustment. He's just going to stay here. I'll come back later and let him know what we're planning to do next."

"An adjustment?"

"He's more comfortable with planes than with people. Fussing with the plane keeps him from having a yak when he doesn't want one."

A gray-haired Aboriginal man got out of the wagon and approached them. Cullen smiled and held out his hand. "Luke. It's been a while."

"Cullen." Luke took Cullen's hand with a smile as warm and shy as John's.

"My dad here?" Cullen asked.

Luke shrugged, as if he couldn't say. "Winnie, she tell me to pick you up and bring you in." He glanced at Liana and gave another smile. "Her, too."

"That's what you should do, then." Cullen hefted both their

bags in one hand and followed Luke to the wagon. Liana followed him.

"Winnie?" Liana said.

"Probably the housekeeper."

"No one you know?"

"When I was a boy, Dad couldn't keep a housekeeper."

Luke spoke from the front. "She been with the boss now for a long time. Harry, her husband, he been with the boss long time, too."

"What's Harry do?" Cullen asked.

"Harry, he's the manager."

Cullen whistled softly. "Dad lets someone else manage the place?"

"Too right. The boss getting old. Just like me."

Cullen sat back. "Luke here is the best stockman in the Territory," he told Liana. "Nothing he can't do."

"Those days gone," Luke said cheerfully.

"Luke, I've rung Dad several times in the past day or so, and no one answered the telephone."

"Bloody stupid machines, telephones."

They pulled up in front of the house, and Liana registered details as she looked for Matthew. She had hoped that he would be waiting for them on the front porch. But nothing stirred in the early afternoon heat.

"It's lovely," she told Cullen, because she didn't want her disappointment to infect him. "An oasis. After Mei's story, I didn't know what to expect."

"Dad built it for Mum."

"Was she happy here? Or can you remember?"

"She was. It was a good life for all of us while she was still alive." Cullen got out and so did she. Luke waited until they had gotten their bags from the back; then he drove off to park. "I guess we find Winnie," Cullen said. "And hopefully a couple of Llewellyn men."

Winnie was waiting just inside the door. Liana took in the flowered polyester housedress, the tightly permed curls, the seamed cheeks. But nothing was as telling as the look on Winnie's face. Liana closed her eyes as Cullen introduced them. Their son was not here. She had seen pity in Winnie's eyes.

"You've missed your dad," Winnie told Cullen without prelude.

"Have we missed our son, as well?"

Winnie didn't pretend not to understand. "Yes, it seems you have."

Liana made a noise low in her throat, and Cullen put his arm around her. "Tell me whatever you know," Cullen said.

"I've made tea. Come into the kitchen for a cuppa."

Liana looked up at Cullen, and he nodded to assure her it was necessary. "Thank you," she said stiffly. "We could use some."

The kitchen was large and airy, scrubbed as clean as a hospital operating room. Winnie motioned them to a table. "I reckon you sat there often enough as a lad," she told Cullen. "I hear you could charm a biscuit out of any and all of the cooks who came through here, even the ones who hated children."

"Please, Winnie," Liana said. "Tell us what's going on. We've been worried sick. We didn't even know Matthew had come to Australia until yesterday—"

"Day before," Cullen said. "I think."

Jet lag was still tugging at her, but terror was winning. Time had stopped the moment she'd discovered her son was missing.

Winnie poured tea from a brown pottery teapot. Then she brought over a tray, complete with sugar cookies. She joined Liana and Cullen at the table, handing them cups before she settled back with her own.

"I'll tell you everything, because I know what you must be feeling. And because there has been enough heartbreak in this house to last another century. Your son arrived..." She spread her fingers and appeared to count backwards. "Tuesday. Yes, that's right. Tuesday. Your father had no idea he was coming. He got a call from a woman over at Cadwale Gap. The Myrtles have a place there, just a hotel of sorts and a little store. Cater to some of the bus tours, or blokes from the road trains. That sort of thing. It's a way to make money…''

She sipped her tea. ''As I was saying, Helen Myrtle rang the boss and told him that his grandson and a girl—''

''Girl?'' Liana said.

''Yes, dear. A girl. I'll explain.'' She proceeded to. When she had explained about Matthew's arrival, about Tricia and Tricia's parents, she sat back. ''It surprises me you figured out so quickly where he was.''

''Winnie, I rang the station just about the time you're telling us Matthew arrived, and I asked for my dad. Someone said he was off at the far end of the place and wouldn't be back for a few days.''

''Yes, I know. That was me, and I'm not proud I didn't tell the truth. But I guessed who you were right away. You sound like your father on the telephone, you know. And I knew why you must be calling. I wanted…''

''What?'' Cullen demanded.

''I wanted them to have some time together, you see. Roman and Matthew. I was afraid you'd make your father send the boy home right away. I knew the boss would make Matthew ring you eventually, and he did, of course. I suppose I was just trying to buy a little time.''

''But we never got a phone call from Matthew,'' Liana said.

''Well, perhaps that's not so surprising. The boy seemed intent on keeping this a secret, didn't he? Perhaps he fooled the boss, as well, when he said he rang you.''

''The boy is *still* missing,'' Cullen pointed out. ''Winnie, where is Matthew? And where is my father.''

Winnie finished her tea before answering, as if she was hoping it would sustain her when she finally spoke. ''You see, that's what I don't know. I'm sorry. I truly am. But yesterday morning I rose early, the way I always do, and made brekkie. I fixed more than usual, because of your boy. He eats, that one does. And he loves sausages.…''

She must have seen the impatience in Liana's eyes, because she cut short her digression on Matthew's appetite. "Then I went to call him. I thought it odd that your father hadn't come to the table. You can set a clock by Roman Llewellyn. Five on the dot every morning, and not one moment later. Every morning of every day. Day in and day out—"

"Please," Liana pleaded.

Winnie looked contrite. "Matthew wasn't in his room. His bed had been slept in. I know, because even though he'd made it, his standards, well, they aren't so high now, are they? But all his things were gone. So I went to tell Mr. Llewellyn. I thought he'd want to know. I knocked on his door, but there was no answer. I opened it. I had to," she added, as if they would find fault with her nosiness. "He's been crook a time or two in the years I've worked here, and I thought perhaps he was again. But the room was empty. The boss was gone, as well. I'm afraid both of them were gone. And no one here has heard a word from them since."

31

Liana prowled the front porch and waited for Cullen, who was questioning Luke and some of the other station employees, including Harold, Winnie's husband. When he finally returned, he launched in without preface. "It looks like they've gone walkabout. There's a car missing, one of the station's Jackeroos. Harold thinks supplies are missing, too. It looks like Dad took a battery, spark plugs, some other extras from a storage area. Nobody travels these roads without spare parts and petrol. If you can't get a car started by yourself in the middle of nowhere, you could sit for days before somebody comes by to help."

"And he didn't tell anybody they were going off?"

"It's odd enough, but he's the boss. He can bloody well do as he pleases."

"What about food and camping supplies?"

"Hard to say. Luke checked, but he just isn't sure. The men come and go, and they take whatever they need." Cullen turned his hands up in defeat. "As dry as it's been, it will be hard to track them. They've had a head start on us."

"If they're the ones who took the car."

"I think we have to assume as much at the moment."

"But what if somebody traced Matthew to Jimiramira, Cullen? What if somebody found him with your father...?'' Her voice trailed off.

"Winnie saw both Dad and Matthew here at the house the night before she found them gone. She served their tea, and she was here until nine or so putting things to rights. No one could take Dad without a real dustup. If there had been a scuffle, someone on the property would have heard.''

"Well, no one heard them leave.''

"Because they were trying to be silent. Even the dogs wouldn't bark at Dad unless they sensed trouble.''

"Why would they take off that way? Without a word to anybody?''

"My father knew eventually I'd figure out where Matthew had gone and come looking for him. For some reason, he doesn't want me to catch up to him yet.''

"Why?'' Liana pushed her hair behind her ears. As she'd waited for Cullen to return from his talk with Luke, she had battled fear and disappointment. They had missed Matthew, and once again they had no leads to where he might have gone. And what about the other person who might be looking for their son? Was he as confused as she and Cullen? Or did he have Matthew in his sights?

"I just don't know, Lee. I need some time to consider this.''

"Maybe they just wanted to spend a little time together. Maybe they'll be back soon.''

"It's not like Dad to nick off and leave everybody else at the station to carry the can.''

"Is there any chance he left a note?''

She watched him consider the possibility. "Dad's ashamed of his penmanship and spelling, and he rarely puts things in writing. That's one of the reasons he insisted I go to university.''

"But this was important enough, wasn't it?''

"Winnie didn't find a note, but we ought to give it a bash. Maybe we'll find something else while we're at it.''

She grasped at straws. "Something else?''

He summoned a smile, nothing more than a twist of his lips, but she could see it was meant to reassure her. "I'm sorry, I don't have anything in mind. At this point, any scrap might do the trick."

"Where do we search?"

"I'm going back to the airstrip to tell John what's happened. I'll see if he can stay over a bit, until we know what to do next. Then I think we should start looking in Dad's private office." He started down the steps.

"Where can I look? Give me something to do."

"Try the room Matthew was using, Lee. Have Winnie show you which one it is. Maybe you'll spot something she didn't."

She suspected this was just busy work, but it was better than staring at the horizon. She watched Cullen climb into the station wagon and take off toward the airstrip; then she went in search of Winnie, who showed her to a guest room on the west side of the house.

"I changed the bed linen, dusted a bit," Winnie said. "So it would be clean when he returned."

The room was surprisingly large, with a window overlooking a huge red gum with strips of tattered bark curling along its trunk. Liana wondered if this had been Cullen's room as a boy. "I'll just look around."

"I'm afraid you won't find a thing." Winnie left her alone.

Liana sat on the edge of the double bed and stroked her hand over the bedspread where Matthew had slept. She wasn't superstitious. She didn't believe that people who loved each other could send thoughts through time and space. But for a moment she tried to clear her mind and put herself in her son's size-ten shoes.

She saw nothing, felt nothing, except her own fear. Shaking her head, she rose and began to methodically search the room. She opened drawers and searched corners. She peered under the bed, into the deepest recesses of the closet, behind cheerful blue plaid curtains. When Cullen returned he found her deep in thought in an armchair whose cushion had been lifted and thoroughly probed.

"Nothing?"

"Matthew picked a fine time to stop leaving things around."

Cullen lifted a dresser scarf and peered under it. "John's working on the landing gear. He claims it will be tomorrow morning at the earliest before we can get away, although I suspect he's just tinkering with perfection."

"Then we'll spend the night here?"

"Unless something else develops."

"Was this your room, Cullen?"

"That seems like a long time ago." He moved to the window, parting the curtains to stare outside. "See that gum?"

She joined him. "Uh-huh."

"At one time there was a limb I could grab if I opened this window. At night, when I was supposed to be sleeping, I'd slide along it to the trunk, then I'd climb higher until I could get to the roof. I'd crawl along the edge until I was directly over the porch that goes off the kitchen. There's a pantry on one side without windows. I could swing down from the roof at that point and leave with no one in the house being the wiser."

"What happened to the limb?"

"I got heavier. It broke in half one night when I was ten or so. I fell on my arm and broke that, too. Dad never said a word. I suppose he thought I got what I deserved. But he had what was left of the limb sawed off. I was glad he didn't do the same to my arm."

Cullen leaned against the windowsill and folded his arms. "I had a lot of dreams in this room, on that bed. Of places I'd go and things I'd do. Of women I'd meet."

"What kind of women?"

"Dark-haired, dark-eyed women with mysterious smiles." For the first time since they'd arrived at the station he grinned, and it seemed almost natural.

"Well, I wasn't dreaming about you. I was dreaming about

wickedly handsome Frenchmen who would whisk me to their extravagant châteaus in private jets.''

"But you settled for a wickedly handsome Australian who whisked you to…'' He groped for a word.

"Hell?'' she supplied.

"Paradise.''

"You wish.'' She smiled, then sobered. "We've got to find Matthew.''

"I've been thinking about what you said, Lee. You may be right and Dad just wanted to show Matthew some of the far corners of the property and didn't want anyone interfering. Wherever they are, he'll keep him safe.''

"If that was true, would we be able to spot them from the air?''

"If John's willing to take the plane up in the morning, we'll try that. But it's too dark for a run, and right now the landing gear's in pieces.''

"I saw another plane on the field.''

"No luck there. Harold says it's been grounded for a month. They're waiting for a part, and the station 'copter is out at one of the camps. In the meantime, we'll keep looking for a note. Let's try Dad's office.''

She followed him through the house. The office door was unlocked, which seemed lucky, since Liana wasn't certain Winnie would have given them permission to search the room. It was spacious, lined with cabinets and files, although there was no equipment except a complicated looking radiotelephone system in one corner. A utilitarian desk sat in the middle of the floor, covered with neatly stacked papers. A brass mirror was the only object adorning the walls.

Cullen did a cursory examination of the desk before he spoke. "Nothing in plain sight.'' He dropped to the chair, lifted a stack of papers and began to read through them.

"Should I check file cabinets?''

"I don't know what you'd look for. Better to check behind them, under if you can. In case a note slipped to the floor.''

She knew what a long shot that was. But she got down on her hands and knees and began a search that led nowhere. Either Winnie or Roman himself was a stickler for cleanliness.

"Nothing here." Cullen set down one pile of papers and took up another. He flicked through them, reading rapidly. "That's quite a view, Lee."

She was crouched on all fours, but she swivelled and shot him a look. "I could check those papers, and you could do this."

"I'm content." He went back to work, trading one stack for another. "Looks as if Dad's introducing more Brahman blood into his Hereford stock. Not an easy task on a property the size of this one. Too many mickey bulls out in the bush..." He went on to another document. "He's paid off some loans recently...."

"Nothing about Matthew?"

"No. Just the sort of papers you'd expect...." Cullen sat forward, wrinkling his brow.

Liana dusted her hands against her slacks. "Did you find something?"

When he didn't answer, she got to her feet and joined him at the desk. "What is it, Cullen?"

"Nothing about Matthew." He continued to read, flipping the top page of a stapled document to go on to the next.

She didn't repeat her question until he had finished. "What is it?"

"The answer to a lot of questions." He set the document on the desk.

She didn't hesitate. She put her hand on his shoulder, automatically rubbing it in a wifely gesture of comfort. "Are you okay?"

He sat back and closed his eyes. She continued to rub his shoulder, then the back of his neck, kneading her fingers into a solid knot of tension. Without considering what to do next, she moved behind him and began a serious massage with both hands.

He sighed audibly. "I always loved it when you did that."

"I'm guessing you still do."

"Do you remember I told you someone loaned Southern Cross enough money to consolidate debts and keep us going after I mucked things up so badly?"

Everything fell into place, and she knew what he was about to say. "I remember."

"It was my dad."

"What were you reading, Cullen?"

"A letter from the bank that arranged the loan for me. A final statement."

"You never suspected the silent partner was your father?"

"I thought Dad was the last person who might help. He expected me to fail when he sent me off. He told me as much when he signed over Southern Cross. He told me it was my inheritance and all I'd ever get from him."

"People say things when they're angry, Cullen. Things they don't mean. God knows, you and I did often enough."

"Why do you suppose he did it, Lee?"

She continued digging her fingers into his flesh. "Maybe he knew what it felt like to lose everything. Maybe he didn't want the same for you."

"You don't know him."

"Apparently you don't, either." She felt a weight lifting from her own shoulders. She had pictured Matthew with a man who was incapable of warmth. Now, she knew Roman was something more.

Cullen hunched his shoulders. "Why did he keep it a secret?"

That part seemed easiest of all. "Because he didn't want to be caught in a lie. He told you Southern Cross was all you'd ever get."

"Maybe."

"And maybe he thought your pride would be destroyed if you knew the money came from him." She rested her fingers lightly at the sides of his neck. "Would you have taken it?"

"No."

She could feel the rapid thrumming of his pulse, the knots of tension that were holding back a lifetime of feelings. She smoothed his hair over his ears. "Cullen, he's a kinder man than you ever thought he was. And he loves you."

"My Lord…"

She thought of all the mistakes that had been made, all the love that had been thrown away, all the tragedies that had befallen their families.

And she thought of Matthew, whose inheritance wasn't Jimiramira, wasn't Pacific International, wasn't Southern Cross, wasn't even the Pearl of Great Price, but instead all the terrible mistakes that both families had made for generations.

Her hands dropped to his shoulders. "We have to find our son. And we have to find Roman. Before something happens."

"I think I know where to look, Lee."

She waited. Afraid to ask.

"They've gone to Pikuwa Creek," Cullen said. "It's Matthew's birthplace. It was Dad's birthright. I think they've gone back. Together."

Matthew braced himself for one more bump in what his grandfather fondly called a track. Yesterday they had driven all day over unsealed road that cut through the heart of Jimiramira and other stations that seemed to have more weathered rock formations, scrub and dry riverbeds than cattle. Today, after a night under the stars and a breakfast of tea and damper, they had gotten up before the sun and driven harder, with only one stop at a rustic roadhouse for petrol and the best steak he'd ever eaten.

"Granddad, why don't you and my father speak to each other?"

Roman swerved to miss a hole which, in wetter country, would be known as a pond. "It's taken you a while to ask."

"It's taken you a while to trust me."

"What makes you think I do, boy?"

"Because you didn't send me home when I showed you the pearl."

"I'm a flaming idiot."

Matthew grinned. "Runs in the family, huh? So why don't you and my father speak to each other?"

Roman didn't answer right away. The sun was beginning to set, their second sunset since leaving Jimiramira. The driving had been particularly rough for the last fifty miles or so, but it would be even rougher in a little while, with the sky turning dark. Matthew let his grandfather concentrate until the road smoothed out. Judging from yesterday, they would keep driving late into the evening, until Roman was just too tired to go any farther.

"Your dad and I never talked much," Roman said at last. "Not even when Cullen was living at home. I guess I never knew what to say to him. He could talk the sun out of the sky, that boy."

"Did that bother you?"

"I never had any answers good enough, I suppose. Later, he got his answers from some of the other blokes around the station, swaggies who'd come in from other properties, sundowners who got what they could at Jimiramira and moved on. I should have watched him more carefully and put a stop to it, but I was always at one end of the place or the other, away from him too long. They taught him to gamble. But they didn't teach him to stop."

"Dad doesn't gamble anymore. He hasn't for a long time."

"So I've heard."

Matthew was surprised. "You have?"

"A man hears things, whether he wants to or not."

"You want to hear about my dad, don't you?"

Roman didn't deny it. "We had a fight one day. I sent him west, to Pikuwa Creek. I thought I'd be better off if I didn't have to worry about him anymore."

"Were you?"

Roman didn't answer.

"He never says anything bad about you, you know," Matthew said. "But he told me that he's coming home someday to make everything right between you. Whether you want him to or not."

Roman snorted. "That just about sounds like my son."

"Your son's the best father in the world!"

"Well, he didn't learn it from me, but if he is, I reckon I've got reason to be proud of him."

Matthew was mollified, then desolate. "I don't think he's going to be too proud of me."

"Don't you?"

"He won't understand what I've done and why."

"And your mother?"

"The pearl's destroying her life. One day she's not even going to be able to leave our apartment. Maybe when the pearl's gone once and for all she'll see why I had to do this."

"And maybe not. People get used to having things. They don't want to see them taken away." Roman slowed. "Look over there, boy."

Matthew followed his grandfather's finger. In the silvery twilight, against a stand of glistening gums, two kangaroos were hopping beside the track. He watched in wide-eyed fascination. There were too few kangaroos in Australia for his taste.

"The big one's a boomer, a male," Roman said. "The female has a joey in her pouch."

"Cool."

"We'll get to Derby tomorrow before midday."

"And you think your mate Pete will lend us a boat?"

"He will, no mistake about it. He's offered in the past, hoping I'd take a bit of a holiday. I told him once I liked to sail as a boy. Guess any bloke who lives in country as dry as this has dreams about the sea."

"But you never borrowed a boat?"

"Don't take holidays. Haven't since your grandmother was alive."

Roman had already told Matthew the story of Pete Carpenter,

a "mate" who had helped Roman ship Jimiramira cattle to Asia during the years when that was the best market. Pete was retired now, living on the coast outside of Derby, which was north of Pikuwa Creek. To keep busy he restored boats, since the best of his own sailing days were over. "Once a sailor gets the sea in his blood, you can't take him too far from it, or he'll wither up like grasslands in a drought," Roman had told Matthew.

"You're sure the two of us can manage a sailboat by ourselves?" Matthew asked now. "Aren't they pretty big?"

"Let's see what Pete has. Then we'll worry." Roman slowed the car and downshifted. "I'm afraid I'm all in, boy."

Matthew thought this looked like as good a place to camp as any. There were scenic gorges and rock formations not far away, the product of an ancient reef that drew visitors from all over Australia. Matthew wished he and Roman could veer north and see them, but he knew Roman was skillfully avoiding any populated tourist accommodations or attractions. His grandfather didn't want to leave a trail. "So, are we going to stop here for the night?"

"No. I just need a rest. How about if you take over for a while."

"Me?" Matthew was sure he'd heard his grandfather wrong.

"Do you see anybody else in here with us?"

"No, but—"

"Good bit of road for the next few kilometers. I don't know why you can't drive it as well as I can."

"But I'm not sixteen." He paused. "I'm not fifteen...."

"I know how old you are, boy."

"It would be okay?"

"Wouldn't have asked if it weren't."

"Wow!" Matthew sat up straighter. Fatigue vanished.

Roman slowed to a halt. "Not much to it. But it seems only right your first lesson should be out here. You're a dinky-di Australian, aren't you?"

"I don't know what I am, but I sure want to drive."

"Then let's do it."

Roman gave Matthew a quick verbal lesson, explaining how to shift gears in the Holden Jackeroo, one of the station's four-wheel-drive vehicles, which, though weatherbeaten, was in top-notch running condition. "Won't matter if we creep along at first," Roman said. "Don't worry about going faster. Just get used to shifting gears."

Matthew got out and circled the car to climb into the seat his grandfather vacated. He was surprised there was so much to remember. But he supposed if he could learn to drive here, where everything was on the opposite side of the car and "power anything" was unheard of, he would be a shoo-in for his license.

Roman reminded him to press the clutch before he shifted into first. Then, hands locked on the wheel, Matthew inched forward. "Wow!"

Roman laughed, the first time Matthew had heard that particular sound. "Your dad said something just like that the first time I put him behind the wheel."

Matthew screwed up his face as he concentrated. There was so much to remember. He couldn't imagine how people did this in traffic. The kangaroos had passed them a long time ago. He wondered if he could catch up to them and doubted it.

"Next gear," Roman called.

The gears ground, but Matthew pressed the clutch harder and they popped into place.

"Good," Roman said. "You've got the touch."

No one had ever said anything better. He felt himself grow an inch taller. He pressed a little harder on the accelerator, and they moved faster.

"Listen to the engine, boy. She'll tell you when it's time to shift again. She starts to strain a bit, and you'll know."

Matthew listened, but there was so much to remember at once. He had to pay attention to staying in the middle of the road, where it seemed safest—since there hadn't been another car for over an hour. He had to remember where the brake was, just in case something ran in front of him or another crater appeared. He was almost sure he wouldn't know when to shift again, but suddenly the car rattled harder. "Now?"

"Told you, you have the touch."

The sun was slipping toward the horizon. Roman reached over and turned a knob below the dashboard, and the road was bathed in the glow of their headlights. This was not the reason Matthew had come to Australia, but for a moment it seemed to be. He felt older, wiser, and infinitely more proud of himself.

He sped up and shifted one final time, working hard, this time to get the car into gear. There was a terrible grinding noise, but Roman covered his hand, just as naturally as if he had often held it, and helped him find the right place. The car wasn't straining now. They seemed to be flying, although Matthew knew he wasn't driving nearly as fast as Roman.

"Why did you come with me, Granddad?" Matthew asked. Behind the wheel of the Jackeroo he felt all-powerful, as if no one could deny him anything, most particularly not the truth. "I thought for sure you were going to try to send me home once I showed you the pearl."

"Just watch what you're doing, boy. We can talk later."

"Please tell me." Matthew concentrated. Roman was silent for so long that Matthew assumed his plea had fallen on deaf ears. Then Roman spoke.

"I found out a few things about time over the years. You always think you have lots of it, Matthew, lots more than you might want. Then one day you see how wrong you were. No one has enough. And sometimes there are things that have to be done while you can."

Matthew wasn't sure if he was confused because he was also trying not to run off the road. "What things?"

"Oh, things, like making sure the Pearl of Great Price never troubles anybody in our family again."

Matthew was still feeling brave. "Things like getting to know your grandson?"

"Bloody hell! Just drive the car, boy."

Matthew grinned and drove.

32

Pikuwa Creek lay on the coast between Derby and Broome, at the mouth of a rugged bay. A hundred years before it had been the supply camp of Somerset and Company. Now it was the center of the world for Sebastian Somerset's great-great-grandson.

Cullen glanced at Liana as John circled the Southern Cross airstrip in preparation for landing. She might always be a white-knuckle flyer, but clearly she would fight any enemy that stood between her and their son.

As if she'd read his mind, she spoke. "Don't get the wrong idea, Cullen. Once we find Matthew, I'll probably crawl under my bed and stay there a year."

"Nah. You won't. You're remembering what it's like not to be all tied up in knots."

"I've never been tied in so many."

"Being worried about Matthew is something different."

She didn't dispute it. "I want him here waiting for us."

That morning they had flown over Jimiramira, searching for the Jackeroo or signs of a temporary camp. They had startled several of the station's stockmen and spooked a mob of cattle, but there hadn't been any sign of Roman and Matthew. By ten they had given up, gone back to refuel and taken off for Pikuwa Creek.

"Winnie promises she'll ring us the moment she hears anything." Cullen peered out the window. "And, Lee, they may be on their way, but we know they haven't arrived yet. Sarah hadn't heard a word when I spoke to her before we left."

"But she's checking with everyone at the farm. You did say that?"

"Once we land, you can ask her yourself." He pointed down below, hoping to take her mind off what might be waiting for them. "See the reflection way out there, just beyond the point to the south? It might as well be silver or gold. Those are aluminum rafts, supporting panels of oyster shell in the water. They were X-rayed before they were brought here, so there's no doubt they contain pearls. The other farm up the coast has even more shell at the same stage."

"Stage?"

"I don't remember exactly how we were doing things before you left. After the divers gather shell in February, it has to recover for four months, sometimes six."

"I remember that part."

"We suspend it in panels just off the bottom, way out at sea where we hope no one will spot it, but even though it's resting, we have to go back and clean it twice a month. The barnacles and other growth compete for nutrition." He sat back. "Then the shell is brought here."

"There are so many rafts."

"We're not the biggest farm. Just the best."

"Matthew's going to be fascinated. Seeing Pikuwa Creek is different from hearing stories. *If* he gets here…"

"He will."

"I keep telling myself he's all right. After all, he's with your father. But I have this feeling…" She shook her head.

"You're his mother."

She turned to him, slate-colored eyes huge against pale skin. "And you, Cullen? You're his father. You have a special bond. What do you think?"

"I think we should stick to facts. We have no evidence that anyone's traced him to Australia except us."

She turned away. "Poker never was your game. You can't hide your feelings."

His voice hardened. "My game right now is finding our son. If that means using my head and ignoring everything else, then that's what I'm going to do."

She was silent until the landing was completed. Then she touched his arm. "I'm sorry."

"We're on the same side."

"For the record, when I remember, I like it."

As a young man, if he'd known how complex life and love could be, Cullen would never have come to Pikuwa Creek and never have involved himself with this woman. She was as eternally mysterious as she had been at their first meeting, and her effect on him was still as mystifying.

He bent to kiss her, knowing that doing so would only make things more complex. She brushed her hand through his hair, but she didn't push him away. His heart hammered against his chest, but he was the one who withdrew.

"We'll find our son, then we're going to talk about possibilities. But one thing at a time." He moved away to gather his gear from the seat across the aisle.

"I can't believe I'm back here." She said the words so softly he barely heard them.

"You'll find everything has changed."

"I've changed, and so have you. Why should Pikuwa Creek be different?"

Because some things stayed exactly the same.

Outside, the sun warmed his arms and hair, and he settled his hat in place. As weather went on the coast, this was a cool day, but he knew it would take Liana time to adjust. He watched from the corner of his eye, waiting for her reaction. To the heat. To being back at Pikuwa. To the changes...

She stepped forward, one tentative step, then she was moving away from the plane and the airstrip. He followed her to the edge, through a dry field. She paused under one of the blossoming moonah trees that framed a view of the house in the distance.

He tried to imagine it through her eyes, but he couldn't. Not really. He couldn't remember what the house had looked like ten years ago, because the changes he'd made had been gradual and therapeutic. What energy he hadn't devoted to Southern Cross Pearls had gone into the bungalow that he and Liana had shared with their son.

"It's…" She turned, and her eyes were shining. "It's spectacular. Cullen, you've darn well worked a miracle."

He hadn't known he needed her praise. He had truly believed that the pleasure—and therapy—he'd gotten from renovating the house and designing the landscaping were enough.

But he had been wrong.

She crossed under the moonah tree bower and started forward. "Did you do this yourself?"

He followed, trying to see the house as she did. "For the most part."

"It's so perfect. I love the red roof. Iron, like Jimiramira?" She glanced at him for confirmation.

"Where would Australia be without it?"

"It looks like a Chinese temple."

"It's Broome style, so the heat rises and water sluices off in the Wet. Of course, if we get a good cyclone whipping through the bay, I reckon it will flap its wings and fly like a Chinese crane."

"No, you're protected here. Well, as much as anyone along the coast can be. The veranda's extended, isn't it? And the latticework along the sides… You've planted so much. Acacia, and kapok and poinciana trees. And that's bougainvillea on the arbor?"

She was not a woman who blathered. He was not a man who sought compliments. For a moment he was uncharacteristically speechless. Then someone stepped out on the veranda, a tall young woman with short blond curls, and the moment was gone.

"There's Sarah now." He rested his hand on her back to propel her forward. "Let me introduce you, and we'll see if she has news."

The pleasure in her eyes faded, and for a moment she didn't look as if she could move from the spot. He knew she was afraid of what Sarah might tell them.

They climbed the porch steps while Sarah waited in the shade. She was a diplomat, which was why she had so quickly risen to assistant manager of Southern Cross. "I'm Sarah." She extended her capable hand to Liana, but she spoke to both of them. "We haven't heard anything from or about Matthew, or Mr. Llewellyn, either, but I've alerted every man and woman on the place to watch out for them. What would you like me to do next? I could call the police stations in Broome and Derby."

Cullen had never been more grateful for her easygoing efficiency. "You've checked my E-mail?"

"Nothing there. I'm sorry."

"It might not be a bad idea to ask the police to watch out for them," Liana said, after murmuring a polite greeting to Sarah.

"I'd better do it," Cullen said. "I can give a better description. Sarah's never met Matthew."

"Haven't you?" Liana asked the other woman. The question sounded more pointed than rhetorical.

"I've never had the pleasure. I can't go to the States when Cullen does. Someone has to stay and run the—"

Cullen cut her off. "Sarah, who's about the farm today?"

She rattled off a string of names. He nodded in punctuation.

"That many?" Liana seemed surprised.

Cullen answered. "It's not the place you knew, Lee. We've a permanent crew of over fifty now, with extra help from time to time during the year."

She didn't hide her surprise. "Here, on the farm?"

"We've expanded since the old days. Some of the crew live out on the water. We have a fiberglass vessel, the *Southern Cross,* that stays out at sea nearly all year. And we have smaller boats, as well, which are out right now turning shell in our dumping grounds and over at our second farm at Yampi Sound. Those crews come and go, three weeks out, one on shore. We fly the crew of the *Cross* back and forth by seaplane in shifts. So the head count at Pikuwa Creek changes from day to day."

"Except for the divers cleaning shell out there." Sarah pointed at the bay. "They're local, for the most part. Some of them live right here, others live in the area. And so do the factory workers."

Liana looked to Cullen for clarification. "We make our own nuclei for seeding now." He pointed north, to a whitewashed building sitting near the water's edge. "There's a canteen down there, a cricket field and comfortable quarters. We even have a satellite dish and a video library. It's not a bad life."

"It's not a bad life at all," Sarah said firmly. "And Cullen's workers know exactly how good they have it."

He had never seen Sarah on the defensive, but he thought he might be getting a preview. "Sarah, give Liana a quick tour, will you? I have to settle up with the pilot who brought us here and ring the cop shops. I've got a few other people to alert, as well. Lee, when you've seen all you want, come back to the house and we'll get you settled in."

"Ready to have a look?" Sarah asked Liana.

For a moment Cullen wondered if she would go along. He wanted privacy to make his calls. He needed to feel free to express his worst fears so the police would take him seriously.

"All right," Liana said. "But, Cullen, if you hear anything, if anything happens…"

"I'll fetch you flat chat."

She smiled. Not the strained attempt at reassurance he'd seen too often, and not the softer, more genuine smile of the girl he'd married. This was the provocative smile of a woman. "Flatter than flat, mate. Don't forget, we're in this together."

* * *

"I really am sorry about Matthew," Sarah said, after Cullen disappeared into the house.

Liana examined Sarah in side glances. She was a tall woman, with a body a personal trainer would take pride in. She was deeply tanned, despite her wheat blond curls and pale blue eyes, and unashamedly casual. But Sarah was no stranger to feminine wiles. She wore a blinding white T-shirt that emphasized both the tan and the perfect breasts, and matching shorts that bared an admirable mile of leg.

As Sarah started off, Liana reluctantly fell into place beside her. "We hope there's nothing to be sorry about except a wayward teenager taking life into his own hands."

"I've never had a child, so I have no idea what one might do or why. But I can imagine how you must feel. And I know Cullen adores his son."

"Matthew thinks Cullen hung the moon."

"That makes it particularly odd, doesn't it, that he chose to take off on his own now, when they could be together?"

"Everything about it is odd."

"You must let me know if there's anything I can do to help, Liana." She paused. "Do you mind if I call you that?"

Liana dredged up a smile. "Please." She didn't want to talk about Matthew anymore, not unless there was something important to say. "Cullen's sent me off so he can have some privacy when he talks to the police."

Sarah paused. "Maybe you'd rather we just sat somewhere and waited until he's finished?"

"No. Why don't you tell me about the farm?"

"Has it changed that much?" Sarah didn't wait for a response. "Of course it has. It's changed by half in the years I've been here. I can't even imagine what it was like so long ago."

Liana felt ancient. Sarah was all of twenty-six. "How long have you been here?"

"Five years. I studied biology at university, but I was raised in Broome, and I was desperate to come back. There's no place like it, is there?''

Sarah was outdistancing her, but Liana knew that when the gap widened noticeably, Sarah would slow her pace. "I'm sure Broome's a very different place than it was then. Just like Pikuwa Creek.''

Sarah slowed with an apologetic shrug. "You won't recognize it. There's quite the cosmopolitan atmosphere these days. It seems we have festivals every month, but it's still the tropics. Everything happens on Broome time.''

Liana stopped when Sarah did. They were at the edge of the white sand beach dipping down to the bay, and she remembered it well. "I always wished Matthew and I could swim here. But the tides would have carried us away if the local croc didn't do it first.''

"The tide is the reason our pearls do so well. An inch a minute. All that nourishment washing back and forth through the shell. This is a nearly perfect environment. Cullen could pack it in at a moment's notice and the other pearlers would be standing in line for this property.''

Liana heard pride in the other woman's voice, but she wondered if there was something more. Sarah had been at the farm for five years. Cullen swore they had no personal relationship, but she wondered whose choice that was.

Sarah stared out into the bay. "What would you like to know?''

"Cullen told me about the rafts on the way in. Is the shell brought here to be seeded?''

"No, now the *Cross* goes to it. That way, the shell doesn't suffer such a shock. Cullen was one of the first to realize the value. The shell is brought on board, seeded, then put flat on the ocean bottom again. But it has to be turned regularly and cleaned for forty days so a pearl will form.''

Liana knew about the seeding process. The shell was opened and a wedge inserted. Then a highly skilled technician made an incision in the oyster's gonad and inserted a tiny nucleus made from Mississippi pig mussel shell covered with some of the oyster's own mantle tissue. Afterwards, over a period of months, the oyster secreted nacre to "heal" the injury. Seeding had always been the most expensive part of a pearl farm's operation. The Japanese technicians flown in to do it had earned many thousands of dollars for only a few days' work.

She wondered if that, like so many other things, had changed. "Have any Australians been trained to do the seeding? Is it more economical now?"

Sarah glanced at her. "Don't you know? These days Cullen does it himself."

"Cullen?"

"He taught himself before I arrived. He's quite the star in these parts. He seeds all his own shell right on board the *Cross*. He's always taken rigid sanitary precautions. He got ahead of the game when some of the other companies weren't producing as well. That's why Southern Cross has grown so quickly."

"Good for him."

Sarah gave her a questioning look. "I'm sorry. This is certainly none of my business, but you seem happy at his success."

"Absolutely."

"Well, then it's even a better story, as it turns out. The overall success rate for seeding's only about 30 percent. Of those pearls, only about 5 percent will be real quality. The others will be baroque—irregular in size or shape...." She stopped, flustered. "I'm sorry. Of course you know that."

"Or keshi," Liana said, remembering how excited she had always been to see each new batch of keshi pearls, which were pearls the oyster had formed on its own, ignoring the nuclei. They had inspired some of her best work.

Sarah was warming up. "I'm partial to keshi, myself. They can be so interesting."

"I always liked working with them," Liana agreed. "Rebel pearls. I—" She stopped.

Sarah gave her first truly genuine smile. "Cullen's success

rate is much higher than the average. Ten, even 15, percent of his pearls are quality. And nearly 50 percent of his implantations are successful.''

"Does he know why?"

"Not precisely. But *I* think it's because he sings while he works on them.''

"You're kidding me.''

"He loves them. He really does. You know what they say about talking softly to your houseplants? Well, oysters are a step up the evolutionary ladder, aren't they?''

Liana could just picture Cullen, whose baritone was delightfully off-key, singing to the oysters as he had so often sung to their baby son.

"And Cullen has wonderful hands,'' Sarah added. "Healing hands. I think there's power in them.''

Liana wondered if Cullen realized that his assistant manager was in love with him.

"Anyway,'' Sarah continued, "the process goes on and on. Three pearls for nearly every oyster. When they're too old to continue, we seed for mabe pearls—five at a time, if we're lucky. Once the oyster is removed, we sell it in Broome or overseas, and then we sell the shell for paint.''

Mabe pearls were grown directly on the shell, using variously shaped nuclei. They were flat on one side and much less valuable. Because they had to be cut from the shell, they were the oyster's last stand, and Liana had never liked working with them.

"It's become quite an industry, hasn't it?'' Liana was still trying to take it all in. Cullen had revived a failing business and turned it into what was obviously a tightly run, profitable pearl farm. Along the way he had inspired fierce loyalty and even love in this woman.

"I'll show you all the buildings, if you like. We're still small, of course. But we're expanding rapidly. Cullen has the knack for this, you know. He knows when to take chances and when to hold steady.''

"'Know when to hold 'em, know when to fold 'em....'"

"I'm sorry?"

"It's a song. About a gambler. When we were married, it was one of Cullen's favorites."

Sarah's voice cooled. "I suppose this *is* the right sort of business for a gambler. But there's nothing reckless about Cullen's decisions. Everyone on his staff has a voice, and we all share in the profits. We've asked him to hold tight when he wanted to try something new, and he listened to us. That's hardly the mark of a gambling man, is it?"

"Cullen and I have a long history, Sarah. It would be difficult to erase it completely."

"You know, I've wanted to meet you. But never under these circumstances, of course."

"Why did you want to meet me?"

"Well, I work so closely with Cullen, I can't help being curious." There was no apology in her voice.

"We were married a long time ago. I'm not sure what that has to do with Cullen's life now."

"You lived here with him. I've seen your work. Cullen still keeps some of your pieces. You're enormously talented. Brilliant, really. He won't have an in-house jeweler, you know. He sells his stones wholesale, even though he could do a good business selling at least some of them in settings right here in Broome. I think..."

"What?"

"Well, I think he's decided that no one else should set his pearls."

Liana didn't want to think about that. She didn't want to think about the art of merging pearl and precious metal into something beautiful and unique. The moments when some nameless part of herself had been made whole by the wonder of creation.

Suddenly the air seemed heavy and still, but her own body was clammy with sweat. She shook her head, then realized it was a mistake when the landscape blurred. "I don't design jewelry anymore, Sarah. I probably couldn't if I tried."

"That seems a pity."

She could feel her heart beating faster, trying to send blood to limbs that were suddenly, maddeningly numb. "People change, and so do their interests."

"Well, I hope mine never change. I love this place, and everything we do here."

Liana had lived in this place for almost five years, loved the man who owned it, hated the same man when he nearly gambled it away. And, in the end, she had taken a gamble, too. She had thrown in the dice and cashed in her own personal chips when she walked away from Cullen and Pikuwa Creek.

And what had she lost as a result? Even as she struggled with familiar panic, the answer was perfectly clear. She had lost her heart, her soul, the muse that guided her hand and her imagination. She'd left a man because he'd made a terrible mistake, and then she had gone on to make her own.

She hated Pacific International and her place in it. She hated the life she had fashioned for herself out of a desperate yearning for security. She hated the woman she had become.

Sarah's brow furrowed. "Liana, you're pale. It's the climate. You're not used to it anymore. And it's Matthew, isn't it? I've been going on and on, and walking too fast, besides. Cullen will give me a real bagging if you faint."

"I'm...not going to faint." Liana took a deep breath as panic surged through her in increasingly forceful waves.

"Let's just get you over to the shade." Sarah took her arm, but Liana shook off her help.

"It has nothing to do with the heat." She squeezed her eyes closed. She was catapulted through time by the fierce thunder of her heart, to a place Sarah had never seen, a tiny pearl farm of dilapidated buildings, of patched-up luggers and workers who only grudgingly appeared after their pay evaporated at the local grog shop.

Despite all she had endured here, she had loved it, sometimes even reveled in the hardships. She had not been driven away by heat or flies, venomous snakes or crocodiles. She had not, as she had told herself for ten years, been driven away by Cullen's mistakes. She had been driven away by a childhood that had left her torn apart. She had not found peace or happiness here, because she had never looked for them in the only place they could be found.

Inside herself.

"Lee?"

She opened her eyes to find Cullen standing in front of her. Sarah was retreating. She didn't know how he had sensed her distress, or if that was why he had come. She didn't even know how long she had stood there, reliving the years of their marriage. This was not the Pikuwa Creek or Southern Cross she had known. This was not the man she had known.

Yet it was.

He cupped her face in his hands. "Your skin's as cold as the water out there."

She covered his hands with hers. "I'm so sorry, Cullen."

"For what?"

"For believing all these years that everything was your fault. For being so afraid Matthew would love you more than he loved me. For leaving you when you needed me most."

He shook his head, as if he, too, had been vaulted backwards in time and understood exactly what she meant. "You had to leave. You were right to leave me."

"There were other ways. I could have stayed nearby. We could have gotten counseling. Even if that didn't work, I could have shared Matthew with you. But I ran so far and shut you out so completely because I still loved you. Can you understand that?"

"I understood it even then."

"And look what you've done. Look what you've become. I gave up on you, even though I knew this was all inside you."

"Don't make that mistake, Lee. It wasn't your duty to stay on and hold my hand. You did what you had to."

"That's the frightening part. I ran away and gave up everything I ever was in exchange for Pacific International. And it's destroyed me."

He was silent, because there was no way he could understand completely.

She turned away from him and stared out at the bay, where seeded silver-lip oysters floated in blissful ignorance of the treasure they harbored. "In ten years I have done nothing but grow more afraid, more insecure, more determined to wall myself off from the world."

"It hasn't destroyed you." He lifted her hair off her neck, twisting it high on her head. Then he gathered her in his arms and gently forced her back against him.

"Maybe it took coming back here to see it clearly."

"It hasn't destroyed you."

"What's left of the woman I wanted to be?"

"You're successful—"

"At a job I despise! I hate Pacific International, Cullen. I hate what we do and the way we do it. We carve the world into smaller and smaller pieces and sell it at bigger profits. I try to make a difference when I can, to protect people who need it, but I'm one voice among many. I have a title but very little power. My father set it up that way. It was Matthew he wanted. The only thing I ever did right in Thomas's eyes was have a son. He told me so when I crawled back to San Francisco and asked him for help after I left you. He made me a figurehead. I can hold Matthew's place until he's old enough to take over Pacific. And as my reward, I get a job there and the pearl. But only because I'll pass it on to Matthew."

"Matthew's our son, and Thomas is dead. We're the ones who have a say in what Matthew becomes."

"Don't you see? Thomas was craftier than I ever thought, because he realized we teach our children by example, not by words. And what has Matthew ever seen from me? I buy and sell the planet, just like Thomas did. I have no real life outside my work. My world is as narrow as the walls surrounding me.

I *am* my father. I am Thomas Robeson. And every day I'm teaching Matthew to be just like me.''

"You're forgetting the differences. You're a terrific mother. You adore Matthew, and he knows it. You've given him everything."

"I've kept him away from the other person who adores him."

"He's a wonderful kid. That's all the proof required."

"He's gone, Cullen!" She turned in his arms and pushed against his chest. "He's gone, and, damn it, don't you see? *I* drove him away! He came here, under his own steam, because I wouldn't let him come home with you. I've tried to control him, exactly the way my father controlled me. Thomas knew that would happen. He died knowing it, the bastard.''

He framed her face, holding her still. She felt tears welling in her eyes, then spilling to her cheeks. Cullen didn't brush them away. "Be quiet and listen. One, we are going to find our son, and then we are going to ask him why he ran away. And until he's told us, we are *not* going to continue to blame ourselves. Neither one of us."

"What do you have to blame yourself about—"

"Two," he said firmly, "from this moment forward we are finished with the past. Done with it. I made mistakes. You made mistakes. Bloody hurrah. We were young. We should have resolved things differently. We didn't. It's over."

"It's not over. We have a son who's missing!"

"It's over, Lee. We've made amends as best we can. And now we have only the future to concern ourselves with."

She stood absolutely still, trying to absorb what he'd said.

"Yes," he spoke for her. "It can be that simple. Let it be that simple."

"I want those years back," she said at last. Her voice was barely audible. "Don't you see? That's what all this is about."

He gathered her close. "But we can't have them. We only

get the years ahead of us. And it will be up to us, won't it, how we live them? Because no matter whose shadow we're standing in, in the end, we're the ones who decide what happens next.''

33

33

Where once there had been small cluttered rooms, now the inside of the bungalow was open and airy. Despite changes in the interior design, there were few personal touches. A carving of a whale embellished a coffee table; framed photographs of Matthew covered the wall behind a plaid sofa. The living area had only basic furniture, although stacks of books and a modest entertainment center testified that Cullen spent at least some time here.

"I made the structural changes, but I never seem to have the time to fix up the place." Cullen moved papers from the sofa and gestured for Liana to sit. "I can turn on the air con if you'd like."

She shook her head. A breeze from the bay swept through the open windows, and the house was comfortable. She sat back and closed her eyes. "You don't have to fuss. I'm feeling better."

"I'll fetch something to drink."

She was drained. As she rested, she could hear waves washing against the shore and the shouts of men in the distance.

"Sarah must have stocked the shelves. I found juice."

She looked up and saw that Cullen was holding out a glass. When she took it from him, she was glad to see that her hand was steadier.

"I put your things in Matthew's room."

"Matthew's?"

"I always think of it that way, even though the house is so different. But it's in the general vicinity of the one he used as a little boy."

"Do you remember when he learned to climb out of his crib and crawled in bed with us in the middle of the night?"

"I remember it could be bloody inconvenient."

He smiled, and she found herself smiling back. Despite everything. "Do you remember his first Christmas?"

The smile disappeared. "Too right. I lost the money we'd saved for gifts."

"That's not what I meant. We had a wonderful Christmas, Cullen. I made mother-of-pearl ornaments for the tree—"

"Bells and stars and angels. I have them."

"Do you?" That both touched and surprised her. "They should go to Matthew someday. They're part of his history."

"You baked biscuits, tiny round ones with chopped cherries. Even though it was hot enough to grill a snake on the veranda."

She made a face. "Grilled snake never seemed festive."

"I made Matthew a truck to pull behind him."

"I made him a teddy bear."

"No, you didn't. You made him a flaming zoo."

"So I overdid it a little. He loved them. He still keeps some in his room."

"I saw them."

They fell silent, both thinking, she knew, of the teenager, not the toddler.

Cullen set down his glass when they'd both thought too long. "The cops will be watching out for him, Lee. They know me. They listened to everything I said. Whitey Pendergast in Derby promised he'll ring up a bloke he knows at Hall's Creek to ask if he's seen or heard anything."

"They should be here by now, Cullen. They left Jimiramira days ago."

"Dad probably stopped off to see the sights. That's all. And this isn't California. He could be by the side of the road somewhere, repairing an axle or the radiator. Matthew's going to see the real Australia."

She was touched again, because he was still trying to protect her. "Look, you must have things to do. Let's make a deal. I'm going to rest. Then I'll rustle up some dinner. You come back whenever you're done. It'll be waiting."

"When was the last time you cooked? Does Sue let you in the kitchen?"

"Whenever I want to be there."

"How often is that?"

She waved off his question. "I haven't forgotten the basics."

He checked his watch. "I'll be back about six. My private line rings down at the office, too, so you don't have to answer it. Sarah or I will get it there."

"Cullen, about Sarah..."

He looked as if he'd been expecting a question. "I'll give it to you one more time, straight-out. I tried mixing business with pleasure just once. With you. I'll admit Sarah would like a relationship. But I'm a dab hand at resisting dangerous impulses."

She raised an eyebrow. "I was going to ask if we should invite her to eat dinner with us."

"That's not what you wanted to know."

"But the other's none of my business, is it?"

"I couldn't begin to say." He jammed his hat back on his head. "I don't know what you'll find in the kitchen, but when you lived here, you did wonders with nothing."

She smiled sadly. "Never with nothing. There was always something here to work with."

Exhausted, she slept on the sofa for an hour; then she prowled the house, inoculating herself against the past by immersing herself in it. He had torn down walls, added a wing and a deck in the back, which he'd screened with white lattice smothered in bougainvillea. She wondered who he entertained here. He denied that he and Sarah were lovers, but he was not a man who would adapt easily to celibacy. She knew there had been women, even if there wasn't one now.

The house was different, but it seemed familiar. It smelled like the sea, like nectar-laden tropical flowers with a cloying, unavoidable note of mildew. The heaviness of the air was a nostalgic serenade against her skin. The rooms were different, but the view remained exquisite. Mangroves to the southwest, teeming with insects and birds. Pikuwa Creek to the northwest, trickling to the bay but promising a torrent of pindan-tinted water when the monsoons arrived. In the farthest distance, the sails of a boat, not the quaint triangular sails of an earlier era, but still a reminder of the ocean's enormous wealth.

Cullen's bedroom had windows all around, as if he couldn't stand to be shut inside, even as he slept. Bamboo blinds and a king-size bed were hints that he didn't always sleep alone. But there was little else in the room except a framed photograph on a wooden chest that Cullen had rescued from an old sailing lugger when they were still married. She lifted the photograph and wondered how Cullen explained it when he brought women to the room. Matthew's likeness stared back at her— this, too, from the days when she and Cullen were still married. But in the shadows, almost like a ghost, a slender young woman stood and watched the little boy.

Liana was that woman. She remembered what Cullen had said about living in the shadows of others, and she wondered if he thought of that each time he saw this photograph.

She was able, somehow, to face all that, to wander the rooms where they had lived as a family. She found the room he'd referred to as Matthew's, a large room now, where once there had been a nursery. She sat on the bed her son should have slept in each summer. She gazed out the window at the view that should have been his.

But she couldn't face her studio. She avoided that side of the house as if it were a murder scene, cordoned off by crime scene tape; as if, once she looked closely, she would see the chalk outline of a body on the floor. Cullen had renovated the space for her in the earliest days of their relationship. Before her pregnancy. Before their marriage. Before things began to disintegrate.

He had taken what was then the largest room in the house, one that looked directly over the bay, and built workbenches and shelves. He had installed a separate diesel generator for her use alone, and wired and plumbed the room to her specifications. He had even installed an air conditioner for the hottest days, although they could not afford one anywhere else in the house. The studio had been her sanctuary, and she had spent blissful hours there, turning Cullen's pearls into art.

And she had been successful. More successful than either of them had dreamed. Her work had been sold in Sydney, Paris and Tokyo, fetching prices that had astounded her. She had considered hiring a production staff, negotiating to bring out a line under her own name, opening her own showroom in Broome or Darwin. Before Cullen's gambling ripped the heart out of Southern Cross. Before their marriage succumbed to a plague of silence, followed by recriminations and lies. Before she snatched Matthew and left her young husband forever to return to San Francisco and her father's tyrannical demands.

Through the years, she had wondered what Cullen had done with her studio. Now, so close to finding out, she couldn't take the final step. Her muse was gone, and she had no hope it would return. But if the studio was gone, too, transformed into a sleeping porch or Cullen's personal office, then the muse was surely dead, entombed in a room used for other purposes. The days when she might have resurrected it would have fled forever.

She completed her tour in the kitchen, where she was bathed in nostalgia. Cullen had done little here, but what did a man who was a ''tinned'' food gourmet need with butcher-block islands, granite countertops or glass-paned cupboards? The same peeling black linoleum covered the narrow counters. The same black and white tiles covered the floor. The refrigerator was new, but small, in keeping with the few fresh supplies he kept on hand. The stove was older now, and even more tired. The round table in the corner was covered with a cherry red plastic tablecloth in an obvious attempt to brighten the room. But except for a few new saucepans under the stove and new glasses in the cupboard, the kitchen was just as she'd left it.

She found rice in the same cabinet where she had always stored it and put it on to steam. She found knives in a familiar drawer to chop vegetables Sarah had undoubtedly stocked. She found a can of boned chicken and marinated it in soy sauce, powdered ginger and chopped garlic as she stir-fried the vegetables. And when everything had been added and the dish was finished, she took out the cutlery and plates she had bought in Broome before Matthew was born.

Cullen was late, arriving well past six. She had listened all afternoon for the telephone, but if it rang, it only rang in his office. When he appeared in the kitchen doorway, he took one look at her expectant face. "I just got a bit of news."

"Did the police call?"

He tossed his hat to a peg beside the refrigerator. "No, they'll ring us the moment they have something to say, but not before. I spent the afternoon contacting all the station managers along the route Dad probably took. No luck there, but I had some luck with Winnie."

"Winnie? What did she say?"

"She rang me to say that no one at the station has heard from Dad. She checked with the neighboring stockmen. Nothing there, either. No one spotted the Jackeroo. But that's to be expected. Those are lonely roads. She did think of something as we talked, though. She disconnected and rang the father of the girl Matthew brought to Jimiramira."

Liana remembered Winnie's story. "Tricia?"

"That's right. She asked him if he would speak to Tricia and see if Matthew had given any indication he might be going somewhere else after he met up with my dad."

"And?"

"As it turns out, Matthew told Tricia he was coming here to Western Australia."

"That's all?" When he nodded, she went on. "Nothing about where or why?"

"I suppose we had a bit of luck just getting that much out of her."

"Then you were right. He *is* coming to Pikuwa Creek. This isn't a wild-goose chase."

"It's little enough, but it's a good omen."

"Would it be like your dad to take his time getting here?"

"It's just been too long. I don't know what Dad's like anymore. I reckon he could be feeling his age a bit and have regrets. It's possible he sees this as his last chance to be part of a family again."

Liana turned back to the stove. Her heart was pounding, not only from the news about Matthew, but from memories, as well. How many nights had Cullen hung his hat on the same peg, then stood in that very doorway watching her put the final touches on their dinner? The past and the present blurred. If she didn't feel twenty-four, how could she feel so many of the same emotions?

"What do you think of the house?" Cullen asked.

"I like it. You've worked so hard."

"You've seen it all?"

She turned off the burner and faced him again, because she couldn't warm the food any more without destroying it. She shook her head in answer. He didn't seem surprised, although she wondered if he could guess what she'd chosen to avoid. "I like the deck," she said. "Could we eat there?"

"I'll just see if the table needs a swipe or two."

"I already took care of it. Let's dish up in here and take everything outside."

"It smells wonderful. You haven't forgotten how to cook."

"I guess it's like riding a bike."

He seemed in no hurry to eat. "It's a different life you lead now, isn't it? Household help. Limousines at your disposal. Designer condo and clothing.''

"Different, yes.''

"Back then, I couldn't have given you any of those things, even if I hadn't been gambling.'' He wasn't apologizing—but he wasn't just making conversation, either.

Neither of them made a move toward putting food on their plates. Liana's breathing grew shallower. She could feel her pulse speeding up, but not in panic.

"I never wanted those things," she said. "I still don't. They came with the package.''

"Package?''

"Security. A position at Pacific International. I had a son to raise. By the time I left Australia, I didn't believe in myself. I wanted to be sure Matthew would always have everything he needed. But I didn't go back to San Francisco for designer clothes and a limo. Those things never mattered to me.''

"You were an artist. You could have supported yourself. Did the job matter so much, Lee?''

"I wanted it," she admitted. "I wanted one sure thing in my life after years of uncertainty. For the first time Thomas actually offered me something I needed.''

"He held it out to you the way the snake in the Garden of Eden held out the apple. Take this and you'll have everything you ever wanted.''

"No, *this* was the garden, Cullen. Pikuwa Creek. And you were the one who offered me the only thing I really wanted, but when I reached for it, I was locked out.''

"What did you really want?''

"Just love.''

"You had it.''

"At the end, I didn't know it anymore.''

"You had it. You have it still.''

For a moment she wasn't sure she had heard him. The last words had been spoken so softly. "You can't mean that.''

"I do.''

She couldn't seem to look away. "We haven't seen each other for ten years."

"I'm not saying I've spent them wasting away. I had as much work to do on my heart as I did on this house and Southern Cross. But when I was done, I knew you were still in it. I've known for some time, and I've tried to make peace with it."

She was so stunned she couldn't speak. He stepped closer, until he was just in front of her. He touched her cheek, and he smiled sadly. "I'm not asking for a second chance. I don't expect anything just because I've told you I still love you."

She closed her eyes. It was the only way she could break the intimacy of his gaze.

"But you wanted love," he said quietly. "You needed it. And you ought to know you've always had it."

She could feel his fingertips stroking her cheek. She knew she had to move away or she would be lost. Here in this place, here with this man, she was in danger of reaching for love again.

"Open your eyes," he said.

She did. His were sad. "We'll go on from here, Lee, just like nothing's changed. Because nothing has, except that now you know the entire truth of it." He dropped his hand. "It's still not too dark to go outside. I'll light the lanterns."

She took his hand and placed it between her breasts, so that he could feel her heart thundering. "No, this is the entire truth of it, isn't it? That you can still make me want you with a few well-chosen words, that my heart still races whenever you touch me?"

"The words are *poorly* chosen. They're the truth, and the truth isn't always pretty, and it doesn't automatically bring happiness. Do you think I want to love you? That I haven't wished a thousand times I didn't? That I don't pray every night to fall in love with another woman and make a life with her?"

"Then do it, Cullen. Because if you do, I won't be tempted anymore, will I?" He started to speak, but she stopped him with a desperate shake of her head. "No, God, that's not true, and now I'm telling lies. Because I would be. My heart would beat just this way. I'd want you no matter what. Even if you were married. Even if I thought you hated me."

They stared at each other, neither breathing. Then she was in his arms with no idea who had moved first. He crushed her against his chest, and she embraced him with every part of her. Hips grinding against hips, breasts flattened, hands moving hungrily across his shirt. His lips were hard against hers, but hers gave no quarter. She kissed him back, tongue against tongue, lips grazing lips, releasing, testing, tasting, demanding.

She moaned, because she was suddenly a creature of deepest, purest need. She needed to soar far and free with him, as she had in the earliest days of their marriage. She needed no assurances, no contracts, no collateral. She thought briefly of Matthew, but tonight all she could do for her son was love his father. In the very depths of their mutual hell, they could give each other solace.

"Say no, and say it now," Cullen said, his lips against her throat. "Or it will be too late."

"Yes."

He swept her off her feet, lifting her easily. Even as a young man, when the flames of desire had licked at every part of their lives, he had never carried her to bed. He did so now, as if even the moments it would take to walk together were too many and too dangerous. He didn't know that she wouldn't, couldn't, change her mind. She felt his fear in the strength of his arms and the grip of his hands.

They undressed each other, or she thought they did. Their clothes were on and then they weren't, belt buckles clanking against the floor, fabric balled at their feet. The bedspread was soft against her back because neither of them took the time to pull it down. His skin was warm, his muscular body taut against hers. They filled their hands with each other's flesh, searching for the familiar and the new. He pinned her body to the bed with his, his weight welcome and seductive, then she was on top of him, limbs sliding along limbs, hearts slamming in the same desperate rhythm.

If sometimes in the deepest sleep she had remembered their lovemaking, if sometimes in the moment before dawn she had ached for his touch, now the man, the waking dream, was so much more than memory had made him. He knew her body, yet he took nothing for granted. Wordlessly he told her how he felt, each touch, each kiss, like rain to parched soil.

The greatest pleasure she had ever known arrived with the least subtle of victories. If for ten years she had yearned silently, shamefully, for Cullen, now she knew he had yearned as often and intensely for her.

There was no final moment of union. In the ways that mattered most, they had united at the first touch. When he finally sank deeply inside her, it was only the culmination and the beginning of release. She cried out when she could not sustain the pleasure even a moment longer.

They ate dinner in bed, Liana draped alluringly in Cullen's unbuttoned shirt, he with nothing but a sheet tangled at his waist. They didn't talk, but they touched frequently. The brush of fingers against a thigh, lips seeking out the curve of a throat or the arch of a shoulder. When they had finished eating, they snuggled under the covers, Liana's hair spilling over his arm as she lay facing him.

For so long Cullen had told himself that making love to Liana again was out of the question, and now he could hardly believe it was true. She touched his cheek with her knuckles, drawing them down to his chin.

"We took a chance, Cullen. Unless you've had a vasectomy?"

Birth control had been the furthest thing from his mind. "You're not on the pill?"

"It's not a good idea at my age."

He was silent, trying to form an apology in his head while his body continued to sing in jubilation.

She sighed. "I didn't think of it, either."

"The last time we didn't think of it, we got Matthew."

"If all the mistakes we made had turned out as well as our son, we'd still be together, wouldn't we?"

"Lee, we are together."

Her hand came to rest between them, no longer touching him. "We're in bed together. That's different."

"Acquaint me with the subtleties, would you? We just made love. We're lying in bed after ten years apart, and it feels like you never left. And even though it's unlikely, we may have just made another baby. Is that together or not?"

She reached down and pulled the sheet higher around her breasts. A breeze had not swept the room, but one swept his heart as she covered herself. She sat up and moved farther from him, tucking the sheet under her arms. "Sex was always great for us. Sex was never the problem."

"And if we'd paid attention to how easily we could please each other in bed, maybe we would have tried harder to please each other out of it."

"There's a lot more to a relationship than orgasms."

"Do you think that's what I'm saying?"

"I don't know what you're saying."

He sat up, propping himself against pillows and the headboard. "I'm saying whatever you want to hear. We can take this a step at a time. I'd say we took a big one tonight. But if that's as far as you want to go at the moment, that's as far as we will."

"At the moment..."

"I want more. I want you back, on whatever terms you'll come. I can wait months. I can wait years. We can sleep together or not sleep together while you sort this out. I'll make you a partner in Southern Cross, or I'll buy property in Broome and live there, if you don't want to live out here in Woop Woop. If you want to spend part of each year in California, I'll find a way to do that, as well. But what I won't do is give you up again."

"What you *won't* do?"

He told himself to walk softly. The most valuable lesson he'd learned as a gambler was that a serene face and a warm word could turn a losing hand into a winner.

"I won't do anything you don't want me to." He raised her fingers to his lips. "But, Lee, you're not the only one to wish the last ten years hadn't existed. If I'm pushing too hard, it's only because I don't want to live another ten without you."

"You don't know what's at stake here." The sleepy look of pleasure was giving way to agitation. He watched her tense, and as she did, his own chest tightened in anxiety.

"What is at stake?" He kept her hand in his and his voice calm. "Tell me. What's at stake, besides a chance to start over?"

"I have a life."

He was confused. There seemed to be something important she wasn't saying. "Too right you do. But not the one you want. You said so yourself."

"But I can't just give it up, Cullen. Maybe ten years ago I should have stayed here and tried to work things out. And maybe if I had, it would have destroyed us both. I don't know anymore. Maybe none of my choices were good and I did the only thing I could."

He could see her moving rapidly away from him. He cursed himself. "This is the wrong time to talk this over. First let's find Matthew. Then things will fall into place. We have the rest of our lives to work this out. Let's just be glad we found each other again and take it from there."

She pulled her hand from his, as if she hadn't heard him. "If I leave California, everything I've worked for will vanish. Maybe I shouldn't have gone home. Maybe I shouldn't have taken my place at Pacific International. But I did. And now you're asking me to give up everything."

"That's not what I'm asking."

"If I come back here to live with you, I lose my home, my job...."

"But you'd always have a job here. You could do what you love. You could design jewelry again. If you didn't want to design for me, you could design for Paspaley or Broome Pearls. Any of them would fight to have you."

"I haven't designed a thing since I left you!"

He hadn't known that for sure, although he had suspected. "Why not?"

"I have a different life and no time for hobbies."

"Hobbies? You're an artist."

"Not anymore."

He could hear himself saying all the wrong things, but he didn't know the right ones. "No worries, then. It doesn't matter. Because I can take care of you and Matthew. You don't need a job, and you have a home. Here, where you belong."

"You're missing the point."

She was right about that. There was still something just out of his grasp, something that he *was* missing, but Cullen knew he was growing too upset to see it. "Bloody hell, we're just making a mess of things again. Let's call a halt to this, before we say things we don't mean."

She looked as if she wanted to say more, but at last she nodded.

He forced an uneven smile. "Will you sleep here, with me tonight? No promises, no pledges. Just sleep beside me?"

For a moment he thought she would refuse, but she nodded again. He slid down and adjusted the pillows, turning to face her. She slid down, too, but she turned her back to him.

He knew he was taking a chance, that he might send her away for good, but he moved closer and settled his arm over her waist, gently positioning her to curl against him. He kissed her hair. "She'll be right, Lee. Whatever it is, we'll make it right."

She didn't move away, but even as he drifted off to sleep, he realized that she was still lying stiff and sleepless in his arms.

* * *

Liana wasn't sleeping deeply when she felt Cullen's hand on her breast. Desire infused her again, fed by the fogginess of dreams. She turned to him before she realized what she had done, then she didn't realize anything again as they came together in the relaxed, indulgent sex of longtime lovers. During their marriage they had often made love this way, as if only in sleep could they bury their problems deeply enough that love and passion could be reborn.

"I love you," he whispered against her hair as he fell asleep again. Her body was satiated, but her heart was too full of emotion to drift off with him. She lay awake, watching him in the half-light of dawn. His brown hair fell over his forehead, and his face was at peace. He was older, but just as desirable now, a man who had emerged from the crucible stronger, and confident in his power.

And who was she? A woman still molded by the flames. A woman who knew what she wanted but was too afraid to reach for it. She had found a tolerable life and a place at Pacific International. She had gained security and an enviable future for their son.

But what had she lost? And what would she lose if she denied her heart?

She stole out of bed as the sky lightened, slipping her arms through Cullen's shirt again and buttoning it as she left. She was drawn by the room she hadn't yet faced, as if within its walls she would find the answers she sought.

Inside, the house was silent, but outside, a cacophony of bird calls greeted the sun. When she had lived here she had done her best work in the early morning hours, while the house was still tolerably cool and the bird chorus sang cantatas to the new day. She remembered the first piece she had created in her studio, the lily-of-the-valley pin that she had given to the homeless man on California Street. She was sorry now that she had parted with it. She hoped the pin had helped him make a new start, the way that once upon a time its creation had made one for her.

The short hallway leading to the southwest corner of the house was wider, she thought. It was foolish to imagine that Cullen hadn't renovated this part of the house when he undertook the rest. She steeled herself to find the studio gone. There were two doors leading off the hallway. She opened the left and found the utility closet that had been there ten years ago. She rested her hand on the doorknob at the right and stood without moving, unable to make herself turn it.

"Go ahead."

She was startled by Cullen's deep voice, and her hand dropped to her side. She faced him. He had pulled on khaki shorts, but his chest was bare. "Go ahead," he repeated. "Open the door."

She had come this far, creeping silently through the house as if she planned to rob it. She couldn't refuse and expect him to retain any respect for her. Trapped, she reached out and turned the knob, pushing the door as she did. It swung open, but not willingly, swollen, she thought, from disuse and humidity.

"There's a light switch by the door," he reminded her.

She hadn't forgotten. She flipped it, wishing he hadn't gotten up, wishing that she could face the younger Liana alone. The room brightened. At her request, Cullen had installed separate lights throughout the studio, over workbenches and sinks, inside display cases. He had bought a reading lamp to place beside an easy chair in the corner, where she had rested sometimes with her sketch pad. It was that lamp that glowed now, illuminating a museum to her past.

"I couldn't bring myself to dismantle it." He came to rest in the doorway as she moved farther inside. "I wanted to. I thought about putting an office in here so I could work at home in the evenings. But every time I'd think I was ready, I couldn't do it."

The room was just the way she'd left it. Hand tools hung neatly from pegboard; a rolling mill, vices and drawplates rested on the sturdiest workbench. One area was partitioned for polishing, the extractor fan set up as if, even ten years later, she could flick a switch to set it whirling. Another area was set up for soldering, with a fireproof mat, blocks and a light shield, so that she'd been able to see subtle changes in the color of heating metal. She wandered the room slowly, trailing her hand over counters, finding them dusty—but only a little. At a glance she could tell that the workstool was still adjusted to her height; the saws had been oiled and cleaned but lay much as she had probably left them.

She turned to Cullen. "Wasn't there somebody who might have used all this? Somebody who could have continued where I left off?"

"I'm fair certain there was, if I'd wanted someone like that."

"Surely you didn't think I'd be coming back?"

"At first I did. That's how I got through the worst times."

"And later?"

"I took it a day at a time. I told myself I could always change things around another day."

"Sarah told me you sell all your pearls wholesale now, even though it would be to your advantage to have some set."

"That's Sarah's opinion, yes."

"What's yours?"

"Look around, Lee. I reckon my opinion's clear."

She didn't know what she had expected. The studio was here. Intact in every way. Ten years had passed, and technology had advanced so rapidly that much of what was in this room was probably outdated. But the bones were here, the basics. She could create wonderful pieces in this room.

If she could create.

She shook her head. Sorrow seeped in to fill the empty space inside her. "When I walked out this door, I left all my talent behind. Everything else is here waiting for me. But not that."

"You're sure?" He sounded skeptical. "Do you know why?"

She did. She was frightened of her talent, of the free-flying exhilaration that came when she trusted her inner voice. She was afraid to take chances now, and what *was* art except chances, each one greater than the last?

She was afraid of this room, more afraid of what she had found here, and frightened most of all of giving up the safety net that ten years ago had halted her plunge into desolation.

"I don't want my talent back." She faced him. "It's that simple, Cullen. I don't want to be that woman again. I'm too old and too afraid."

"That's sounds like a decision. Don't you think it's too early to decide anything? Can't we—"

She cut him off. "No. We can't. You've told me the truth. I owe you the same. I have to keep my position at Pacific International. If I leave, everything I've worked for will be gone."

"What exactly will you lose?"

She looked away. "My father's will was complicated. But boiled down, it says if I stay with Pacific, I'll have everything I need for the rest of my life, and when I die, Matthew will inherit everything. If I leave, I'm cut off completely, and Matthew has to split control of the company with Graham and Graham's children, if he has any."

"That's blackmail."

"That's what it's called, yes."

"And you'll willingly give in to it? You'd give up a chance at happiness here? Pacific International means that much to you?"

"It means that much for our son. It's his future."

"You just said he's going to get a healthy share of Pacific, no matter what you do. And Matthew wants to come to Pikuwa Creek to work with me. He wants to create pearls."

"Matthew doesn't know what he wants. He's fourteen."

"No? Think again. He wanted to run away. So he did. To Australia." He moved closer. "What aren't you telling me? You're paid superbly, aren't you? In ten years' time you've surely saved and invested enough money to be comfortable, even if things fell apart again with me. What else did your father hold over you?''

She didn't answer.

"It's the Pearl of Great Price, isn't it?" he demanded.

She could see it now, the world's most perfect pearl. A natural pearl that glowed against her palm when she held it, that warmed the air surrounding it. A gem any king would covet.

Cullen moved closer. "He bloody well tied that into his scheme, too, didn't he?''

She hedged. "Why would I base any decision on the Pearl of Great Price? It's gone.''

"Because you know in your heart Matthew has it. And you think you'll have it back once we find him. What did the will say about the pearl, Liana? Exactly what did it say?''

Her throat was dry. "I don't know why this matters. I don't have to defend any of my decisions, Cullen. We aren't married anymore, remember?''

"Then it won't matter if you tell me, will it? I have no power over you.''

But he did. More than anyone—except a dead man who had known his daughter too well.

"You owe me the truth," he said, when she didn't answer.

She couldn't find a way to tell him. How could she put into words what she had done, and why? How could she admit that in trying to give Matthew everything, she had denied him his father?

His expression changed. "It has something to do with me, doesn't it?''

She exhaled sharply. It was all he needed. "So it does. Since you won't tell me, let me see if I can think like your dad. He wanted victory over you. He wanted to rule your life, only you wouldn't let him. You escaped, and then you married a man whose family had a claim to your father's greatest treasure. Am I getting close, Lee?''

"Stop, Cullen. It isn't helping anything.''

"Stop, Cullen, because I'm dancing on the edge of the truth?

Let me dance a little closer to the heart of it, then. When you left me and went back to California, your father saw he had one more chance to control your life. Better yet, you had a son, his natural heir. And so he had even more reason to ensure that you'd do what he wanted.''

"Stop this...."

He continued as if she hadn't spoken. "So when you returned to Thomas like a whipped puppy, he knew what he had to do. He had never been able to manipulate you, and he probably saw that once you recovered, he wouldn't be able to manipulate you again. So he used the one thing he had.''

She closed her eyes.

"Our son," he said. "Am I spot on, Liana?"

Her voice was lifeless. "Thomas was ill by the time I got back to San Francisco. A few months later he was dying. He called me to his bedside one afternoon." She opened her eyes. "You and I were just beginning custody negotiations. He told me that he was afraid if Matthew was allowed to come here to visit you, you might try to keep him. He said his attorneys were afraid that if that happened, I might never be able to get Matthew back. I told him he was wrong, that you would never hurt any of us that way, but of course Thomas didn't agree. So he told me he was leaving me the Pearl of Great Price in his will, but only if I agreed not to let Matthew come to Australia until he was eighteen. He claimed that if Matthew came to Australia, you might trade his return for the pearl. He said you were a Llewellyn, after all...."

Cullen was silent.

She recited the rest in a monotone. "He had a brigade of high-powered attorneys. The will is ironclad. If I return to you before Matthew turns eighteen, or if Matthew comes here to visit, the Pearl of Great Price will be sold. I don't care for myself, Cullen. I never have. But that means it will never belong to Matthew, that the pearl my grandfather lost his life to gain will never belong to his great-grandson.''

"If you return to me? That was part of it?"

"Yes," she said softly.

"That frigging pearl!" Cullen swept his hand along the top of the nearest workbench, and tools that had lain there for a decade crashed to the floor. "Never mind you and me, Lee. That's one thing entirely. You kept Matthew away from Pikuwa Creek because of the pearl?"

"I made sure you had a month every year with him. Thomas wanted to arrange it so you didn't see him at all. I wouldn't let that happen. I managed—"

He cut her off. "Does Matthew know any of this?"

"I don't know," she said miserably. "It's possible."

"Well, he's bloody well here in Australia now, isn't he? So you've lost the pearl anyway, haven't you?" He stared at her, and suddenly she saw new comprehension in his eyes. "No, you haven't, have you? Because nobody at Pacific International knows he's here. They think he's off in Arizona somewhere. That's why you agreed to keep this trip a secret. You weren't just worried about his safety. You were worried about your inheritance!"

"Not mine! *His!* Matthew deserves that pearl! It's his birthright."

"Once we find him, you're hoping to slip him back into the country, put the pearl in your safe and go on the way you have for ten years, aren't you?"

"How can it be any other way? I owe him this. I owe Matthew the world. I'm his mother."

"You owe him your love! You owe him a good start and the wings he needs to fly when the time's right. You damned well owed him a father, and you owed him a mother who knew what was important and what was extortion, but that's all! No pearl, and no corporation."

"You don't know anything about it! That pearl is all the security Matthew will ever need. He can do anything he wants, be anything he wants—"

"It's not about Matthew, Lee. It's about you! The bloody thing represents your entire life, doesn't it? You've never struck a balance between freedom and security. Your mother gave you freedom without security. Your father gave you security, but he bound your hands.''

"What does my childhood have to do with this?"

"You think that pearl is both rolled into one perfect iridescent sphere. But it's not! It's a freak of nature. It's one oyster's attempt to heal itself, but there's something you've forgotten. In the long run, that pearl was responsible for the oyster's death. Well, it won't heal you, Lee, but it can bloody well kill the best parts of you.''

He paused only for a moment. "Maybe it already has." He turned and left the room.

She wanted to call him back, to remind him that ten years ago she'd had every reason not to trust him. To explain that if she'd known the ways he was going to change, she would never have agreed to Thomas's conditions. She wanted to scream that he had driven her to this, that she had been alone and terrified that she would never be able to do enough for their son by herself.

But she didn't. Because even though all those things were true, so were the things that he had said. By her actions she had earned the Pearl of Great Price for Matthew. But Matthew had needed more: his father's companionship and his mother's integrity.

Somewhere in the far recesses of the house she thought she heard a telephone. The sun was just coming up, but the pearler's day began at sunrise. Cullen might dress and leave, and what would she do? Sit on the porch and wish Matthew would appear, so she could spirit him home without anyone knowing that he had left the country? Sit on the porch and ask herself if at any time in the last ten years she had made even one good decision?

She put her face in her hands, so tired and disheartened that she didn't know if she could face another day of waiting. She had chased Cullen away with nothing more than the truth. Had she done the same with Matthew?

"Lee."

She looked up to find Cullen in the doorway. She waited.

"That was the Derby police."

Instantly alert, she forgot everything else. "Have they seen or heard something?"

His face was impassive, as if he didn't want to share even the most basic emotion with her. "There's been a murder. An old man named Pete Carpenter, a bit of a recluse, apparently. But someone in town recalled a man and a boy asking for directions to his house yesterday. The boy fits Matthew's description. The man introduced himself by his first name."

"Roman..."

Cullen nodded curtly. "Get dressed. We're going to Derby."

34

Whitey Pendergast, a middle-aged officer of the Derby police, was waiting for Cullen and Liana when they arrived at what was left of the old seaside shipyard where Peter Carpenter—Old Pete, to his mates at the pub—had gone to live after retirement. The shipyard had belonged to Pete's father. Now it was nothing but smoke and rubble. As they walked down to the water, Whitey, a thin man with an incongruous beer belly, filled them in on Pete's history.

"Kirby Carpenter, that's Old Pete's dad, was a fair enough shipwright. He built more than a few seaworthy vessels in his time. But this place had gone to gundy by the time Old Pete came back to end his days."

Near the water's edge, Whitey brushed his booted toes through a pile of glowing cinders that had once been a shed. "Pete fixed up the house a bit, just so it was liveable. He was really more interested in the property. He rebuilt the jetty with the help of a couple of mates. Then he brought in a small fleet, odd vessels of different sorts that he'd collected over time. Some to repair, some to restore or sell, I suppose. What you see is all that's left."

Cullen stared out at the water. The fire that had raged through the house and yards had spread to the jetty and the boats anchored along it. The tide was low, and one flat-hulled sailboat lay like the skeleton of a beached whale on the mud flats closest to the house. What remained of the others—he counted five—listed and smoldered in the water beyond.

Whitey had already explained that whoever had set fire to the house and property had untied the boats first, then doused them with petrol before setting them aflame. Pete's body had been found in the hold of a trawler, which looked to be his latest work in progress. The arsonist and murderer hadn't reckoned with the swift tides, which had lifted the fishing vessel from the mud flats before it turned to ash. Pete had not vanished on the floating funeral pyre. The flames had gone out, and the first men at the scene had removed his body before the trawler capsized. It hadn't been charred badly enough to disguise the bullet hole to his temple.

"The first to arrive didn't find anyone?" Cullen asked.

"Whoever did it was gone. You know how long it takes to respond to fire in a place like this one. If there hadn't been surveyors on a parcel of land to the west, the flames might be leaping still."

The air remained heavy with smoke. Liana coughed and cleared her throat. "Could there be more bodies?"

Cullen was surprised she had put the question so bluntly. As Whitey had acquainted them with the situation, Cullen had struggled with a less direct way to phrase it.

"I won't lie," Whitey said, without meeting her eyes. "It's still possible. But I don't think so. We've searched all the boats and what's left of the house, the sheds, even the boot of his car."

"Some of the boats are under water."

"Two of the surveyors swam out and poked around. We'll be hauling what's left to shore as soon as we're able, but I don't think we'll find bodies."

Cullen didn't glance at Liana. He had tried to look at her as little as possible since informing her of the murder early that morning. "I'm going to send a couple of my divers up here, just to be certain. Now tell me again what you know about Matthew and my dad.''

"We don't know it was your son." Whitey removed his hat and used it to fan himself. "An older man and a boy stopped at a restaurant outside of town yesterday afternoon and asked about Old Pete. The place is called the Diver's Inn. The proprietor's a man name of Dick Jones...." He frowned. "You know Dick?"

At Cullen's nod, he continued. "Dick gave them directions. When he heard about the fire, he drove out here to tell me. He said the boy was tall, maybe eighteen or so, brown hair, sunburned. The man was in his sixties. A wiry bloke. Dick didn't remember much, but he remembered the name Roman."

"Matthew could pass for eighteen," Liana said.

Cullen's voice was cold, even to his own ears. "We'll have to take your word on that, since I haven't seen my son for a year."

If Whitey heard Cullen's resentment, he gave no sign. "Did your dad know Old Pete? Has he ever spoken of him?"

"Dad lives in the Territory, between Darwin and Alice, off the Buchanan Highway. I don't know how they would have met."

"Cattle station?"

"That's right. Jimiramira."

"Pete worked for a company that shipped cattle from Wyndham. That was his job for years. Might explain how they knew each other."

"It might."

"You said your son was missing...."

"Right-o. He came to Australia to see my dad at Jimiramira, and they took off together. We thought they might be coming down to Pikuwa Creek. Matthew hasn't been there since he was small."

"We'll be watching for them. They might be the last to see Old Pete alive...besides whoever murdered him."

"You don't think my dad and Matthew had anything to do with this?"

"I didn't say that. But it's odd, isn't it, that they came looking for him, and he was killed just afterwards."

Liana stepped closer, so that neither man could avoid her any longer. "Whitey, it's possible somebody might be after Matthew."

Cullen had been reluctant to mention that until he collected all the facts, but Liana was right. The time had come.

Whitey pulled his hat over black hair slick with sweat. "After him?"

Cullen told the story of Matthew's disappearance and the aftermath in as few words as possible. Whitey listened, his frown deepening. "Why would anybody want to catch up with the boy?"

Cullen turned to Liana. "Suppose you tell him."

She met his eyes. Hers were sad, and for the first time since their conversation in her studio, he felt a flicker of compassion. She lifted her chin and turned to Whitey. "Have you ever heard of the Pearl of Great Price?"

Cullen said next to nothing on the trip into Derby, and Liana didn't know what to say. They drove directly to the Diver's Inn to show the proprietor Matthew's photograph. Dick Jones, who winked at Liana and tried to shout Cullen a drink, thought it might just be the same boy. They stopped and asked others who might have seen Roman and Matthew, or the Jackeroo. When that was unsuccessful, they drove back to Pete's, but nothing else of interest had turned up in the ashes.

"There is one thing," a soot-streaked Whitey said, as Liana turned back to the ute Cullen had driven to the site.

"What's that?"

"We got a call back at the station. I haven't had time to investigate. Bloke over at a petrol station in Broome says that yesterday Pete brought in a car for repairs. Claimed it belonged to somebody else. Pete told this bloke, Ralph Nakamura, that he was going to fix it himself, but he needed a part he didn't have. He dropped it off and got a ride back with one of the surveyors.''

"What kind of car?" Liana asked.

"I didn't talk to him. I just got the message a little while ago." Whitey fumbled through his shirt pocket and handed Cullen a piece of paper. "Here it is. You find anything at all, I want to know," he warned.

"Done." Cullen folded the paper and stuck it in his pocket.

Liana got into the ute and braced herself for what would be another bumpy ride to the highway. She waited until they were on their way before she spoke. "Do you think it might be the Jackeroo?"

"It might."

They had gone at least a mile before she spoke again. "Cullen, you can't forgive me, can you?"

"I have more important things to think about right now."

"All those years ago, I didn't understand how much you loved him. You had just gambled away his trust fund."

"I know what I did!"

"I didn't know you would change and become..."

"Become what?"

"The man I thought you could be."

"You never gave me a chance to prove myself, did you? You held my son and my heart hostage to a pearl."

"Matthew turns eighteen in a little over three years. Everything will belong to him then."

"Are you trying to say that in three years I can have my son back, Lee? That if I just wait patiently for three more years I can have my son here in Australia, and maybe you, as well?"

She didn't answer.

His knuckles whitened as he gripped the wheel tighter. "You sold us all for a flash chunk of calcium carbonate."

She didn't know what to say. Her life had changed so drastically since Matthew's disappearance that she had been off balance ever since. For ten years she had carefully constructed

an existence, and now its very foundation was under attac'
Not just from Cullen. Not just from her beloved son. But fro
her own fragmented heart.

They arrived in Broome sooner than they should have, b·
Cullen was obviously in no mood to think about speed limit
The town flew by as he sped to the petrol station. Broome ha
been spruced up beyond her wildest imaginings, a frontier tow
that was now as charming as it was interesting. Bougainville
bloomed in lush fountains of color; exotic boab trees provide
sculptured focal points. Architecture with an Asian flavor pro
claimed that Broome was unique and proud of its heritage, an
the colorful racial mixture of people in the streets proved tł
heritage would continue.

"You can stay in the ute," Cullen said as he parked unde
a palm tree swaying in a light breeze.

"I'd rather come with you."

"Suit yourself." He got out, and she followed.

Cullen found the owner, a man with dark skin, Malaya
features and a Japanese surname. Cullen explained what the
were looking for. The man, who was busy with another cu·
tomer, gestured to the back of the station, where cars sat in a
otherwise vacant lot. "Third car." He fished through his pock·
for keys and handed them to Cullen.

Liana followed Cullen behind the station. A four-wheel-driv
vehicle was third in the makeshift row. "There it is," Culle
said. "Now let's see if it belongs to the station."

Liana was sure of the answer, but she followed him to tł
car and saw by the logo that it was a Holden Jackeroo. Culle
unlocked the door and slid into the driver's seat. It took onl
a moment of rustling through papers to find what he was lool
ing for. "It's Jimiramira's."

She could almost smell smoke. She visualized the smolde·
ing ruins of the shipyard. "So they were there at Old Pete's.
Her voice cracked.

He got out, conflict twisting his features. Then he sighed an
put his arm around her. "She'll be right, Lee. It's not the wor

news. They were at Pete's. We know that for certain now. But Pete was the one who drove the car here and left it. If Dad and Matthew had still been with him, Dad would have brought it here himself.''

''Where are they, then? They had plenty of time to get to Pikuwa Creek if they borrowed another car from Pete.''

''If that's where they were going.''

''What do you mean? Where else?''

''If they'd borrowed a car they'd be at Pikuwa Creek. But it wasn't a car they borrowed.''

She straightened, but she didn't move far away. ''What?''

''We don't know how many boats Pete kept at the old shipyard, do we? He had a collection. We know that. He made them seaworthy. That was his hobby.''

''Matthew and your father on a boat? On one of Old Pete's refurbished sailboats?''

''It's been staring us in the face. Matthew isn't coming to Pikuwa Creek. He's taking the pearl back to the place where it was found. That's why he needed Dad's help.''

''But why? It just doesn't make any sense. It's his inheritance. Matthew's ancestors died to keep that pearl.''

Cullen's eyes were sad. ''Matthew understands what you never have, Lee. The pearl has destroyed before, and now it's in danger of destroying the person he loves most. He's going to put it back in the ocean to save you.''

''I thought there would be more wind.'' Matthew stood at the bow of the motorsailer *Argonaut*, which he and Roman had borrowed from Pete Carpenter, and watched his grandfather trim the mainsail.

''You're in some kind of a hurry, boy?''

''I don't think I have my sea legs.''

''You're not crook, are you? Hang your head over the side if that's what this is about.''

Matthew didn't feel sick, exactly, just odd, as if parts of his body weren't where they were supposed to be. Nothing, not hands or feet, and particularly not his stomach, felt familiar.

"It was nice of Pete to let us use this boat."

"I reckon he's a good mate, at that."

"I wish it was a real pearling lugger."

Roman grunted. The boat was picking up speed, although at the rate they were traveling, he had already informed Matthew it would be tomorrow or later still before they reached their destination. "You wish for a lot, don't you? You'd have to wish for a full crew, besides."

Matthew knew when to draw the line. He was amazed that he and his grandfather had come this far. The fact that the *Argonaut* had never been a pearling lugger meant very little. But going to the Graveyard meant everything, and that was where they were headed, thanks to Pete, who had showed them exactly how to get there.

"Couldn't we use the motor, just until the wind picks up?"

"Not unless you want to take a chance on not having enough fuel to get us back."

Matthew hadn't thought about that. The hold was stocked with fuel, but he supposed the boat would burn it quickly. He knew now that there was a lot he hadn't thought of when he made his plans to come to Australia. Luck had been on his side. For once the pearl had brought good luck instead of devastation.

Matthew braced himself as the sailboat picked up speed. Roman might not have sailed for years, but he hadn't forgotten the basics, and his old touch had returned once he'd had some time to experiment. "Does it seem strange to be going to the place where Archer killed Tom?"

Roman settled at the helm. "You're the one who's a Llewellyn *and* a Robeson. You tell me."

"Well, I guess Tom might understand, but Archer would think I'm really stupid."

Roman was in an unusually chatty mood. "I never knew my grandfather. He'd been dead for a long time before I was born. Just before he died, my dad did tell me the story of the pearl."

"Did he tell you how Archer murdered Tom?"

"He did. Years after Archer's death, an old swaggie who had lived in Broome came through Jimiramira, and he told my father everything he knew. My father said the story didn't surprise him, that he'd always known something terrible had happened in Broome, something his father felt guilty about. When Archer drank too much he saw ghosts...."

Despite himself, Matthew shuddered.

Roman continued. "Dad said that after fire destroyed the homestead and killed my grandparents, the stockmen didn't want to build a new homestead in the same place. They believed the pearl was still at Jimiramira, and if they searched the rubble, they might just find it. So when they built a new house, they built it up the hill a bit. For years, in the evening, the men would poke through what was left of the old place, and when they did, Dad was always sure he could hear his mother moaning."

Matthew's stomach churned, but he tried to sound nonchalant. "What's on that spot now?"

"When the time came for me to build a house for my Joan, I built it on the old site. I cleared every speck of the ruins away. Not that much was left by then, I reckon. What the men hadn't carted off, white ants and storms had taken. I stood over that place and said a prayer or two. Luke's a tribal leader, and he and some of the others came late one night and had a bit of a corroboree at the spot. I don't know what they did, exactly. Maybe just something to make us all feel better. Great psychologist, Luke. But when it came time to break ground for the new house, nothing went amiss. It's just a house, and for a long time, it was a happy one."

"It can be happy again, Granddad."

Roman actually smiled. "I don't need a house to make me happy, Matthew. I have a grandson. As far as I'm concerned, that's bloody well done the trick."

35

Back at Pikuwa Creek, Cullen turned off the ute's engine, but he didn't get out immediately. "You don't think Mei will be sleeping? It's just past nine in San Francisco."

Liana noted sadly how effortlessly he could calculate the time difference between the two cities. "If Aunt Mei's asleep, I'll have Betty wake her. But I have to speak to her. She may be the only person who knows where Matthew and your father have gone."

"The museum will have an answer before long."

Liana was sure Cullen realized that "before long" might be too late. Broome's historical museum in the former customs house was long on atmosphere but understandably short on personnel. The curator had searched to see if any documents in their possession mentioned the place where the Pearl of Great Price had been taken from the ocean. But by the time Cullen and Liana started back to Pikuwa Creek, she still hadn't been successful.

Liana opened the door. "I'll phone my aunt. You'll radio the *Southern Cross* and ask the captain and crew to watch out for Matthew?"

"Right, and he'll radio anyone in range and ask them to pass along the message." He paused. "But it's a fair cow of an ocean, and we don't know what sort of vessel they borrowed.''

''We'll find them.'' Again she didn't add the obvious. *Before whoever murdered Pete Carpenter found them first.*

She and Cullen headed separate ways. Now past the first flush of anger, he had been formally courteous, even considerate, during the difficult morning. But she wondered if he had pondered the irony of this newest twist in their lives. If Matthew really had stolen the pearl and now he tossed it into the ocean, Liana had fewer reasons to keep her son in California. Her own reason to stay was diminished, too.

The pearl might vanish forever, exactly the way her chance to make a new life with Cullen had vanished forever that morning.

Inside, she took a moment to acquaint herself with Cullen's telephone system, located at a desk in an alcove off the kitchen. Then she waited for an operator to connect her with Mei's Chinatown apartment. She willed her aunt to be awake and strong enough to speak to her. She willed herself to be calm and clear, so that she wouldn't frighten Mei.

The telephone seemed to ring forever. Finally a woman's voice came over the line, and Liana recognized Betty. Quickly she explained that she was calling from Australia. ''I need to talk to Mei about Matthew. It's urgent.''

''She's gone to bed,'' Betty said. ''But I heard her coughing a moment ago.''

''I have to speak to her right now.'' Liana clasped the receiver as Betty went to alert her aunt. They were hemispheres apart, yet Betty's voice had been clear, with only a faint echo to point out the distance between them. Mei's hearing was not the best, but the volume on her bedroom telephone was enhanced. They would be able to communicate.

She paged restlessly through a desk calendar as she waited for Mei to pick up the phone. Cullen had scribbled notes everywhere, and she felt a tightening in her chest as she scanned them. April: ''Tell Matthew about J. and the sea snake.'' May:

"Read M. article in the *Broome Advertiser* about the Stairway to the Moon." Early June: "Tell M. news about this year's Shinju Matsuri and the parade."

Matthew had not been allowed to visit here, but Cullen had found ways to make their son feel part of Broome and Pikuwa Creek. Her eyes stung with tears, and she closed them, unable to continue reading.

"Liana?" Mei's quavery voice sounded over the line. "Is this Liana?"

"Auntie Mei." Liana took a deep breath. "I'm in Australia. With Cullen. We think Matthew is here."

When Mei didn't answer, Liana wondered if her aunt was assimilating this new information or simply waiting. "Cullen and I think Matthew may have gone on a sailing trip with his grandfather—"

"Grandfather? Bryce's son?"

"Yes. Roman Llewellyn. We know Matthew visited him, then they took off for parts unknown. But Cullen and I think they may have gone off to see where the Pearl of Great Price was found. We have to find them right away. It's important. But we don't know where to look. Did your mother ever tell you exactly where the pearl was discovered?"

Mei was silent again.

"Auntie Mei, are you trying to remember?"

"He has taken the pearl," Mei said at last.

Liana could deny it no longer. "Yes, I think he has. Cullen thinks he's planning to drop it back into the ocean." Suddenly her heart beat faster. "How did you guess?"

"I know Matthew."

"Did he tell you he was going to do this?" Liana demanded sharply. "Have you known all along?"

"I as much as told you."

Liana gripped the receiver harder. "You didn't! You told us about Jimiramira and Bryce. That's all!"

"Liana-ah, I told you the same story I told your son."

"Where is Matthew, Auntie? I have to know."

"Is he in trouble?" Mei asked, worry in her voice.

Liana knew better than to upset someone of Mei's advanced years. "Nothing like that," she said, in a gentler tone. "Really. But it's time for this to end. Until Cullen and I have him back, we're going to worry. We just need to be sure he's all right."

"You want...the pearl."

"No!" She swallowed, too confused to know if she had told a lie. "No, I just want my son. Please, Auntie Mei. I need to be sure he's all right. That's all. Can't you tell me where the pearl was discovered? You must have been the one who told Matthew."

"I cannot remember what I ate for supper. But I can tell you where the pearl was found."

"*Will* you?"

"A place called the Graveyard. How could I forget such a name?"

Liana shuddered. "Thank you. That's what we needed."

"The boy is the best of two families. This is what he was meant to do. He will be safe."

Liana wished her aunt had not filled Matthew's head with superstitious nonsense, but she loved the old woman too much to criticize her now.

"I hope you're right," Liana said. "I'll phone you again, just as soon as we find him." She paused, then added before she hung up, "Auntie, don't tell anyone I called or where I am. Please, don't tell anyone Matthew's in Australia."

She went in search of Cullen. The office was near the canteen, a simple frame building with a steeply angled iron roof like the one on the house, and tall windows with top-hinged shutters that doubled as awnings when they were open. Here, closer to the water, she could see a small fleet of workboats and men farther up the shore working on one of them. Someone was sunbathing on the cricket field, and soft music and voices sounded from the canteen where the noon meal was probably in progress.

Inside she found Sarah, who pointed toward a closed door.

"He's talking to Nigel Finch, captain on the *Cross*. And he just spoke to Whitey Pendergast, as well."

"Do you know what Whitey said?"

"Our divers just arrived at the Carpenter property, and they're in the water now. No sign of anything so far."

The "anything" in question was bodies. Liana flinched. "Sarah, have you heard of pearling grounds called the Graveyard?"

"The Graveyard?"

"That's what it was called early in the century."

Sarah got up to search a map tacked to one wall. "I haven't. Is that where Matthew's gone?"

"It's possible."

"It's not on this map. But perhaps the name's been changed or that was just something the crews called it? Cullen might know.... Better yet, we'll ask my father...." She went to her desk. "I'll ring him and he'll have a bash at it."

"Your father?"

"A third-generation pearler, my dad. He scraped along for years when pearl shell wasn't good for anything but ballast. He knows every bit of the coast."

Cullen came out just as Sarah hung up.

"The Graveyard," Liana told him. "Aunt Mei remembered."

"It's one of the bays up in King Sound," Sarah said. "Dad says too many divers died there, which is why it was christened something so grisly."

Cullen waved his hand impatiently. "Cygnet Bay."

"You know the area?" Liana said.

"Too right. I nearly lost a diver there last year."

"How?"

"To a whaler shark that was larger than he was."

Cullen knew better than to hope Liana would stay at Pikuwa Creek while he searched for Matthew. "I'll grab a change of clothes," she told him after he strode to the map and pointed out the bay known as the Graveyard. "Do you want me to pack anything for you?"

He kept a bag in the office for emergency trips and told her as much. She was gone before Sarah spoke again. "Do you want me to come? You may need help."

"No, I need you here. We'll fly up to Yampi Sound and take the *Robinette*. She's light, and she'll get us there quicker than anything else. Call ahead and tell Ken to stock her. Then ring up Whitey and tell him where we're going and why. He might be able to help us search as soon as we get a crew for the *Windrun*."

The *Windrun* was one of Southern Cross's luggers and might be available to sail into King Sound as early as the next morning.

"Cullen, if Pete Carpenter's death had something to do with your son—"

He grimaced. "It did."

"Should you be out there alone?"

"I'll be armed."

"What about the *Cross*? Are you going to ask Nigel to meet you?"

"They're too far away to do any good."

"I wish I could do more."

He knew what she really wished. She wanted to give him comfort, even love. Instead, he was tied to a woman he could never have again. "Just sleep here in the office tonight, will you? I'll stay in touch as long as I'm able. Let me know if Nigel or anyone else calls in."

"I've slept here before."

"You need a life, Sarah."

"That I do." She tried to smile, too. There was nothing else to say.

He was down at the water's edge talking to one of his workers when Liana joined him. He introduced her. "Ellis will fly us to Yampi Sound. Our other farm's on an island there. It's closer to the Graveyard, and we'll be taking one of our workboats from there.'' Cullen gestured toward the center of the bay, where a small seaplane floated on the water. ''Better roll up your pant legs.''

She did so without complaint. He shouldered their bags, and they waded out to a dinghy. Ellis, who was descended from generations of Greek fishermen, started the motor with one expert tug, and in a moment they were speeding toward the plane.

''Is he coming with us on the boat?'' Liana shouted.

''The lighter we travel, the better.''

''We might need him.''

He knew she wasn't talking about an extra hand to crew. He had considered asking Ellis or one of the men at the Yampi farm to accompany them, but he didn't know what he and Liana would face out on the water. He didn't want another person for whom he was responsible.

He didn't want another witness.

''We'll travel faster alone,'' he said.

She didn't object, although she looked uneasy.

By the time they landed in a small inlet of Yampi Sound, the *Robinette* was waiting, primed and ready to go. Every craft in Pikuwa Creek's fleet was kept in top condition, because the lives of Cullen's crews depended on it. The little utility boat was the only thing he could really count on in the hours ahead.

''Throw our stuff below.'' He tossed their bags in Liana's direction, turning back to Ellis and Ken, the Yampi manager, for a last-minute conference. Then he waved them off.

Liana resurfaced as he made a quick check of their equipment. ''You're carrying a handgun, aren't you?'' she asked.

''Abso-bloody-lutely. If you have a problem with that, this isn't the right place for you.''

''Do you have two?''

''When did you learn to shoot?''

''Right after I moved back to San Francisco. I never bought a gun, though. I decided Matthew and I were safer without it.''

''I just have the one, a .38 caliber semiautomatic. And a

rifle, besides, in the cabin. Once we're out on the ocean, you can practice off the side. Just in case.''

"All right.''

"This isn't a game, Lee. I can still call Ellis to take you back.''

"I know it's not a game.''

In the old days he might have said "That's my missus.'' But not now. Instead he started the motor and listened to it purr, every valve perfectly synchronized. "Sarah made sure they put tucker on board. Find us something to eat while I take her out of here, would you?''

They lunched on canned fruit salad, beans and crackers. They dined on cheese sandwiches and apples. As darkness deepened, Liana made tea in the galley and brought a cup up to Cullen. He cut the motor, and they drifted on calm waters as they sipped in silence.

She was surprised at the beauty of the Buccaneer Archipelago. Cullen had told her that the northwest coast had some of the most extreme tides in the world, peaking at twelve meters in King Sound, where the *Robinette* now drifted. The severe tides exposed mudflats and hills, along with reefs that masqueraded as islands. Sandy beaches played hide-and-seek with brooding mangroves, and narrow cliff-lined passages snaked into hidden bays.

They had passed islands of countless varieties, some that seemed formed of nothing but bird life, others stark and barren, with tormented shrubs and red-boulder shores. They had been forced to delay their entrance into the sound to avoid sucking, teeming riptides that, over the years, had taken pearling luggers and tossed them on rocky shoals.

They had not made the progress they had hoped to. They still had hours before they reached the Graveyard.

"There won't be enough moonlight to do any good.'' Cullen slapped his palm against the railing in frustration. "I'd hoped to go until midnight. But there's no point. We can't see anything in the dark.''

She joined him at the side and stared at the water. The moon was a splinter of light, and gathering clouds veiled the stars. ''Is a storm brewing?''

He didn't look at her. ''The sound's calm enough here.''

''But the sky's full of clouds.''

''The Graveyard was the place the first pearlers came to ride out cyclone season. But we may have some trouble by morning,'' he admitted.

She was numb. Trouble just sounded like more of the same. ''This isn't the best boat to ride out a big blow, is it?''

''It might be better than whatever Matthew and Dad are sailing.''

''You were hoping we'd find them today, weren't you?''

''There are so many flaming variables, I don't know what to hope for. I don't know what sort of vessel Pete loaned them. I don't know what kind of time they're making, exactly where they're going, or how they intend to get there. Dad's no sailor, and these waters can be treacherous. Even if he's headed for the Graveyard, I don't know if he'll find his way.''

''And you don't know if someone else caught up with them, do you?''

''Don't think about that now.''

''None of the things I *can* think about are much better.''

''Then maybe it's time to get some sleep. We'll be up before dawn.''

''What time is it in San Francisco?''

He glanced at his watch. ''About 4:00 a.m.''

''Then I won't get to sleep. This is usually when I wake up. My body thinks it's prime time to toss and turn.''

''When we were married, you slept like the dead. I had to stand you upright in the shower every morning.''

She could no longer risk those memories. ''Are you coming down, too?''

''No, I'll sleep up here.''

"You want to keep watch, don't you?"

He didn't deny it.

"I'll stay up here with you, then. Two sets of eyes and ears."

"No point in both of us being uncomfortable."

She thought of the cramped quarters below, two narrow bunk beds with a narrower aisle between. She took his empty cup and started down the steps. "Two can listen and watch better than one. Want me to bring up a sleeping bag for you?"

"No, have a wash and get what you need. I'll come down when you've finished and do the same."

A little later they were settled in sleeping bags in the small space available. The waves had picked up, and the *Robinette* rocked gently. Liana thought of all the places she'd slept since Matthew's disappearance. Strange, threatening places, yet for the first time in years, she was nearly panic-free. She was on a boat out on open waters, her life in ruins around her, yet she was strangely calm.

"The eye of the hurricane," she said.

"What?"

She hadn't realized she had spoken out loud. "The eye of the hurricane. What you call a cyclone. The center of the storm, when everything is peaceful, but you know the worst is yet to come. That's what this is, Cullen. We've been through hell, and tomorrow we'll go through it all over again. I'm terrified for Matthew, but I'm not afraid of anything else. For the first time in a long, long time. I wonder why."

"Don't you know?"

She opened her eyes. He was close enough to touch, although she didn't. "Why?"

He lay on his back with his head resting on his hands. "The pearl, Lee. It's out of your hands, isn't it? In every single way, for the first time since you left Australia, that pearl and everything that goes with it is out of your hands."

Matthew put the finishing touches on two mugs of stew right out of the can. He never ate this way at home, and even though he missed Sue's cooking, he liked the simplicity of eating whatever he wanted, whenever he was hungry. He took the stew up the stairs to Roman, who had dropped anchor for the night.

Roman's eyes were closed, and Matthew felt a stab of guilt. His grandfather was not a young man, and the trip was obviously exhausting him.

"Granddad?"

Roman opened his eyes. "Took you long enough, boy."

Matthew grinned. The day had been one of the finest of his life. He'd gotten his sea legs, and he'd caught on to his grandfather's commands. He was storing up memories. The thrill of catching the wind, darting between islands and reefs; watching raptly as a school of dolphins cavorted behind the sailboat like family pets.

Once Roman had taken his portion, Matthew flopped down on the seat beside him. They ate in silence until Matthew was almost finished. With his appetite appeased, he was able to put into words something he'd been considering all day.

"I've been thinking, maybe we've gone far enough. Maybe we don't have to find the exact spot where the pearl came from. This is close enough, isn't it? We could drop it overboard now. Before we go to sleep. Then everything would be over."

"I've been thinking, too. You know, a pearl's just a pearl, Matthew. There's no magic in it. It's the way the pearl makes people feel that's the key, isn't it?"

"I guess."

"You had it with you a long time before you got to Jimiramira, didn't you?"

"Uh-huh."

"And did you feel any different?"

He thought about Tricia, but he doubted that was what his grandfather meant. "I'm not sure people can tell if they feel different or not."

"Did you do anything you don't usually do?"

"Sure. I broke into my mother's safe. Then I charged an airplane ticket on her account. I lied to everybody." He decided not to mention the encounter with Charlie. "I left my dad waiting at the airport. I—"

"Bloody hell! I get the picture."

"I know it's worth a lot of money."

"That it is."

"In a way, when I get rid of it, I'm stealing from my own kids. But at the same time, I'm protecting them."

"The tide may have turned, boy. There's no reason to think your children will be changed one way or the other by what you do."

"My mom will. And I will. I don't want to think about it ever again. I want to decide for myself who I am and what I'll do, without thinking about the pearl. I just want it gone."

"You could give it to a museum. Once it's really yours."

"By then I might not be able to. I might do terrible things to keep it, like everybody else."

Roman was quiet for a moment. "Then let's do it right. Let's find the dinky-di spot and do it the way it's supposed to be done."

Matthew had the uncomfortable feeling that his grandfather was just trying to delay the inevitable. Roman probably hoped that Matthew would change his mind if they waited another day. But there was nothing he could do about that tonight. Roman had the pearl in his pocket. From the moment he had learned that Matthew had stolen the pearl, he had refused to help unless Matthew gave it to him for safekeeping.

"Are you really going to let me decide what to do when the time comes?" Matthew demanded. "Because I'm not going to change my mind."

"When the time comes, the decision will be yours," Roman said. "On my word."

36

As Liana watched two huge turtles gliding through the waves just beyond them, Cullen did some calculations. "We'll be entering the Graveyard before long. I thought the wind had thrown us farther off course, but it hasn't."

All morning Liana had hoped to sight another boat, but as far as she could see, the choppy waters of King Sound were deserted. Even though storms were unusual in June, it looked as if they would get one. Unfortunately, gray skies made searching more difficult. Sea and island melted into sky, and the waves were steadily picking up.

She swept her hand in a broad arc. "No one's out here. I thought Sarah said these grounds were still popular."

"It's not the right time for gathering oysters, but we might see a pirate ship or two. The waters are remarkably rich. Lots of trouble with fishermen from other countries coming to gather trochus in our waters. They make so much money from one load of shell, it's worth risking time in our jails."

"If Matthew and your dad ran into one of their boats…"

"They'd be safe. No worries. It might be better than being out on these waters alone."

Or almost alone. Liana knew that the bigger threat was from whoever had killed Pete Carpenter.

She shaded her eyes with her hand, even though there was

no glare off the water. "Cullen, if they're not there, are we going to turn back?"

"We'll spend the rest of the day having a look there and in some of the nearby bays, then we'll decide what to do."

She was afraid they had run out of options. They had surely run out of conversation. She sat back with the binoculars as Cullen maneuvered reefs and riptides with precision. With the approaching storm, she was doubly glad to be with someone who knew the waters. Thunder rumbled in the distance, but she and Cullen were still silent half an hour later as he carefully guided the *Robinette* into the Graveyard. Once past the mouth of the bay, she saw there were islands here as well, and hills far beyond, rising like the walls of an ancient fort, protecting and sheltering the waters.

She had hoped the bay would be compact enough that sighting another vessel would be a simple matter. But there were mangrove creeks coiling away from the main waters, as well as islands densely forested with gum trees and paperbarks that hid wide stretches of the bay.

"What's that?" Cullen squinted at the eastern horizon and pointed.

She didn't see anything until she put the binoculars up to her eyes. Then she saw the faintest shadow against a distant island. "It might be something. Shall we check?"

He headed southeast.

She hadn't spent much time on the water in recent years. In the early days of their marriage, she had sometimes gone out with Cullen and his divers, just to be closer to him. But she had forgotten the way that distances couldn't be measured this far from shore. She strained to see, but they seemed to be treading the tossing waves, not moving through them. Only when the shadow began to lengthen and develop shape was she convinced it wasn't a mirage.

"It's a boat," Cullen said at last. "Probably a small sailboat of some sort. Not a fishing boat."

"The right size for a crew of two?"

"Looks that way."

They covered the rest of the distance in silence. Once the sailboat was in plain sight, there was no thrill of recognition. They still had no idea what sort of craft, if any, Matthew and Roman had borrowed. But there was an instant of awareness like none Liana had ever felt when the gap closed and with the help of binoculars she recognized Matthew.

"Cullen!" She pointed. "It's Matthew! Look!"

"Easy, Lee."

She turned and saw that Cullen had taken out the semiautomatic she had practiced with yesterday. "What are you doing?"

He shoved it in the waistband of his shorts. "We don't know who's on board with him."

She spun around, straining to see. "It looks like one other person. An older man. It's probably your father."

"Come here and take the wheel."

She did, handing him the binoculars. He focused, then he grabbed the wheel again. "It's Dad, all right."

"There's nobody else on board, unless they're below."

"Let's find out."

She gripped the railing as he sped toward the sailboat. Thunder boomed, amplified now and extended, but the approaching storm no longer seemed important. Minutes passed. Matthew grew larger. She watched him peering over the side at their approach; then she tossed the binoculars on a seat when she could see her son without them. Cullen cut the engine, and they drifted to the side. Cullen took the line and tossed it through the air toward a gawking Matthew.

"Grab it, son, and tie us off."

Matthew did as he was told. Roman joined him at the side. When the boats were secured, Cullen addressed his father. "Your place or ours, Dad?"

"We're not the ones who came looking for you," Roman said gruffly.

"That you didn't." Cullen held out his hand to help Liana to the foredeck of the sailboat. Then he joined her.

She made her way toward Matthew, grabbed him in a bear hug and felt his arms close convulsively around her. She held him for a moment, then she shoved him away. "Do you have any idea what you've put us through?"

Matthew still looked stunned. "What are you doing here?"

"What am *I* doing here?" She shoved him again with the heel of her hands, harder than she had before. He stumbled backwards. "You lied! You ran away. You broke into my safe and took the pearl, and you're asking me what I'm doing here?"

She felt Cullen's hand on her shoulder. "Give the boy a chance to speak."

She couldn't stop. "We were afraid you were dead!"

"I'm okay, Mom. I can take care of myself. I just had some things to do."

He was taller. She could swear he was taller. His hair had been long. Now it was short and streaked from the sun. He was sunburned.

He was alive. She hugged herself and swayed in rhythm with the swelling waves. He was alive.

Cullen turned to his father. "Matthew's fourteen. A four-teen-year-old boy doesn't have the best judgment. So where was yours? Don't you know what it's like to worry about your own kid?"

"You gave me plenty to worry about."

"You had no right to keep Matthew's presence here a secret."

"I did what I had to."

Liana glanced at Roman for the first time. She hadn't been prepared for the resemblance to Cullen. Or to Matthew. "What about me? Didn't I count, either?"

"Stop it," Matthew said. "I talked Granddad into this. He did it for me. If you want to be angry at somebody, be angry at me. Okay?"

Liana lowered her voice and was momentarily drowned out by another clap of thunder. She started again. "How could you have done this to us, Matthew? Your dad and I have been worried sick."

"You know why he did it, Lee," Cullen said. He faced his son. "We know, Matthew. You stole the pearl and brought it here. You thought you were helping everybody by getting rid of it. It's gone now, I suppose."

Matthew exchanged glances with his grandfather. "It's gone. We—" Thunder cut him off.

"No, it's not gone," Roman said when the thunder died. "I have it," he told Cullen. Then he turned to Matthew. "It's time for honesty, boy."

Matthew turned pale under his sunburn. "But you said this would be my choice," he told his grandfather. "You gave me your word."

Roman slipped his fingers into the pocket of his well-worn white moleskins and carefully lifted out a tiny jeweler's case. "Your mother kept her rings in this whenever she was tidying the house," he told Cullen. He snapped open the lid and held out the Pearl of Great Price, nestled on a square of linen. It gleamed as if in full sunshine, an iridescent sphere, seemingly perfect in every way.

Roman didn't smile. "The boy's superstitious, but maybe I am, too. Joan was a good woman. I reckoned we could use her blessing."

As Liana watched, hardly daring to breathe, Roman pinched the pearl between index finger and thumb. But he didn't give it to her, as she expected. He turned. "Hold out your hand, Matthew."

Matthew's eyes widened.

"Don't do this, Dad," Cullen said. "He's fourteen. He can't be expected to make this kind of decision."

"Hold out your hand, Matthew," Roman repeated.

Matthew stared at his father, then at his grandfather. Finally he unclasped his fingers and held his hand palm up. The boat was rocking harder now, and only streaks of distant lightning brightened the gloom. Matthew's hand was unsteady.

"The pearl is yours, boy. You're the one who took it, after all. So it's your decision. What'll it be? Will you steal this from your mother a second time? Are you smart enough, good enough, to decide for everybody what's the right thing to do? Because it's your decision now." Roman set the pearl in Matthew's palm, then he folded the boy's fingers around it. "God help you, though, if you make the wrong one."

Liana didn't dare to breathe. She was certain that if she moved toward her son, or even looked as if that was her intention, Matthew would throw the pearl into the bay. Even in the calmest weather, the waters of the Graveyard were too treacherous for them to have any hopes of retrieving it. It would be lost forever.

"It brings out the worst flaw in anybody who has it," Matthew said. "Mom, you were getting worse and worse. You could hardly leave the house. You were so unhappy...."

Liana felt tears streaming down her cheeks. "Not because of a pearl, Matty."

"You've done a lot of things because of it. You stayed at Pacific International, even though you hate it."

She wondered if he knew that, at least partly because of the pearl, she had also kept him from Australia and his father's life at Pikuwa Creek.

The first drops of rain dotted the deck. Matthew clenched his fist, and his knuckles turned white with strain. "I've seen some of your jewelry, Mom. And Dad told me that you used to love designing it."

"The only thing you'll accomplish if you throw that pearl in the water is to prove you don't trust your mother," Cullen said. "You're telling her she's not strong enough, or even smart enough, to take care of herself. Well, she's both. Your mother will do whatever she has to, no matter the consequences."

The words sounded like a tribute. But Liana knew exactly what Cullen meant.

"I believe in you," Matthew told her. "But you can't control the pearl. It's evil."

"Do you really know what's right for everyone, Matthew?" Cullen said. "Is that *your* greatest flaw? Is that what stealing the pearl has done to you?"

Matthew looked stricken. The *Argonaut* was pitching from side to side in the water. Liana held on to the lifeline with one hand and extended the other, slowly and carefully. "It's not your decision." Despite the thunder, she spoke softly, as if she were pacifying a younger Matthew. "It never was. I love you so much for wanting to protect me. But you can't. In the end we're all responsible for ourselves, no matter how much the people we love want to help us."

"I hate it!" His voice was choked with tears.

"It's a pearl," Roman said. "Just a pearl. Not good, not bad. A pearl that inspires people to act like fools and criminals. But that's all, boy. And maybe you can change that now. But not by throwing it in the bay."

Matthew swallowed. Liana wanted to put her arms around him again, to hold him tight, to change him back into the infant she had nursed and comforted at her breast. But Matthew was almost a man, and this was a man's decision.

At last he stepped forward and held out his hand. She extended hers a little farther, palm up. She felt oddly disoriented, as if she were not one but many people, the embodiment of generations, who had held out their hands just this way, yearning for whatever they needed most. Archer, who wanted to fulfill his dreams of land and cattle. Tom, who blindly valued loyalty and friendship more than life. Viola and Willow. Bryce and Mei, and even Thomas, who had hoped that one flawless pearl would save him forever from the shame of his ancestry and the childhood terror of a city collapsing around him.

Yet, in the end, the pearl had promised each of them everything and given them nothing.

Matthew dropped the pearl into her hand, and it lay shining against her skin, dewed by raindrops, lit by lightning. His voice shook. "When it's mine, I'll bring it back here and bury it forty fathoms deep."

"When it's yours, I'll help you," Cullen told him.

Liana's fingers closed around the pearl. Her grandfather had died for it; Cullen's great-grandfather had killed for it, and she had sold her soul to keep it. She felt no pleasure and no relief. The Pearl of Great Price was no hotter than the air surrounding it, but it seared her palm.

A new voice spoke. "I don't think it *will* be yours, Matthew."

Liana looked up as the men turned. Frank Fong stood in a powerboat just at their stern. For a moment she froze, unable and unwilling to comprehend what was happening. In a blur of movement beside her, Cullen drew the .38 from his waistband and aimed it, but not quickly enough. Frank lifted his arm and fired first. The revolver clattered to the deck and slid into an open hatch. Cullen fell to one knee.

"Dad!" Matthew pitched himself at his father, trying to hold him up. Roman started toward Frank, but Frank swung the gun toward him. "You're next, old man."

Roman faltered.

"What are you doing?" Matthew shouted. "This is my dad, Frank. You shot him!"

Liana knelt beside Cullen and saw the blossoming of blood on his shirt, well below his collarbone. She was trembling, but her voice was steady. "Frank, put the gun away. Everything's fine here. You've misinterpreted the situation."

"Oh, have I?" Frank, who had climbed on board the *Argonaut*, sounded as if she'd told him that he had mistakenly dialed a wrong number. "Now that was stupid of me."

Liana pocketed the pearl and tore open Cullen's shirt. The wound was ragged and bleeding hard. She ripped off her jacket and folded it, pressing it against the wound to slow the blood loss.

"What do you want?" Cullen demanded of Frank, nudging Liana aside. "What is it you...want here?"

"Sunshine?" Frank raised his eyes to the sky. "Darn. I come all the way to the Southern Hemisphere to soak up a few rays, and you're having a freak storm."

Liana heard Cullen gasp as she tied the jacket sleeves tightly around his shoulder and under his arm. He turned paler, and his head dropped forward. She was terrified for him, but for the moment there was nothing else she could do. She rose and faced her cousin. "Frank, you're my cousin, my friend."

His smile died. For a moment he looked genuinely sorry. "I really *was* your friend. But then, your father and my grandmother were twins, weren't they? And that didn't stop him from stealing the pearl from her."

The boat was rocking harder now, and rain glazed her skin. The thunder had drowned Frank's approach, and the dark skies had made it impossible to see his boat in whatever tidal creek or inlet he had hidden it in on the other side of the island. In the emotion of their reunion with Matthew, she and Cullen had foolishly forgotten that a killer was stalking their son. A few minutes of carelessness had been enough.

Liana placed her hand over the pocket of her jeans. Her eyes flashed to Cullen and Matthew, then back to Frank. "So it's the pearl?"

He smiled patiently, regret forgotten. "Of course. By rights it belongs to my branch of the family." He trained the gun on her. "Look what Grandmother went through to get it."

"You want me to give you the pearl? That's all?" she said.

"Now that's why you're the lady boss and I'm your flunky."

She played for time. "You want to know what else I've figured out?"

"Something about old man Carpenter?"

She felt sick, although she had already guessed that Frank was the one who had murdered Pete. "Aunt Mei was the one who set this up. You know that, don't you, Frank?"

He laughed, and the sound was almost conspiratorial. "Oh,

lease. Grandmother has nothing to do with this. You think she
sent me here? She loves you like a daughter.''

"I know she didn't send you to threaten us, but she sent
Matthew to steal it. Aunt Mei told Matthew the story, all the
stories about the pearl, every single time she saw him. And she
hoped, she *knew*, eventually he'd steal it and rid our families
of its curse. Do you know why?''

"I'm all ears," he said pleasantly.

"Because she must have known you were becoming obsessed with it. She adores you, and she knew if you continued
to dream about the pearl it would destroy you. Just the way
it's destroyed everyone else. It wasn't even yours, but it was
already bringing out the worst in you.''

"It's just a pearl, Liana. Nothing special. Except that it's
worth probably a million or more to the right collector.''

"Aunt Mei thought she could save you, and she believed
Matthew was strong enough to risk it.''

"Then she was wrong. Can't salvage me, cuz. I'm selfish to
the core.''

"No, you're not." She slipped her hand into her pocket, then
swung her arm over the water. "Matthew was right. Aunt Mei
was right. And I've been so blind. I let the pearl rule my life.
But not anymore.''

Before he could threaten her, before he could turn the gun
on Matthew or Cullen and use their safety as a weapon against
her, she unclasped her fingers. She didn't watch the Pearl of
Great Price's descent back into the waters that had nourished
it. Suddenly her hand was empty, but her heart was full. As
Cullen pushed Matthew away and rose unsteadily to his feet
beside her, she felt the dawning of a new millennium.

She had expected Frank to rush to the side, perhaps even to
dive in. Instead he stood absolutely still, and his gun didn't
waver. "I am deeply touched by your altruism. Deeply.''

She clasped Cullen's hand, a hand that was much too cold
and unsteady. "Please, it's over, Frank. The pearl's gone.
There's nothing to be gained from killing any of us. Dump our

fuel, slash the sails. Leave us here. You can be wherever yo
plan to escape to before anyone finds us.''

Matthew stood, too, and for a moment Frank trained the gu
on him until he seemed certain the boy wasn't going to tr
anything. The storm was moving overhead now, and lightnin
fragmented the sky. Frank had to raise his voice to be heard.

"Do you know how easy it was to install a video camera i
your office, Liana? Because of our friendship, no one ques
tioned my right to be there, even when you were gone.''

For a moment she thought he had lost his mind. "What ar
you talking about?''

"I'm talking about the way I discovered the combination t
your safe. Months ago. You've always been so particular abou
your privacy. No surveillance cameras. No one watching you
So there wasn't anything to stop me when I decided to do
little filmmaking. And I knew every time you'd be opening th
safe. You always had me arrange security. So I installed
camera one evening, just in time. You'd be amazed how ad
vanced the technology is. I filmed you the next day, then on
day in April I opened the safe and took it. Just like that.'' H
snapped his fingers.

She spoke as if he was a child. "Frank, Matthew took th
pearl. And now it's gone forever.''

Rain dripped off Frank's nose and chin; his hair was plas
tered to his forehead, but his expression was casual, almos
good-humored. "Nah, cuz…Matthew took the pearl I put in
side the safe. It's a fake, but a darned good one. The French
made it. Fish scales and mother of pearl dust held together wit
resin. It's as heavy as the real thing, not like most fakes. Culle
can tell you, can't you?'' He pointed the gun at Cullen.

"No one who knows pearls would mistake a fake…for th
real thing,'' Cullen said.

Liana knew what it was costing Cullen to stand. His han
seemed to grow colder. She gripped it harder. "You stole th
Pearl of Great Price?''

"You're catching on.'' Frank swung the gun toward Roman

who had said nothing but had managed somehow to move a little closer to him. "Old man, another inch and you're dead, just like that friend of yours in Derby."

"Pete?"

Frank grinned. "Old fart. He died without telling me where you were headed. But I grew up on Grandmother's stories. Once I figured out he was in Australia, I knew exactly what Matthew would do. By the way, it was good of you to make that phone call to the office, Matthew. One of the secretaries who doesn't know you just happened to mention it. It set me on the right track."

"If you stole the pearl," Matthew said, "why did you follow us here? Why did you care what I did with a fake?"

"This is a smart boy," Frank told Liana. "A credit to the family." He smiled at Matthew, as he had so often in the past. "I had the real pearl, but I knew eventually somebody would discover it was gone, and I was afraid if it was hot it might be harder to sell once I was ready. So, when you took the fake, I just wanted to be sure you got rid of it. Then later I could pass the Pearl of Great Price off as an unknown pearl and do whatever I wanted with it."

Liana tried to distract him, praying for a way out of the inevitable. "You're the one who broke into my apartment and accessed Matthew's E-mail. And when Cullen and I figured out where he'd gone—"

He shrugged. "Then I knew I had trouble. So Plan B was born. I tried to follow you quietly. Right up until the end, I hoped everything would come right by itself and you wouldn't catch up to Matthew in time. Then I wouldn't have to kill anybody. But while you were waiting for Matthew to show up at the pearl farm, I did some scouting on my own. I traced him to the shipyard, but he was already gone by then. Then Old Pete caught me stealing a boat, and once he was dead, I didn't have that much more to lose, did I?"

"So you followed him here?"

"No. I got here first. And then I waited. Deserted, treacherous bay, terrible storm, an ocean just filled with all manner of creepy crawlies.'' He pretended to shiver. ''If anyone finds what's left of you, it'll be a miracle. They'll assume the pearl went down with Matthew, of course. No pearl. No more Llewellyns.''

He swung the gun toward Cullen. ''I don't have a grudge against you. Maybe your great-grandfather killed my grandfather. I don't care. Let bygones be bygones. But I'm going to kill you first, because, even wounded, you're the most dangerous.''

''No, Frank!'' Liana moved between Cullen and Frank, but Cullen pushed her aside with what remained of his strength. ''If you do kill me...or anybody here, you'll never have the real pearl.''

Frank laughed. ''I *have* the real pearl.''

''With you, I suppose?''

''Darned right.''

''Guess again, mate.''

The smile on Frank's face dimmed a watt. ''Really? You have ten seconds to explain.''

''The real Pearl of Great Price...is in my safe at Pikuwa Creek.''

''And how do you figure that?''

Cullen spoke slowly, resting at the end of sentences, as if each breath was more difficult than the one before. ''I was...in the U.S. in April, too. Did you...know?''

''So?''

Cullen hesitated just a moment, and Frank steadied the gun.

Matthew stepped closer to his father. ''You figured out the combination to the safe, didn't you, Dad? The way I did.''

''Stay out of this, Matthew,'' Frank ordered.

''I knew you would figure out what I'd done,'' Matthew continued, as if Frank hadn't spoken. ''But you must have figured it out first.''

''Shut up!'' Frank shouted, swinging the gun toward Matthew.

Liana's heart filled her throat. "Matthew, be quiet!"

"No, Mom. Don't you see? I didn't need a camera like Frank. I figured out the combination on my own. It wasn't just random numbers, not the way everybody thought. Dad was the one who gave me the idea. He warned me once I should never use my birthday or anything personal as my computer password."

"Well, you didn't listen to that bit of advice, did you?" Frank said. "I figured out your password in ten minutes."

"Yeah? Well, when I used Aunt Mei's address, I didn't know I'd have a thief and a murderer tracking me!"

"Matthew!" Liana started forward to try to protect him, but Frank waved her back with the gun. He didn't fire. Even in her terror, she knew that killing Matthew was not going to be easy for him.

"All right, Llewellyn," Frank said. "Your son figured out the combination. Now you're saying—"

"Dad liked to play keno," Matthew said. "He told me he used to choose numbers that meant something to him. And that's what my grandfather Thomas did, too."

"Shut up, Matthew," Frank warned. "Or I'll shoot your father at the next word! I swear I will! What numbers is he talking about?" Frank swung the gun back to Cullen. "This is your big chance, Crocodile Dundee."

Cullen was panting, and Liana's own breath was coming in short bursts. "That's easy. The day...of the San Francisco earthquake. That was the worst moment of Thomas's life. He wasn't a man who would choose a happy date, was he?"

Frank laughed. "You know, you and the kid almost had me going. But I know my California history. The earthquake was April 18, 1906. That's four, eighteen, right? I remember the combination, and it doesn't begin with a four. Bang, you're dead."

"No, it's the date *and* the time. Backwards," Matthew shouted. "Twelve, five, six, nineteen, eighteen, four. I figured it out from stories about Thomas. I was fooling around with it one day while I was waiting for Mom to finish a meeting. Four for April, eighteen for the eighteenth, 1906 at 5:12 a.m. We'd just studied the earthquake in school. I wrote a paper about it. When the numbers didn't work in the right order, I reversed them. When the safe opened, I knew I had to steal the pearl."

Frank was no longer laughing.

Cullen didn't look relieved or surprised. For once his expression was a perfect poker face. "Now do you believe…I nabbed it from the safe?"

Frank leveled the gun at his heart. "Not a chance. Matthew just fed the whole thing to you."

Cullen nodded. "Good on ya…mate. Because…you're right, it's all a lie."

"Dad!"

"Be quiet, son." Cullen struggled for another breath. "Matthew did figure out…the combination. But I never even got near Lee's office. Only, I still have the real pearl. Do you…want to know how…I got it?"

"You're wasting my time!"

"Your grandmother…discovered that you stole it, Frank. She found it…on one of her visits to…your house.… You kept it…at home, didn't you?"

"Where?" Frank demanded.

Liana knew Cullen, like Matthew, was just playing for time. The boat was rocking harder, and rain was sweeping across the deck. Roman was inching closer to a fascinated Frank. Cullen was gasping, as if trying with all his strength not to lose consciousness.

"She would never say. But she saw what it…had done to you, and she knew your only hope…was for me to bring it…back here to Australia. She never got over stealing it from my grandfather.… She thought it should belong to…me. Because of Bryce. So she wrote me a letter, and I flew to San Francisco.… There was a family gathering that weekend, a birthday, I think. She said…she was too tired to go, then she made Betty take her…to your condo while the family…was together. She replaced the Pearl of Great Price with one I brought for her, the biggest pearl ever to come...out of Pikuwa Creek. And that's...where the Pearl of Great Price is waiting for you. At Pikuwa Creek, in my safe. You can have it, Frank. But not if we're dead. Our lives for the pearl.''

"I don't believe you!''

"No? How closely have you looked at yours? It's a big stone, all right...but it's not perfect. Not by a bloody long shot. It's flawed.... It's not even a sphere. Anyone who looked closely at it, anyone who knew pearls...could have told you. One X-ray is all it takes...to reveal the nucleus.''

Liana felt Cullen slumping against her. She was frantic to finish what Cullen had started. She put her arm around Cullen to try to hold him up, and Matthew grabbed him from the other side. "But you didn't show the pearl to anyone, did you, Frank?'' she said. "You couldn't, until you were sure the other one was gone. That way you could pass off your pearl as something entirely different.''

Another sky-rending streak of lightning showed the indecision in Frank's expression. Liana could almost feel his desire to take out his pearl and look at it, just to be sure Cullen was lying.

"Lee was right. Mei knew...what you had become.... It's like her to understand these things, isn't it? It's like her...to worry about everybody....'' Cullen fell limply against her, and even with Matthew's strength, Liana was unable to brace herself enough to stop his slide to the deck.

"You've killed my dad!'' Matthew shouted.

"Shut up!'' Frank ran his fingers through his hair, but the gun didn't waver.

"Let's go back to Pikuwa Creek and get the real pearl,'' Liana pleaded. "It's a small price to pay, Frank. Please...''

"Shut up!'' He pointed the gun directly at her. "All of you shut up!''

The boat was rocking harder now, and the *Robinette* was banging against the side with every toss, making the sailboat even less stable. Frank stood his ground like a seasoned sailor, but after a moment, the strain was too much. He felt in his right pocket with his left hand, glancing down for one heart-stopping moment when the angle proved difficult. Roman edged closer, then halted when Frank glanced up again.

With the utmost care, Frank pulled a ring case from the watch pocket of his jeans. "Don't anybody move." He held the case in his left hand and tried to flick it open with his thumb. When that didn't work, he rubbed the side against his belt buckle, but opening the case was a job for two hands.

Liana prayed that Roman would see there was going to be only one small window of opportunity. She could see Frank's indecision, his desire to know the truth, and, at last, the greed that eclipsed common sense. The gun wavered momentarily as he used both hands to open the box and take out the pearl.

Roman sprang.

The gunshot was louder than thunder. Liana saw Roman stiffen, but he fell against Frank, pushing him backwards against the lifeline. The gun clattered to the deck, and the boat rocked wildly under the shifting weight. Then both men were overboard.

"Granddad!" Matthew started toward the side.

"Stay where you are! We'll tip!" Liana felt along the deck for Frank's pistol, all but invisible in the darkness. Her breath came in short sobs, but her hands didn't tremble. She found the gun and knelt at the side, training it on the men in the water. Even with the storm overhead and the waves tossing furiously, she could see both men thrashing several yards from the stern, but not clearly enough to take aim.

"Roman, get away from him," she screamed. "I have the gun."

She could see a fist high above the water, and two hands clasping it at the wrist. She thought she saw blood pooling around the two men, although she couldn't be sure. "Roman! Get away!"

"I've got to help!" Matthew crawled up beside her.

"Get an oar. Do it right now!"

He crawled toward the bow. She peered into the waves, ready to go in after Roman. The fist wavered. She saw shoulders, but only one head, although it was too dark to tell whose. Matthew returned with an oar and held it over the side.

"Roman, the oar!" Liana shouted. "Grab the oar!" She was stripping off her shoes, ready to dive in. She shoved the gun at her son. "Matthew, can you shoot if you have to?"

"You can't go in there, Mom!"

Something grabbed the oar. She saw hands, then a head with silver hair. The gun clattered to the deck again. "Hold on, Matthew. Pull!" She leaned over and grabbed Roman's shirt, tugging hard until she could get an arm under his. He kicked feebly with his legs, as the boat rocked harder beneath them.

"Slowly," she shouted. "Matthew, a little at a time, or we'll tip."

They got him on board at last.

Roman was gasping. "Wouldn't let go of that pearl...to save himself.... I held him under, but he was treading water with one hand. He wouldn't let go—"

Liana felt for the gun and trained it on the water. "Frank!" she shouted. "We'll get you out, but I've got a gun on you."

As they had struggled to rescue Roman, the boats had drifted in circles closer to the island, caught in a sluggish whirlpool. Everything looked different now, and for a moment she was disoriented. She couldn't see Frank, and she wasn't sure where to look. The storm was passing, but the waves were still fitful enough that a man could be hidden between them.

"Frank!"

His answer was a terrified scream. She saw thrashing, wild, terrible thrashing, far beyond where she had expected Frank to be, twenty yards or less from the island. She thought frantically of Cullen's diver, nearly taken by a shark. Then she saw the Australian archangel of death, the Neanderthal outline of a huge saltwater crocodile, winding through the waves from the direction of the island, drawn by the blood of the man now safely inside the boat.

She grabbed Matthew and turned him away, wrestling him like a younger child so that he wouldn't see. The scream died quickly. She hoped, for Mei's sake, that the man had died quickly, too.

"Granddad." Matthew fell to his knees sobbing. "He shot you."

Roman limply batted his hand away. "Don't fuss, boy."

She knelt beside Roman. Like Cullen's, his shirt was stained with blood. She ripped it open and spread it wide. Frank's bullet had grazed Roman's side, taking its share of flesh, but, cleansed by saltwater, the blood was already beginning to clot.

"Watch him, Matthew."

She crawled toward Cullen, praying. She reached him and lifted his arm. The makeshift dressing had slowed the bleeding, but his clothes were soaked with all he'd lost. Much too much. She used a shirt Matthew or Roman had discarded, loosening the jacket sleeves and slipping the shirt beneath it for more pressure against the wound, then she sat cross-legged and pulled his head into her lap. The bleeding slowed, but she was still worried about shock or worse.

"Lee…"

"Cullen." She smoothed his hair back from his forehead. "Frank's dead. We're going to get you out of here right now. We'll take the *Robinette* and flag down the first boat we see. You're going to be fine."

"The pearl…"

"Fuck the pearl!"

Somehow he managed the shadow of a grin. "I didn't…"

She saved him an explanation. "I know Frank's pearl was the real one. You weren't a gambler for nothing, were you? You knew if Mei had found the pearl she would have done exactly what you said."

"I was just bloody well…making my final bet…."

"I knew that."

"How did you…?"

"Because you never would have taken it. No matter how angry you were at me. Even if you could have." She began to sob. "I'm so sorry about everything. I love you. Don't die on me, Cullen. Promise me!"

"The pearl?"

"Gone forever."

"Then I reckon I'll have a good chance of making it…through this alive…at that."

She was sobbing, but she didn't care. "I'll stay with you. I'll take care of you, if you'll have me."

"You threw…it away, Lee. Just…like that."

"I threw away a fake! But it's the thought that counts, isn't it?"

"It was always…the thought. Never the pearl."

"I don't care which it was. It doesn't matter anymore. I just want you and Matthew. I want our life back. I'm going to make it happen."

"You say…you'll stay with me?"

"Oh, Cullen, if you'll forgive me. If you'll have me."

"Get me home, Lee."

"Nothing's going to stop us, mate. Not ever again."

He lifted her hand to his lips. "That's…my missus."

37

Matthew perched on one of the coolibah rails outlining a ring where Luke had been working with a snow-white filly. The horse was alone inside the enclosure now, but every time Matthew spoke to her, she edged closer. She was one of Jimiramira's own, descended from thoroughbreds, spiced with the blood of champion quarter horses and fleet-footed Arabians. Earlier in the day Roman had told him that tomorrow, on his fifteenth birthday, she was to be his.

He had named her Pearl.

"So, what do you think?"

Matthew swivelled to find his grandfather standing just behind him. He supposed Roman's silent approach had been perfected in the bush. "You're supposed to be napping."

"The day a hoon like you can tell me what to do with my life is the day I won't climb back into anybody's boat."

Matthew was unperturbed. "I'm not telling you. Dr. Keller's telling you. You're still supposed to rest in the hottest part of the day."

"He doesn't know a thing about me."

Matthew hopped down to stand beside him, just in case Roman needed someone to lean on. "She's beautiful. She's the best gift ever."

"You have to come visit her. I reckon I'm not going to waste her on a boy who never comes to ride her."

"Pikuwa Creek's not that far away. We'll be coming back every chance we can. I'll come on school holidays. And in between, you'll be coming to see us. Dad said you promised him."

"I was talking about visiting the horse, boy, not me." Roman offset the words with a half grin.

Matthew looked beyond his grandfather to the couple slowly walking side by side toward them. Cullen and Liana were absorbed in each other and didn't notice that Matthew was watching. Cullen's face remained pale, but his strength was returning. As Matthew looked on, Cullen reached over and tucked a stand of Liana's dark hair behind her ear. He might not seed his own pearls this season, but by the fall he would be in charge again.

Liana's arm was tucked inside Cullen's, but Matthew's father was the one who needed the support. By the time Whitey Pendergast and the crew of one of Southern Cross's luggers had found them at the mouth of the Graveyard, Cullen's lung had collapsed and he had lost enough blood to send him into shock. Only the expert intervention of a medic on board had saved his life.

Liana had stayed at Cullen's side throughout his recovery, refusing to leave him for even a moment. And, more often than not, Matthew and Roman had joined her there.

Matthew was still startled to see his parents together, even though he'd had most of a month to get used to the sight. As a child, he had never imagined a reconciliation, or even hoped for one. Yet here they were, together, and now his own life had changed forever.

"I like her," Roman said gruffly. "She's a strong woman. Just so you know."

"Do you like him?"

"Mind your manners, boy."

"It's a good question."

"I always liked him. I reckon I just didn't like me." Roman was silent for a moment. "You won't miss San Francisco?"

"We'll go back to visit." Matthew thought of the designs his mother had shown him last night, drawings of jewelry she would craft from his father's pearls. She had talked of opening a boutique in San Francisco where she could sell her work, as well as one in Broome. She had promised that they would travel back to California as often as they could to see friends and Aunt Mei, who needed their love more than ever now. Even Uncle Graham was planning an Australian vacation, just to be sure they didn't forget he was part of the family. Liana had promised she would do everything possible to help Matthew make the adjustment to Pikuwa Creek, as if living there hadn't always been his heart's desire.

Matthew spoke his greatest fear out loud. "I think she's still afraid."

"Afraid?"

"She's worried about making things easy for me, but living in Australia will be hard for her." He tried to think of a way to explain. "It's like Pikuwa Creek is a brand-new game for me, one I always wanted to play but was never allowed to. She played it a long time ago and lost."

"She'll be right. She's got everything she needs to make a go of it. And she'll have your dad to help her adjust."

"She will, won't she?"

"I reckon it looks that way."

Matthew watched his parents, who had stopped just out of hailing distance. They had their heads together, and Matthew thought his father was laughing. Liana rose to her tiptoes and kissed him, and Cullen scooped her closer.

Roman rested his hand on Matthew's shoulder. "Frankly, boy, I think it's time you stopped worrying about everybody else. From what I see, your mum and dad can take care of themselves and each other just fine. You just work on becoming a man."

Matthew pictured one flawless pearl, buried forever at the

bottom of Cygnet Bay. Something eased inside him, like a hand opening slowly, a burden disappearing between one wave and the next.

He nodded at his grandfather. "Maybe I will."

Behind him the filly, Pearl, snorted defiantly. He turned and extended his hand between the coolibah rails, clucking softly. He wasn't even surprised when she sidled close enough to rub her velvet muzzle against his palm.

If you enjoyed what you just read,
then we've got an offer you can't resist!

Take 2 bestselling
love stories FREE!
Plus get a FREE surprise gift!